Praise for *Flying Blind* by Max Allan Collins

"Highly entertaining. . . . Collins offers quite a few nonfiction studies of Earhart that offer a variety of theories on her fate. Readers who delight in snappy dialogue and jet-paced action undoubtedly will prefer his."   —*Los Angeles Times*

"Plausible. Compelling. It's a reasonable bet that Collins, who has been nominated for an unequaled eight Shamus Awards, could be in line for number nine."   —*Booklist*

"I suffer from severe envy of Max Allan Collins. He creates period mysteries around real characters and incidents. And he's damn good at it."
—*The January Review*

"Buckle your seat belt and get ready for a journey into a world of intrigue, espionage, betrayal and a rousing good time. Collins is at his best."
—*Mostly Murder*

"Max Allan Collins brings us Nate Heller-meets-Amelia Earhart in his ninth Nate Heller book. And once again he manages to combine fact and fiction in a plausible, highly readable manner that mere biographers can only aspire to."
—*Mystery News*

"Nate's ninth is an entertaining case."
—*Kirkus Reviews*

continued on next page . . .

THE MEMOIRS OF NATHAN HELLER:

Flying Blind
Damned in Paradise
Blood and Thunder
Carnal Hours
Dying in the Post-War World
Stolen Away
Neon Mirage
The Million-Dollar Wound
True Crime
True Detective

FLYING BLIND

A NATHAN HELLER NOVEL

Max Allan Collins

A SIGNET BOOK

SIGNET
Published by New American Library, a division of
Penguin Putnam Inc., 375 Hudson Street,
New York, New York 10014, U.S.A.
Penguin Books Ltd, 27 Wrights Lane,
London W8 5TZ, England
Penguin Books Australia Ltd, Ringwood,
Victoria, Australia
Penguin Books Canada Ltd, 10 Alcorn Avenue,
Toronto, Ontario, Canada M4V 3B2
Penguin Books (N.Z.) Ltd, 182–190 Wairau Road,
Auckland 10, New Zealand

Penguin Books Ltd, Registered Offices:
Harmondsworth, Middlesex, England

Published by Signet, an imprint of New American Library,
a division of Penguin Putnam Inc.
Previously published in a Dutton edition.

First Signet Printing, September 1999
10 9 8 7 6 5 4 3 2 1

 REGISTERED TRADEMARK—MARCA REGISTRADA

Printed in the United States of America

To Mike Wynne—
who suggested this flight
of fancy and fact

Although the historical incidents in this novel are portrayed more or less accurately (as much as the passage of time, and contradictory source material, will allow), fact, speculation and fiction are freely mixed here; historical personages exist side by side with composite characters and wholly fictional ones—all of whom act and speak at the author's whim.

"I think it's too bad when aviation movies depend for their excitement on plane wrecks and lost fliers and all that sort of thing. Perhaps that's good drama but it certainly isn't modern aviation."

—Amelia Earhart

Prologue

February 14, 1970

One

The press called her "Lady Lindy," but her family called her Mill. Schoolgirl pals preferred Meelie, certain friends Mary (Fred Noonan among them), she was Paul Mantz's "angel," and her husband used "A. E." To the world she was Amelia Earhart, but to me, and only me, she was Amy.

I hadn't thought of her in a long time, at least a week, when that damned Texan came around, stirring memories. For all the mentions of her in the media, even after so many years—some screwball was always mounting an expedition to "find her"—I'd managed to keep her real in my mind, not just a famous name, not just a "historical enigma" (as Leonard Nimoy called her on some silly TV show), always a person, a friend, someone I missed, with that bittersweet kind of longing you feel more and more, the older you get.

Old age is a combination, after all, of hard and soft, a senile sundae of cynicism and sentimentality, with much of your time spent reading, both aloud and silently, from a laundry list of bastards and sweethearts you spent a lifetime compiling. And not all of the sweethearts were women, and not all of the bastards were men.

My wife—my second wife, the marriage that took—and I had not given up our home in suburban Chicago, yet; I was telling people I was "semi-retired" from the A-1 Detective Agency, lying to myself that I was still in charge. I was still in charge like a brain-dead billionaire on life support is still in charge of his finances.

But at age sixty-four (with sixty-five a few months away), I didn't need to work. My one-room agency in Barney Ross's old building on the corner of Van Buren and Plymouth, established in 1932, had turned into suites of offices in six cities now, not to mention two floors of the Monadnock Building. I wasn't the President of the A-1 anymore, but Chairman of the Board. We no longer did divorce work; our specialties were "anti-industrial espionage" and "security consultation." I had become so successful, I didn't recognize my own business.

So when the Texan came calling, I was still kidding myself that I was only "wintering" in Florida. We had a nice little rambling three-bedroom ranch-style on a waterway where we could sit and watch boats glide by, first in one direction, then the other, sometimes chased by water skiers, some of whom were pretty young girls. We could have had an oceanfront place, giving my tired old randy eyes even more ready access to sweet young things in skimpy bathing suits, but the "villa" available shared a wall with a next-door neighbor. Maybe that was a villa in Florida; in Chicago, we called it a goddamn duplex.

Our life in Boca Raton was fairly simple. I rarely played golf, though we had country club privileges (our house was part of a "neighborhood association"), because golf was a social pastime I had put up with for business purposes. I've always had better things to do than hit a little ball with a stick and chase the ball and then hit it with a stick again. Nor did I go fishing; I'd caught plenty of big fish in my time, but not the aquatic kind—fishing, it seemed to me, existed solely to provide the world with a more boring pastime than golf. My wife loved to garden, and I loved to watch her bending over in ours; she had a green thumb, and a great ass for an old gal. I told you I was a randy old bastard. Or is that sweetheart?

Anyway, my days were spent in a lawn chair, watching the boats go by, sipping rum and Coke, reading, occasionally accompanying my wife shopping, just as she would more than occasionally accompany me to the track. Evenings it was often cards, bridge club with my wife, poker with my buddies, retired cops, mostly. Since I'd only smoked during the war and was a mild drinker, my health was excellent, save for the sporadic aches and pains, never quite escalating into arthritis or bursitis, that a son of a bitch with as many healed-over bullet and knife wounds (even a machete scar) as I have ought to expect after a lifetime of merriment.

I had also started to write the memoirs of which this is the latest installment; but I had not yet come to the realization that writing those memoirs would become my salvation. That a man who had lived a life as eventful as mine, who was no longer of an age where that eventful life could be further pursued, could find, if not meaning, relief from the malaise of old age, in reliving that life. Besides, I had a fat advance from a publisher.

So I was noodling on a yellow pad, when the Texan strolled up, blotting out the sun like an eclipse with a pot belly.

"You're Nate Heller, aren't you?" With that drawl, only the word "pardner" was missing.

"I'm Nate Heller," I said, and I was, even if I was Nate Heller in sunglasses, a Hawaiian-print shirt, chino shorts and sandals. No trench coat or fedora, despite the goofy pictures I'd posed for, for *Life* magazine, a hundred years ago. "Private Eye to the Stars," they called me. We'd opened up our Los Angeles office, by then.

Anyway, the Texan. He was as big as . . . a Texan. He wore a multicolor Hawaiian shirt that looked like a paint factory drop cloth, unlike my own tasteful purple and white affair. A young guy—maybe fifty-five—he wore new blue jeans and wraparound black sunglasses, and his hair was white at the temples and suspiciously black everywhere else and curly and dripping with more Vitalis than a Sam Giancana bodyguard. He had a bucket head and a shovel jaw, and the hand he extended was smaller than a frying pan.

I just looked at it.

He took no offense, just reeled in his paw and sat on the edge of the deck chair next to mine, sort of balancing precariously there, asking, after the fact, "Mind if I sit myself down?"

"Who else is gonna do it for you?"

He grinned—his teeth were as white as well-polished porcelain bathroom tiles; caps or dentures. "You're a hard man to find, Mr. Heller."

"Maybe you should've hired a detective."

An eyebrow arched above a sunglass lens. "That's partly why I'm here."

"I'm retired." That was the first time I didn't use "semi"; dropping the prefix was either an admission to myself, or maybe just a lie to cool this Texan's interest.

"You never answered my letters," he said. He pronounced "my" like "mah." Like a lot of Southern men, he managed to sound simultaneously good-natured and menacing.

"No," I said, "I never did."

"Least you're not pretendin' you never got 'em. Did you read 'em?"

"About half of the first one."

A motorboat purred by, pulling a shapely blonde whose hair was made even more golden by the sun; the blue water rippled, and so did the muscles on her tummy.

"The rest you just pitched," he said.

I nodded.

"Left messages at your office. You never answered them, neither."

"Nope," I said, speaking his language.

"Thought when I come up with your home number, there in, where is it? Forest Park? Thought we'd finally connect. But you got one of them tape machines. Pretty fancy hardware."

I gestured with my rum and Coke. "That guy James Bond, in the movies? He was based on me."

He chuckled. "Actually, I wouldn't be surprised. Your name turns up in the damnedest places."

Peering over my own sunglasses, I said, "I know you've come a long way, Tex. So I'm going to do you the courtesy of lettin' ya speak your piece."

"And then you're gonna tell me to haul my fat Texas ass out of here."

"I would never insult a man's home state."

"You knew her, didn't you?"

"Who?" But I knew who he meant.

He stared at my sunglasses with his sunglasses. "Anybody but me ever track you down, on this subject?"

". . . No."

"I mean, you been talked to enough. I dug back through the files. There was a time you gave plenty of interviews, droppin' all them famous names."

"Stirring up business." I shrugged.

He made a click in his cheek, and his words made me sound like a pecan pie he liked the taste of. "Crony of Frank Nitti and Eliot Ness alike. At the Biograph when Dillinger got his. Pal of Bugsy Siegel's." He shifted his body from side to side, like he was really settling into this one-way conversation. "Were you really one of Huey Long's bodyguards, night they plugged him?"

I sipped my drink. "Another proud moment."

He filled his chest with air; it was like a dirigible inflating. Then he breathed it out, saying, " 'Course, there are those people that say you got a line of bullshit a mile wide and two miles long."

"Question is, how deep?"

"People that say you took all sorts of credit, for all sorts of famous cases, made yourself ten kinds of important, just to build up your business. That none of this wild shit you talk about ever really happened to ya. You really have an affair with Marilyn Monroe?"

I took my sunglasses off, tossed them on the grass. "I think you're about there."

The bathroom tile grin flashed again. "Out the door, you mean? Or knocked on my tail? . . . I figure your connection with Lindbergh's how you and A. E. hooked up. You worked that kidnapping, a while, didn't you? Only weren't you still on the Chicago police, at the time?"

I sat up, swiveled and faced him. "Is there something you want? Or are you just another mosquito, buzzing around a while? Before you draw blood."

"And get swatted? Can I just show you somethin', 'fore I head out? I mean, I come a long way . . . from Dallas?"

He withdrew a piece of paper from the pocket of his paint-splotch shirt; unfolded, it was a photocopy of a fairly crude drawing, about on the level of a really poor police artist's sketch.

"One of my associates has what you might call a modicum of art training," he said, "and worked this up from a native's description."

The drawing, rough as it was, was clearly a portrait of a ruggedly handsome young man in a priest's collar.

"Several natives we showed this to," he said, "remembered this priest, though not his name. They say he had reddish-brown hair . . . kinda like yours must've been, 'fore the sides turned white. About your size . . . six foot . . . your build, 'fore you got that little paunch. No offense. Ain't near the spare tire I'm carryin.' "

"Natives where?"

Now his smile turned sly. "Little bitty slice of paradise in the Pacific, no more'n five miles long, fifteen wide. In the Mariana Islands?"

I said nothing.

" 'Course the first time I seen it," he said, "it was about the opposite of paradise, Saipan was. Never saw such a landscape of total fucking devastation. You see, I was there with the Second Division."

"Marine, huh?"

"Twenty-fifth Regiment. I was there when Captain Sasaki and five hundred other Jap sons of bitches tried to break through at Nafutan Point."

"So I'm supposed to warm up to you now, 'cause you were a jarhead, too?"

"You know what they say—*Semper Fi*, Mac. Guadalcanal, weren't you?"

I thought about cold-cocking him, but only nodded.

"Got out on a Section Eight, I understand. Funny. You don't look like a nutcase to me."

"You might be surprised."

"Of course, according to that *Look* magazine article, it was battle fatigue. They even made you sound like a kind of hero, holdin' off the Japs in a foxhole with your boxer pal, Barney Ross. He was a drug addict, wasn't he? What a life you've led." He folded the photocopy back up and returned it to his pocket. "You want me to leave now?"

I didn't say anything. Another boat was streaking by; no pretty girl tailing this one, though.

"Nobody ever connected you to Saipan before," he asked cagily, "did they?"

"No," I admitted.

"I mean, you been talked to about her. You mentioned her in passing, to this reporter and that one. More of your celebrity name-dropping, to feather your business nest. I know you were her bodyguard for a while, in what, 'thirty-five? Least they didn't bump her off under your nose, like they done with Mayor Cermak and the Kingfish."

My hands were turning into fists. "I'm sure there's a point to this."

"But nobody ever noticed your name come up in the Mantz divorce proceedings. I never saw that in print anywhere—did you?"

"You have been digging."

He gave a shrug of the head. "So have a lot of people, for a lot of years. I've made three trips back to Saipan so far . . . and I got another one coming up. I want you to come with me."

I just laughed. "I don't think so."

"You know, there've been lots of expeditions . . ."

"They haven't found squat."

His smile was small but knowing. "So . . . you paid attention. You followed the news stories. You read any of the books?"

"No," I lied.

"Not even Goerner's? CBS news correspondent, that's hot shit. Then there's Davidson, and Gervais—"

"And you. Speaking of which, who the hell are you?"

"I won't tell ya unless you shake my hand," he said, shambling to his feet. "I mean, I already put up with more indignity than any good Texan had ever ought to suffer. If you won't shake a fellow jarhead's hand, then fuck you and goodbye, Nathan Heller."

"I don't know whether to throw your ass out," I said, "or invite you in."

"Well, make up your mind, pard. Either way, I come prepared for a good time."

And he stuck the paw out again.

I laughed once, and shook the goddamn thing.

"Let's go inside," I said. The sun had gone under and the afternoon was slipping away, cool dark shadows shimmering on the waterway; no more pretty girls today.

His name was J. T. "Buddy" Busch, and he was from Dallas; there was oil money in his family, but he'd made his fortune in real estate. In recent years, he'd been pursuing various exotic business ventures more for "the sheer fucking fun of it" than profit.

Amelia had fascinated him since childhood, from when she was first in the news for crossing the Atlantic in 1928; officially the "captain," she'd been a passenger to a male pilot and male navigator, though that fact was sluffed over, in the press. But later—five years to the day after Charles Lindbergh—she became the first woman to make a solo Atlantic crossing. Lady Lindy had set many records in her Lockheed Vega monoplane, her feminine yet tomboy image sending mixed but intriguing signals to a public that included a little son of Texas named Buddy Busch.

Buddy was an aviation buff who never learned to fly; later I learned he had retained his childish enthusiasms, as evidenced by movie posters (*Tailspin Tommy*), comic books ("Flyin' Jenny") and vintage model planes (*Spirit of St. Louis*) in a museumlike room of his Dallas near-mansion.

But right now we were in the three-bedroom Heller palace, in the kitchen-dining area, where my wife was serving us coffee and macaroons after bacon-lettuce-and-tomato sandwiches. She disappeared off to watch television while Busch and I talked into the evening.

"You know, I realize all of a sudden this is Valentine's Day," he said chagrined, "and here I drop in and you and your wife probably had plans. Didn't mean to spoil 'em . . ."

"We had a romantic little luncheon together," I said. "We did what all Chicagoans do to honor the day."

"What's that?"

"Shot up a garage." I munched a macaroon. "So Saipan trip number four is coming up? Aren't you taking a childhood interest a little far?"

"I didn't set out to try to find Amelia," he said. "A

pal of mine and me, we went to the Marshall Islands, what was it, now? Four years ago, five? Anyway, I had it on good authority that a whole slew of Jap warbirds were just waitin' for the pickin', on Mili Atoll."

"I suppose they did abandon a lot of planes," I allowed, sipping my black coffee, "when our boys started advancing. So you figured you could reclaim a bird or two?"

He nodded. With his sunglasses off, he had sky-blue eyes with long, almost feminine lashes, curiously beautiful in a craggy male face. "I had a couple museums on the hook, eager to buy planes to restore and display. But it never panned out."

"Never found any?"

"Oh, hell, there was a passel of 'em, all right. Zeros, mostly. Only in shit-poor condition. Planes either past restoration or too difficult to pry loose from the underbrush and overgrowth. Did some diving, too, 'cause we knew some planes went down; but what with rust and corrosion . . . It was a fool's errand, and you're lookin' at the head fool."

I studied him. "Did you think you were going to find Amelia's Lockheed?"

"Not hardly." Now the blue eyes had a twinkle. "You see, I know what happened to that 'flyin' laboratory' of hers. I saw it."

That perked me up. "When in hell?"

"The *first* time I was in Saipan . . . July 1944."

"You saw the plane."

"We'd just captured Aslito Field. You or your wife mind if I smoke?"

"Go ahead."

He dug out a pack of Lucky Strikes and fired one up, waving out the match as he said, "I was one of several Marine guards posted outside this padlocked hangar. Some of the brass were arguing with this fella in a white shirt, no sidearm, and you know sidearms were mandatory for officers in combat zones. Some kinda intelligence spook, I gathered. . . . Seems Major Greene discovered this American plane in Jap storage, and wanted to make sure the Marines got credit for it. But this guy in the white shirt was backing 'em off—and they were taking it."

"Did you see this plane?"

"Yes and no. A buddy of mine said they rolled her out and actually flew her. I didn't see that. That night, off duty—we were bivouacked a half-mile away—we heard an explosion, over at the airfield. Bunch of us went over there and this plane, a Lockheed Electra, civilian plane, was the hell on fire. Like somebody'd poured gas on and lit her up like a bonfire. Still, I could make out an ID number—NR16020—which meant nothin' to me at the time."

That was the registration number of Amelia's Lockheed Electra, the one she'd taken on her final, ill-fated flight around the world. She and her navigator, Fred Noonan, had taken off on the last leg of the landmark flight, from Lae, New Guinea, on July 2, 1937. Their destination was tiny Howland Island, 2,556 miles away. It was the most famous unfinished trip in history.

"Jap sabotage?" I asked, referring to the burning plane. "There would've been plenty of our little yellow friends left on the island, in the hills and trees and caves."

"I don't think so," he said, shaking his head, no. "I think somebody was destroyin' evidence. That fella I saw? In the white shirt? He had a real familiar face. I recognized him from the papers, or anyway I knew I should have recognized him from the papers. He was somebody."

"Did it ever come to you, who he was?"

He snorted a laugh. "Only the goddamn Secretary of the Navy. Remember that guy? James Vincent Forrestal!"

Names from the past can have a funny effect on you. Sometimes a warm feeling flows through you; my stomach had just gone cold. Colder than my wife's coffee could ever cure.

The blue eyes tightened. "You all right, Nate?"

We'd gone to first names, a long time ago. Sometimes I'm not all that easy to read; but I guess the blood had drained out of my poker face.

"Yeah. Sure. Get back to your story, Buddy. Trying to reclaim those old warbirds."

He grinned again; dentures, I'd decided. "I guess I am gettin' ahead of myself, jumpin' around. . . . Anyway, while we were on Majuro, misguidedly mountin' a machete expedition into the jungle to try and liberate one of the better-preserved Zeros, this fella . . . he was in charge of this heavy equipment yard where we were rentin' some stuff? This fella asked me the same question you did."

"What question is that?"

"He asked if we were looking for Amelia Earhart's plane. Then he told us how in 1937 he'd worked for a company supplying coal to the Japanese Navy. How one night he was refueling a ship called the *Koshu* when a crew member friend of his told him the ship was about to leave to search for an American airplane that crashed."

"That was his whole story?"

He gestured with a Lucky Strike in hand, making smoke streaks. "That was it, but it was enough, coming when it did. I mean, we were stuck in the Marshall Islands, about to throw in the towel on my warbird expedition. My friend who gave me the lead on the abandoned planes? Well, he'd also told me about these islanders, hundreds of miles apart, all with the same story to tell . . . a story of two American fliers, a man and a woman, captured by the Japs and held as spies, before the war."

"You were an Earhart buff already, Buddy. You'd read the books."

"Sure, casually. I knew the stories of her and Noonan windin' up on Saipan, the theory that Amelia was on some sort of secret spy mission, and got shot down and captured. Never took it too seriously, though. 'Course I kinda liked the romance of it. Right out of the movies, you know?"

"And you were in the neighborhood, so you decided to see for yourself."

"Yes, I did. Got an ashtray?"

"Use your saucer."

He put his Lucky out, then sat forward, the coolness of his blue eyes at odds with an expression that had grown intense. "And I talked to all sorts of people . . .

on Majuro, Mili and Jaluit, three little atolls in the middle of the South Pacific.''

He told me of some of the islanders he'd spoken with.

Bilimon Amaron, a respected storeowner on Majuro, related that as a sixteen-year-old medic, at Jaluit, he was called to a military cargo ship, where he tended to two Americans, "one lady, one man." The man had some minor injuries from a plane crash, and the woman was called, by the Japanese, "Amira."

Oscar De Brum, a high-ranking Marshallese official, told of hearing from his father (in 1937, when De Brum was in the first grade) of the capture of a lady pilot who was being taken to the Japanese high command office in Jaluit.

John Heinie, a prominent Majuro attorney, recalled attending a Japanese school as a child in 1937 and witnessing, one morning, just before school, a ship towing a barge with a silver airplane on it, into the Jaluit harbor.

Lotan Jack, a Marshallese working in 1937 as a mess steward at the Japanese naval base on Jaluit, told of hearing officers discuss Amelia's plane being shot down between Jaluit and Mili atolls; that she'd been routed to Kwajalein and on to Saipan.

On Saipan, a respected local politician, Manuel Muna, told of talking to a Japanese pilot who claimed to have shot the Electra down, and also took Buddy for a tour of the ruins of Garapan Prison, where he said the American prisoners—Amelia Earhart and Fred Noonan—had been held.

"We've made three trips to Saipan," Buddy said, "with limited results. At first, the Saipanese, the Chamorros, seemed less willing to talk than the other islanders."

"Why do you suppose that is?"

"Well, for one thing, they still fear reprisals from the Japanese."

"Even now?"

"There's still a strong Japanese presence on Saipan, Nate, strong economic ties. Then there's a general distrust, no, more a . . . hell, a downright fear of Americans, 'cause up till recently the CIA had a secret training center on the island, behind a security fence, not unlike the kind of fences the Japanese put up, in the old days."

"And the Saipan natives were afraid of the Japs, so now they're afraid of us."

"Right. Just another foreign military presence to be feared. And they got worries from within, too—a good number of Saipanese collaborated with the Japs, vicious goddamn thugs, carrying clubs, beating and torturing their own people. Many of those mean old bastards, who were on the Japs' 'local police force,' are still alive, and might retaliate if old secrets were revealed. . . ."

"You'd think after the war, these snakes would've been rounded up and shot."

"That's not the way of the Saipanese. Yet gradually we did get natives to talk to us. Dozens of them, with similar stories of the lady pilot held in the hotel, and the man who'd come with her, kept in the prison."

"So why bring me into it?"

He tapped the pocket where the photocopy was folded up; it crinkled under his prod. "You were on Saipan, Nate, well before the war . . . probably in 1939 or maybe '40. Weren't you?"

"Do I look like a priest?"

"You sure don't look like a Jew. Even if your name is Heller. That's 'cause your mama was a good Catholic girl; that's where you get your Irish good looks."

"What would I have been doing on Saipan in 1930-whatever?"

That bathroom tile grin flashed again; dentures, all right—you didn't smoke that many cigarettes and keep them white like that unless they reside in a glass overnight.

"Same thing I was doing there in 1967 and '69," he said. "Looking for Amelia."

"She's been dead a long time."

"Probably. But where did she die? And when? And where's the body?"

Out the glass doors of our patio, moonlight glimmered on the waterway; but even with the moonlight, the night seemed dark.

I said, "Buried somewhere on that island, I suppose."

He pounded a fist on the table. "That's why I'm going

back. To find her grave. To prove she was there, and give her a proper burial, and her rightful place in history as the first courageous casualty of the Second World War."

I looked at him like he was the one who'd been mustered out on a Section Eight. "Then go dig her up. You don't need me for it."

The blue eyes narrowed and bore in on me like benign laser beams. "I think you'd be useful company, Nate. Might be interesting, seeing if that mug of yours stirs any memories, loosens any tongues. You'll see some familiar faces. Remember a badass named Jesus Sablan? He was the head of the Saipan police—worst of the collaborators."

My stomach grew cold again; my eyes felt like stones.

When I didn't say anything, Buddy said, "Funny, I thought maybe you might remember him. One of the stories about the Irish priest involves Sablan. . . . They say Sablan's the one that killed Fred Noonan. Some of them say that, anyway. Quietly, they say it. Secretly. Praying it never gets back to Lord Jesus."

"Still alive." My voice sounded hushed, distant, like somebody else was saying it, somewhere else.

A sly smile formed; blue eyes twinkled. "Oh, you do remember Jesus Sablan, then?"

I gave him my own sly smile. "I never confirmed your theory, Buddy. Never said I'd been to Saipan before. This could all just be another horseshit Amelia Earhart yarn."

"Could be."

"Remember your research. Remember all those people who dismiss Nate Heller's ramblings as bullshit self-aggrandizement."

"Good point. Of course, another thing I read about you, they say you like money. You don't turn down a good retainer."

"I'm old and rich, Buddy. Anyway, rich enough. And old enough, to ignore you and any offer you might make me."

"Ten grand, Nate. For ten days. Are you so well off ten grand don't matter?"

Actually, I was.

But I said, "Okay, Buddy—I'll take your money. Just don't ask me to go on record about that priest business."

"No problem." He rose from the table. "We leave next week. I'll mosey out so you can break it to your wife . . . no wives on this trip."

"Good policy."

"Please do thank her for the hospitality, and my regrets for messin' up Valentine's Day evenin'. Passport in order?"

I nodded. "I'll phone my office in Chicago and get you a contract."

"I'm disappointed," he said as I walked him to the front door. "I figured you'd want cash."

"That was a long time ago, that Nate Heller. I'm a different man, Buddy."

And I was, or at least I thought I was, till I heard those names: Amelia Earhart, James Forrestal, Lord Jesus Sablan.

Buddy Busch was giving me an opportunity I'd never dreamed I'd get: before I really retired, I would return to a place I'd never expected to see again, to a job I'd left unfinished, a very long time ago.

And finish it.

Ceiling Zero

March 11–May 16, 1935

Two

Searchlights stroked the evening sky, motorcycle cops kept the traffic moving, and hundreds, hell, maybe thousands of gawking pedestrians lined the sidewalks, the flashbulbs of the press popping, as limousine after limousine drew up on Washington Street near State, where a doorman in green and gold livery helped women draped in diamonds and furs step to the curb, followed by husbands in black tie and bemusement. What might have been a Hollywood premiere was only another attention-attracting attempt by a floundering department store to regain its footing in dark Depression days.

The famous showcase windows of Marshall Field's remained tasteful tableaus of prosperity, the classic Queen Anne opulence of a few years before replaced by Art Moderne; but the faces reflected in their glass belonged to window shoppers whose dreams of lives of luxury were as abstract as the streamlined geometry on display. Retail sales were down and wholesale was a disaster aided and abetted by the Merchandise Mart, the Field Company's $30,000,000 white elephant, the world's biggest (mostly empty) building, that mammoth warehouse conceived on the eve of the Crash.

Marshall Field's clearly needed help, and the heroine of the hour was finally arriving.

The man in uniform opened the door for her and Amelia Earhart seemed to float from the backseat, an angelic blur of white. Then, as she paused to wave at the cheering crowd—her shyness and self-confidence a peculiar, peculiarly charming mix—she came into focus, tall, slender, tanned, loosely draped in a white topcoat, its large mannish collar and lapels those of a trench coat.

The applause and huzzahs ringing around her seemed to both embarrass and amuse Miss Earhart, her wide-set eyes crinkling; with Hollywood-style makeup, the elongated oval of her face would've seemed pretty, but her features were barely touched with the stuff, a little lipstick, a little powder. Her hair was a dark honey-blonde tousle, her nose small but strong, her mouth wide and sensuous.

Just inside the bank of doors, two men in tails were scrutinizing engraved invitations and checking off names from a guest list limited to 500 of the Midwest's well fixed. Waiting with them was a handsome devil, also in tails, about thirty, six strapping feet with reddish-brown hair.

Me.

Stepping outside into the crisp March air, where breath plumed from every mouth, I crossed the red carpet to meet our honored guest, halfway. It was the least I could do.

I introduced myself: "Nathan Heller, ma'am. I'm the chaperone your husband arranged."

Taking in my tux, she flashed me just a hint of an apple-cheeked, winsome, if gap-toothed grin. "You don't look much like a bodyguard, Mr. Heller."

She didn't bother working to be heard above the noisy crowd; she seemed to know I'd be able to hone in on the low-pitched, Midwestern musicality of her voice.

"You don't look much like a pilot," I said, taking her arm.

Her smile froze, then melted into an ever better one. "You don't impress easily, do you, Mr. Heller?"

"No."

"Good."

I selected a door and opened it for her. Inside, no one asked to check our invitation. We moved down the long wide main aisle; though this was after normal business hours, the first floor was open, brilliantly illuminated and fully staffed. Some of the wealthy guests were pausing to pick up this and that at the curving plate-glass counters, bright showcases of fine lace, jewelry, perfume, embroideries and notions. As Amelia strolled by on my arm, eyes turned our way and oohs and aahs accompanied us.

"How lovely," Amelia said, looking skyward.

She was taking in the fabled Tiffany dome, a million and a half or so pieces of iridescent glass, blue and gold, shimmering six floors above.

"Hell of a lampshade," I granted.

She laughed gently, then her eyes widened and brightened. "You're that detective Slim told G. P. about!"

Slim was Charles Lindbergh.

"I've heard of you, too," I said. "I guess you know your husband's already upstairs."

"You've met G. P.?"

George Palmer Putnam, formerly of G. P. Putnam's publishing, part-time consultant to Paramount Pictures, full-time husband and manager of Amelia Earhart.

"Oh yes," I said. "He's been choreographing things here all afternoon, the management, the staff, the press, me, you name it."

"That's G. P. Obnoxious, isn't he?"

She had a wicked little smile going; I gave her half a smile, just this side of noncommittal, in return.

"That's an opinion I wouldn't care to express, ma'am, at least until my expense account had been approved."

The smile widened and made her face crinkle in all sorts of interesting ways; wind and sun had left their signatures on the once-fair, now-freckled skin. But to me the beauty of those blue-gray eyes was only emphasized by the fine lines at their corners.

She damn near hugged my arm as I escorted her to the elevators where the middle one was being held for us. Then, except for the good-looking elevator girl (Field's only hired the prettiest—Dorothy Lamour started in one of these cages), Miss Earhart and I were alone.

"Rent the tux for the occasion?" she asked, looking me over, finally stepping to one side, releasing my arm.

I gestured to myself with both hands. "This is mine."

An eyebrow arched in amusement. "Really? I didn't know private detectives owned tuxedos."

I patted under my left arm, where the nine-millimeter

was nestled in its holster. "You got to be well-heeled to guard the well-heeled."

Childish enthusiasm turned her into the tomboy she'd most likely been, growing up. "There's a *gun* under there?"

"Tailor on Maxwell Street gave me a special cut. Wouldn't want to create an unfashionable bulge. 'Specially not when I'm guarding a big-time dress designer."

Which she was, in her way: Marshall Field's was the exclusive outlet for the Earhart line of clothing, outfits for sports, travel and spectator wear, sold under franchise by one merchandiser in each of thirty metropolitan areas. Macy's had New York.

She had a wry smirk going. "I'm not exactly Coco Chanel."

"Coco Chanel never flew the Atlantic, not to mention the Pacific."

The latter had been Amelia's latest accomplishment, a Pacific crossing from Honolulu to California, a little two-day jaunt in January.

"You see, it's a routine now, Mr. Heller." The low, melodic voice was weary and resigned. "I set a record and then I lecture on it . . . even though I hate crowds. And I sell books—which I do write myself, mind you— and clothes, which I do design myself—and even, Lord help me, cigarettes."

"Don't tell me you roll your own."

"No. I detest smoking. Filthy habit."

"Then why endorse Lucky Strikes?"

Her smile was as sad as it was fetching. "Because I love to fly—and it's an expensive obsession."

Our cage shuddered to a stop, and the pretty elevator girl opened the gate and we stepped onto the sixth floor, and Amelia took my arm again. A handsome young man in a gold and green uniform, looking like a chorus boy in a Victor Herbert operetta, took Amelia's topcoat and ushered us into the salon's lavish oval foyer, with its beige oak walls and matching carpet and Regency furnishings.

"Miss Amelia Earhart," a butler intoned. He had an English accent that was almost convincing.

She swept into the salon with her distinctive combination of self-confidence and humility. Applause—of the fingertips in the palm variety, but applause nonetheless—echoed in the main rotunda. She waved it off and began to circulate, shaking hands, saying little, listening to effusive compliments with the patience of a priest.

The spacious circular room, broken up by curtained-off alcoves, had plump, comfortable chairs for plump, comfortable customers to plop down in around the central, beige-carpeted area, where wafer-thin models in costly clothing normally would do their preening, whirling routine.

Tonight, however, the joint was standing room only. Wealthy women, from younger dolls in slinky sparkly gowns to older gals who seemed to be wearing the dining room drapes, took center stage, their tuxedoed husbands at their sides like personal butlers.

In her casual white sheath with its distinctive black-and-white sash, Amelia would have seemed out of place, had she not been the focal point of wide-eyed admiration. Waiters served champagne from silver trays, waitresses ferried *hors d'oeuvres* and a pianist in tails tickled the keys with Cole Porter. I didn't tag after my charge, but kept her in sight. With a crowd this select, this controlled, it wasn't like my experience with the pickpocket detail was likely to come in handy; still, the ice hanging off these dames made Jack Frost look like a piker.

The most suspicious character in the crowd was probably Mr. Amelia Earhart, that is, G. P. Putnam. There was something wrong with the guy; something that just didn't fit, though he certainly wore his tuxedo well. He had the tall, broad-shouldered build of an adventurer; but his big square head with its close-cropped dark hair was taken over by the mild features of a college professor, particularly the cold dark beady eyes behind rimless glasses.

And yet, as I'd seen this afternoon as he manipulated everybody at Field's from the top brass down to the salesgirls, orchestrating the evening like Florenz Ziegfeld putting on a new Follies, he was one glib son of a bitch, whose fast-talking charm was a thin layer over his general disdain for the human race.

So what if he was a con man with a scholar's puss and

the build of a linebacker? He was paying $25 for the evening, better than double my usual rate, so he was okay by me. The job had come in over the phone—he'd called me from his home in Rye, New York, a few days before—and had been a referral from (as he had pompously put it) "our mutual friend, Colonel Lindbergh."

Right now he was working the room himself, in the company of Field's amiable president, James Simpson, who was introducing him to Mrs. Howard Linn, one of the local arbiters of fashion.

Stocky, round-faced Bob Casey from the *Daily News,* looking about as at ease in his tux as a dog in a sweater, came trundling over with a glass of champagne in hand. "You're a little out of your league, aren't you, Nate?"

"And when did you start covering the fashion beat?"

"When Lady Lindy picked up a needle and thread. Did she give the photogs a chance to snap her, downstairs?"

"Sure. She stopped and waved at the crowd. They probably got some swell shots."

"Great. It'll be nice gettin' some pics of her without the lens louse in 'em."

"Who?"

He jerked a thumb toward Putnam, who was smiling and laughing as he spoke with Mr. and Mrs. Hughston McBain; McBain was the store manager. "Ol' G. P. He shoves himself into every interview, every photograph he can. For every ten words you get out of the Queen of the Air, you get a hundred from the Bag of Wind."

"Well, he's sure had the Field's crowd jumping through hoops all afternoon."

"Shame on them," Casey snorted. "He's a cheap flimflammer."

Putnam looked anything but cheap in his rimless glasses and tails, hobnobbing with Chicago's elite, who seemed enthralled by his wit and wisdom; or maybe they were just impressed, looking at the guy who slept with Amelia Earhart.

Casey wasn't through with his critique: "He took over a great publishing house and cheapened it with those fabricated books of his."

"Fabricated books?"

He sipped, almost slurped, his champagne. "Overnight opuses wove out of headlines. By Admiral Byrd and your pal Lindy, and this big-game explorer, and that deep-sea diver. Ol' Putnam virtually cast your date, there, in her role."

"What do you mean, 'her role'?"

Casey shook his head, his grin a Chicago cocktail of contempt and admiration. "He sold so many copies of Lindbergh's book, he had a regular casting call, lookin' around to find a *woman* to fly the Atlantic, so he could publish a follow-up."

The reporter nodded toward Amelia, who was patiently, smilingly, listening to an overweight, diamond-flung patron of fashion prattle on.

"The belle of the ball, there," Casey continued, "she was just a social worker in Boston, a weekend flier, till a pal of Putnam's noticed her resemblance to Lucky Lindy, and the fabricated-book king made a star out of her."

"You sure you newshounds aren't just irritated, Bob," I asked innocently, "that Putnam's found a way to reuse your stuff for something besides birdcage liner?"

Putnam had spotted me talking with Casey, and he smilingly excused himself from Simpson and a small group of high hats, and made his way toward me, as Casey slipped away.

Hard-edged words emerged from a thin smile in a face as pale as his wife's was tan. "Hope you're not giving away trade secrets to the press."

"I don't know any to give away, Mr. Putnam."

He put a hand on my shoulder. "I told you, Nate— we're on a first-name basis. Call me G. P. I'm not some damn snob."

Nice way to tell me I was beneath him. And since when was "G. P." a first name?

"Well," I said, "you've scored at least one coup tonight."

"I think we've scored more than one," he said, pointlessly defensive. The mouth moved quickly, the eyes remained unblinkingly still. "I think we've done extremely well, and the night is still young."

"I was referring to that sourpuss over there."

He followed my nod and took in the grumpy visage of a stocky, white-templed character in dark-rimmed glasses and a tux that fit like a glove, if the hand in it were missing a finger or two from an industrial accident.

"Is he somebody?" Putnam asked, machine-gunning his words nervously. "I've never seen him before, he's nobody to me."

"That's Robert M. Lee. That may sound like he's a Confederate general, but he's considerably more important. He's the editor of the *Trib*'s Sunday section."

Putnam's thin upper lip pulled back over very small, white teeth, and his eyes widened with delight. Then the hand settled on my shoulder again and he whispered chummily in my ear: "How about that, Nate? We're too big to ignore. Even by that fucking Colonel McCormick."

Considering publisher McCormick's legendary hatred for FDR, there had been considerable doubt that the *Tribune* would cover this event, what with Amelia's well-known connections to the White House, particularly with the First Lady.

But now Putnam's joy had faded; a frown clenched his high forehead. "This character won't make us look bad, will he?"

"He looks grouchy," I said, "and he is grouchy." I'd known Lee a long time; he'd been in a bad mood ever since his legman Jake Lingle got plugged under his (Lee's) city editorship. "But the photogravure section's not exactly where the muckraking stuff gets run. You're probably safe."

Suddenly he shook my hand. "You're doing a great job, Nate. You're everything Ben said you were."

He was still gripping my hand; he was trying too hard to show me his strength and his he-man temperament— sort of like using a word like "fucking" in a Marshall Field's dress salon.

"Ben?" I asked. "Which Ben told you what about me?"

"Hecht," Putnam said, and at first I thought he'd said "Heck," which was better than "fucking." "Aren't you and Ben Hecht old friends?"

". . . Yeah. Sort of . . ." Former newsman Hecht,

who'd long since traded Chicago for Hollywood, had been part of the Bohemian coterie that used to hang around my father's radical bookshop on the West Side, when I was a kid. "How do you know him, G. P.?"

"I published his first novels," Putnam said, touching my chest lightly. "Now, when we wrap up here, I want you to accompany A. E. and me out for a late dinner . . . not as a bodyguard, but as a valued friend."

And then he got back to gladhanding more important suckers than yours truly, leaving me to wonder who had really recommended me—Hecht or Lindbergh . . . and what made me such a big deal, anyway? Just what the hell had I accomplished here, tonight, that was so gosh darn fucking phenomenal?

Pretty soon affable Field's president Simpson was introducing their honored guest.

"As the fashion center of mid-America," he said, a glass of champagne in hand, Amelia standing shyly just behind him, G. P. looming behind her like a square-shouldered shadow, "we are proud to add to our distinguished list of designers . . . Hattie Carnegie, Adrian, Norman Norell, Oscar Kiam and Pauline Trigère . . . Miss Amelia Earhart!"

More applause followed, and Amelia stepped forward, clearly embarrassed, gesturing for the applause to stop; after a while, it did.

Simpson said, "You know, Miss Earhart, you've set many impressive records, but tonight you've really pulled off a remarkable feat. . . . This marks the first time spirits have been served on these premises."

A mild wave of tittering moved across the room; all present knew of the Field Company's conservative nature.

"But it was necessary so that we might honor you with a proper toast," Simpson said, and he raised his glass of champagne. "To Amelia Earhart—Queen of High Flying . . . and High Fashion."

At the end of the toast, Amelia—who had no glass of her own—stepped forward and said, "I'm afraid you've broken your longstanding rule just to honor a teetotaler."

More laughter followed.

"I thank you for your gracious introduction, Mr. Simpson, but I'm not here to make a formal speech. I would like to join you for what I understand will be a lovely presentation of the rather simple fashions I've come up with . . . not high fashion, really, but I hope you'll take a liking to our line of functional clothing for active living."

With a bashful smile and a step backward, Amelia indicated this was all she had to say.

But a male voice from between two dowagers in tiaras chimed out: "Miss Earhart, you're of course to be congratulated on your recent success . . . the first solo flight from Hawaii to California. . . ."

The voice belonged to the *Trib*'s Robert Lee, who stepped forward.

"Thank you," Amelia said, uneasily. Just behind her, Putnam frowned at this intrusion.

"But this was a very dangerous flight," Lee said, "already accomplished by a man . . . and had you been forced down at sea, the search would have cost the taxpayers millions."

Putnam stepped forward, but Amelia raised a hand gently.

"I wasn't forced down at sea," Amelia said, softly, "and the gentleman who preceded me flew with a navigator, not solo. But I do feel, frankly, that the appreciation of my deed is out of proportion to the deed itself. . . . I'll be happy if my small exploit draws attention to the fact that women, too, are flying."

A smattering of applause, accompanied by expressions of irritation turned toward the *Tribune* representative, was interrupted by Lee's next volley: "Perhaps 'deed' isn't the correct word, Miss Earhart. There are those who say this was a reckless stunt, bankrolled by Hawaiian interests campaigning against the sugar tariff."

"I assure you that I'm more interested in aviation than sugar," she said, rather tartly, and G. P. held up a palm like a traffic cop.

"Please," he said. "This is not a press conference. It's a social event and you're quite at risk of spoiling the evening, sir. With all due respect . . ."

Bob Casey couldn't resist; he popped out with: "Now

that you've pulled off a Pacific crossing, is an around-the-world flight next?"

Casey's tone was friendly enough and Amelia answered, "Everyone has dreams. I like to be ready. . . ."

"We all admire you very much, Miss Earhart," Casey said. "But I for one would like to see you abandon these dangerous ocean flights."

"Why?" she asked, as if she and Casey were having a casual conversation over coffee. "Do you think my luck might run out?"

Casey arched an eyebrow. "You have been very lucky, Miss Earhart. . . ."

Nothing defensive in her tone, she asked seriously, "Do you think luck only lasts so long, and then lets a person down?"

Putnam took his wife's arm and said, "If you gentlemen of the press would like to arrange an interview with my wife, please speak to me, privately. Right now, we have a fashion show to present. . . ."

The press conference was over, the reps from the *Herald-Examiner* and *Times* not even getting in a lick, though I saw them taking Putnam up on his offer, buttonholing him on the sidelines as the guests retreated to the circumference of the room and models began showing off Amelia's wares, with the designer herself providing a low-key play-by-play.

"The tails of the blouse are long enough," she said as a slender girl loped through the room in a white blouse and pleated navy slacks, "not to ride up and reveal the midriff . . . and the silk detailing on the blouse is parachute silk."

An aviation theme ran cleverly throughout the collection: silver buttons in the shape of tiny propellers; hexagonal nuts fastening a jersey dress; a belt with a parachute buckle. Cool pastels and washable fabrics made for a shockingly sensible fashion show.

"This coat is Harris tweed," she said, "with an innovation we think will catch on . . . a zip-in, washable lining."

The simple, somewhat mannish lines of these practical clothes—broad shoulders, ample sleeves, natural waistlines—had a classic elegance that appealed to the starstruck crowd, and by the end of the evening, Field's salesgirls were doing a brisk business, with frocks and mix-and-match outfits going for as little as $30.

I asked her about that, at dinner, over my Hungarian goulash with spätzles. "Those upper-crust types aren't really who you're aiming for, with your line, are they?"

Amelia, her husband and I were at a table in the Victorian Room at the Palmer House, the hotel where they were staying. I was a frequent diner at the Palmer House, only normally in the basement lunchroom, at the counter. The plushly elegant white and gold room with its draperies of crimson was dominated by a large oil portrait of Queen Victoria; this was at the other end of the room and did not affect our appetites.

"Not really," she admitted, touching a napkin to her full lips, having just finished a house specialty, the fried squab Ol' Man River with pan gravy and pimento. "I think my audience is working women, particularly professional women."

"Well, we're not going to last long in the market-place," Putnam said, "if you insist on high-quality fabrics and low prices." He'd been the first of us to finish eating, polishing off the potted brisket of beef like it was his last meal.

"Working women need washable, non-wrinkle materials," she said, sounding like a cross between a commercial and a political statement—not that there was much difference.

"We're not making a profit yet," Putnam said.

She shrugged as she pushed away her plate. "The luggage line is doing well."

"That's true," Putnam granted her, obviously not wanting this to turn into an argument. "Very true, and with the lecture series coming up, we should soon be in better shape."

She glanced at me, obviously uneasy that their personal business was being discussed in front of a stranger. Like me, she didn't seem to understand why, exactly, I was here.

"Also," Putnam said brightly, cold eyes glittering behind the rimless glasses, "there's something I'd like to show you, dear . . . perhaps after we've had dessert."

She looked at him with what might have been suspicion. "What?"

His eyebrows went up, then down, like Groucho Marx, only not so funny. "Something you'll like. Something potentially very profitable."

"May I ask . . ." She turned to me again, her smile warm and apologetic. ". . . and I mean no offense, Mr. Heller . . ." And now she turned back to her husband. ". . . if there's a reason why we're discussing business in a social setting?"

"I think you probably already know the answer to that one, A. E."

"Simpkin," she said to him, a nickname she'd already used several times over our sumptuous, expensive meal, "I've told you a dozen times I don't take any of that seriously. It's the sort of thing people in the public eye just have to put up with."

"I disagree," he said with a frown, then flicked a finger in my direction. "At least you could do me the courtesy of getting a professional opinion from Nate, here. After all, security is his field. Didn't he do a fine job this evening?"

Amelia smiled and shook her head, then said to me, again, "I mean no offense, Mr. Heller, but—"

"I agree with you," I told her, giving up on the goulash. "I'll be damned if I know what your husband is so impressed with about me."

Putnam's thin line of a mouth flinched in a momentary scowl; then he said, "To be quite honest, A. E., I did some checking around about our guest."

"Slim recommended him," she said, with a tiny shrug. "You told me."

"Actually," Putnam said, "it was George Leisure who first mentioned Mr. Heller."

He really had been checking up on me. "How do you know George Leisure?" I asked, almost irritated. *Who the hell had recommended me to Putnam, anyway?* Leisure, a top Wall Street attorney, had been second chair to Clarence Darrow in the Massie trial in Honolulu in 1932; I'd been Darrow's investigator.

"Golfing pal," Putnam said. "Mr. Heller, I'm told you're

discreet, and you have a certain familiarity with the special needs of the famous. Of celebrities."

There was some truth in that, though the retail credit firms I did the bulk of my work for—not to mention the husbands and/or wives looking to get the dirt on their spouses that made up most of the rest of my accounts receivable book—weren't exactly household names.

"I suppose so," I said, just as the waiter arrived with dessert. We had all ordered the house specialty—Creole Juanita, a yam pudding—and Putnam and I were having coffee with it. Amelia had cocoa, explaining she drank neither coffee nor tea. A non-tea-drinking teetotaler.

"My wife has received some threatening letters," Putnam said, spooning his pudding.

"Everybody in my position receives threatening letters," she said, mildly impatient.

I touched her sleeve, lightly. "Now it's my turn to ask you not to take offense . . . but there is no one in this country, no one in the world, who's in your position. I'll be glad to listen to what's been going on, and give you my best reading . . . no extra charge, no obligation."

She had a lot of nice smiles, but this one—faint but fetching—was my favorite so far. "That's very decent of you, Mr. Heller."

"Hey, you paid for my services this evening," I said, dipping a spoon into my Creole Juanita, "and bought me a nice meal. How can I help?"

Putnam didn't have the notes with him, but as he described them, this seemed fairly typical celebrity harassment—letters were assembled via cut-out words lifted from newspapers and magazines, not asking for a ransom—just hateful, threatening messages: YOU WILL FALL TO EARTH, THE CRASH IS COMING.

"How many of these notes have you received?" I asked.

"Three," Amelia said. She was eating her pudding, not terribly worked up about this subject. The stuff was pretty much pumpkin pie without the crust, by the way.

I asked, "Where did you receive them?"

"At my hotel, in California. Before we left for Honolulu, and the Pacific flight."

"Did you go to the cops in L.A.?"

"No. I've had other crank mail, before. I think G. P.'s upset primarily because these are so . . . nasty . . . with the cut-out words and all, which make it . . . creepy."

"Did the notes come in the mail?"

"Yes." She pushed her pudding cup aside, half-eaten. Maybe this was bothering her, after all.

"Then you might be able to take this to the FBI or the postal inspectors."

"Please understand," Putnam said, his pudding finished long ago, "there's a history of sabotage, where female fliers are concerned. During the first Women's Air Derby, Thea Rasche got a note with cut-out words like the ones A. E.'s been receiving and got grounded with sand in her fuel tank . . . the rudder cables of Claire Fahy's plane were weakened by acid, and Bobbi Trout was forced down with sand, or maybe dirt, poured in her fuel."

Amelia made a face. "Jiminy crickets, Simpkin, that was 1929."

"I would prefer to be safe than sorry," he said crisply. Then he formed a businesslike smile and those unblinking eyes fixed upon me. "Nate, Amelia's about to embark on a brief lecture tour . . . ten days, twelve appearances . . . on her way to California, where she'll prepare for our next long-distance flight."

"Going after another record?" I asked her. "So soon?"

But Amelia, who had brightened at her husband's last words, ignored me and leaned toward Putnam, her voice breathless as she asked, "Then we're on for Mexico City?"

He smiled and patted her hand. "We're on."

She was almost bouncing in her chair, an eager child. "Simpkin, how on earth did you manage it?"

He sipped his coffee and then, too casually, said, "Merely persuaded the President of Mexico, our new friend Lázaro Cárdenas, to have the words 'Amelia Earhart Good Will Flight' . . . in Spanish, of course . . . printed on a limited-edition Mexican twenty-cent airmail stamp. Of the less than eight hundred they're printing, we get three hundred first-day covers to have you autograph and sell to collectors."

"Well, naturally, I'm pleased. . . ."

A mild frown creased his forehead. "What's wrong, dear?"

Her childish glee was gone. "It just seems a little . . . undignified."

"Flying around setting records is terribly expensive," he said, and this was obviously not the first time he'd said this, or something close to it, "and we have to accept legitimate returns where we can get them."

She nodded. Sipped her cocoa. Asked, "And . . . selling these stamps . . . this will cover our expenses?"

"It's a start," he said. He turned to me. "Nate, I can't accompany A. E. on this lecture tour, nor can I join her, immediately thereafter, in California. I have preflight preparations to make, service and fuel to arrange, magazines and newspapers to contact, and several other sponsors I need to finalize before the flight. . . . I would like you to accompany A. E. on this lecture tour, and provide personal security for her, at the Burbank airfield, as she prepares for the Mexico City flight. Are you willing to do that?"

Amelia was staring straight ahead, sipping her cocoa.

I hadn't anticipated a job of this scope. "Well, uh . . . when would we leave?"

"The day after tomorrow."

I shrugged. "I would have to make some arrangements to cover my regular clients with other agencies . . ."

Now he shrugged, in a matter-of-fact, take-it-or-leave-it manner. "Twenty-five dollars a day and expenses. I'll write you out a retainer check for five hundred dollars before the evening's through." He pushed away from the table and rose. "Give it some consideration. . . . Excuse me, for a moment. They're holding something for me at the desk that I'd like to show you." He was speaking to his wife and had a pixie smile going below the professorial glasses. "I think you'll be very pleased."

And he walked briskly from the dining room out into the lobby.

I sipped my coffee, then looked her way and asked, "Are you comfortable with this arrangement, ma'am?"

She laughed inaudibly. "Why don't you stop calling

me 'ma'am,' and I'll stop calling you 'Mr. Heller.' If that's all right with you . . . Nate?"

"It's jake with me, Amelia. Do you really think you need a bodyguard?"

She frowned a little. "It's difficult to say. It's true there's a lot of jealousy among the women in aviation."

"Gets a little catty, does it?"

Her eyes flared at that. "Actually, there's a great deal of camaraderie. . . . Have you heard of the Ninety Nines? That's an organization of women pilots, and I'm a past president."

"Presidents get assassinated, now and then."

"Well . . . truth be told, there's a lot of petty malarkey because of the attention I get. Or, I should say, the attention G. P. gets me."

"You have mixed emotions about that, don't you?"

"I do. But G. P.'s right—going for flying records is costly."

"You did say you had an expensive obsession. . . . Listen, if I take this job, we won't be . . . flying from one town to another, or anything, will we?"

At the corners of the blue-gray eyes, amusement crinkled. "Don't you like flying? Or is it flying with a woman?"

"I just prefer train travel. . . . You know, I imagine a lecture tour's like a whistle-stop political campaign, where you need to be able to rest up between engagements."

"So you're thinking of my welfare, my convenience. . . ."

"Well, that's part of my job, isn't it? I'm not casting aspersions on you, ma'am . . . Miss Earhart . . . Amelia. It's not that I'm afraid to fly with a female pilot, particularly one with your reputation. I mean, I was up with Lindbergh. . . ."

"Knowing Slim, and his sadistic sense of humor, he probably tried to scare the heck out of you."

"Not the 'heck,' exactly."

She patted my hand; her touch was cool, and her voice was soothing, somewhat sarcastically so, but soothing.

"We'll be traveling by car, Nate. . . . Not enough of these towns have suitably situated airstrips. Hope you won't be terribly disappointed . . . that we won't be traveling by train, I mean."

"Like you said. Just thinking of you."

Putnam was coming back into the dining room, carrying a paper sack that seemed incongruous with his tux, and wearing a tight, self-satisfied little grin. Before he sat, he grandly withdrew from the sack a flimsy reddish-brown suede hat with a silk band.

The band bore a facsimile of Amelia Earhart's signature, and the thing was cheap-looking, like it had cost about a quarter.

"This costs twenty-five cents to manufacture," Putnam said, sitting, as she took the hat from him and turned it in her hands, studying it with a blankly pensive expression. "And retails for three dollars."

"What is it?" she asked.

"Well," he said absurdly, "it's a hat."

She passed it to me. "What do you think of it, Mr. Heller?"

I thought I wouldn't want to get caught in the rain in a hat made out of cheap felt like this one, but all I said was, "It's a little small."

"It's a girl's hat," Putnam said. "A little girl."

"This is a hat for a child," Amelia said. Her voice sounded strangely cold.

"Yes, it is. Small hats to make a small fortune."

"No," she said. "I won't approve this. I won't have my name used to cheat children."

For the first time that I noticed, Putnam blinked. "But they're making them now. . . ."

"Tell them to unmake them."

"That's impossible! I've already signed the contract. . . ."

"Well, then that puts me in a difficult position," she said. "I obviously can't sue the manufacturer. But I can sue you."

He touched the front of his tux with a splayed hand; his eyes showed white all 'round. "Me? Your husband?"

"I never granted my permission for my name to be used in this manner . . ." She dropped the hat into the paper bag on the floor between them. "Do you want me to sue you for abusing my power of attorney?"

His voice was hushed, but loud with humiliation. "Of course not."

"Then you will call the . . . the hat people, first thing in the morning, G. P., and cancel that contract."

He just sat there, stunned, for a moment, struck dumb; then nodded.

Now she looked at me with a blandly sweet expression; the blue-gray eyes seemed as hard as they were beautiful, and as soft. "Mr. Heller? Nate?"

"Yes?"

She rose and offered me her hand; I took it, which is to say, shook it—she had a firm grip, but didn't overdo it. Not like her husband.

"We'll discuss the arrangements of the lecture tour tomorrow. I realize you gentlemen have some business to do . . . a matter of a retainer, I believe . . . so I'll excuse myself and go on up to our room."

She left the table, and the eyes of the high-society types around the dining room—a judge here, a senator there—were upon her, partly because she was an attractive woman who walked in a pleasingly, flowingly feminine manner; but also because that tousled-haired head of hers bore one of the most famous faces in America.

Putnam sighed. "That little attack of conscience is going to cost me royally."

I didn't say anything.

He stopped a passing waiter and ordered a Manhattan; I asked for a rum and Coke.

While we waited for our drinks, he asked, "What do *you* think of the hat?"

"Would you mind making out my retainer check first?"

"That bad, is it?"

"Hat's a piece of shit, G. P."

"Well, hell, yes, of course it is, but a profitable piece of shit. You mind if I smoke a cigar?"

"Not at all."

"Care for one yourself?"

"No."

He lighted up a big Havana number, waved out the match and took a deep draw off the cigar, the eyes behind the round rimless glasses narrowing to slits.

Then he said, "Now . . . would you like to know why I *really* hired you?"

Three

The wax-mustached, bunny-nosed "Managing Director" of the Coliseum—a buff brick building between Locust Street and Grand Avenue in Des Moines, Iowa— had proudly told me, earlier that evening, that the facility in his charge played an important cultural role in Des Moines, citing as a recent example a presentation by the Russian ballet. I decided it would be less than gracious to mention that the bulletin board in the lobby heralded the upcoming poultry show as his next attraction; and anyway, I needed him to help me set up a folding table for tonight's speaker, after her presentation, to sign copies of her most recent book, *The Fun of It*.

My role as bodyguard entailed any number of activities I hadn't expected, including hauling in from the trunk of her Franklin a slide projector, a reel of 16-millimeter film, a carton of books and of course a small tin cash box for me to make change out of, being the guy who'd be selling *The Fun of It* (it would be undignified for the author to do so herself).

The capacity of the joint was 8,500, and that was exactly how many butts were fitted into the seats. Mine was not among them—I was standing, arms folded, my back to a side wall, fairly near the stage, where I could keep an eye on the speaker and the crowd. They were mostly ladies, dressed in their Sunday finery, though this was a Thursday evening—feathered chapeaus and pearls and lacy gloves that would have waited till Easter if such an important guest hadn't come to town. A few men in suits and ties were sprinkled around the hall, and nobody looked like a farmer, nobody seemed to have manure on their shoes. Nobody looked like somebody who might have sent Amelia Earhart a fan letter comprised of cut-out words from magazines and newspapers, either; still, you never know.

The stage was rather large, empty but for an American flag at one side, an Iowa state flag on the other, a silver-white movie screen, a lectern and a single armchair, near the state flag. A murmur of anticipation was rumbling across the room, like a motor warming up.

We were in the second week of our lecture tour. We had stayed in Chicago the first night, where she'd spoken at the Orchestra Hall to a group of 1,000 4-H members, and had done De Kalb last night, at Northern Illinois State Teachers College, speaking to a much smaller group, coeds mostly ("We welcome home an Illinois girl"). Then it had been on to Gary, Indiana, and Battle Creek, Michigan, and a blur of cities and towns that gradually curved back westward.

Onstage, Miss Earhart displayed an unpretentious grace and an effortless command, with a deceptively casual, off-the-cuff manner (though she gave one basic speech with little improvisation) that made the audience members feel she was speaking directly to each of them.

But I knew that right now, in the dressing room backstage, she was sitting quietly, head lowered, hand over her eyes, in a zombielike state, having already thrown up, once or twice. I'd found out the hard way that she, like Garbo, wanted to be alone. She needed at least fifteen minutes to gear herself up for the ordeal of facing a crowd.

The house lights went down as the movie projector began its whir, and black-and-white images came up on the screen, the sonorous voice of Lowell Thomas, made tinny by tiny speakers, elucidating newsreel footage that began with the lonely unattended Boston takeoff of the Fokker seaplane *Friendship*, followed by a mob in Southhampton, England, where Amelia got her first taste of fame; then ticker-tape parades, Amelia with Lindbergh, cheering onlookers at airfields where she'd set various speed and altitude records, Amelia with President Hoover, Amelia flying the ungainly goose that was an autogiro, takeoffs, landings, swarming crowds, Amelia with President Roosevelt and Eleanor. . . .

Then the footage ended and the lights came up and there she was, no longer an image flickering on a screen, but a sweetly pretty young woman seated primly on stage, in the armchair near the Iowa state flag. Hands folded in her lap, like a schoolgirl, only the faintest smile acknowledging the immediate, ringing applause that filled the hall, she did not rise. Perhaps because she was seated, and her willowy height was not yet apparent, the impression she gave was of an improbably slight figure, for a woman of such accomplishment; in a gray chiffon frock of her own design, coral beads at the curve of her long, lovely neck, she was perfection, with only the studiously tangled mop of dark blond hair to hint at the daredevil within.

In bow tie and tweeds, the bunny-nosed Coliseum director was at the lectern, smiling prissily, as if all that applause had been for him. He informed the crowd of Miss Earhart's graciousness and friendly manner, how she put on none of the airs the famous frequently brought with them; and he spoke, rather eloquently, of her bravery, and her devotion to the cause of equality for women.

Through all this, Amelia gave no sign that she was being spoken of, or stared at; neither proud nor embarrassed, she gave no clue that experiences like these were far more frightening to her than flying across an ocean.

"Gertrude Stein has called us a lost generation," the Coliseum director said.

I didn't know how to break it to him, but I didn't think Gertrude Stein had Des Moines in mind.

"But," he continued, "no generation that could produce our speaker could ever be considered 'lost.' She displays better than any other young woman of her generation the pioneer spirit and courageous skill of our Midwestern forefathers . . . and need I remind you that she is a Des Moines girl, come home to share her story with us tonight. . . . Ladies and gentlemen, the Queen of the Air, Lady Lindy—Miss Amelia Earhart!"

She winced, just barely, at that "Lady Lindy" sobriquet, which followed her everywhere, and annoyed her no end. And as the most resounding applause of the night followed her introduction, she rose with easy grace, moving fluidly to the microphone, where she thanked the director and patted the air with one hand, gently, till the applause abated.

"It's true," she said, in that low, rich, yet very feminine voice, "that I saw my first airplane here in Iowa, at the State Fair. It was six years after the Wright Brothers made their historic flight at Kitty Hawk, and it was their celebrated plane on display, behind a fence. . . . My father told me it was a flying machine. To me, it was a funny-looking crate of rusty wire and wood. I was much more interested in the merry-go-round at the time."

Laughter rippled through the hall.

"In his generous introduction, Mr. Cornelison mentioned our courageous pioneer forefathers," she said solemnly, "and I realized suddenly what a terrible mistake I'd made . . ."

The grave timbre of her voice quelled the laughter.

". . . being born a woman," she said, her voice now mischievously lilting, "and not a man."

Laughter almost exploded from the women in the hall, their menfolk smiling nervously.

"When heavier-than-air craft were first invented," she said, "women followed just a few years behind in flying them. Today women hold various records, and I'm lucky enough to hold a few of those myself . . . though one recent article in the French press concluded, 'But can she bake a cake?' "

Gentle laughter, now.

"More important in my view than record-setting is the everyday flying done by five hundred cake-baking women in this country, on missions of business and pleasure. How many of you have flown? Show of hands."

Around the hall, perhaps twenty men raised a hand, and only four women.

"Please keep in mind that the flights I have made were simply for the fun of it . . ."

This reference to her book was contributed by Putnam, I would bet.

". . . and have really added nothing to the progress of

aviation. The time will soon come when what Colonel Lindbergh and I and a few others have done will seem quaint. Safe, regularly scheduled transoceanic flights will take place in our lifetime."

This exciting news caused a mild wave of whispering to break out.

"Could I have the lights dimmed, please?" she asked, and they were.

Then, using a pointer but never turning her back to the crowd (a nice piece of public-speaking savvy), she guided them through a lively, personalized slide show of her Atlantic crossings and other record-setting adventures. Throughout she maintained an unaffected, friendly tone, rarely getting overly technical, and even then projecting so much enthusiasm about her subject, her audience never grew bored.

When the lights came up, she shifted subjects, with the startling statement, "Sex has been used too long as an excuse by incompetent women who like to make themselves and others believe that it is not their incompetence holding them back, but their womanhood."

The crowd didn't know what to make of that one, and I could spot a few frowns, though they seemed to be thought-induced. And the men were shifting in their seats, fidgeting; the word "sex" spoken in public, when a husband was seated next to his wife, was apparently unsettling. In Des Moines, anyway.

"Don't take me wrong," she said, and flashed that gap-toothed, just-one-of-the-girls, just-one-of-the-boys smile, "I'm no feminist. I merely indulge in modern thinking."

And she spoke of science having cut back on household drudgery, that a woman could run a home and have a career, that husbands could and should share household and child-raising duties.

This all sounded pretty good, but when I plugged Amelia Earhart and her husband George Palmer Putnam into the equation, something didn't add up—I couldn't quite picture either one of them doing a dish or pushing a sweeper, and I figured both were too self-centered to ever have a kid.

But it made for a good, mildly controversial speech,

which received a standing ovation, the Coliseum director returning to the microphone to let the crowd know that, shortly, Miss Earhart would be signing copies of her book in the lobby. Soon I was making change and dispensing full-price copies of a three-year-old volume that was available in a cheaper edition, but not here.

Amelia signed three hundred and some copies of her book, and spent time with every customer, shaking hands, laughing, listening, each treated as an individual, and if she felt any condescension for any of her public, her eyes did not betray it; she did the same with those who bought no book, merely came through the line with a program to sign.

With Amelia piloting her big, powerful, twelve-cylinder Franklin, we left the Coliseum shortly after ten o'clock and, following the practice that was a constant over our two weeks of appearances, set out immediately for the next stop on the schedule—Mason City, the easiest drive of the tour. We checked in at the Park Inn, a Frank Lloyd Wright-designed hotel, around midnight.

Usually we drove all night, checking into hotels at dawn, frequently granting the press an interview over a room-service breakfast prior to getting in a few hours of sleep before the next lecture. She gave the reporters more outspoken stuff than her lecture audiences.

"If women were drafted," the dyed-in-the-wool pacifist modestly proposed to a gaggle of golfball-eyed Iowa scribes, "they would share the privilege with men of killing, suffering, maiming, wasting, paralyzing, impoverishing and dying gloriously. There'd soon be an end to war."

For the first several days and nights, she and I had said little, nothing beyond polite conversation; Amelia was cordial, if not quite friendly, and seemed distant, if not quite cold. I didn't understand it, since I felt we'd hit it off pretty well at the Field's opening and at the Palmer House dining room, after.

But driving through the night, in the Franklin, with her at the wheel more often than not (she loved that big car, loved to drive it, and I didn't mind letting her, because it handled like a boat), we sat in silence. I didn't take offense; hell, I just worked here.

Everywhere we went, it seemed, Amelia was claimed as a native daughter—whether at a Women's Christian Temperance Union meeting in Lawrence, Kansas ("What a pleasure to welcome home a Kansas girl"), a Zonta International tea at St. Louis, Missouri ("This outstanding woman grew up here and really took our 'Show me' state motto to heart!"), even an American Association of University Women lecture in Minneapolis ("Minnesota's own!").

She got $250 for each appearance—I was frequently handed the payment checks, as I was mistaken for her manager—and she earned her dough. Detroit was particularly grueling.

At the Hotel Statler (where we'd arrived at 2:00 A.M. the night before, Battle Creek being our previous stop), Amelia held a press conference in her suite over an omelet, six pieces of toast, a cantaloupe and a pot of hot chocolate. A morning tour of the Hudson auto plant (where the Essex was made—the car she was currently endorsing, despite the Franklin she preferred, which was from a previous endorsement deal) was followed by a Women's Advertising Club luncheon in the Detroit-Leland Hotel dining room, where she did not speak but received a warm ovation as guest of the Detroit Automobile Dealers Association. This made necessary a mid-afternoon tearoom stop with key members of the association, after a photo for their company publication was taken outside the three-story brownstone rooming house which a bronze tablet announced as the birthplace of Charles Lindbergh. Her lecture followed dinner for the auto dealers association at the Yacht Club and, finally, she made an appearance—but not a speech—at an auto show at Convention Hall, between Woodward and Cass Avenues, where an enthusiastic crowd turned ugly, pushing, shoving, trying to get a closer look at her, waving pens and pieces of paper and hollering for autographs, pawing at her clothing, till it seemed they might tear themselves some souvenirs.

These were not the refined ladies in feathered hats and figured frocks we'd encountered at luncheons and lectures, nor the polite businessmen in suits and ties who made up the rest of her usual audience; these were real people. Blue-collar working stiffs, hard-working house-wives, salt of the earth, backbone of America.

You know—goons.

"We got a problem here!" I said to the Hudson rep who was Amelia's official escort. Arms outstretched like an umpire, I was doing my best to keep the clawing crowd away from an increasingly spooked Amelia; she was behind me, and we were backed up to a Hudson Eight on display there.

The Hudson rep was a little guy with George Raft's hair, Clark Gable's mustache and Stan Laurel's face. "What do you suggest, Mr. Heller?"

Arms were flailing, hands pawing the air, like the crowd was drowning in its own tidal wave of bad breath and body odor.

"Where are the keys to that buggy?" I yelled, nodding to the Hudson.

He blinked. "Under the floor mat—why?"

A housewife who only slightly outweighed me was climbing on me like she wanted to procreate. I put my hand in her face, like Jimmy Cagney feeding Mae Clarke a grapefruit, and shoved her back. Then I straight-armed a ten-year-old kid and took Amelia by the arm, yanked open the driver's-side door and said, "Get in."

She gave me only a moment's look, to determine whether or not I was crazy, saw that I was and got in; so did I. She crawled over into the rider's seat and we both rolled up the windows and locked ourselves in. I reached down and fumbled around under the mat and finally found the car keys. Wild eyes and yellow teeth and waving arms were the view out the windshield.

I started the engine but nobody seemed to notice; the hubbub out there was a dimwitted din a mere Hudson motor couldn't hope to be heard over. Then I leaned into the Hudson's horn and it bleated like a cow a tree fell on, and they heard that. In fact, it scared the hell right out of them, and gave them notice to get their asses out of my way.

Putting the Hudson in gear, I guided that streamlined baby right down the center aisle, through the convention hall, startled, pissed-off auto show attendees getting out of my way, bowling pins avoiding an oncoming ball. For people at an auto show, it was like they'd never seen a moving car before; hell, I was only doing five or ten miles an hour.

When I neared the exits—a row of doors clearly designed for people, not Hudsons—I braked, put the car in park, gave her a glance that told her what to do, and we hopped out on our respective sides, leaving the motor running, and she came around the front of the Hudson and took my hand.

A couple of uniformed cops near the exits were viewing this escapade with wide eyes and open mouths; one of the cops yelled, "Say! You can't do that!"

We were halfway out the door, still hand in hand, when I nodded toward my partner and said, "But this is Amelia Earhart," and the cop was thinking about that when we were gone, scampering like a couple of kids out the Convention Hall's high arched entrance where we grabbed the first of a row of waiting cabs.

In the backseat of the cab, she threw back her headful of tousled curls and laughed and laughed. I wasn't laughing, but I was smiling to where my cheeks might burst, and my heart was hammering. The excitement was like a drug rushing through my veins.

"Oh my goodness!" Tears of delight rolled down her apple cheeks. "You're amazing, Nate! Simply amazing!"

"I just drove a damn car from one end of a convention hall to the other, is all," I said. "It's not like I flew across an ocean or anything."

"What wonderful fun. You do have a reckless streak, don't you?"

"I've been accused of that."

And that night—though she'd just endured fourteen hours of public scrutiny and abuse—we set out in the Franklin for the next stop on our itinerary, Fort Wayne. Not that she didn't show some of the wear and tear of the long day; she looked frail, wan, the lovely blue-gray eyes surrounded by not so lovely puffiness. For a change, she allowed me—in fact, implored me—to do the driving. She curled up in her seat, like a cat, in a blouse and chino slacks, the curve of her back to me as she slept, and her rather nice backside. . . .

"Those threatening notes are quite real," Putnam had

told me, back in the Palmer House dining room. "The bodyguard aspect of your job is every bit the way I explained it to you."

"Then what's the idea of asking me," I said, "do I want to know the 'real' reason I was hired?"

He drew on the Havana cigar, leaning back in his chair, a man of means, about to discuss his prized possession. "My wife's an attractive woman, wouldn't you say?"

"Well, I wouldn't say, but now that you mention it, sure. She's a peach. You're a lucky guy."

"Perhaps." He sat forward now and those unblinking eyes revealed something new, something besides self-absorption and mild lunacy: sorrow. "I believe my wife is having an affair."

This was not the first time I had heard a male client say this of his spouse; normally, it was news about as shocking as the sun coming up. But this I hadn't seen coming. Perhaps it was in part the setting, the fancy dining room with its background sound of a string quartet and the clink of fine china and occasional clunk of silverware and polite conversation with laughter mingled in. The waiter was delivering our drinks and I grabbed and sipped my rum and Coke, rolling the liquid around in my mouth as I rolled Putnam's words around in my brain.

Quietly, I spelled it out: "You mean, this is a divorce job? You want me to get the goods on your wife, so you can sue for divorce?"

Savoring a sip of his Manhattan, he shook his head, no. "Nate, I'm hoping that if I can confront my wife with proof of her . . . indiscretions . . . she will abandon this . . . this fling . . . and return to my arms."

Those arms were folded, right now, and he seemed about as loving—and concerned—as a broker discussing stock options; still, the sadness in the glazed eyes behind the scholarly round-rimmed glasses could not be denied.

"How sure are you that she's dallying?" I asked.

"Fairly sure. Quite sure."

"Which is it? There's a big difference between fairly and quite."

"His name is Paul Mantz." He took another sip of his Manhattan; in fact, he took two sips. "He's a pilot, a

stunt pilot in the movies. Cocky little pipsqueak, six
years younger than A. E. Fast-talking, glib son of a bitch,
full of himself.''

That latter could have been a description of Putnam.

"I brought him into the fold myself,'' Putnam said, a
twitch of disgust flicking in one corner of his mouth.
"Met him when I was publicist on the picture *Wings*,
where he put together a small team of pilots to stage
the dogfights. I thought he'd be the ideal man to help
A. E. prepare for the Honolulu-Oakland flight.''

"Why a stunt pilot for that job?''

Putnam shrugged. "To give the devil his due, Mantz
is more than just a stunt pilot. He's an engineer, set his
own share of speed records, he's president of the Motion
Picture Pilots' Association. Successful businessman, too,
with a charter service, maybe you heard of it—the Honeymoon Express?''

"Can't say I have.''

"It's for Hollywood bigwigs and stars. You know—
quickie Reno weddings and divorces. Las Vegas, too. Or
just for celebrities to take weekend getaways, in Arizona
and so on. After all, somebody in Hollywood is always
fucking somebody else's wife.''

I was swirling my drink in its glass, studying the dark
liquid, as if looking for moral guidance; perhaps not the
best place to look for it. "I don't know about this, Mr.
Putnam.''

"It's 'G. P.,' and what the hell is there to feel uncom-
fortable about? You do divorce work, don't you?''

"All the time. . . . But this is kind of a shady business,
leading your wife to believe I've been hired for one
thing, getting me into her confidence, when actually I'm
working against her.''

He gestured with an open hand, reasonably. "As I
said, the threatening notes are very real. She may well
be in danger from a deranged fan or some jealous
competitor . . . most of these women fliers are dykes,
you know, and are by nature frustrated.''

"You're asking a lot for twenty-five bucks a day. This
sounds like two jobs to me.''

Amusement turned his thin lips into a curve. "Is that
what it takes to salve your conscience, Nate? Well, fine.

We'll make it twenty-five dollars a day for bodyguard duties, and another twenty-five dollars a day for . . . these other . . . investigative services. *Fifty* a day . . ."

He reached into his inside tuxedo jacket pocket and withdrew a checkbook.

". . . and we'll make that retainer not five hundred dollars, but one thousand dollars. Plus reasonable expenses, of course. . . ."

And he uncapped a fountain pen and wrote my name and that very attractive amount on the check; it was upside-down from where I sat, but I could read it. Glistening there—my name attached to a thousand bucks. It was like an actor seeing his name in lights.

So I took the job. I didn't like myself for doing it, but I did like the thousand bucks. The thousand bucks was swell.

And now I was at the wheel of Putnam's wife's Franklin, and she was snoozing next to me, curled up cutely, and for the first time, in any major way at least, I felt bad, even guilty. We'd had a nice moment together, this evening, she and I. She was warming to me. And I was a heel.

But a well-paid heel.

She woke up around 2:00 A.M., and announced she needed a rest stop. I pulled the big bus of a Franklin in at the Junction Diner at Angola, on U.S. 27, just a few miles over the state line into Indiana. While the outside of the little boxcar all-nighter had that sleek modern look—a stainless steel bullet edged with blue porcelain enamel in the neon glow of its sign—the interior was dominated by the warmth of oak and gumwood woodwork. A truck driver sat at a counter stool having pie and coffee, but the place was pretty dead, just a blowsy blonde waitress and the occasional glimpse of the bleary-eyed, blue-bearded short-order cook at the window of his hole of a kitchen. We ordered at the counter and carried our hot chocolate (hers) and black coffee (mine) to our cozy booth.

"You saved my tail today," she said, dipping a spoon into the whipped cream atop her cocoa.

"I figure it was worth saving," I said. That was about as flirty as I'd got with her.

She gave me half a smile as she nibbled whipped cream off her spoon; no makeup, hair even more a tangle than usual, face puffy from sleep and still cute as a paper doll. "I admire that kind of courage," she said.

"Is that what it is?"

She was stirring the hot chocolate, now. "Call it guts, then. . . . I'm sorry if I've been a little, I don't know . . . hard to get to know."

The coffee was bitter. "Don't be silly."

"I learned a long time ago, not to confide in just anybody."

"I like to think I'm not just anybody." I saluted her with the coffee cup. "There are times I fancy myself somebody."

She laughed. "Don't be so anxious to be somebody. Look how much fun *I* have."

"Like almost getting crushed to grape jelly in that crowd? You got a point. Since we're talkin' like a couple of humans, you mind if I ask you something just a touch on the personal side?"

"I think that would be all right," she said, not quite sure.

"Where the hell *were* you brought up? Seems like every state in the union claims you as theirs."

She chuckled and blew on her hot chocolate; steam shimmered off it. "That's 'cause I was raised in just about every state in the union. . . . Well, not really. Just Illinois, Kansas, Missouri, Iowa . . ."

"Minnesota?"

"Minnesota, too. Not Michigan, that I can remember. My father moved us around a lot. He was an attorney working for the railroad. Rock Island Line."

"Ah."

"Actually, he had a lot of jobs. He drank." She sipped her chocolate. "My mother is a fairly cultivated lady, from a well-to-do background, and it was hard on her, when her attorney husband turned out to be a . . ."

She didn't say it, but the word hung in the air: *Drunk.*

All she did say was: "Kind of strange for us kids, too."

"How many of you are there?"

"Just my sister Muriel and me. We would stay with my grandparents, my mother's parents, part of the year, growing up. They were well off and I think it's rather hard on kids, seeing how the other half lives, then going back to the other side of the tracks."

I nodded. "I know what you mean. My uncle was wealthy, my pop was a diehard union man. An old Wobbly."

"Ha! Old boyfriend of mine took me to a Wobbly meeting once."

"It can be a good place to pick up girls."

"Ah, well, Sam already had a girl, didn't he? Though not for long. Your father wasn't much for capitalism, huh?"

I sipped my coffee. "That's the funny thing. He was a moderately successful small businessman. He ran a radical bookshop for years, in Douglas Park."

"Douglas Park," she said, nodding. "I know where that is."

I grinned at her. "You really did live in Chicago, then?"

"For about a year, when I was seventeen. We had a furnished apartment near the University of Chicago. I did a miserable stint at Hyde Park High. Hated the teachers there like poison and I think the other girls thought I was a weird duck."

"Were you?"

"Of course! In the yearbook they called me 'the girl in brown who walks alone.' "

"And why did they do that?"

"I guess because I wore brown a lot and—"

"Walked alone. I get it." I walked alone over to the counter with my coffee cup and got a refill; Amelia seemed to be doing fine with her hot chocolate.

Sitting back across from her, I asked, "Why flying? If you weren't a rich kid, how did you manage that, anyway? It's not a very proletariat pastime."

She pretended to be impressed by the big word, saying, "Your father really was a Marxist, wasn't he? . . . Jiminy crickets, I don't know, I get asked that all the time, but never know what to say. How did I do it? Scrimped and saved and worked weekends at airfields, any job they'd give me. Why did I do it? I always did love air shows. . . . Probably got the bug in Toronto."

"Toronto? Don't tell me you're Canada's native daughter, too?"

"Not really. Muriel was going to college there, and I'd lost interest in my own schooling, so when I went up to visit her, and saw all the wounded soldiers—this was, you know, during the war—I had an impulse to try to help. I took a job as a nurse's aide at a military hospital."

"That sounds like a lot of laughs."

Her eyes widened. "It was an education. I only lasted a few months. Those poor men, with their poison gas burns, shrapnel, TB. . . . I made a lot of friends among the patients, many of them British and French pilots. One afternoon, a captain in the Royal Flying Corps invited Muriel and me to an airfield and he did stunts in his little red airplane." She drew in a breath and her eyes were lifted, as she remembered. "That plane said something to me when it swished by."

"So that's where it began, you and your love for little red airplanes."

"Maybe. But then, too, I remember one air show particularly, on Christmas Day, must have been, oh . . . 1920?"

"I don't know," I said, "I wasn't there."

"I think it was 1920, in Long Beach. They had races, wing-walking, aerobatics. I was enthralled! Then, three days later, at Rogers Field, off Wilshire Boulevard in Los Angeles . . . only in those days, it was more like the suburbs of Los Angeles . . . anyway, I went up for a ride with Frank Hawks, who was nationally known for setting speed records. . . . He took me up two, three hundred feet over the Hollywood hills, and I was a goner. I *knew* I had to fly."

"Love at first flight."

She showed me the gap-toothed grin. "That's about right. My goodness, Nathan . . . you mind if I call you 'Nathan'? It's so much more elegant than 'Nate.' "

"I prefer to think of it as 'suave,' but sure. Nathan's fine."

She leaned forward, her hands gathered around the cup, cupping the cup, as if holding something precious; those blue-gray eyes were alive—it was like looking into a fire. "Nothing could've prepared me for the physical and emotional wallop of that flight. To me, it's the perfect state, the ultimate happiness. . . . It combines the physical and the intellectual. . . . You soar above any earthly concerns, responsible to no one but yourself."

"I feel the same way about draw poker."

She laughed, once. "That's what I like about you. You don't take anything too seriously, yourself included . . . yet I feel, deep down, you're a very serious person."

"I am deep. So's a drainage ditch."

Now her expression was almost blank as she studied me. "Does it bother you?"

"What?"

"Seeing someone so . . . obsessive about something? So committed? Isn't there something *you* love to do?"

I sipped the coffee, shrugged. "I like my work, for the most part."

"But do you *love* it?"

"I love working for myself. Not answering to anybody but the bill collector."

Amusement tickled her mouth. "Well, then . . . you fly solo, too, don't you?"

"I guess so. And . . ."

"What?"

"Nothing."

She sat forward again, urgency in her voice. "Are you embarrassed? Were you going to share something with me? Hey, I've opened up to you, mister. And that's not my style. Don't clam up on me . . . Nathan."

"Okay, Amy. I'll level with you."

"Amy?"

"Yeah. Amelia's a goddamn maiden librarian. And 'A. E.' is a stock broker or maybe a lawyer. Amy's a girl. A pretty girl."

Her eyes and lips softened. "Amy. . . . Nobody's ever called me that."

"It's all I'm ever going to call you, from here on out."

"I guess nobody ever called me that because it's my mother's name. . . . But that's okay. I like my mother, except for having to support her and the rest of my family."

"One of the prices of fame."

"You started to say . . ."

"Hmmm?"

"You were going to level with me."

I sighed. ". . . Yeah, I guess there is something I love about my work. Back in Pa's bookshop, I used to read Sherlock Holmes stories and dime novels, about Nick Carter the detective. . . ."

"And that's what you wanted to be. A detective."

"Yeah."

"And it's what you turned out to be, too."

"Sort of. Mostly what I do isn't like the stories. It's routine work, sometimes boring, sometimes shoddy, sometimes shady. Security work. Retail credit checks. . . ."

She nodded. "Divorce cases, I suppose."

"Yeah. But now and then something comes along, and I get to be a real detective . . ."

Another gap-toothed grin. "Like the magazines: *Real Detective, True Detective* . . ."

"Right. I help somebody. I solve something. A puzzle. A riddle. A crime."

She was nodding again, eyes narrowed. "And in those instances, you feel like a detective. And you love that."

"I guess I do. But it's like what you do, Amy—it's dangerous work. Sometimes you soar, and sometimes you crash."

"You've done both?"

"Yeah. But the problem with what I do, I'm only flying solo where the business end is concerned . . . I'm really messing in people's lives. Sometimes I get hired by the wrong people. Sometimes people I like get hurt."

"And when that happens, you don't love what you do."

"No." I was staring into my coffee; my face stared back at me from the liquid blackness. "Last year a young woman . . . young woman died because of me. Because I made a mistake. Because I believed a man's lies, a man who said he was her father but was really her husband. Because I wasn't as smart or shrewd as I thought I was."

Suddenly her hand was on mine. "Oh, dear. . . . You loved her, didn't you?"

Why the hell had I opened that can of peas?

"We better get back on the road," I said, drawing my hand away, slipping out of the booth, digging a nickel from my topcoat pocket and tossing the tip on the table-top. "We can blab just as easy in the car, you know."

"All right. My turn to drive."

"Okay," I said. "You're the captain."

She looped her arm in mine as we walked out. "You're not such a bad co-pilot to have along for the ride, Nathan."

We talked more that night, and many nights after that; we became friends and there were times, when I walked her to her hotel room, where I felt perhaps our friendship might be more, moments when I almost had the nerve to kiss her.

But, of course, that would have been wrong.

After all, I was working for her husband.

Four

Despite a blunt nose and wooden construction, the Vega was twenty-seven feet of streamlined design; with its fresh red paint job, the monoplane looked as if it were fashioned of metal. Though Amy indicated she was something like the fifth owner of the single-engine aircraft, the Vega awaiting us on a runway of Lambert-St. Louis Municipal Airport might have been brand spanking new; even its propeller had been polished to a silverlike sheen.

This reflected work that G. P. had commissioned. In one of the hangars of the sweeping modern airport with its radio-controlled towers, the Lockheed craft had been reupholstered and repainted, and refitted with extra fuel tanks.

"I didn't exactly lie to you," she had said the night before as we paused at the door of her room in the Coronado Hotel in downtown St. Louis.

Looking attractive if every one of her thirty-seven years, she wore a pale blue crepe gown of her own design; she was obviously weary after another long day on the personal appearance trail, having just spoken in a hotel dining room for the Daughters of the American Revolution (introduced as "a ray of hope in these bleak times"), where the only males in the room were the waiters and me.

"Sure you lied to me," I said, leaning a hand against the wall, pinning her there, her back to her doorway. "You said no flying."

"No I didn't." Amusement tickled her full, sensuous

mouth; she had her hands tucked behind her back. "I said we wouldn't be traveling by train."

I waggled a finger in her face. "You said we wouldn't be flying from town to town on this little lecture tour."

Her chin lifted and she aimed her cool gaze down at me. "And we didn't. The lecture tour is over, and now we're flying to California. . . . What did Slim do to you, up in the air, to spook you so?"

"He had the stick jimmied somehow so that his pal Breckinridge would lose control of the plane. And I just about lost control of my bodily functions."

Her laugh was humorless and not unsympathetic. "My goodness but that Lindbergh has the sickest sense of humor I've ever met in a man. . . . I once saw him pour a pitcher of ice water down a child's pajamas."

She was right about Slim, but I sensed a resentment for, and even jealousy of, America's most famous flier, from his nearest rival—who happened to be saddled with the Lady Lindy moniker.

"It's early," she said. I could tell by her eyes that she had another of the sinus headaches that plagued her. "Want to come in for a moment?"

"You need another neck rub?"

Half a smile settled in the corner of a cheek. "Am I that transparent?"

"Not to most people."

She had a suite, with a sitting area—this was an extravagance G. P. put up with so that she could receive the press on her own terms. Soon I was sitting on the couch and she was sitting on the floor like an Indian, her back to me, tucked between my fanned-out legs as I massaged her neck. Room service was on its way with some cocoa for her and a bottle of Coke for me.

We were great pals now, Amy and me, having shared the special intimacy of late-night gabfests as we rolled over the roadways of America in the middle of the night and the wee hours of the predawn morning; that big lumbering Franklin became a confessional, as the blanket of stars in clear Midwestern skies lulled us both into sharing confidences.

I knew the bitterness she felt for her family—her mother and sister, who she had to support, her late fa-

ther, who had boozed their family into periodic poverty.
I knew she had still not overcome the guilt for her "manufactured fame," since on her first and most famous
flight, the Atlantic crossing on the *Friendship,* she had
really just been a "sack of potatoes" passenger.

And she knew that my idealistic leftist father had
killed himself in disappointment over his only son joining the corrupt Chicago police department; shot himself
in the head with my gun, a gun I still carried with me,
the closest thing to a conscience I had.

These were not things we shared with just anyone.

Even so, I was keeping two secrets from her. One, of
course, was that her husband had hired me to spy on
her, to see if she were a faithful wife. The other was
that I could feel my friendship for her deepening into
something else. Of course, if I did something about the
latter, it might clear up the former.

"That's so good . . . so good, Nate. . . ."

I could feel her neck and shoulder muscles loosening.
Then I began working my fingers into the tousled curls,
digging at her scalp. Her moans of painful pleasure
sounded almost orgasmic. Or maybe I just wanted
them to.

"Why do you work so hard?" I asked, rubbing her
scalp.

"For the money."

"Your expensive obsession."

"Yes, but also to buy books and clothes, and send my
dear mother her monthly allowance to blow on my sister
and her no-good husband. And I like to live
comfortably . . . in a nice house with my bills paid and
money in the bank."

"You're mostly living in hotels."

"Oh yes . . . more of that . . . more of that. . . ."

She had given herself completely over to my touch. I
could smell her perfume—Evening in Paris—and her
hair whispered the scent of all-American Breck. A raging hard-on was inches from the back of her head and
she didn't even know it. A thief with a pistol in his
pocket had entered her shop and she didn't even realize
her valuables were at risk.

I said, "I always figured your husband was rich."

"That's what *I* thought. . . . But a lot of people aren't as rich as they used to be."

She meant the Crash.

"Anyway," she continued, moving her head in a slow circle as I continued loosening up her muscles, "he still has access to money. He's got the kind of tongue that attracts it."

"Don't you get tired of it?" I asked, referring to her grueling schedule, but she thought I meant something else.

"Of course I do," she said. "Marriage doesn't come naturally to me . . . but this is more a . . . business partnership. And I'm grateful for what G. P. has done for me . . . but, still . . . the endless schemes, his passion for celebrity, not to mention that ugly temper of his. . . ."

"How ugly does it get?"

She peeked over her shoulder at me, for a moment, as I rubbed. "Does he get physical, do you mean? He knows I'd never put up with that. Ooooo, do that . . . do that. . . . A man raises his hand to me, he's out of my life."

"You sound like maybe you've had some experience in that department."

"Not really. . . . Well, didn't I tell you about my father and the bottle of whiskey?"

We had shared certain childhood secrets on our long rides through the Midwestern nights.

"No," I said. "I don't think so. . . ."

"He was supposed to not be drinking anymore . . . supposed to've taken 'the cure.' I guess I was seven or eight . . . yes, right there, right there, feel that knot there? . . . I was probably seven and he had to go on a trip all of a sudden. Sometimes he investigated accidents for the railroad and he'd have to drop everything and just go. So I decided to help him pack and I found a bottle of whiskey in his sock drawer. I was pouring it down the bathroom sink when he noticed me."

"Oh, brother," I said. I was working my thumbs at the muscles between her shoulder blades.

"He only struck me a few blows, before my mother intervened," she said, "and spared me from a real beating . . . but I swore no man would ever hurt me again. Ouch!"

"Was that too hard?"

"Maybe a little. I think that's enough, Nate."

"I'm not tired. I can rub you some more."

"No." She wiggle-turned around and now was facing me, still seated Indian-style. She was working her head around on her neck again. "Do any more and it'll just start to hurt. . . ."

That was when I decided not to try to kiss her. And when my erection wilted.

Room service finally brought our cocoa and Coke, and she sat beside me, but not right beside me, and we talked for maybe another hour.

"I don't know what I'd've done without you on this tour," she said at one point, her cocoa down to the last sip or two. "It's getting nasty out there."

"Yeah, I thought maybe those D.A.R. dames were gonna start busting chairs over each other's heads, for a while there."

She laughed; it was almost a giggle. "No, ladies like tonight, that's one thing, but these public appearances . . . the shoving, shouting. . . . I mean, my goodness, what kind of way is that to express admiration? They even cut pieces of fabric from the wings of your plane. Someday a souvenir hound will carry off a vital part and there'll be a crash."

"You think that's what this is about?"

"What what's about?"

We had spoken little about the threatening notes; I had moved from bodyguard to trusted confidant to friend, and it had just never come up, even if my erection had.

"Could one of your admirers be behind those sick notes?"

She made a goofy face and waved that off. "Why would an admirer threaten me?"

"To stand out from the anonymous crowd. To be special in your life."

"It doesn't make sense to me. Of course, then, neither does G. P.'s theory."

"You mean, that it's a rival aviatrix."

She nodded. "I'm sure there's jealousy, but my peers know I've been their champion, that nobody's worked harder for the betterment of female pilots than Amelia Earhart."

I was aware, from the question and answer portions of her lectures, that as a founding leader of the Ninety Nines she had worked to make that organization of women pilots a central information exchange on job opportunities.

But I also knew that efforts like that could be dismissed as self-aggrandizement and politics.

"People can be pretty damn petty," I pointed out. "Besides, Amelia-Earhart-who's-done-so-much-for-the-betterment-of-female-pilots, trust me . . . anybody who refers to herself in the third person has enemies."

She pretended to be annoyed. "You think I'm self-important?"

"For a celebrity, not particularly."

"Is that what I am? A celebrity?"

"It's what puts the gas in your airplane, Amy."

Now it was the next morning and the gas was in the plane. The tall, slender woman I'd lusted after the night before was standing next to me on the tarmac, near her ship, buckling a tan helmet under her chin, flashing me that gap-toothed grin she hid from photographers. The weariness was gone, her eyes a piercing blue-gray, her chin firm, and she made a striking Lindberghesque figure in her brown broadcloth chinos and boots befitting a farmer, and of course a properly wrinkled, oil-stained leather flying jacket with its collar winging up, zippered a casual two or three inches, blousing open to reveal a brown and tan plaid shirt with a brown bandanna knotted gaily about her graceful throat.

"So is the Vega a good plane?" I asked, working my voice up above the airfield noise. It was windy enough to make my suit and tie flap; my fedora was flattened to my skull with a hand trying to prevent the hat's takeoff, and with my small suitcase in the other hand, I looked like a door-to-door salesman who wandered off his route.

"It's fast," she said.

"That wasn't the question."

"Well, the heat buildup in that cramped cockpit can get pretty disagreeable; that's why I don't need a flying suit."

"The question was, is it a good plane?"

"Yes and no."

"Tell me the 'no' part."

"It can be a little tricky near the ground. That single-chassis construction, with the no-longer-on fuselage, won't take any plane of the year awards."

"Why's that?"

"Folds up like an accordion in a crackup."

"Jesus! What do you do about that?"

She shrugged. "Don't crack up."

And she climbed the small ladder leaning against the plane by the wing, opened the isinglass cockpit cover and crawled in.

With that heartening observation to cheer me, I boarded through the cabin door toward the middle of the aircraft, crawling over massive fuel tanks to take the single remaining seat, where I buckled myself in. Glancing around at the boxlike tanks that provided less than reassuring company, it occurred to me I was seated in the middle of a flying bomb.

Though she was somewhat above me, I could still get a good view of Amy in the claustrophobic cockpit, her legs resting practically up under the engine mount. No wonder it got hot up there. She started the engine, and while it idled she watched the response of the panel of round dials, checking oil and fuel temperature and engine revolutions per minute.

Curling her long, feminine, artist's fingers about the stick, she taxied down the runway, turning into the wind, holding the brakes steady and hard, yanking the stick all the way back into her midsection. Revving the motor, she reached up and turned a switch; the sound of the engine's thrum shifted, and apparently this was what she wanted to hear, because her smile was reflected in the windshield.

With her left hand, she advanced the throttle, slowly, easily, and the churning of the propeller grew to a hard fast roar, as the Vega built speed, racing down the runway. She eased the throttle ahead, to its limit, keeping

the stick forward, bringing up the tail; the plane seemed
to want to get into the air but she wasn't quite ready to
let it.

Then she yanked back on the stick and the plane rumbled off the runway, riding the wind, climbing to ten
thousand feet and lending me a fine view out my little
window of the rolling countryside, shades of brown alternating with emerging green and occasional patches of
snow, threaded by sun-glistening rivers and tributaries,
interrupted by the occasional town of toy houses.

We didn't talk much, not with her crammed into that
cockpit and the Vega's deafening prop and engine noise.
She was allowing two days to make the nearly two-
thousand-mile trek, and had assured me we'd land well
before sundown, in Albuquerque.

The trip was mostly uneventful. I ate a box lunch and
read the latest issue of *Ring* magazine and even dozed
off, periodically, though late in the day, flying over New
Mexico, I got jostled awake by bucking bronco turbu-
lence.

I unbuckled and, moving with the grace of a drunk on
an ice floe, made my way to the opening between cabin
and cockpit and stuck my head up and in; even right
next to her, I had to yell: "Anything I should know back
here? Like where my parachute is?"

She hollered back: "We've run into some rapidly shifting winds! Don't panic!"

She was already making her descent toward the runways and hangars of Albuquerque Municipal Airport,
where a wind sock on a pole was twirling like a New
Year's Eve noisemaker.

"You were kidding with that 'folds up like an accordion' remark, right?"

She was sitting forward and her hands clutched the
yoke. "More like a Chinese lantern. . . . Get back and
buckle yourself in, Nate! I never lost a passenger yet."

I did a clumsy native dance back to my seat, buckled
in and then she shouted at me: "I'm going to have to
take the shortest runway! That's going to mean an
abrupt approach. . . ."

The Vega was riding the wind like a motorboat on
choppy waters.

"What do you mean," I asked, " 'abrupt'?"

And she answered me by dropping the plane into a steep forward sideslip. My as-yet-undigested box lunch (tuna salad sandwich, apple and chocolate chip cookie) damn near made a crash landing. Then the ship began a series of wide fishtails, like the Vega was waving hello to New fucking Mexico.

"Shit!" I yelled. "Are we out of control?"

"That's on purpose! It cuts speed!"

Maybe the plane's, but not my pulse rate.

The runway was looming before us, and yet she was flying the plane virtually onto the ground, the throttle opened up. We seemed to be running out of runway; she sideslipped so as not to overshoot it and as I waited for the sound and feel of the Vega's fixed wheels touching tarmac, and as Amy pulled the stick back to set down, a gust of wind suddenly ballooned the Vega back up twenty feet . . . and then just as suddenly, that gust of wind died.

And left us there.

Before we could drop like a stone, Amy slammed the throttle forward, the wind came back and the Vega set down without a bounce, though we were still at full throttle; fortunately, the runway was built on something of an incline, dissipating the plane's forward speed. We careened around the arc of the taxi circle at the runway's end and finally, blessedly, drew to a halt.

In the dining room of the Hilton Hotel on Copper Avenue that evening, I asked her, "What the hell happened today?"

"When?" she asked, nonchalantly cutting a bite of a big medium rare filet of beef.

"When we almost landed," I reminded her, "then had to land again?"

She shrugged. She was still in her plaid shirt and knotted scarf—we hadn't taken time to wash up for dinner, Amy being too hungry to bother. "Technically," she said, "we were in a stall."

"Jeez, I hate it when a plane crashes on a technicality."

She smirked, waved that off, chewed, swallowed, not wanting to be impolite and talk with her mouth full.

"We didn't crash, silly. We were just caught in a momentary vacuum. . . . It's as if all the air pressure got suddenly sucked from the controls."

"So you put the plane on the ground at full throttle."

"That seemed to me to be the best option."

"Isn't that a pretty good trick?"

"It is if you can get away with it."

I raised my rum and Coke to her; it was all I was having. "Here's to one hell of a pilot."

She liked that. "Thanks, Nathan." She raised her water glass to me. "Here's to one hell of a guy."

That was one of the few times I ever heard her swear, and I took it as a high compliment.

At the door to her suite, I asked, "Need a neck rub tonight? Or maybe just some company?"

Halfway inside already, she smiled almost sadly and said, "No, I don't think so, thanks. I have to call G. P., write a few letters, then I want to get to bed nice and early."

I'd been hoping to get to bed nice and early myself; only, not alone.

Maybe she could read my mind, because just before she shut herself in her room, she touched my face, tenderly, with the tips of those long tapering fingers. "Cheerio, Nathan. . . . We have another long day in the air, tomorrow . . . and I want to be alert, in case it's eventful."

But it wasn't, really. Smooth flying over the brown and tan and salmon vistas of New Mexico, Arizona and California, canyons and mesas and only the occasional stray city-boy thought that surviving a crash in this country would mean keeping company with sand and lizards and cactuses. She would dip down low enough to provide a good look at this delightful desolation, the Vega's cool shadow racing across the godforsaken landscape, where occasional dabs of green were like parsley sprigs on a big empty plate.

The late-afternoon landing at Burbank was blessedly free of unexpected crosswinds and technical stalls. We were close to the ocean now and desert vistas had given way to a breathtaking view of green hills bordering the fertile San Fernando Valley, mountain ranges beyond, some snow-capped, with Burbank and its United Airport nestled in the flatlands between.

The runways below were the five spreading arms of a flattened octopus whose head was a sprawling terminal identified by white letters painted on the tarmac before it: UNITED AIRPORT. On the runways at left and right of the modernistic, T-shaped terminal, giving it plenty of breathing room, were buildings that from my cabin window looked like flat square matchboxes but were actually massive corrugated-metal hangars, their roofs labeled UNITED and BURBANK respectively. Amy set gently down, with none of the melodrama of yesterday's landing, and we taxied, pulling up before a huge hangar door, over which white painted letters added up to UNITED AIR SERVICES LIMITED.

We were greeted by a trio of the airfield equivalent of grease monkeys, one of whom provided the ladder for Amy to climb down from the cockpit; she greeted them by name ("Howdy, Jim!," "Hey, Ernie!," "Tod, what do you know?"). A fourth man, who brought up the rear in the confident manner of a commanding officer who allows his troops to lead the charge, wore a gray suit and a lighter gray shirt with a gray and black tie and looked as dapper as a movie star, or anyway a movie executive. Small but with a solid, square-shouldered build, he was almost handsome, with bright dark brown eyes, a jutting nose, and a jaunty jutting chin; his slicked-back black hair and slip of a mustache were apparently on loan from Clark Gable.

He and Amy embraced and patted each other on the back like long-lost pals. Both had smiles that threatened to split their faces.

"How's my girl?" he asked her. "Ready for another foolhardy adventure?"

"Always," she said, unbuckling her helmet, yanking it off, shaking her mop of curls. "Paul, this is my friend Nathan Heller; he's been my one-man security team on this lecture tour. Nathan, this is Paul Mantz—he's the mastermind behind my record flights."

I had already guessed as much, but extended my hand and said, "Mr. Mantz, I've heard big things about you."

Amy glanced at me, wondering what those big things

might be, and I wondered if I'd misspoken: she had never mentioned Mantz to me—everything I knew about the man had come from G. P.

"Call me Paul," he said, as we shook hands, his grip showing off his strength a little, "and I'll take the liberty of calling you Nate . . . and as for what you've heard about me, it's just possible some of it's true."

"Well, for one thing, I hear you're the best stunt pilot in Hollywood."

He twitched a smile and I sensed some annoyance. "Actually," he said, "I'm not really a stunt pilot . . . what I am is a precision pilot. I leave stunts to the fools, kids and amateurs. By which I mean, the soon to be deceased."

Amy allowed the three mechanics to take over the Vega, and, with her in the middle, she and Mantz and I walked slowly toward the looming hangar. He had his arm around her, casually; it was hard to tell whether it represented a brotherly familiarity or something else.

"What have you got in mind for me and my baby?" she asked him.

"Angel, the boys in St. Louis have already increased your fuel capacity. I've got new magnetic and aperiodic compasses to install and check, we're upgrading the directional bank and turn indicators, adding improved fuel and temperature gauges, plus a tachometer and a supercharger pressure gauge."

"Is that all?" she asked mockingly.

"No. I'm gonna have Ernie overhaul the Pratt and Whitney again."

She frowned at him. "You really think that's necessary? That engine purred like a kitten, all the way from St. Louis to here. I ran into a wind shear landing at Albuquerque and it performed like a well-tuned race car. You can ask Nathan."

My opinion, which was that the landing in question had scared holy hell out of me, may not have shed any light on this discussion of technical matters.

But we never got to my opinion; Mantz was already shaking his head, no. "Better safe than sorry. And as for you, young lady, I've got a new toy for you to play with . . ."

We were inside the cavernous hangar now, the golden dying sun filtering in lazily through the many-paned high windows. Half a dozen monoplanes were parked within the tool-littered hangar, including a Vega like Amy's, only this one was painted red and white with the words "Honeymoon Express" painted on the side, in a heart pierced by cupid arrows. Amy had told me earlier that her Vega had no nickname (unlike her famous *Friendship* and Lindbergh's *Spirit of St. Louis*) because G. P. figured giving the plane a name and a personality might detract from Amelia Earhart.

"Here's your new best friend, angel," Mantz said, stepping away from her, gesturing like a ringmaster to his center ring attraction. "The Link blind-flying trainer."

And here was another little red plane, only this really was a little red plane, not much bigger than the ones that kids went 'round and 'round in at Riverview Park. With its tiny white wings and a precious white-scalloped tail and the words UNITED AIR SERVICES stenciled on its side, the squat fat-nosed trainer had a cockpit lid with no windows, and was elevated from the ground like a carousel horse.

"You're joking," she said.

But he wasn't.

"Angel, as long as you insist on letting that goddamn Gippy con you into these long-distance flights . . ."

"G. P. doesn't con me into anything," she said firmly.

"Well, then, if you insist on trying to prove to yourself that you really are that Amelia Earhart person they write about in the papers, you had better learn some goddamn discipline."

"I've had plenty of blind-flying training," she said dismissively. "Anyway, I don't like that term."

"Call it instrument flying, then. Or dead reckoning— and dead is what you'll be, angel, if you don't face the reality of how often your life depends on an ability to fly precise compass headings through the shittiest weather known to God or man."

"Let's call it zero-visibility flying."

"Fine. Call it Mickey and Minnie Mouse in the Tunnel of Love, as far as I give a damn. But over the next several weeks, angel, your pretty behind resides in that red tin can."

And he gave her pretty behind a couple playful pats, and she laughed and said, "All right, all right, you evil man," and somebody cleared their throat.

Actually, somebody cleared *her* throat, because it was a woman doing it, a redhead with green eyes and a pert nose and full red-rouged lips and a complexion like fresh cream and a chassis better constructed than any plane on that airfield.

"Isn't this a cozy sight?" she said, her voice high-pitched, with a hint of Southwestern twang.

It was the least attractive thing about her. She was poised just inside the hangar, and for a fairly small woman, she threw a long shadow. Her frock was a sheer white polka-dot organdy with a draped cowl neck and bare arms, which were folded under the rounded wonders that were her breasts; she had her weight on one leg, though both legs—judging by the sleekly nyloned and well-turned ankles—were worth considering.

"Myrtle," Amy said, and her voice seemed warm, as did her smile, "how delightful to see you!"

And Amy walked toward the woman with her arms outstretched.

Mantz whispered to me, "That's the little woman."

"You're a lucky man."

"There's all kinds of luck."

Amelia Earhart had now reached Myrtle Mantz, whose icy demeanor seemed suddenly to melt and the redhead accepted, and reciprocated, the hug Amy offered.

I was still trying to figure out what to make of that when they walked toward us, hand in hand, Myrtle's high heels clicking on the cement floor, echoing in the high-ceilinged space like gunfire. Myrtle was smiling, now; a dazzler it was, too, with no gaps.

"Have you seen the torture chamber your husband's arranged for me?" Amy asked Myrtle, and the two girls—chums now—peeked in and around the little red plane. Myrtle stood on tippy-toe and, under the organdy dress, the globes of her perfect behind were like firm ripe melons; as much as I admired Amy's tomboyish pulchritude, Mantz was definitely a guy who didn't need to leave the house to find a pretty behind to pat.

Shortly thereafter we recommenced to the Union Terminal's Sky Room, a quaint mix of linen tablecloths, airplane memorabilia and cumbersome dude ranch furnishings. Birds tweeting in cages spoke more of captivity than flight, while a wall of windows looked out over endless runways where the bigger birds of United, Western and TWA came and went; as dusk turned to evening, floodlights turned the tarmac to instant noon.

Mantz sat beside his wife but across from Amy; I was next to Amy and across from Mrs. Mantz, who was so gorgeous I instantly composed a private, filthy limerick about her, utilizing the word "pants" as the punchline.

A cocky, swaggering little guy, Mantz did most of the talking at dinner, frequently laughing at his own jokes. But mostly he was coaching his star pupil.

"You know you have a tendency to push your engine to the limit," he said to Amy. We had finished our dinner—everyone had fresh seafood of one kind or another, delicious—and he was working on his third frost-rimmed martini.

"Of course," Amy said, over her inevitable cup of cocoa. "The extra power makes up for the headwinds."

"That's no way to fly," he said, exasperated. "It's a foolish goddamn dangerous method to use on life-and-death long-range flights."

Myrtle Mantz had said little through dinner; she was watching her husband and his charge talk about flying as if she were overhearing them pitching woo at each other. But neither Paul nor Amy seemed to notice the daggers in those green eyes.

"Listen," he said to Amy, "when this Mexico flight is over, why don't you leave the Vega with me? I can add it to my charter service. You can make a little dough, angel."

Every time he called Amy "angel," a furrow like a cut appeared between Mrs. Mantz's finely plucked eyebrows.

Amy considered Mantz's offer, shrugged. "I don't see why not. How's business been?"

"You know flying—up and down." He chortled at this

prime witticism, then said, "The big money's with the
Hollywood jobs, but when the weather's bad and production schedules are slow, I fall back on the ol' Honeymoon Express."

Myrtle, finally acknowledging my existence, gazed at
me with hooded eyes. "This is where Paul starts dropping names. It's one of his least attractive traits."

Mantz sipped his martini and said to me, "Don't listen
to her, Nate. Ever since Jean Harlow kissed me at that
air show in '33, she's been like this." And he said to
her, "Baby, that's how Hollywood is. They kiss and they
hug and it don't mean a goddamn thing. It's like a hand-
shake to these people."

"He had Cecil B. DeMille in his plane last week," she
said to me. "I doubt there was much kissing and hugging
on that flight."

Then Mantz said to me, "Ask her if she didn't beg
me to come along on the Douglas Fairbanks charter."

Generally it's not a good sign for a marriage when
the husband and wife speak to each other through a
third party.

Suddenly Mrs. Mantz, her tone suspiciously civil,
asked, "Amelia, where are you staying while you're in
town?"

"I haven't lined anything up yet," she said. "Maybe
the Ambassador. . . ."

"Nonsense," Myrtle said. "The Ambassador's all the
way downtown, and we have plenty of room. Stay with
us."

"Oh, I don't want to impose again," Amy said.

Again? Had she stayed with the Mantzes before?

"Oh you simply must," Myrtle said. "I won't even be
underfoot, much . . . . I'm leaving tomorrow afternoon,
to visit my mother in Dallas."

"Well . . ." Amy looked at Mantz. ". . . if it won't
put you out."

"Not at all," Myrtle said.

"It'll give us a chance to put our heads together at
night," Mantz said, and he patted Amy's hand. "You know
how hectic it gets out here at the field. . . . I've been
working up charts with Clarence, and he'll consult with
us, too."

Clarence Williams, Amy later explained, was a retired Navy navigator who'd been helping prepare the charts of her long-distance flights since the solo Atlantic crossing.

Amy looked at Myrtle searchingly. "If it's really not an imposition. . . ."

"Don't be silly," Myrtle said. "I want you to come."

And she lifted her own frost-edged martini glass in a little toast to her invited houseguest, with a smile just as frosty.

Five

The almost-full moon was an off-white spotlight, casting an ivory spell upon the precious storybook houses of Valley Spring Lane. This was Toluca Lake, a district poised between Burbank and North Hollywood like a backlot positing an imaginary America that existed only in the movies. Small houses mostly, cottage-size—though on nearby Toluca Estates Drive I'd seen some larger ones, modest movie star mansions where perfect couples like Dick Powell and Joan Blondell had settled; but even those had a movie magic tinge, here a perfect Tudor, there a quaint gingerbread, and the occasional Spanish colonial-style, like this pale yellow stucco number with the green tile roof and matching front awnings, a dream bungalow in the bushes of which I was crouched by a side awningless window with my Speed Graphic with infrared film and the world's most inconspicuous flash.

The role I was playing, in this ambitious production, was bedroom dick. I wasn't proud of working the divorce racket, but there are those who would say I was typecast.

This was my third night in southern California. After dining at the Sky Room with the Mantzes that first evening, Amy had presented me with the keys to a blue '34 Terraplane convertible she and G. P. kept in California, a perk from the Hudson company for her current endorsement deal.

"*I'm* going to do the driving?" I asked, mildly surprised that I was being chosen to pilot the stylish little streamlined coupe, which was parked outside Mantz's United Air Services hangar.

"Not when I'm along," she said, needling me gently. "But Paul and Myrtle'll take me home with them tonight, and you'll need something to get to your motel."

She—or perhaps G. P.—had made reservations for me at Lowman's Motor Court on North San Fernando Road.

"I thought we were staying at the Ambassador," I said.

"No, I knew Paul would insist I stay with him. I always do."

Every mention of Mantz from her lips gave me a twinge of jealousy. Funny attitude for a peeper trying to get the goods on a cheating wife.

"And," I said, "G. P. wasn't about to spring for a nice room for me if he didn't have to."

Her half-smile made a deep, wry dimple. "I would say that's an insightful reading of my husband's character."

The next day I watched from the sidelines as Amelia followed Mantz's lead, working all morning in the little red Link trainer. She wore a red and green plaid shirt with a tan bandanna and chinos and all she lacked to be a cowgirl in a Gene Autry picture was the right hat. Mantz, when he wasn't flying, maintained an image that was part executive and the rest dashing playboy; he wore a nubby brown sports coat with a light blue shirt and blue striped tie, his pants navy gabardines.

Amy was a dutiful pupil, for the most part, though at lunch, in the Sky Room again, she showed impatience when he told her about a gadget that next-door neighbor Lockheed was going to install in the Vega.

"It's called a Cambridge analyzer," he said. "You use it to know how to reset your mixture control, and get maximum miles per gallon."

"Oh for Pete sakes, Paul," she said, gnawing on a carrot stick like Bugs Bunny, "you take all the fun out of flying."

"There's nothing fun about running out of fuel over the goddamn Gulf of Mexico."

"You're still stewing about that?"

Mantz's concern for her ran deep; but I still couldn't

read whether it was a lover's caring or that of a teacher or friend.

"It's stupid," Mantz spouted, "cutting across a body of water that size, when you don't have to. Jesus, angel, it's seven hundred miles, half an Atlantic!"

"I flew a whole Atlantic, before. . . . Look who's here!"

She grinned the gap-toothed grin and waved enthusiastically.

"Toni!" Amy called. "Over here!"

I turned to see, checking in with the hostess at the register, a slightly chunky but still nicely put-together woman, medium height, perhaps thirty, decked out in a goggled tan flying helmet, white blouse with a red and yellow polka-dot knotted scarf and brown jodhpurs; her features reminded me of a slightly less attractive Claudette Colbert. It struck me she didn't need the helmet indoors, but maybe she wanted to make sure people knew she was a flier.

In which case, you'd think the woman would relish public attention from the most famous female pilot on the planet. But the response to Amy's zealous hello was tepid; the round, makeup-less face twitched a polite smile. Then the woman took a seat alone, near one of the birdcages by the far wall.

Amy frowned. "I don't understand. . . . Toni's a friend. I haven't seen or talked to her in some time, but—"

"Maybe she's holding a grudge," Mantz offered.

"Whatever for?"

"Didn't you turn her down when she wanted you to partner up for the refueling-in-flight endurance record?"

"Well, yes, but I just couldn't do it . . . G. P. had me so heavily booked with lectures. . . . Anyway, she got Elinor Smith to go with her, and they set the darn record."

"Sure. And didn't get near the publicity if Amelia Earhart had been along."

Amy's mouth tightened and she rose. "I better go talk to her. . . ."

She went over to the woman's table and began speaking very earnestly, a hand to her breast, standing before

a cool, seated audience. The woman had removed her
helmet to reveal a boyish black-haired bob with
pointed sideburns.

"A lot of jealousy between the girls who fly," Mantz
commented.

"Who is that?"

"Toni Lake. Ever hear of her?"

"No."

"Well, she's pulled off as many aviation feats as our
girl Amelia, a real slew of altitude and endurance records in fact, and yet you've never heard of her. And
that's why she's so royally pissed off, I'd guess."

But something interesting was happening over at that
side table. Toni Lake was standing and the two women
were suddenly hugging, grinning, patting each other on
the back. Amy had won her over.

Hand in hand, the two rival aviatrixes came over to
the table and joined us. Amy made introductions (I was
her "bodyguard and chief bottle washer") and Toni
Lake sat next to Mantz, across from Amy and me.

"Paul," Amy said, "you've got to hear this. . . . Toni,
tell Paul what you told me."

"Tellin' you's one thing, hon," the woman said.
"Spreadin' it around, tellin' tales outta school, makes me
look like Miss Sour Grapes of 1935."

To tell you the truth, with her scorched-tan, leathery
complexion, Toni Lake didn't look like Miss Anything;
but she did have lovely brown eyes and lashes longer
than some store-bought I'd seen.

"G. P.'s done Toni an awful injustice," Amy said; she
was pretty worked up about it.

"Go ahead, Toni," Mantz said, sitting back. He was
working on one of his trademark frosted martinis; this
was lunch so he'd only had two. "Let me warn ya,
though—nothing you tell me about Gippy Putnam's
gonna much surprise me."

But it was Amy who began the story, blurting, "G. P.
tried to hire Toni to an exclusive contract to fly with me
in the Women's Derby."

The Powder Puff Derby, as Will Rogers had dubbed
it.

"She was to pretend to be my 'mechanic' but do most of the flying," Amy said, indignantly.

"He said you weren't 'physically strong enough,'" Lake said with a humorless smirk. "Her loving husband offered me a two-year seventy-five-bucks-a-week contract to co-pilot Amelia, only she had to seem to be doin' *all* the flyin'. You know, I'm not some damn dilettante or socialite, I'm just a girl who likes to fly and was lucky enough to have an old man who's a pilot and runs an airfield. Seventy-five bucks is big money to this little girl."

Amy was shaking her head, mortified.

I asked, "How the hell did G. P. figure you could make it look like Amelia was doing all the flying?"

Lake shrugged. "When we made stops, I was supposed to either get out of the way of the photographers, or stand to the left so I came second in the captions."

"You have to believe me, Toni," Amy said, and she seemed close to tears, not a frequent state for her, "I knew nothing of this. I would never have stood for it. Oh my goodness, how he could even think—"

"That's not the worst of it," Toni said. "When I refused to sign the contract, he blew sky high, started swearin' like a stevedore, said he'd ruin me and all. Said I'd never fly professionally again and even if he hasn't quite managed that, he's put all sorts of barriers in my path . . . officials causin' me problems, sponsor contracts fallin' through. And I can't get press coverage to save my life, anymore. They used to cover me like a movie star. Now I could fly to the moon and they'd just report an eclipse."

"Toni," Amy said, "I couldn't be more embarrassed. I promise you, I swear to you, I will take care of this."

"Well, even if you can't—"

"I can, and I will, Toni. Count on it."

"Sweetie, I'm just glad to know you weren't in on it. I mean, everybody knows that your husband works against the other women pilots—"

"I *didn't* know."

"Just ask anybody. Ask Lady Heath, ask Elinor Smith, ask 'Chubby' Miller. . . ."

"I will," Amy said, her mortification giving way to

resolve. Suddenly I almost felt sorry for old G. P. "In the meantime, join us for a nice lunch. On me."

That afternoon, to Mantz's displeasure, Amy abandoned her flight preparations for the company of Toni Lake, who owned a pair of Indian Pony motorbikes. The aviatrixes spent hours racing up and down the runways on the bikes, flight helmets and goggles on, like a couple of schoolgirls having the time of their lives playing hookey. Chasing small planes, cutting figure eights, pursuing each other like cowboys and Indians, they attracted something of a crowd, when word got out one of the two naughty children was Amelia Earhart.

During part of this gleeful exhibition, I retreated to the office of Paul Mantz, who had requested a word with me.

The glassed-in office was in the left rear corner of the hangar, a good-size area with light tan walls that went up forever, with more signed celebrity photos than the Brown Derby—James Cagney, Joan Crawford, Pat O'Brien, Wallace Beery, Clark Gable, Jean Harlow, Eleanor Roosevelt. Occasionally Mantz was in the photos, and there were shots of Amy and Lindbergh and pilots I didn't recognize, as well as a sprinkling of aerial stills from movies he'd worked on, *Wings*, *Hell's Angels*, *Airmail*.

What was most impressive, however, was how straight all those framed photos were hanging. Mantz's office had a neatness that approached unreality, or lunacy. His big maple desk with the glass top was fastidiously arranged, blotter, ashtray, framed photo of his wife, desk lamp, several flying trophies topped with metal model planes. Papers were stacked neatly. Stapler, phone, perfectly arranged. Squared up. Symmetrical. It was a desk not in life, but in a movie.

And Mantz, in his natty sportcoat and tie and swivel chair, was like an actor playing a big shot, and a slightly miscast one. He was a pretend big shot in a pretend office.

"I expected to see your wife around today," I said. Compared to Mantz I was underdressed in the spiffy summer clothes I'd brought for my California jaunt, rust-color rayon sportshirt and sandstone tan worsted slacks. "Isn't she flying out to Dallas?"

"Red doesn't like to fly. She took the train."

"Ah. What did you want to talk about, Paul?"

"I wanted to talk about why G. P. really hired you," he said, leaning back as he lighted up a cigarette selected from a wooden box with a carved airplane on its lid.

I thought perhaps he was on to me, but I played it out, asking, "As security on the lecture tour, why else?"

"The lecture tour's over."

"But the Mexican trip's coming up."

"So what? We've never taken on extra security before any of the other flights."

"Has Amelia mentioned the threatening notes?"

He frowned, sat forward. "What threatening notes?"

I filled him in.

He thought about what I'd told him; flicked some ash into a round metal tray. "Well, I can see a celebrity like her attracting envy, all right," he said. "And or cuckoo birds. But something about this sounds a little too familiar."

"How so?"

"Let me ask you somethin', Nate—what do you make of Gippy?"

"He's a fine human being, as long as he pays me in full and on time."

"And if he doesn't?"

"Fuck him."

That made Mantz laugh—one of the few times I heard him laugh at anything but his own jokes.

"Let me tell you something, Nate," he said, stubbing out the cigarette. "Gippy Putnam's one of the vilest bastards on the face of this sweet earth."

"Who's married to one of the sweetest angels on the face of this vile earth," I said.

"Couldn't agree more." And he was rocking in his swivel chair now, looking past me, summoning memories to share. "But let me spin ya a little bedtime story about Gippy. Back when he was still in the publishing business, not long after the Crash, when he was in need of dough, he put out this book by the nephew of the Italian premier that Mussolini deposed. This character was the first

guy to escape from some fascist penal colony or somethin'. Anyway, the book spoke out against Mussolini,
and Gippy was in Paris, doin' advance publicity on the
thing, when he went to the Sûreté and showed them an
anonymous letter he got, threatening his life if he went
ahead and published this book. He had a press conference and puffed up his chest and said nobody was gonna
frighten Gippy Putnam outta publishing an important
book. Then he went to London, for more advance promotion, and took two more of these threatening notes
to Scotland Yard—"

"What did these notes look like?"

"Pasted-up letters cut out from newspapers and magazines. 'Pig—you will never reach New York alive.' Stuff
about blowin' up the Putnam publishing offices in both
London and New York. He had another press conference, same bullshit; but this time he gets round-the-clock
police protection, till he sails home on board the S. S.
France."

"You know, this is jogging my memory—"

He was waving out a match, having lighted up a fresh
cigarette. "It should. It got lots of play in the papers,
both here and abroad. The book was a big bestseller; it
pulled the Putnam publishing nuts outta the fire."

"Why do I think you think Putnam sent those notes
to himself?"

A sneer of a smile formed. "I don't just think it—I
know it. He brags about it, to his family and close
friends. He uses it as an example of how clever he is."

"You can go to the pokey for fraud like that."

He blew a perfect smoke ring and watched it dissipate
as he spoke. "Yeah, but to Gippy, it's just another publicity stunt. And he prides himself on stirrin' up the
press."

"And you think he's doing the same thing now."

"He's capable of it. Sitting by himself some night, cutting out those words from papers and magazines, pasting
them up, feeling like he's one smart son of a bitch."

"Then why would he hire me to protect Amelia?"

Of course, I knew the answer to that: because I was
really hired for a completely other purpose.

"Probably for authenticity," he said with a shrug. "To

show his concern for his wife, when he leaks this to the papers."

"Does Putnam know how low your opinion of him is?"

"He suspects."

"Why do you do business with him, then?"

"He's got a great wife. She's only a so-so flier, but she's got a great heart and more courage than a Marine battalion."

"A so-so flier?"

He grunted a laugh. "You know how many crashes that sweet girl has had? At least a dozen."

"Nobody told me that before I went flying with her."

A Cheshire Cat grin formed under the pencil mustache. "To a pilot, a crash don't count unless it kills you. If you can walk away from it, it's just another successful landing . . . even if your plane blows up a few seconds later."

"You're worried about her, aren't you?"

The grin vanished; his forehead tightened. "You're goddamn right, I am. Each one of these feats of hers has to be bigger than the last. She's running out of impressive baloney to pull off. She's no spring chicken, either."

I sat forward. "Why do you help her, then? I can see she respects you. Why don't you just tell her to retire? Famous as she is, she ought to be able to rest on her laurels, and let G. P. market her fame for the rest of her life."

He'd started shaking his head no about halfway through that. "She wouldn't listen to me, Nate. As disenchanted as she may be with Gippy, she knows the bastard *invented* her."

"Svengali?"

"Yeah, or Doc Frankenstein. Besides, Gippy's a tightwad, a stingy fucking bastard . . . but he pays top dollar when he really wants something."

"So he's buying you, too."

"Yeah. I'm not proud of it, but I'm a pilot in Hollywood . . ." He gestured to the gallery of famous faces. ". . . and Hollywood is a town of glamorous whores. . . . Like it or not, I fit in."

I knew what he meant. He was at home in Hollywood like I was at home in the bushes of his Toluca Lake bungalow with my Speed Graphic. I didn't like what I was doing, particularly, but it was a living, and I was good at it.

It was ten o'clock at night, after a day that had included another half-day of training for Amy in the little red Link and an afternoon here at Mantz's house, where I had not been in the bushes, but relaxing in the living room. Shoes off, spread out on a couch, I read movie magazines and took catnaps while Mantz, Amy and retired Navy Commander Clarence Williams, a dark-haired sturdy guy with a beaky nose and a dimpled chin, were gathered around the kitchen table going over charts and maps. Williams was no-nonsense in a military manner that got Amy's attention.

On the afternoon trip to Mantz's place, Amy had done the driving, tooling the sleek Terraplane past the farms, ranches and lush orange groves beyond the airport to the shaded streets of residential Burbank, where the foot soldiers of the dream factory lived in modest cracker-boxes.

Toluca Lake was another story, from the wide flawless sidewalks to the cozy interesting homes ("Lots of art directors live in Toluca," Amy explained) and an eclectic array of shade trees, elms, oaks, redwoods, and, for the requisite Hollywood tropical touch, palms. She pointed out several movie star homes ("Bette Davis lives there. . . . That's where Ruby Keeler lives") and indicated a golf course beyond Valley Spring Lane.

"Do you play golf?" she asked.

"Only under duress."

"I rather enjoy it. Would you consider joining me some afternoon, if I can get out of Paul's clutches?"

"Sure. Is that a public course or a country club?"

"It's a country club."

"Might be a problem."

"Why, Nate?"

"Most country clubs are restricted."

"Oh . . . I'm sorry . . . I forgot . . ."

"I'm Jewish? That's okay. I forgot it myself, a long time ago. Trouble is, other people keep bringing it up."

Amy, Mantz and Commander Williams had slaved over the charts till around six, at which time we all headed over to a steakhouse in Glendale where we hooked up with Toni Lake. Dinner was nice, though I was glad Amy was paying—it was a pricey seventy-five cents a steak, à la carte—and I dropped Amy back at Mantz's bungalow, ostensibly heading back to Lowman's Motor Court.

Only I didn't head back. The Terraplane was parked over on Toluca Estates Drive, in front of Mary Astor's house (always had kind of a yen for her and wouldn't have minded a glimpse, but no luck). The night was cool and dry, a breeze riffling leaves, including those of the bushes I was snuggled behind; I was in a sportshirt and slacks and didn't look much like a private detective, more like a peeping tom . . . if there's a difference.

The blinds on the window were shut, but I could see around the edge of them, and—thanks to light from a lamp out of my range of vision, presumably on the bed-stand—catch a view of the doorway and a dresser next to it; also the edge of the bottom of the bed. This angle would not give me the prize-winning *in flagrante delicto* shot I craved, but if this bedroom were the site of a man and woman making whoopee, sooner or later the two of them might appear together within my view, enjoying a before or after hug and kiss, in dishabille.

I'd done this kind of work plenty of times before, but tonight I had a sick feeling and a racing heartbeat. To tell you the truth, as close as I'd gotten to Amy, as much as I liked her, I might have ditched G. P.'s snoop job, if I wasn't so goddamn jealous of Mantz. What did he have that I didn't have? If she'd had the good sense and better taste to have an affair with me instead of Mantz, I would have never considered ratting on her to her husband.

I'm just that kind of guy.

Around ten-fifteen Mantz came in, alone. He was already in striped maroon pajama bottoms, and his chest was bare and hairy; he had a well-muscled upper torso, and a magazine was rolled up in one fist, as if he were going to swat a bug with it. For a moment I thought he might be coming after me, but he disappeared toward the bed and I could hear the box springs squeak as he climbed in, and even from my limited perspective could see that he'd gotten under the covers.

Presumably, he was reading the magazine.

No sign of Amelia. Was he waiting for her? Was she already in bed and I couldn't see her from this angle?

It didn't take long to figure out the latter wasn't the case. Though the window was closed, the night being cool enough to warrant that, I'd been able to hear the box springs clearly when he climbed into bed. Presumably, the sound of conversation, and certainly the joyful noise of lovemaking on that mattress, would have found their way to my ears.

Half an hour later, he was still alone, and apparently still reading. No Amy.

Knowing where the guest room was, I worked my way around to the other side of the house and a new set of bushes. The window here was closed, as well, the blinds down, and furthermore the lights were out. But bedsprings were squeaking, so somebody was in there all right, possibly tossing and turning . . .

Only from the sound of it, that somebody was having one hell of a restless night. Either that, or getting their ashes well and truly hauled.

Puzzled, I returned to my previous post, wondering if Mantz had managed to perfectly time it and leave his bedroom and climb in with Amy just as I was circling the house to switch windows.

But Mantz was apparently still in bed, the bedstand lamp aglow; I would have sworn, listening closely, I could hear the pages of his magazine being slowly turned.

And so back to the guest bedroom window I went, where a bedspring symphony was still in full sway. Two voices, emitting muffled, restrained but very audible grunts, groans, sighs and cries, accompanied the squeaking springs. Snugged between bushes and the stucco exterior of the bungalow, poised at the edge of the blinds, my Speed Graphic and I waited for things to settle down, hoping a light would eventually go on and satisfy my professional, not to mention prurient, curiosity.

Finally a light clicked on.

Amy had reached for the bedstand lamp and filled
the guest room (the yellow plaster walls of which were
decorated with framed Mantz aviation movie stills) with
a golden luster appropriate to the afterglow of a satis-
fying amorous event. She wore the maroon pajama top
that Mantz had apparently loaned her, but the person
next to her in bed wasn't Mantz, rather a nude woman,
or at least nude to the waist because that was where
the sheet fell. The woman was voluptuous bordering on
plump, her torso pale next to her dark-tanned leathery
face and short black boyish hair.

Nonetheless, there were less pleasant things in the
world to view, particularly for a lech like me, than a
nude-to-the-waist Toni Lake.

I backed away from the window, and the bushes behind me rustled like the wings of startled birds. Afraid
I might have given myself away, I ducked down, hiding
under and within the shrubbery like the weasel I was.

Shaking, sweating despite the night's coolness, I didn't
know what the hell to think. I felt ashamed that I'd
intruded upon such a scene, even though my intrusion
wasn't known to my victims; and I felt sickened, not
by Amy's sexual perversion—I was never one to sit in
judgment of other people's sex lives, being primarily interested in my own—but at the thought that this special
woman, toward whom I'd been developing ever-deepen-
ing feelings, some carnal, some not, was in a sense a
stranger to me. She was not who I thought she was, and
I would never be close to her.

It just doesn't pay for a guy to fall in love with a
lesbian.

Crouched there in the bushes, thoughts racing, I knew
one thing for certain, and one thing only: I would take
no candid photos of Amy and her friend Miss Lake. If
that was what Putnam had been after, he'd have to find
another sleazy private eye to do it. This sleazy private
eye had had his fill.

So I left my nest under the bushes, and was skulking
away from the house toward the sidewalk, when a car
came moving down Valley Spring Lane, very slowly, and
with its lights off. Finding this curious, I slipped behind

a palm tree and watched as the car, a snazzy red and white Dusenberg convertible, drew up in front.

I recognized the car, because I'd seen it out at United Airport the day we'd arrived: it belonged to Myrtle Mantz, who had left on the train yesterday afternoon, to visit her mother in Dallas.

Only she hadn't.

Myrtle Mantz was in Toluca Lake, driving the Dusenberg.

With the lights out.

She parked, got quietly out of the car. She was wearing a lime blouse and hunter-green slacks, her long red hair pinned up, and looked very pale in the ivory moonlight; she seemed to have no makeup on and her pretty face was immobile, her eyes glazed. She stood on the sidewalk and gazed at her house as if she were a ghost that had returned to haunt it.

She had something in her right hand that I couldn't make out too well, but it might have been a gun. . . .

I scurried to the back door, ready to shoulder it open but found it blessedly unlocked; I moved through the dark kitchen where the Frigidaire was purring, left my Speed Graphic on the table where the charts and maps were still spread out, and slipped through the hall and into the guest bedroom where the bedstand lamp was still on and Amy was in bed, pillows propped behind her, while Toni Lake was off to one side of the room, where she'd been getting dressed, in fact was pretty well back into her white blouse and brown jodhpurs.

Lake scowled at me, not appreciating this invasion one little bit, and Amy's eyes were wide with surprise and the beginnings of indignation, but I didn't let her say a word.

Instead I whispered, "Myrtle's coming up the front walk with a gun. Go out the back way. Now!"

Amy scurried out of bed, grabbing her bathrobe, and Lake followed us out into the hall and through the kitchen, Amy getting into and belting the bathrobe as she went; I could hear the front door opening—Myrtle had opened it quietly, but I was listening for it, whereas Mantz wouldn't be.

"You got a car?" I whispered to Lake.

She nodded.

"Get yourselves the hell away from here," I said to them both, opening the back door for them. "Sleep somewhere else tonight."

Amy frowned at me, as if she didn't know whether she loved me or hated me, although now that I knew what I did about her, what was the difference?

Then they were gone, and I went over and stood hugging the Frigidaire and peeked past it down the hall, where Myrtle was going into Mantz's bedroom.

And I got a good look this time: it was a gun all right, a .32 revolver, a Smith and Wesson maybe, just a little bitty thing that could fit in a handbag, but you still wouldn't want to get shot in the eye with it.

I didn't have a gun with me. My nine-millimeter was in my suitcase at Lowman's Motor Court; I was not licensed to carry a firearm in the state of California and, besides, this was the kind of assignment where you packed a camera, not a pistol.

So armed only with my wits—no remarks, please—I sneaked down the uncarpeted hallway, which was empty now; she was in Mantz's bedroom—actually, it was her bedroom, too, wasn't it?

And from the hallway as I crept along, I could hear her saying, with a Southwestern lilt, "Where's your angel, Paul?"

"What are you doing here?" His response registered surprise, but not fear; maybe she had the gun behind her back. "She's in the guest bedroom, where do you think she is?"

Myrtle's voice was musical as she said, "Look what I've got, Paul. . . ."

I figured that gun wasn't behind her back, now.

"Put that down, Red. You don't . . ."

That was when I came in and grabbed her from behind, bear-hugging her, pinning her arms, flattening her fine breasts with my forearms, but she managed to fire the gun anyway, shattering the bedstand lamp even as Mantz dove out of bed, just under the bullet's trajectory. The room was dark now, though some light filtered in from the hallway.

"Let me go!" she squealed, not knowing who had hold of her.

And Mantz came scrambling forward, his face tight with rage, and he belted her in the jaw with a fist, and she went limp, the gun clattering to the hardwood floor, where we were lucky it didn't go off again.

"You didn't have to do that," I spat at him, easing the unconscious woman over to the bed, laying her out gently, there. I hadn't been holding her like that so he could fucking slug her! Blood trailed from the corner of her mouth; even in this state, she was a lovely thing. Too bad when she got jealous she went around with a gun.

"She tried to shoot me!" Mantz said, understandably worked up, hopping around like a mustached monkey in his bare chest. "She's lucky I didn't knock her block off! . . . Where's Amelia?"

"I got her and her pal out the back door," I said, switching on the overhead light. "Your wife never saw them, or me. So we were never here, remember? In about two seconds, I'm slipping out, myself."

"What should I do?"

"Call the cops."

He frowned, calming down a little. "Do I have to?"

"Your neighbors probably already have. If you don't, it'll look bad."

He smirked. "Doesn't it look bad enough?"

"I don't think so. Take it from somebody who's done his share of divorce work, this marriage isn't working out . . . and in the settlement, Myrtle coming after you with a .32 is going to speak better for you than her."

He was mulling that over, looking at his out-cold, incredibly beautiful, crazy-as-a-bedbug wife, when I got the hell out, before it occurred to him to ask me what I was doing there.

Six

Stained ivory in the moonlight, the foothills of the green Verdugo Mountains provided a majestic backdrop for the humble skyline of the pink adobe cabins of Lowman's Motor Court. Exotic as this vista may have been, I had begun to long for the simple pleasures of Chicago, Illinois. In the red blush of the motel's nearby hovering neon sign, I pulled the Terraplane into the stall at Cabin 2, put the buggy's top up in case the forecast of rain was correct, and trudged inside, where I began to pack.

I had decided to quit. The women on this job were either sleeping with each other or waving guns around, and that was enough to send this Midwestern lad back to where girls were girls and boys were boys and guns were carried chiefly by cops and crooks, if you'll pardon the redundancy. Furthermore, I wanted work that did not involve a client who very likely sent his wife death threats before hiring me to protect her, and/or work which also did not require me to fly with a pilot who considered crashing her plane an interesting variation on landing.

True, this job paid well, but I had been on it long enough to rack myself up a pretty little pile of money, which I was now prepared to gather up and take home with me. On the train. Sitting on the edge of the bed in the small square room, I used the nightstand phone to make a reservation; I could get a Union Pacific sleeper at two-forty-five tomorrow afternoon.

With the exception of my clothes for tomorrow, toothbrush and powder, hairbrush and oil, and the white boxers I had on for sleeping, my bag was packed. It lay open like a clamshell on the luggage stand at the foot of the bed, the Speed Graphic nestled among the clothing like a pearl; my nine-millimeter was similarly buried.

Bare-chested like Gable in *It Happened One Night* (and Mantz in what happened tonight), I lay atop the nubby pink bedspread, reading *Film Fun* magazine, which was mostly jokes and pictures of pretty girls; I never claimed to go in for Proust. The cabin was sparsely furnished in ranch style, its pink plaster walls broken up occasionally by a framed print of a cactus or burro; but one amenity, at least, was a table model radio by the bed. I had it going fairly loud, in hopes of drowning out my thoughts, the Dorsey Brothers playing their theme song, "Lost in a Fog," live from the Roosevelt Hotel's Blossom Room, when the knock came at the door.

I didn't put my robe on, because I didn't have one. And I didn't bother putting my pants on, either, because I figured this was probably the manager asking me to turn my radio down. The windows were open, after all, wind whispering in, fluffing the green-and-yellow cotton curtains with their geometric Indian-blanket design. Clicking the radio off as I climbed from the bed, I figured my problem was already solved.

As Proust would say, little did I know.

"What?" I asked my closed door.

"It's me."

Amy's voice.

I cracked the door and looked into her lovely, weathered, somewhat puffy face, expressionless as a bisque baby's, though the blue-gray eyes were filigreed red. Her mop of dark blonde curls looked even more tousled than usual.

I asked her, "What are you doing here?"

"Let me in," she said.

"I'm not dressed."

"Neither am I."

I opened the door a little wider and saw that she wasn't, at least not properly: she still wore Mantz's maroon-striped pajama top and a pair of dungarees that were parachute-baggy but short, her ankles showing.

And her feet were in moccasin-type slippers.

Bewildered, I let her in, shut the door, asked, "How'd you get here?"

"Toni loaned me her car. What happened at Paul's? Is he all right?"

I climbed into my pants as I told her.

"I hope he called the cops, like I advised him," I concluded. "If so, I'm sure he'll leave you out of it."

"I can't believe she actually shot at him." Amy was sitting on the room's only chair, in the corner between the windows and the dresser, shaking her head; her hands were folded in her lap and she had the aspect of a repentant naughty child.

I sat on the edge of the bed and said, "I don't know that she shot *at* him. . . . The gun just kind of went off, when I grabbed her."

Amy gave me a sharp look. "Did she see you?"

"No. Myrtle probably thinks *you* grabbed her . . . but she didn't see either one of us in the house . . . or your friend Miss Lake, either."

She sighed deeply. "I'm suppose I'm lucky you were there . . ."

"If you came here to thank me, it's not necessary."

"Thank you?" She stood; her arms were straight at her sides, her hands were fists—she looked a little comical in the pajama top and short baggy jeans (on loan from Toni Lake, I'd wager) but I didn't feel like smiling. "*Thank* you?"

She walked to my open suitcase and plucked the Speed Graphic from amidst my underthings. Then she strode over to where I sat on the edge of the bed, planting herself before me, holding the camera in my face as if I were on the witness stand, she were the prosecuting attorney and the camera Exhibit A.

"What's this?" she asked, the second word hissing through the space between her teeth. "A party favor?"

"You know what it is."

Her lip curled in a tiny sneer. "I knew what it was when I noticed it on the kitchen table, at Paul's, too."

She had good night vision; but then she was a pilot.

"You were spying on me, Nathan, weren't you?"

"I didn't take any pictures, Amy."

She flung the camera. It smacked into the far wall, carving a notch in the plaster, springing open like a jack-in-the-box, exposing the unshot film, which unspooled, pieces of the camera flying off, broken to shit. Now I really was expecting a call from the manager.

"I thought we were friends," she said, voice quavering with anger.

"I was hoping we might be more than that," I said. "But I guess I'm not your type."

She slapped me.

It rocked my head and my cheek stung like a burn, tears springing to my eyes, and I tried like hell to keep them there. The wounded like to cling to their dignity, shredded though it may be.

"And here I thought you were for equal rights," I said.

She spit the words at me: "What are you talking about?"

And I stood and got almost nose to nose with her and, my cheek on fire, spit words back: "God help the man that raises a hand to *you*, but you can hit a man. . . . That's always a woman's prerogative, isn't it?"

She sucked in air and raised a fist, as if to hammer me with it, only it froze there, her eyes going to that fist, as if her hand had had a life of its own and was surprising her with its actions.

Then her hand wasn't a fist anymore, it was an open palm that covered her mouth and then both hands were enveloping her face as she seemed to crumple, and I caught her in my arms, folded her close to me, and surprisingly, she let me. Maybe she was just too upset to stop me.

"That was cruel of me," I whispered in her ear.

"No . . . no . . . I should never have struck you. . . ."

She pushed away a bit and, still in my arms, looked at me; the eyes, bloodshot though they were, were lovely and clear, more blue than gray, the color of a clear winter sky, and she fixed them on me, her tear-streaked expression regretful as she touched my cheek, gently.

"I'm sorry, Nathan . . . sorry. Forgive me. . . ."

"I deserved the slap. I'm a lousy goddamn bastard and I don't deserve your apologies. . . ."

She was shaking her head side to side, the tears welling again. "I don't believe in hitting people. I hate being struck, and yet I struck you. . . ."

I placed my hands on her shoulders and looked right at her. "I hit you in another way. I betrayed our friendship, and Christ, I couldn't feel like a bigger heel. Amy, I'm sorry."

She hugged me, her hands warm on my bare back.

"It's not you," she whispered. "It's G. P. He's a corrupting influence. . . . No one knows that better than I."

"Amy, I wasn't lying," I said into her ear, in a rush of embarrassed words. "I didn't take any pictures. I would've quit this dirty job days ago if I hadn't got jealous of Mantz. . . ."

She pulled away a few inches, her expression quizzical and almost amused. "Jealous?"

"Guess that's kind of silly now. . . ."

"I never knew you felt that way about me, Nathan. I thought we were just . . . pals."

"We are pals, Amy. And I won't say a word to that son of a bitch you're married to."

She touched my cheek again, just with her fingertips. "I'm sorry I hit you."

"Stop it," I said gently.

She kissed my cheek. A tender little kiss.

I smiled at her. "Still friends, then?"

She smiled back. "I don't think so. . . ."

And she kissed me again, only not on the stinging cheek, but full on my mouth, not at all tenderly, but urgently, eagerly.

Those warm, full lips were everything I'd hoped they'd be, salty with her tears, and this was no friendly kiss, it was passionate, a hungry confession of feelings that she'd harbored, too, and her hands clutched at my back, desperately, and if I'd held her any closer, I'd have crushed the life from her. We kissed again, and again, and I was crying too, and it wasn't from the slap, it was the emotional fucking roller coaster I'd been on this evening, tears of joy because a woman I desperately wanted and had abandoned hope of ever having had her tongue in my mouth.

Then we were fumbling at each other's paltry clothing,

my hands unbuttoning the man's pajama top, exposing the creamy skin beneath, and she was unbuckling my belt, then tugging my pants down over the white boxers, both of us flailing in comical, out-of-control desire.

And then she was nude to the waist, justifiably unashamed of a shapely form that might have belonged to a teenage girl, not a woman approaching forty—small, beautifully formed tip-tilting breasts, prominent rib cage, and a waist I could put my hands around. Confronted by the tentpole at the front of my white boxers, she had a sudden burst of modesty and reached over and switched off the bedside lamp.

Then she stepped out of her baggy dungarees and the white cotton step-ins beneath, and I got out of the boxers, and we rolled as one onto the bed, embracing, kissing, caressing, saying nothing except each other's name occasionally, and when it was time, under a framed cactus print, she rolled the lambskin onto me and mounted me.

The cabin's darkness wore the red patina of the motel sign filtering through the cotton curtains, and with her atop me, flushed with passion and suffused neon, eyes half-lidded, lips parted as she panted, she remained in control, ever the pilot. She was like no woman before or since in my experience, tall, lean, muscular yet pliable, her skin satin-smooth except for her sweet freckled weather-punished face, her legs endless though sumptuously fleshed, her breasts perfect girlish handfuls, tipped with bullets. For being of such a modest, even prudish upbringing, she knew things; she had a contortionist's limber frame, and an athlete's stamina, and she took me new places.

But her co-pilot had flown before too, and when she finally arrived at our destination, back on top again after a world tour, she came with a shuddering intense glee and a final shower of tears before she collapsed into my arms.

Out of gas.

We were both still breathing hard, and she was snuggled against me and I was on my back, looking at the ceiling, which wore the reddish blush of motel neon.

"Can I ask you something personal?" I ventured. I

was using a tissue from the nightstand to remove the lambskin.

"My goodness," she said, "I think at this point you can risk it."

"Do you like boys or girls?"

"Yes," she said.

And I was trying to think of something to say in response to that when I realized she was asleep, gently snoring.

Perhaps an hour later, I heard something, woke and she wasn't next to me. The red-tinged darkness was cut by a shaft of light from the bathroom where the water was running. Then she was in the bathroom doorway, in just Mantz's pajama top, silhouetted there.

Sitting up, I said, "Hey, you."

"Don't look at me," she said, though only her legs were showing, and hadn't she been a stark-naked cowgirl riding me not so long before? She clicked off the bathroom light, ran to the bed, threw back the covers and scurried under them; we'd been sleeping atop the bedspread, so I got around under there with her and leaned on my elbow and looked at her. She was on her side, facing me, face half-hidden by the pillow.

"What brought on that sudden attack of ladylike reserve?" I asked.

"I hate my body."

"Well, I love your body, and anyway all I could see was your legs."

"I hate my legs."

"I have fond memories of your legs."

"I have fat thighs. I hate my thighs."

"Well, let's have a look, then. . . ." I flipped the covers back.

She squealed and pulled the covers up and said, "I'll hit you again."

"Go ahead," I said. "I like where that led last time. . . ."

Then we were in each other's arms, giggling, kissing, and then the giggling ceased and the kissing continued and this time around was not at all frantic, but the sort of luxurious, lingering lovemaking characteristic of a couple who know each other well.

Later, I was half-sitting up, two pillows behind me, and she was snuggled against me again, my arm gathering her near, her head resting against my chest.

"There will be no more scurrilous remarks about your thighs," I said.

"Okay," she said. She was leaning on her elbow, now, chin propped on her palm. Gazing right at me. "Nathan, there's something you should know about those threatening notes—"

I cut her off: "Mantz told me about your husband's history in that regard. Do you think G. P. sent them?"

"Not really," she said, but not confidently. "Why would he?"

"Publicity, for one thing. To remind the world how important you are."

"He hasn't released anything about it to the press."

"Yet. . . . Or maybe it's to provide a cover for what he *really* hired me to do."

Her eyes narrowed. "And what was that, Nathan?"

"He said he wanted me to find out if you were having an affair with Paul Mantz."

Now the eyes widened, as if I'd just proposed something ridiculous. "With Paul?"

"Yes. Are you?"

"Am I what?"

"Having an affair with Paul?"

"Are you crazy?"

"Don't change the subject. Are you having an affair with him?"

"No! He's not my type. . . ."

"Amy, now please don't get mad, but considering the events of the evening, I'm having just a little difficulty ascertaining who or what your 'type' might be."

She ducked the question. "Maybe I should say I'm not *Paul's* type. You've seen Myrtle. She's his type."

"Armed and dangerous, you mean?"

She snorted a little laugh. "That's no joke. He likes flamboyant, outgoing, drop-dead gorgeous 'dames.' . . ."

"You ain't chopped liver, kid."

The sheet around her had fallen down below the

small, perfectly conical breasts. "No, but I'm no curvy cutie-pie, no dolled-up starlet. And on a daily basis, half the little Jean Harlots in Hollywood are throwing themselves at Paul."

"But is he catching?"

"Yes! Which is why poor old Myrtle is half-bonkers. I'm probably the only woman in California under forty he's *not* having an affair with. He's a ladies' man, a tomcat from the word go, which is also why he's not my type. He doesn't respect women."

"He has great respect for you. You're his star pupil."

Her eyes and nostrils flared. "That's what I mean! He's a stunt pilot, and a good one, but he doesn't begin to have the list of records I have. What sets him above me?"

"Why do you put up with him, then? I would've guessed you were very fond of him."

She shrugged, sighed. "I am. I guess I look at him and see a kindred spirit. He loves to fly, and he's got adventure in his soul."

"Well, tonight he had a wife with a .32 in his bedroom."

"Maybe he's a little too adventurous. And *I* respect *him.* He's got connections in the aeronautics industry second to none; the guys at Lockheed love him. He knows people, and he knows his stuff."

"But he's also a cocky little bastard."

"Yes. Can I ask you something, Nathan?"

"Shoot . . . as long you're not packing a .32."

"What do you think these are?" she smirked as she pulled the covers up over her breasts. "Listen. You were around the two of us, Paul and me, and even knowing me as well as you do, you thought the two of us might be having an affair, correct?"

"I was convinced of it. I was hoping it wasn't true, because I couldn't imagine why any sane woman would prefer that little son of a bitch to a handsome so-and-so like yours truly . . . but sure. I made you two for an item."

She mulled that over. "Then G. P. really may have sent those notes himself."

"Why do you say that?"

"Nathan, tonight . . . when you saw me in bed with Toni . . . what did you think?"

"What do you think I thought?"

"Probably that I like to be with women."

"A reasonable assumption."

"Yes, but . . . I like women, uh . . . You see, I went to several girls' schools, and that's where I had my first, oh . . . this is embarrassing."

"Then don't talk about it."

She swallowed, steeled herself. "There have been women in my life, casually . . . and a few men, too. . . . Does that shock you?"

I gave her my best smartass smirk. "So you fly a biplane. So what?"

She tapped my chest, with a playful fist. "I'll hit you again. . . ."

"It doesn't shock me, Amy. I'm from Chicago. Takes a cattle prod to shock a Chicagoan."

"Good. Because I need you to understand my relationship with G. P., and it's not, uh . . . *Saturday Evening Post* material."

"Not something Norman Rockwell might paint?"

"Not exactly. I was sort of G. P.'s . . . discovery."

"I know. He cast you as 'Lady Lindy' to make a bestseller. Then the bestseller was such an enormous success, he decided to latch onto you for the sequels."

"That's about it, but the whole truth is, I also latched onto him. . . . Nathan, I didn't have money. I'm a nurse, a social worker, a teacher, and flying is an expensive . . . obsession."

"I remember."

"He was married, when we were first associated. It sounds ugly, but it's true: I wrote my first book, about the *Friendship* flight? Under his and his wife's roof. Dorothy was wonderful to me . . . I even dedicated the book to her."

"I'm sure that made up for you taking away her husband."

"Go ahead, be snide, I deserve it; I'm not proud of what I did. He claimed their marriage was over before I came along, and I could lie and say I rejected his advances until after the divorce, but I won't. We slept together, when he accompanied me on lecture tours. . . . My goodness, Nathan, why didn't you kiss me when we were alone in those hotel rooms? Do you know how much time we've wasted?"

"Please . . . no salt in the wound. So there was love between you, in the beginning?"

"I never felt that for him."

"How did he feel about you?"

"I've never been sure whether he viewed me as a valuable property he secured or really did love me, but I do know he . . . lusted after me. My goodness, this sounds like a meller-drama, doesn't it?"

"All G. P. lacks is the handlebar mustache and the whip."

"He was aware of my . . . proclivities. He knew that despite my fairly modest demeanor, that I, uh . . ."

"That still waters ran deep."

"Thank you. What a generous way to put it. Anyway, I had a well-known, publicly stated aversion to marriage, but, uh, at the same time, the normal biological urges of a young woman and, perhaps in the view of some, some not so normal ones, as well. But I did, if not love him in those early days, admire him. He was an impressive man to me. I thought he was fascinating . . . publisher, explorer, socialite. . . ."

"So you had a normal sexual relationship."

"Yes. We, uh . . . don't have much of one, now. He . . . he makes me feel dirty."

"In bed?"

"No. Everywhere else. He's the management, Nathan, and he still does a good job, but he goes too far. You're a case in point. . . . He had no right to hire you to spy on me. We had an agreement, G. P. and I, before our marriage, not a formal agreement really, but I did put it in writing . . ."

"A prenuptial agreement, you mean?"

"Not exactly . . . just a letter I gave him on the eve of our wedding. But he accepted the terms."

"The terms."

"Yes. I told him I wouldn't hold him to any medieval code of faithfulness, nor would I consider myself bound that way to him."

"And has he been with other women?"

"Almost certainly, but it's no concern of mine, is it? Then in the early days of our marriage, when we were more romantically active, he started getting possessive, and finally I did agree . . . Nathan, this is embarrassing for me, please forgive my reticence . . . I agreed that any future dalliances would be with members of my own sex."

"You mean, it was okay with George if you fooled around as long as it was with other females."

"That's it."

"But he wanted to be the only man in your life."

"That's right. Otherwise, it would be an affront to his manhood."

I winced at the weird logic. "And you finding satisfaction in the arms of another woman wasn't?"

"No. Frankly, I . . . I think he found the idea exciting. Is that a common male fantasy?"

"I think most fellas figure if two girls were going at it, and a real man happened onto the scene, he could straighten 'em out."

She began to laugh. She laughed so hard, tears were rolling.

"Was that funny?" I asked. Usually I know when I'm kidding.

"You should write for the Marx Brothers. . . . Nathan, I believe I'm something of an exception, feeling as I do toward both sexes. But the notion of a 'real man' trying to make a 'real woman' out of Toni Lake, for example, is about as likely as a dog turning a cat into Rin Tin Tin. . . . Have I disappointed you? Did you think you'd made a real woman out of me tonight?"

Now I laughed. "Anything's possible. Didn't I make myself into a real fool?"

"A sweet fool." She nestled under my arm again, the long tapering fingers of one hand entwining themselves in the hair on my chest. "You know, Nathan, this begins to make sense. If observing Paul and me together led you to believe we were 'an item,' then G. P. might have come to the same conclusion."

I worked my fingers gently in her tousled curls. "Which

means your husband might very well be behind those threatening notes."

"It's highly possible. . . . Nathan, your suitcase . . . is it my imagination, or is it packed?"

"Well, everything but my camera, if I can find the pieces."

"I'm sorry. . . . Was it an expensive camera?"

"That's your husband's problem, 'cause it's going on the expense account. So G. P. wouldn't care about you and Toni Lake getting friendly?"

"Well . . . I'd rather you didn't mention it to him. I learned some nasty things, from Toni, about what G. P.'s been doing to my colleagues, and I'd like to try to remedy that, but from within."

"He wouldn't mind you sleeping with her, but talking to her is another story."

"Something like that." She looked up at me. The blue-gray eyes were wide and clear; she had no makeup on at all and I never saw a lovelier face. "Will you protect me?"

"Of course."

"I don't just mean by withholding information from my husband. I mean, will you unpack and stay, till the start of the Mexican flight?"

"Why?"

She pushed up on her hands and put her face so close to mine, the tips of our noses nearly touched. "Why not? We can spend some time together. . . . We're pals, remember?"

"I remember."

She began chewing on my earlobe. "Besides, what if G. P. didn't write those notes? Somebody else might be lying in wait to sabotage my plane. I have enemies, you know."

"Sure. G. P.'s made you plenty, sounds like."

She kissed me; by the end of the kiss, she was back on top of me, a lanky woman in a man's pajama top and no bottoms.

"Will you stay?" she asked.

"Well, your husband did hire me to be your bodyguard."

"That's right."

"So, uh . . . I guess I have a responsibility to guard your body."

She nodded. "Day and night."

"You know, that isn't the throttle . . ."

"Sure it is. . . . Don't you want to go for the record?"

"Is three times your record?"

"Four would be."

"Four?"

"My goodness, have you forgotten? You're not my first tonight. . . ."

"Oh, you are a dirty girl underneath it all. . . . What you need is a real man in the cockpit. . . ."

She yelped at the funny filth of that, and laughed and laughed, even as I slipped another lambskin over my throttle and prepared for another flight.

Seven

The flight was scheduled for April 19, a Friday night, according to a strategy worked out by G. P. Putnam that would have Amy reaching Mexico City on Saturday afternoon, in time for a story in the Easter Sunday papers.

Mantz had installed in the Vega his various new and improved gizmos, several engineers from neighboring Lockheed had worked their technological magic as well, and mechanic Ernie Tisor pronounced the plane in ship-shape condition, ready for the five hundred gallons of fuel that with other special equipment would send its weight up to a staggering six thousand pounds. Amy took the fully loaded and fueled-up Vega up for numerous test spins and seemed delighted at the way the plane handled. I declined to accompany her.

Meetings at the Mantz bungalow ceased, Paul having moved out at Myrtle's request, and resumed in Mantz's office at the United Air Services hangar. There, Amy spent many hours with Mantz and Commander Williams going over charts and maps (Rand McNally overviews of the United States and Mexico, and state maps of both countries); she would have to compute her position from compass readings and elapsed time using tables that showed distances covered at various speeds. Mantz created specific exercises for her in the blind-flying trainer based on Williams's charts, and she dutifully carried them out.

But she and Mantz continued to have the occasional row, as when she complained about the inconvenience of a trailing antenna for her two-way radiotelephone, which she had to unwind from a reel under the pilot's seat, after takeoff, and then reel in again before landing.

"Listen to Papa, angel," Mantz said condescendingly, "and take it along."

"With our weight problems," she said, "why bother with it?"

"Since you've never learned how to use a telegraph radio, and you don't know how to take celestial sightings, it's your principal aid to navigation. Or were you planning to pack a Ouija board?"

He laughed at his own joke as she stomped off—but that was the end of it, and she agreed to take the trailing antenna along. No matter how she may have resented him, Mantz was the final authority on all technical matters.

On Tuesday night, with G. P. Putnam due to arrive the next afternoon by train (he liked to fly even less than I did), his wife and I said our goodbyes in the cabin at Lowman's Motor Court where we'd spent every night together following the incident with Myrtle Mantz and her .32. Officially, Amy had moved from the Mantz bungalow to the Ambassador Hotel, but my cabin was her home away from home.

We were in bed. She was in the crook of my arm and we were both naked and rather melancholy. I don't suppose either one of us had any illusions that our affair was anything but a passing if memorable moment in our lives. But several weeks of intimacy had made us a couple, and it was difficult to let go.

"Myrtle Mantz is suing for divorce," she said.

"Stop the presses."

"I've been named as corespondent."

"I'm sorry. . . . You can't be surprised."

"No. I'm not even worried about the bad publicity. Myrtle's own disgraceful behavior lets the world see exactly what she is . . . but I don't know how G. P. will take it."

"Why do you care?"

She gazed up at me like a worried child. "What are you going to tell him, Nathan?"

"How about, I'm convinced his wife isn't having an

affair with Paul Mantz because she's having one with me?"

She frowned and laughed. "You're terrible."

"He's terrible. If you believe he's the kind of man who would send threatening letters to his own wife, if you find his business practices disgusting, if anything tender you might once have felt for him has gone completely cold, then you have a responsibility to yourself to dump the son of a bitch, pronto."

"Quite a speech."

"Thank you."

She twirled circles in my chest hair with a forefinger. "So. Are you suggesting I dump him and move to Chicago? We could raise little Hellers. I could take in laundry, a little sewing . . ."

"No," I said, not appreciating her sarcasm; like most sarcastic people, I only appreciated my own. "I'm looking for something in a wife a little less interesting than a woman who flies six thousand pounds of fuel and aircraft over the Gulf of Mexico in her spare time."

"Really?"

"You don't need G. P. anymore. You're more famous than Wrigley's Spearmint Gum. You hang around with the President and Eleanor, for Christ's sake. You're at a stage where you can attract all kinds of backing and sponsorship without the help of that slick operator."

She leaned on an elbow, her expression solemn. "I don't approve of everything G. P. does . . ."

"No kidding."

"But he put me where I am, and he knows how to keep me there. He doesn't push me around, Nathan, I can handle him; there are going to be some changes made about how he goes about things—"

"But not a change in management."

"No. I'm going to stick with G. P."

"Even if he sent those notes?"

"Even then." She smiled a little. "But someday . . . who knows?"

I snorted a laugh. "Laundry and little Hellers?"

"Who can say? I only have a few good years in the air left in me, a few good flights . . . and then it is my firm intention to leave G. P. Putnam behind and find myself a tropical island. Maybe it'll be a tropical island in Illinois."

I slipped an arm around her, gathered her close. "Why don't you quit now? Or at least after this Mexico City flight . . ."

She shook her head, no, and though her eyes looked right at me, they were distant. "I need to go out on something bigger, Nathan. Something with wings so wide it'll carry me to the end of my days . . ."

Did she know how arch that sounded?

"Jeez, what the hell's left, Amy? I mean, no offense, but don't you think the public's interest in record-breaking flights has pretty much subsided? When you got airlines flying people coast to coast, like some Twentieth Century Limited of the sky, the bloom's off the rose, my sweet, the novelty's plumb wore off."

Her eyes tightened. "It has to be something *really* big. . . ."

"What are you thinking? What have you got cooked up under those Shirley Temple curls?"

Her expression turned pixieish. She tapped my nose with a fingertip. "What would you say to *two* oceans, Nathan?"

"What? . . . An around-the-world flight, you mean?"

She withdrew from my arms and flopped onto her back and folded her arms across her bare breasts, and stared at the ceiling as if it were the sky, her eyes alive with a dream. "A female Phileas Fogg . . . in a plane. Wouldn't that set 'em on their ears?"

I leaned on my elbow and studied her like a moron stumped by a trigonometry problem. "Didn't Wiley Post do that already?"

"Wiley's not a woman. . . ." She frowned in thought. "Only I'll need something better than the Vega to do it. A bigger plane, with two engines. . . ."

"Does G. P. know about this latest scheme?"

"Of course. He's all for it."

It was probably his idea.

"Isn't it a little dangerous?"

Her response was lilting: "The most dangerous yet."

"Jesus. What if it kills you?"

"I think G. P. would grieve—after he got a ghostwrit-

ten book out of it." She tossed a wry little smirk my
way. "Then he'd find himself a new young wife and get
on with his life."

"What about you? So, do you want to die, Amy? Does
dying in the drink sound like a fun adventure?"

"If I should pop off, it'd be doing the thing I always
most wanted to do. Don't you think the Man with the
Little Black Book has a date marked down for all of us?
And when our work here is finished, we move on?"

"No," I said, angry to hear such romantic horseshit
coming from an intelligent woman. "I don't believe that
at all. If a guy with a scythe comes around to collect me,
I'll grab it from him and slice his damn head off."

"Nothing wrong with that. I never said I was in favor
of going down without a fight."

"Amy, tell me, please, I'm just an ignorant workaday
rube—what exactly would a flight like that do for the
cause of aviation?"

Her full lips pursed into a kiss of a smile, which unfolded as she admitted, "Not a darn thing . . . but for
the cause of women, everything . . . not to mention set
me up with a reputation bigger than Slim Lindbergh's,
allow me to retire to a life of respect, an advisor to
presidents, writing, lecturing—but at my own pace, perhaps a college teaching position. . . ."

There was no talking to her. I was at least a little in
love with her, and maybe somewhere in the back of my
self-deluded brain I thought she might come back to me
one day, when her final flight was over and she'd di-
vorced that machiavellian bastard. But I wasted no more
breath in trying to discourage her from reaching her
goal, even if it did involve her staying with G. P. Putnam.

Who, on Thursday afternoon, spoke privately with me,
though we were in the mammoth echoing United Air
Services hangar.

We were not alone—Ernie, Tod and Jim, the team of
mechanics assigned to the Vega, were at work on Amy's
plane. But they were on the other side of the hangar, the
clanking and clinking of their tools, and their occasional
chatter, providing a muffled accompaniment to our conversation, just as oil and gas smells provided a pungent
bouquet. Putnam and I stood in the shadow of the wing

of Mantz's bread-and-butter ship, the red and white
Honeymoon Express.

I was wearing a lime sportshirt and dark green slacks,
fitting in nicely with the casual California style; but Putnam was strictly East Coast business executive. His wide-
shouldered suit was a gray double-breasted worsted that
had not come off the rack; his black and white striped tie
was silk and probably cost more than any suit I owned.

"Is she sleeping with that little cocksucker?" Putnam
demanded, looking over toward the glassed-in office
where Amy and Mantz hunkered over the desk looking
at a map or chart, Commander Williams opposite them,
pointing something out.

"No," I said.

"You're absolutely positive?"

"I was in the bushes looking in the windows, G. P."

"Did you get pictures?"

"There was nothing to get pictures of. They had separate bedrooms. Then when Mantz's wife filed divorce
papers on him, he had to move out, and your wife went
to the Ambassador."

He gestured with open palms. "If there's nothing between them, why has Myrtle Mantz named Amelia in
this divorce action?"

"Because Paul Mantz can't keep his dick in his pants
and your wife's been a houseguest. It's a natural
assumption."

He began to pace, over a small area, two steps forward, two steps back. "But an incorrect one, you're
saying?"

"That's right. Your wife and Mantz get along pretty
well, I mean they work together fine as a team . . . but
she resents his superior attitude."

"Well, he is a patronizing little son of a bitch," Putnam snapped.

Funny thing was, I'd overheard Mantz complain to
Williams about the same thing where Putnam was concerned: "Where does that prick in a stuffed shirt get off
treating me like an employee?"

Williams hadn't replied, but it occurred to me the answer might be: Because Mantz was on G. P.'s payroll.

It also occurred to me that that "stuffed shirt" dressed similarly to Mantz.

On the other hand, Mantz had a point. He probably considered himself Amy's business partner, because she was going to consign her Vega to the United Air Services fleet, plus they'd been discussing, over lunches at the Sky Room, the possibility of a flying school that bore the Amelia Earhart imprimatur.

"Have you received any more threatening notes?" I asked Putnam.

His pacing halted and the cold eyes did something they rarely did: blinked. "What? Uh, no. We've been fortunate in that regard."

"You'll be interested to know there haven't been any sabotage attempts. No breaking and entering, here at the airport; no suspicious characters hanging about; no lovesick fans carrying a crush too far."

He smiled tightly, nodded. "That's a relief to hear."

"I mean, because you were concerned about your wife's welfare, right?"

"Of course I was."

"This wasn't just about me snooping on her, to see if she was cheating around."

"Of course not."

"It's not like you sent those threatening notes yourself or anything. To make it look good."

A groove formed between his eyebrows. "What are you implying?"

"Nothing. It's just that Paul Mantz told me an interesting story about how you promoted a book, a few years back. That Mussolini exposé?"

He sucked air in and huffed, "Are you accusing me of sending those notes myself? That's patently absurd."

"It is absurd, and I also don't give a damn, as long as your checks don't bounce . . . but I wouldn't be surprised, once the dust settles, and this Mexico City flight's behind you, if that sweet little aviatrix of yours doesn't sit you down for a spanking."

His chin lifted and the cold eyes peered down at me with unblinking contempt. "Mister, I don't like your attitude."

"You didn't hire me for my attitude. You hired me

for my low moral character. I wormed my way into your wife's confidence and betrayed her . . . just like you wanted me to."

"After Amelia takes off tomorrow," he said, stalking off, glaring, "I won't be needing your services any longer."

"I don't think you ever needed them, really . . . but thanks for the work. Times are hard."

The rest of that day, Putnam said not a word to me, and final preparations went on without a hitch, with the slight exception of a guest appearance by Myrtle Mantz, who dropped by to scream at her husband.

Wearing a dark green dress with jagged streaks that might have been lightning bolts, she cornered Mantz in his office during Amy's final stint in the Link trainer. The glass of his glassed-in office rattled as she yelled at him, and pounded his desk.

I was lounging in a folding chair, reading the boxing results in the sports section of the *Herald Express*, when the brouhaha began. And I would have stayed out of it, but Mantz started yelling back at her and took a swing at her, which she ducked. I had a feeling these two sparring partners had been in the ring before.

Nonetheless, I'm the old-fashioned chivalrous type who doesn't like to see guys belt gals even when they deserve it, and went in there and got between them with outspread hands like a referee.

"Save it for the lawyers, you two," I said.

Myrtle curled her pretty mouth into a sneer, and snarled, "Who appointed you sheriff, big boy?"

Normally, a good-looking redhead calling me "big boy" would have perked me up; but I had little interest in even good-looking women who shot target practice in the bedroom.

"Get her the hell outta here!" Mantz was yelling. "Crazy greedy dame!"

I walked her out of his office—she was yelling back at him, but not flailing around or anything; I think she was glad to get out of there before Mantz actually struck her. On her way out, she did hurl a few epithets at Amy, who Putnam was helping down out of her little red trainer.

"Adultery's a sin, you snooty bitch!" she shrieked. "I hope you crash! I hope you drown in the ocean!"

Though Putnam was getting an eye- and earful, Amy merely turned her back to Myrtle, as I kept walking the estranged Mrs. Mantz toward the door.

Ushering her outside the hangar to where the flashy Dusenberg was parked, I found she'd calmed down, some. "No-good lousy husband of mine canceled my charge accounts," she explained.

"Steer clear of that guy," I said. "You don't want to lose any of your pretty teeth."

Myrtle touched my cheek with a cool hand and, laying on the Southwestern accent, said, "You are a sweet one, aren't you? Wish I'd run into you a long time ago."

She ran into me in the bedroom at the Mantz bungalow; she just didn't know it.

And when she'd driven off, I went back into Mantz's office and said, "Hey, Paul, if you want to come out of that divorce with your shirt and maybe a pair of socks or two, I'd suggest not belting that broad."

He didn't say anything, but I had to wonder if the reason Myrtle resorted to a firearm was because he'd been smacking her around.

With the flight due to begin around ten that night, nobody came in the next day till around one in the afternoon, including the mechanics.

Shortly after I got to the United Air Services hangar, I stuck my head into Mantz's office and asked if he had a moment, and he waved me in. He was in a tan shirt and black tie, seated behind his desk, going over the pile of charts and maps, looking a little frazzled.

I took the chair opposite him and asked, "Are you aware that Amelia's talking seriously about makin' her next flight a little around-the-world number?"

Mantz sighed, tossing a chart onto the stack. "Maybe she ought to survive this flight first. . . . Yeah, I know. She and Gippy have been after me to help 'em prepare—and work my connections at Lockheed to get 'em a good price on a twin-engine plane."

"Will you?"

"Probably. I mean, if she's got it in her head, then she's going to do it, and if she's going to do it, I want

to see her tackle it as close to the right way as she's
capable of."

"How capable is she?"

Mantz waggled a finger. "Never forget that Amelia
Earhart won her reputation first, then set about earning
the right to havin' it. . . . She has zero experience in
twin-engine piloting technique."

"Can she learn it?"

"You've seen how impatient she can be, where training's concerned."

"She's worked hard in that trainer of yours."

"Hey, she's a good pilot, but a woman's pilot. These
dames all jockey the throttles—"

"*Paul!*" Ernie Tisor, his face pale and long with worry,
had stuck his head in the door. The mechanic was wiping
some grease off his right palm onto his coveralls. "Something nasty. . . . You gotta see this. . . ."

I tagged along as Mantz followed Tisor to the Vega,
where a small metal ladder up to the cockpit was in
place. The other two mechanics, Jim and Tod, were
standing around wearing spotless coveralls and dazed
expressions.

"Take a look down by the rudder pedals," Tisor was
saying, gesturing to the ladder, which Mantz quickly
scaled.

Mantz wasn't up in the Vega cockpit long before his
head popped out and his face was as white as powdered
sugar, only his expression was anything but sweet.

"Who's been around here?" he asked Tisor.

"Nobody," Tisor said, shrugging. "I unlocked the
place just a little before one. . . . Tod and Jim were
waiting outside when I got here."

Mantz was clambering down the ladder. "Nobody's
been around the Vega?"

"Not that I saw. Boys?"

The other two mechanics shook their heads, no.

"Shit," Mantz said.

Tisor asked, "What do you make of it, Paul?"

"Drop or two of acid, maybe." He placed a hand on
Tisor's shoulder. "God bless you, Ernie, for catching it.
Can you repair those cables?"

"That shouldn't be any big problem."

"Fine. Get that done, then go over every rivet and nut and bolt on this baby. I want this patient to get a complete stem-to-stern physical, boys—look down her throat, and up her ass, understood?"

The three mechanics nodded, and quickly got to work.

Mantz turned to walk back to his office and I fell in step with him. "What's going on, Paul?"

"Here's Amelia and G. P.," Mantz said, nodding to where Amy and her husband had just entered at the front of the hangar. "I'll fill everybody in at the same time."

They were walking toward us, Amy smiling, sporty in a plaid shirt and chinos, Putnam wearing his perpetual frown and an impeccably tailored blue twill suit.

Soon we were all seated in Mantz's office with Mantz standing behind his desk. "I'm going to recommend we postpone," he said, leaning his hands on the maps and charts before him.

"Why in hell would we do that?" Putnam demanded, seated but almost climbing out of his chair.

Next to him, between us, was Amy, who said quietly, "What's happened?"

Mantz grimaced. "Your rudder cables—somebody left you a present, angel . . . a few well-placed drops of acid. The wires are almost eaten through."

"What in God's name . . . ?" Putnam exploded.

"Acid?" Amy asked, as if she wasn't sure of the meaning of the word.

"Probably nitric or sulfuric," Mantz said. "You'd have flown a while, maybe a few hours, then they'd have given way . . . snapped like twigs."

"Sending my plane out of control," Amy said, hollowly.

Putnam thrust an accusatory finger in my direction. "This is just the kind of sabotage you were hired to prevent!"

"I wasn't hired to sleep overnight in Paul's hangar," I said. "There's nighttime security here at the airport, right, Paul?"

It was a question I knew the answer to, that having been one of the first things I asked Mantz about.

"Certainly," Mantz said, "a full detail of highly competent night watchmen . . . but of course the airport is open well into the wee hours . . . and if someone who had a key to my hangar . . ."

"Like your wife Myrtle," I said.

"Yes!" Putnam yelled. "We all saw her yesterday, yelling and screaming, and out of control!"

Mantz sighed and nodded. "Yeah. I'm afraid this may be Myrtle's doing. She'd love to get back at me . . . and you, too, angel."

I asked, "Is this something Myrtle would know how to do? I mean, I wouldn't know a rubber cable from a bagpipe."

"Myrtle was a student pilot of mine," Mantz said. "She knows how to fly. She knows planes."

I frowned. "You told me she hated flying."

"She doesn't like to fly unless she or I are at the controls . . . at least, that's how it used to be. Kind of doubt I'm her favorite co-pilot, these days."

"Paul," Putnam said, suddenly calm and reasonable, "you may not be aware of this, but one of the main reasons Mr. Heller was hired was because Amelia had received threatening notes in the mail. They were post-marked California."

Putnam had never mentioned the California post-marks before. Of course, I'd never actually seen any of the notes.

Putnam continued, asking Mantz, "Do you think your wife might have been capable of sending them?"

Mantz, who was after all the first to peg Putnam for sending those notes himself, said only, "Well, Myrtle's been jealous of Amelia for a long, long time . . . and she knew this flight was coming up. . . ."

"We should call the cops," I said.

"No police," Putnam said.

"I agree," Mantz said.

Now I exploded, half out of my chair: "You guys are nuttier than Myrtle! You got somebody trying to sabo-tage Amelia Earhart's airplane, and you look the other way? Jesus, G. P., I'd think you'd want the publicity . . ."

"Not this kind," Putnam said. "It's tainted by this di-vorce scandal."

Appearing not at all upset, Amy asked, "Are there any other signs of sabotage?"

"No," Mantz said. "We're giving the Vega a complete inspection. Still, I'd feel more comfortable if—"

"If your people don't find anything else," Putnam said, "we go ahead with the flight. . . . That is, of course, if that's my wife's desire . . ."

"It is," she said.

"You have no business," I said to Amy, rather crossly, "getting on a plane, on a flight that's dangerous under ideal conditions, when you've discovered sabotage like this."

She didn't answer; she wouldn't even look at me.

Putnam said, "If you'd done your goddamn job, Mr. Heller, we wouldn't have this problem, would we?"

"I did my job for you," I said, "remember?"

Putnam blanched at that, knowing it was my way of reminding him of what he'd really hired me to do, but he bellowed on: "No police, and no postponement. If we postpone, we lose our coverage in the Sunday papers. We've got maximum press attention out of Amelia's previous three long-distance flights, with these Friday take-offs, and I see no reason to miss another golden opportunity . . . unless, of course, Paul, your people come up with some other act of sabotage."

But they didn't.

I despised G. P. Putnam. He was a reprehensible son of a bitch whose wife was a property for him to exploit and if her flying life were endangered along the way, he didn't give a flying shit. Of course, I'd been taking fifty dollars a day from this reprehensible son of a bitch, to find out if his wife was cheating on him, and then slept with the woman myself. So maybe when it came to reprehensible sons of bitches, it took one to know one.

Around nine-thirty that night, the hangar cluttered with reporters from both the L.A. papers and the international wire services, I managed to get Amy alone for a moment, over by the *Honeymoon Express*.

I said to her, "You know I'm against this."

She looked jaunty and unconcerned in the leather flying jacket with red-and-brown plaid shirt, a red scarf knotted at her neck; her tan flying helmet was held in one hand.

"The boys didn't find anything else," she said. "They've repaired the rudder cables. Everything's fine."

"You're probably right. There probably won't be any other problems. Because for one thing, I don't think Myrtle put the acid on those cables."

She laughed in surprise. "Well . . . who did, then?"

"I don't know who did it, but I can guess who hired it done."

"*Who*, Nathan?"

"The management . . . your ever-lovin' husband."

Her eyes tightened. "What? Why?"

"I accused him yesterday of sending those threatening notes himself. I think he hired somebody . . . maybe one of Mantz's mechanics . . . to perpetrate a little act of sabotage. Something that could be discovered, and quickly remedied . . . and which would make G. P.'s phony notes look like the real thing, making him seem innocent, and somebody else . . . Myrtle Mantz . . . guilty."

That made her wince. "Nathan, do you really think he's capable of that?"

"Does Garbo wanna be alone? Listen, you want me to take hubby off in a corner and beat a confession out of him? Be glad to do it—no extra charge. I'm a former Chicago cop, remember—I know how."

The full lips curved into a lovely smile, and she touched my face, gently, where she once had slapped it. "That's one of the sweetest, if most violent, offers, I've ever had . . ."

God, how I wanted to kiss her right then; I like to think she was wishing the same thing.

Finally I said, "I got a sleeper out tonight, at midnight."

The smile settled into a smirk. "Yes, G. P. mentioned he'd discontinued your security services, as of tonight. . . . But I'll see you again."

"These have been special weeks to me, Amy."

"I love you, too, Nathan."

And, Putnam waving her over, she went off to chat

with a few members of the press, before climbing into the cockpit of her nameless red Vega.

At nine fifty-five, under the blazing floodlights of the Burbank airport, I watched her rumble down the endless runway and, finally, when her speed overcame the six thousand pounds of loaded-down, fueled-up Vega, she lifted into a clear but moonless night sky, which soon swallowed her up.

I didn't say anything to Mantz or Putnam, who I'd handed the Terraplane keys over to, earlier. I just found my way to the United Airport terminal and went out front and got a cab to the train station.

Amy's record-setting flight to Mexico City was fairly uneventful. She threw Commander Williams's elaborate flight plans away and flew south, following the coastline until she figured she was parallel to Mexico City and took a left. When she couldn't find it, she landed in a dry lake bed and asked directions of a farmer.

Delayed by weather, her eventual return to Newark (which included crossing the Gulf of Mexico, despite Mantz's warnings) found her mobbed by fifteen thousand admiring fans who pawed at her and tore her clothing. Putnam reaped substantial publicity benefits from the flight, and had arranged for several honorary degrees and awards to be presented her in the glow of this latest accomplishment.

Within a week of her return from Mexico City, Amelia Earhart was in Chicago, Illinois, to accept a medal from the Italian government at a conference of two thousand women's club presidents, every one of whom represented a potential lecture booking on a future tour. I was employed by the Emerson Speaker's Bureau, at Miss Earhart's request, to provide security.

Her husband did not accompany her on the Chicago trip.

And since Putnam had essentially fired me, it was necessary that, in doing this job for his wife, I remain undercover.

Reprehensible son of a bitch that I was.

Dead Reckoning

March 17–July 19, 1937

Eight

Press coverage was minimal when Amelia Earhart (and an all-male crew) lifted off in her twin-engine Lockheed Electra 10E from the Oakland Airport on St. Patrick's Day, 1937, on what was, technically at least, the first leg of her round-the-world flight. Heavy rains had caused numerous postponements, and many reporters—who, frankly, were probably a little bored with Amelia Earhart by now, anyway, finding her a relic of a quaint, earlier era of pioneering aviation—had bailed out. But one memorable photo—which appeared all over the country, including Chicago—caught the Electra, shortly after takeoff, poised above the almost-finished Golden Gate Bridge.

When they arrived at Honolulu fifteen hours and forty-seven minutes later (setting a record), Paul Mantz handled the landing, due to fatigue on Amy's part. At least, this is what Mantz later told me, dispelling the official word that the twenty-four-hour delay before beginning the first true leg of the flight (and the most dangerous)—Honolulu to tiny Howland Island, more than 1,800 miles away—was due to shaky weather forecasts; in fact, it was to give Miss Earhart time to rest up for the physically demanding flight. Mantz, who was only along for the Oakland-Honolulu leg, took advantage of the delay and flew one last test flight of the Electra, to check out a few last-minute adjustments that had been made.

The papers were referring to the sleek, all-metal, silver Electra with its fifty-five-foot wing span as "the Flying

Laboratory" (a G. P. Putnam touch, no doubt) and I knew the ship was a great source of pride to Amy.

April of the year before, back on the lecture circuit (interspersing speaking engagements with campaign appearances for President Roosevelt's reelection), she had been glowing about it.

"They've put fifty thousand dollars into a research fund," she said, "can you imagine?"

I knew all about huge sums of money; I figured I had at least six bucks (factoring in tip) invested in our tables d'h‹te (filet of sole with Marguery sauce for her and filet mignon for me). The elegant oak-paneled Chez Louis on East Pearson Street near the Gold Coast was one of the handful of places in Chicago where a celebrity could dine unaccosted, though many eyes were on my tall, slim companion in her canary shirt, string of pearls and tailored gray slacks. Amy was the first woman I knew who chose slacks as evening wear.

"So they gave you fifty thousand clams," I said matter-of-factly, carving myself a bite of rare filet. "Who is 'they'?"

"Purdue University. Or anyway, Purdue's 'Amelia Earhart Research Foundation' . . . whatever that is. Probably some rich alumni whose arms G. P. twisted."

"Why Purdue University?"

"Didn't I tell you? Since last fall, I have two positions with Purdue: I'm their aeronautics advisor but I'm also a consultant in the Department for the Study of Careers for Women."

"Is that what they're calling Home Economics now?"

A wry smile dimpled an apple cheek. "You tread a thin line with me, sometimes, Nathan Heller. . . . I spend several weeks a semester there."

"So it's not just an honorary title, then?"

"No," she said, touching her napkin to her lips, finished with her sole, "I live right in the dorms with the girls, eat in their cafeteria, sit elbow to elbow with them. I let these young women know they don't have to settle for being nurses, they can be doctors; they don't just have to be secretaries, they can be business executives."

"That's a swell sentiment, Amy, but do you think it's realistic?"

Amy smiled at the colored busboy removing her plate. "Oh, I let them know they'll be facing discrimination . . . both where the law is concerned, and good old-fashioned male stupidity."

"It was probably good old-fashioned stupid males who ponied up your fifty grand. . . . You wouldn't have your eye on a new plane, by any chance? That twin-engine job you've been craving?"

The waiter was delivering our desserts.

She licked her upper lip in anticipation of the delicious parfait before her; or she might have been thinking about her new plane. "Two motors, dual controls, capable of a twenty-seven-thousand-foot altitude. It's an Electra."

I had a parfait too and spooned a bite of the frozen confection. "Isn't that a passenger plane?"

"Yes, seats up to ten. But Paul's going to strip it for auxiliary fuel tanks; he says we'll have a capability of four thousand five hundred nonstop air miles."

"That's a long time between pee breaks," I said.

Famous for subsisting on nothing but tomato juice on her long-distance jaunts, Amy had once confided in me that she turned her nose up at the tubular gadget used by the military for urination ("I never tinkle on a flight").

"I may have to change my ways," she admitted, dipping her spoon into the parfait glass. "Oh my goodness, Nathan, this Electra is my dream airy-plane. Paul's fixing it up with all the latest gadgets: Sperry autogiro robot pilot, a fuel minimizer, wind deicers, blind-flying instruments. . . . There'll be over a hundred dials and levels on the control panel."

"But will you bother to learn how to use them?"

"Of course! We're calling the plane our 'Flying Laboratory.' . . . I mean, it's a research project, after all."

"Right. For the Amelia Earhart Research Foundation. You can study the bladder capacity of a woman nearing forty."

Digging for the final far-down bite in the glass, she gave me a tight-lipped, chin-crinkled smile, then asked, "And what experiment are you conducting? How many smart-aleck remarks a man can make and still get invited up to an emancipated woman's hotel suite?"

I licked the last bite of parfait off my spoon and innocently asked, "Have I mentioned lately how much I admire Eleanor Roosevelt?"

And of course I received (and accepted) my invitation to her hotel suite, though I was disheartened by all her "good news": it meant G. P. Putnam still had his hooks into her. Through various machinations, he was going to deliver her a new "airy-plane"—and in fact he did, on July 24, her thirty-ninth birthday.

When she took off for Howland Island at dawn from Honolulu's Luke Field near Pearl Harbor, Paul Mantz—just an advisor on this trip—stayed behind. He had slipped a paper-orchid lei over Amy's head before she followed her co-pilot navigator Harry Manning and assistant navigator Fred Noonan aboard the Electra.

Manning was beside her in the co-pilot's seat with Noonan in the rear at the chart table against a bulkhead by a window—the Electra's cabin stripped of seats, replaced with fuel tanks—when Amy started the engines and motioned to the ground crew to remove her wheel chocks.

The Electra began to roll down the wet runway but it gave no sign of lifting off before it began to sway in the crosswind, its right wing dipping down; Amy corrected by reducing power to the left engine and the plane yawed to the left, out of control, its right wheel and undercarriage sheared away in a scream of metal on concrete, the silver bird sliding down the runway on its belly spewing sparks and spilling fuel.

When the plane finally skidded to a stop, the hatch cover popped open and a white-faced Amelia Earhart emerged, shouting, "Something went wrong!" She and Manning and Noonan were unscathed and sparks had never met fuel, so there was no exploding plane, no fire, though fire trucks and ambulances were racing their way as the crew stumbled from the plane to safety.

Amy quickly regained her composure and told reporters, "Of course the flight is still on!" The Lockheed would be shipped back to the Lockheed factory in Burbank for repairs.

One of G. P. Putnam's first voiced concerns, I understand, was to make sure the 6,500 presold first-day-of-issue philatelic covers be recovered from the wreck.

Traveling by commercial airliner, Amy stopped in Chicago in April, on her way to New York; we spent an evening together, in my apartment on the twenty-third floor of the Morrison Hotel, where in the glow of a single table lamp, with a soft backdrop of the Dorsey Brothers playing on the radio, we enjoyed a middling room service meal and each other's company.

But this was not the Amy I'd dined with at Chez Louis, a year before—not the bubbling, optimistic Amy almost giddy with anticipation of obtaining her dream "airy-plane."

This was a thin, wan, middle-aged woman, her weariness reflected by the dark puffy patches under her clear blue-gray eyes and lines above and at the corners of her wide sensuous mouth. Still a handsome creature, she was curled up on my couch beside me in a white blouse and navy blue slacks and white cotton anklets, possessed of a slim leggy frame that a much younger woman might have envied.

Nestled under my arm, sipping a cup of cocoa, she had just told me her version of the Honolulu crackup, which laid the blame on a tire blowout, when she looked up with her eyes wide and guileless. "Aren't you going to ask, 'Are you going to try again'?"

"No," I said. I was working on a bottle of Pabst Blue Ribbon. "And by the way, I hope you don't."

"Why? Don't you want me to be rich and famous?"

"Aren't you already?"

She made a clicking sound in one cheek. "Just halfway . . . I'm afraid we're pretty darn near broke, Nathan."

"Then how can you expect to repair your plane and try again?"

"Unless I find fifty thousand dollars, I can't."

"What about the Purdue Institute for Female Bladder Research?"

She elbowed me, then sipped her cocoa and said, "They ended up kicking in eighty thousand in the first place," she said. "That's what the Electra and all its bells and whistles cost. . . . Now I need another thirty grand for repairs, and twenty for incidentals."

"What's that? Your cans of tomato juice?"

"Flight arrangements are expensive, permissions from countries and lining up airstrips, having mechanics ready, and fuel waiting. . . ."

"Why can't you just plug into what you had set up before?"

"Before I was flying east to west; this time we're going west to east."

I frowned. "Why?"

"Changing weather conditions, G. P. says."

"What does he know about it?"

She gave me a stern look. "He's the one who's finding that extra fifty thousand dollars."

"That makes him an expert?"

"Would you do me a favor, Nathan?" She gestured to her head, then her neck. "I have one of my sinus headaches. I could really use a neck rub."

Soon the nearly empty cup of cocoa was on the nearby coffee table, which had been pushed aside, so that she could sit on the carpet, Indian-style, her back to me, between my legs, as I worked the muscles of her upper back and neck.

"If G. P. doesn't put this together," she said, "I'm all washed up."

"Don't be silly. You have money."

"Not much. I can't even afford to support my family anymore. . . . I couldn't afford the upkeep on my mother's house and we've taken her in with us. . . . Did I tell you we bought a house in Toluca Lake, just down the street from Paul's old place? Muriel I had to cut off entirely and now . . . oh yes, right there . . . she's out peddling interviews about me to the press."

"That's a shame."

"We had to shut down the fashion line . . . we were barely breaking even. I've invested in several business ventures with Paul but it's too early to see how that's going to come out . . . oh yes, yes, there. . . ."

"Is that what this New York trip's about? Raising cash?"

She nodded her hanging head. "Whatever's necessary.

I've mortgaged my future on this one . . . but what are futures for? Did you hear me on *The Kraft Music Hour*?"

"Can't say I did. What's Bing Crosby like?"

She threw me a smile over her shoulder as I worked my thumbs in it. "Funny. Nice. But can you imagine how scared I was? How much I hated that?"

"Yeah." I thought back to the lectures she endured, those necessary evils to pay the freight; sitting backstage paralyzed with fright, puking her guts out, then going on with a smile and poise a princess might have coveted.

"And in New York," she said, "I'll be appearing in the Gimbel's eleventh-floor restaurant to personally help sell an additional one thousand first-day covers."

More stamps, yet.

"What happened to the batch from your first try?"

"G. P. had them imprinted with the words: 'Held over in Honolulu following takeoff accident,' or some such. These new ones will be marked in some special way. . . . Ouch!"

"Too hard?"

"Yes . . . just rub in circles for a while, then maybe you can go after that knot again. . . . I'm signing a new book contract. That's the major reason for the trip."

"What's the book about?"

"The flight, silly. I'll keep a diary along the way and when I get back spend a week or two polishing it up, and, presto . . ."

"Another instant book."

"We're pulling out all the stops this time."

"Sounds like you and G. P. are quite a team."

She turned and looked up at me. "Are you jealous?"

"Of your husband? I don't know why I would be. I mean, it's not like you sleep in the same bed or anything."

"Actually, we do . . . but it's not like that between us, anymore. I think he has a sense that . . . well, he knows this partnership is winding down. . . . Uh, that's enough, that was wonderful, thank you. . . . Listen . . . I have something for you. . . ."

She scooted her butt around and, still seated before me, dug in her breast pocket. She withdrew something

130 Max Allan Collins

the size of a folded-up handkerchief, which she pressed
into my hand.

I unfolded it and it became a small silk American flag.
"What's this for?"

She had an impish smile. "Just a lucky keepsake. I
took it along on all my long-distance flights."

"Don't you think you should take it on this one, too?"

"No, no, I . . . I want you to have it now."

I held it out to her. "Give it to me when you get
back."

She shook her head, no. "Better take it now."

I frowned at her. "What? You have some kind of
premonition . . . ?"

Her eyes popped open. "No! No. It's just . . . a
feeling."

"If you have that kind of feeling, Amy, for Christ's
sake, don't go!"

She crawled up on the couch and nestled in next to
me, again. "Nathan, as far as I know, I only have one
real fear—a small and probably female fear of growing
old. I won't feel so completely cheated, if I fail to
come back."

"I don't want to hear that kind of talk."

"Nathan . . ."

"It's fatalistic bullshit." I held the little flag out to her.
"I don't want it. Take it with you."

She took and refolded it, placed it back in her pocket
and was clearly hurt. Which was fine with me.

"What's got you thinking like this?" I asked her.

"Nothing." She had her arms folded now, and was
still next to me, but not nestled, her back to the sofa. "I
don't really have misgivings . . . except maybe for Fred."

"Fred?"

"Fred Noonan."

"Oh, yeah. He's your navigator?"

"And co-pilot if necessary, though I'll do all or most
of the flying myself."

"What about that other guy—Manning?"

"He dropped out after Honolulu. Scheduling conflict."

I bet that conflict arose about the time the Electra
went skidding on its belly trailing sparks and fuel down
the runway at Luke Field.

"So what's the story with Noonan?"

"Paul recommended him. He's experienced, easy-going . . . I like him well enough."

"So why do I still sense misgivings?"

Her response was unconvincingly chipper. "He has a background in ocean navigation, and a great reputation for putting that to use in air navigation."

"You haven't answered my question."

"He's really a remarkable man . . . a merchant marine as a kid, joined the British Royal Navy during the war; one of the first flying-boat pilots for Pan Am, navigator on the *China Clipper*, its first year."

I said, "Answer my question."

"What was your question?"

"Don't play dumb."

The blue-gray eyes went hooded. ". . . He's a drinker."

"Ah." Teetotaling Amy of the cups of cocoa, the little girl who'd been slapped by her drunken father, did not suffer drunken fools gladly. "Has it been a problem?"

Her smirk was humorless. "I think he got drunk the night before the Honolulu takeoff."

Actually, it had been an attempted takeoff, but I thought not correcting her was the gentlemanly thing to do.

"Was he in some way responsible for the crackup?"

"No. No. Not at all. And he seemed quite clear-eyed and sober and lucid, that morning."

"That's all you can ask."

"He and his wife . . . he got married recently, to a lovely girl, Mary's her name. . . . Funny, 'cause that's what he calls me, too. It's my middle name . . . Mary. Anyway, driving back from their honeymoon, in Arizona someplace, they had this head-on collision with another auto."

"Good God."

"He wasn't hurt, but his wife suffered some minor injuries, though not, thank goodness, the woman driving the other car . . . or her toddler. Fred was cited for driving in the wrong lane."

"Was he drunk?"

She wouldn't look at me. "Well, drinking, anyway."

So I tried a conciliatory tone: "He just got married. Maybe he was celebrating."

Now she looked at me. "Or maybe he was still upset about the Honolulu crackup. I know that upset him."

"Why, if it wasn't his fault?"

"Pan Am fired him for drinking. He apparently views this round-the-world flight as a last chance to vindicate himself . . . and make himself employable again. He says he has the backing to open a navigation school, if we pull off this flight."

I put my hand on her shoulder. "Amy, can't you find anybody else? Or is it that, you can't bring yourself to fire somebody who needs this job so bad?"

"He's really very good. Paul thinks the world of him."

"Paul isn't risking his life."

"G. P. insists on Fred."

"G. P. isn't risking his life, either. Why does G. P. want Noonan?"

". . . Because Fred's . . . never mind."

She looked away from me again.

I pressed: "What?"

"I think it's because Fred's an . . . economical choice."

"Oh, Christ!"

She returned her eyes to mine and her gaze was almost pleading. "Nathan, most of the good navigators are military and they obviously can't be accessed. Fred Noonan is the man who charted all of Pan Am's Pacific routes—"

"Didn't you say Pan Am fired him?"

"Please don't be cross, Nathan. I didn't look you up so I could spend the evening wallowing in my problems . . ."

This was one of those rare times when she seemed near tears.

I gathered her into my arms and kissed her on the forehead. "You mean, you were lookin' for a good time? Did you find my name scribbled on a phone booth wall? . . . I'm sorry, Amy. We won't talk anymore, about any of this."

She kissed my nose and said, softly, "This is the last flight, Nathan. When I come back, I'm going to have a different life."

Was she implying I'd be part of it? I was afraid to ask. I preferred to think she was. In my bed that night, city lights filtering through sheer curtains like neon stars, her slender white form had a ghostly beauty as she rode me, cowgirl-style. She seemed lost in the act of lovemaking, just as I was lost in her, and I like to think she found a joy with me, in our sexual flight, that rivaled whatever it was in the sky that drew her there.

When Amy began her around-the-world-at-the-Equator flight, she took steps to keep it from the press, telling reporters on May 21 that she was heading out on a shakedown cruise to Miami, to test the Electra's special equipment. With Noonan, her mechanic "Bo" McKneely and her husband, Amy flew to Tucson that afternoon, one of her engines catching fire shortly after landing. She requested an overnight checkup for her ailing plane, knowing that her Electra had a history of malfunction, having flown it in the 1936 Bendix race in which the oil seals leaked and the hatch blew off.

From Tucson she flew the repaired Electra to New Orleans, arriving at 6:00 P.M. Saturday evening at Shushan Airport; checking in at the airport hotel, she and G. P. spent a quiet evening out with Amy's old friend Toni Lake. All of these tidbits I picked up in the papers, following my friend's flight long-distance, and even having to work at it somewhat, as the press didn't seem to care all that much, this time around.

She was strictly an inside-pages phenomenon now, even when at Miami, the next morning, she brought her silver bird in with a shocking thud. She climbed from her cockpit after this "almost" crash landing to be quoted as saying, "I sure smacked it down hard that time!"

The Electra was misbehaving again: faulty shock absorbers, leaking fluid all the way from New Orleans, had caused the hard landing. The oil lines were also leaking, and McKneely led mechanics in an all-out assault on the problems.

On May 29 Amy told the press she would be taking off from Miami Airport, flying east to west on Pan Am's route through the West Indies and then on down along South America's east coast. Leaving G. P. and McKneely behind, Amelia Earhart and Fred Noonan lifted off at

5:56 A.M. on June 1 with five hundred fans in attendance, held back by a line of policemen, her loyal admirers waving and cheering their heroine of the skies.

The papers were less easily impressed. In Chicago the headlines of the next day's papers belonged to the police riot on the South Side of Chicago in which ten striking Republic Steel workers were killed; and the next day, every front page seemed devoted to Edward of England marrying Baltimore's Wallis Simpson.

Over the next six days, to modest press attention, the Electra glided over the east coast of Central and South America, with stops at San Juan, Puerto Rico; Caripito, Venezuela; and Paramaribo, Dutch Guiana; and—after a ten-hour flight, crossing 1,628 miles of jungle and ocean—touched down at Fortaleza, Brazil, with Natal her last stop before crossing the South Atlantic.

According to the papers, on her overnight stops, she was up at three or four in the morning after no more than five hours of sleep. But the flights themselves, in the noisy plane with its cramped cabin, were the real endurance test: she mostly communicated with navigator Noonan by sending him notes fastened to a pulley line with a clothespin. Otherwise one of them had to climb over the bulky auxiliary fuel tanks between her cockpit and Noonan's navigation table.

The flight over the Atlantic went well, despite some headwinds and rainstorms, with the Electra's performance finally on the beam and Noonan providing ace navigation. But when they neared the African coast on June 7, Amy ignored Noonan's counsel to turn south for Dakar and instead headed north, flying fifty miles along the African coast. When she sighted St.-Louis, almost two hundred miles north of Dakar, she sent back a note to Noonan asking him what had put them north. His response: "You." She later admitted as much.

They landed at St.-Louis, their revised destination, where barracks-like accommodations, complete with bedbugs and primitive toilet facilities, awaited them. But their first week had been successful: four thousand miles in forty hours.

After a short hop to Dakar, Amy met two days of bad weather; impatient, she switched her destination

from Fort Niamey to Gao in French West Africa, finding
a corridor between sandstorms to the north and a tornado to the south, and making the 1,140-mile flight in
seven hours and change. The next morning she made
the nearly one-thousand-mile trek from Gao over the
Sahara Desert to Fort-Lamy in French Equatorial Africa. The heat was so punishing that the Electra could
not be refueled until after sunset, as the gasoline might
ignite upon touching the hot metal. Then it was on to
El Fasher in Anglo-Egyptian Sudan and, on June 14,
another twelve hundred miles to Assab on the shores of
the Red Sea, stopping for lunch at Khartoum in the
Sudan and taking tea at Massawa, Eritrea. She was, at
the end of her second week and fifteen thousand miles
from Miami, better than halfway to her objective.

The next day she crossed the Red Sea, then the Ara-
bian Sea to Karachi, Pakistan. Here she stayed for two
unpleasant days in the unremitting desert heat, taking
two camel rides, and the time to stop at the post office
to choose stamps and supervise the cancellation of the
7,500 first-day covers in her keeping. On June 17 she
and Noonan headed for Calcutta, but even in the air, no
relief from the blistering heat could be found: at fifty-
five hundred feet, the temperature was a brutal ninety
degrees. Finally the heat let up, and rainstorms took
over, including air currents that sent the Electra up and
down at a rate of one thousand feet in seconds.

When she took off from Calcutta's Dum Dum Airport
on June 18, the Electra struggled off a water-soaked runway, barely clearing the trees, and monsoon rains accompanied them over the Bay of Bengal on the way to
Rangoon, Burma. She didn't make it to Rangoon, settling on Akyab, but on June 19, they reached their destination, where they took in the Golden Pagoda, taking
off the next day for Singapore. Word awaited her that
mechanics would be on hand to overhaul her plane at
Bandoeng, Java, which she made on the last day of her
third week out. Her landing was an unsteady one, however, and she undoubtedly was suffering from what Paul
Mantz later described as "extreme pilot fatigue."

She had, after all, flown in 135 hours an amazing
twenty thousand miles. She had slept in unfamiliar,

sometimes primitive, even bizarre, surroundings; she had
eaten little, slept less, and suffered from heat exhaustion,
diarrhea and nausea.

Three days of scheduled repairs for the Electra turned into
six, and it wasn't until June 27—suddenly behind schedule,
playing hell with G. P. Putnam's plans to have her back by
the Fourth of July for some grand press attention—that
she and Noonan landed at Koepang on Timor Island, having given up on reaching Port Darwin, Australia, before
nightfall. High on a cliff, Amy and Noonan and some
villagers staked down the Electra on the grass-covered
field, bordered by a stone wall designed to keep out wild
pigs. She rose at 4:00 A.M., hoping to reach Lae, but was
forced by headwinds to settle for Port Darwin, where
she set down at 10:00 A.M. Some minor repairs were
made, and—after a seven-hour-and-forty-three-minute
and twelve-hundred-mile journey—the Electra reached
Lae, Papua New Guinea, on June 29.

Weather and instrument problems delayed takeoff till
Friday, July 2, when at 10:22 A.M., the Electra—carrying
more than one thousand gallons of fuel, as well as Amelia Earhart and Fred Noonan—wheeled lumberingly
down a crude dirt runway a mere one thousand feet
long. A 2,556-mile flight lay ahead, with navigator Noonan responsible for pinpointing tiny Howland Island
somewhere in the mid-Pacific.

At the end of the runway was a cliff, a dropoff into
Huon Gulf, and—providing spectators with a literal cliff-
hanger—the Electra's wheels stayed on the dirt runway
until the final fifty yards, her propellers churning up
puffs of red dust. No wind to help liftoff on this hot,
clear morning. Spectators said it was as if the plane had
jumped into the ocean, committing suicide; and indeed
it did seem to fall off the runway, dropping behind the
edge of the cliff.

When it reappeared, the Electra seemed to ride the
gulf, no more than five or six feet above the surface,
props throwing spray. It took a long time, the spectators
said, for that plane to finally rise from the ocean's surface into the sky, but at last it did. And on this clear
morning, the Electra stayed visible for a long, long time.

Then, finally, it disappeared.

* * *

For the first seven hours of her flight, Amy stayed in contact with a radioman on Lae. On course, 750 miles out, still clearly heard, she was advised to maintain the same radio frequency until further notice. But that was the last she was heard on Lae.

The U.S.S. frigate *Ontario*, midway between Lae and Howland in the Pacific, waited to provide navigation and weather updates; the Electra should have passed over the ship where three sailors kept watch and a radio operator stood by. No sign of her. Of course, the good weather had turned bad after midnight, a nasty squall kicking in and holding on till dawn. This might have slowed Amy down and/or caused her to use up a considerable amount of fuel, outmaneuvering the storm, and unintentionally escaping the *Ontario*'s sight.

The Coast Guard cutter *Itasca* lay anchored just off Howland Island, assigned to help Amelia Earhart with radio direction signals, voice communication and surface smoke. But starting at midnight, *Itasca*'s radio room had sent weather reports on the hour and half-hour, and Amy had not acknowledged any of them.

Then at 2:45 A.M., the chief radioman—with two wire service reporters, eavesdropping at the off-limits radio room doorway—thought he recognized her voice; so did the reporters, and at 3:45 they heard her again, more clearly now, saying, "Earhart. Overcast. Will listen on 3105 kilocycles on hour and half-hour." So at 4:00 A.M., the radio operator called on 3105, asking, "What is your position? When do you expect to arrive Howland? Please acknowledge."

But she didn't, though at 4:53 A.M., as the operator was issuing a weather update on 3105, Amy interrupted with a faint, muffled, garbled message, with only "partly cloudy" discernible amidst static.

Fifteen minutes before she was due at Howland, at 6:14 A.M., Amy's voice could be heard saying: "Want bearing on 3105 kilocycles on hour. Will whistle in microphone." But her whistle got lost in the harmonic whines of Pacific radio reception at dawn, and the operator couldn't get a fix on her.

At 7:42 Amy's voice, stronger, said, "We must be on

you but cannot see you . . . gas is running low. Been unable to reach you by radio. Flying at altitude one thousand feet." A minute later, interrupting *Itasca*'s frantic transmissions, Amy's voice, louder yet, chimed: "Earhart calling *Itasca*. We are circling but cannot hear you. . . ."

The radio operator on the *Itasca* sent messages by voice and key and listened on every frequency that Amy might use. Her final transmission, at 8:44, was shrill and frightened: "We are on the line of position 156-137. Will repeat message. We will repeat this message on 6210 kilocycles. Wait. Listening on 6210 kilocycles. We are running north and south."

With no frame of reference, her "position 156-137" and "running north and south" were meaningless. Until 10:00 A.M., the radio operator continued trying to make contact.

At 10:15 A.M., the commander of the *Itasca* ordered full steam, beginning a desperate search at sea, soon to be joined by the minesweeper *Swan*, the battleship *Colorado*, the aircraft carrier *Lexington*, and four destroyers in a sweeping mass rescue effort the likes of which had never before been expended on a single missing aircraft.

Amelia Earhart was back in the headlines.

Nine

I was drawn into the matter of Amelia Earhart's disappearance well before she got around to disappearing.

Midafternoon on Friday, May 21, in my office, in my swivel chair with my back to the uninspiring view of the El and Van Buren Street, a warm, barely discernible breeze drifting in the open window, I sat hunkered with a fountain pen over a stack of retail credit check reports, when the phone rang.

"A-1," I said, over the street noise.

"Nate Heller? Paul Mantz."

Even in those four words, I could tell he was worked up in some sort of lather; and since our only common ground was Amy, that got my attention. I shut the window to hear better, though the connection was remarkably good for long distance.

"Well hello, Paul . . . is everything all right with our girl's round-the-world venture?"

"No," he said flatly. "It's gone seriously to shit. She's taken off."

I sat forward. "Isn't that what pilots do?"

Bitterness edged his voice: "She took off on a 'shakedown flight' of the Electra, she told reporters, but really she's headed to Miami. She's on her way."

"Where are you, Burbank?"

An El train was rumbling by and I had to work my voice up.

"No, no, I'm in your back yard . . . St. Louis. Down here with Tex Rankin, we got an air meet at Lambert Field. Flyin' competition aerobatics."

"I thought you were working full-time as Amelia's technical advisor."

"So did I. February, I put all my motion picture flying on hold to give myself over to this cockeyed world flight. But when this air meet came up, Amelia and Gippy encouraged me to take a little time off and go."

"Are you saying they double-crossed you? She sneaked off on her big flight while her top advisor was out of town? Why the hell would she do that?"

"I think it's Putnam's doing. Listen . . . this thing stinks to high heaven. We got to talk."

"Isn't that what we're doing?"

". . . You want a job?"

"Usually. What do you have in mind?"

"You free this weekend?"

"I'm never free . . . it's going to cost you twenty-five bucks a day." Since G. P. and Amy were paying Mantz $100 a day, I figured he could afford it. Besides, I'd have to cancel my date Saturday night with Fritzie Bey after her last show at the Koo Koo Club.

"I'll pay you for two days," he said, "whether you take the job or not. I'm flyin' the air meet all day tomorrow, but nothin' on Sunday, and we're not headin' home till Monday."

"You want to come to me, or should I come to you?"

"You come to me . . . We can meet at Sportsman's Park, Sunday afternoon—playin' craps the other night, I won a pair of box seats for the Cardinals and Giants, should be a hell of a game. Dean and Hubbell on the mound."

That might be worth the trip alone. Baseball wasn't my first love—boxing was my sport, growing up on the West Side with Barney Ross like I did—but, after all, Dizzy Dean and Carl Hubbell were to the diamond what Joe Louis and Max Schmeling were to the ring.

"You take the train down here tomorrow," Mantz continued, "and I'll reimburse you. I'll have ya booked into the Coronado Hotel."

That was where Amy and I had stayed on the lecture tour; where I gave her that first neck rub. . . .

"Is that where you're staying?" I asked him.

"No! I'm at a motel out by the airport. I don't want us to hook up till the game."

"Why the cloak-and-dagger routine, Paul?"

"It's just better that way. Safer."

"Safer?"

"I'll leave your ticket for the game at the Coronado front desk. You in?"

"I'm in," I said, not knowing why, unless it was my love for Amy, or maybe my love for $25 a day with a Cards-Giants game tossed in.

Sunday afternoon in St. Louis, baseball fanatics from all over the Mississippi Valley squeezed into Sportsman's Park, nearly thirty thousand of them bulging the stands. Many of them had driven all night to see Dizzy Dean try to stop master of the screwball "King" Carl Hubbell's winning streak, which stood at twenty-one straight; here sat an Arkansas mule trader, there an Oklahoma dry goods salesman next to a WPA foreman from Tennessee, sitting in front of a country farm agent from Kansas, men in straw hats drinking beer, women in their Sunday best fanning themselves with programs, as the annual heat wave was getting a nice early start. Despite the heat, and the anticipation, the crowd wasn't surly, laughing and applauding the pregame horse and bicycle exhibition and a drum and bugle corps show. The sky was blue, the clouds white and fleecy, and there was just enough of a breeze to flutter the flag above the billboard ads of the outfield fences.

Perched in a box seat along the first base line, I sported a straw fedora, light blue shantung sportshirt and white duck slacks, doing my best not to get mustard from my hot dog on the latter. No sign of Mantz; even with the game delayed half an hour to jam in all these fans, Amelia Earhart's technical advisor did not get the pleasure of seeing the boyishly handsome, Li'l Abner-like Dizzy Dean stride cockily to the mound, flashing his big innocent smile to the bleachers, a faded tattered sweatshirt under the blouse of his red-trimmed white uniform.

His first pitch was a fastball that sent the Giants' lead-off batter, Dick Bartell, to the ground. The crowd ate that up, and the umpire did not complain, and for the rest of the inning Dean, master of the beanball, behaved himself. In the second inning, with Hubbell on the mound, Joe Medwick had just knocked a high curveball into the left field bleachers for a 1–0 lead for the Cards. I was on my feet with the rest of the crowd, cheering (a somewhat different response from yours truly than if the Cards had knocked a Cubs ball into the Wrigley Field stands) when I realized Mantz was standing beside me.

We shook hands and, with the rest of the crowd, sat down. As usual, he had a dapper look, a light yellow shirt with its sleeves rolled up and collar open and crisply pleated doeskin slacks. But his usual cocky expression was absent, the somewhat pointed features of his face set in a pale blank mask, his mouth a straight line under the straight line of his pencil mustache.

With no greeting, no preamble of any sort, he started in: "I just got hold of that bastard Gippy, in New Orleans."

"What's he doing in New Orleans?"

We kept our voices down and only occasionally were shushed by those who were there to see the game.

"That's where he and his wife spent the night," Mantz said with a humorless smirk. "Today she's off to Miami and from there . . ."

"Sky's the limit," I said. "So—did G. P. have an explanation for the sneak departure?"

On the mound the tattered sleeve of the right arm of Dean's sweatshirt hung to his thumb, and when he whipped his arm forward to release the ball, the loose cloth snapped in the wind like a cat o' nine tails.

"None," Mantz said. "He just claimed it was Amelia's decision and let it go at that. Jesus, Heller, the repaired Electra was only delivered just last Thursday."

"The day before she took off?"

"Yes! Just three days ago! Hell. . . . She'd had no flying time in it whatsoever. And she knew damn well I was leaving—and after she and I talked about how we'd spend a week, at least, in preflight preparations, and test flights!"

"What was left to do?"

His eyes saucered. "What the hell wasn't? I needed to check her fuel consumption levels—I worked out a

table of throttle settings I needed to go over with her—
and I had a list of optimum power settings for each leg.
Shit, now she's flying by sheer guesswork!"

Dean was loping down off the mound with a cocky,
tobacco-chewing grin; another perfect inning.

"She has radio equipment, doesn't she?"

Mantz lifted his eyes to the heavens. "I didn't get a
chance to check *that* out, either, and give her proper
instruction. Hell, man, we never covered actual operation of the radio gear—you know, little things like taking
a bearing with a direction finder, or how about just con-
tacting a damn radio station?"

"Well, you must have showed her the ropes on the
radio gear before the first attempt," I said.

"No," he admitted with a shrug. "Remember, she had
a co-pilot, Manning, along that time, and he knew his
stuff, where the radio was concerned."

Left-hander Hubbell had just struck out Pepper Mar-
tin, to the displeasure of the crowd.

"Are you saying she went off completely unpre-
pared?"

He shook his head, no. "When we flew that first Oakland to Honolulu leg, before the Luke Field crackup,
she showed real improvement. Held to her magnetic
compass headings within a reasonable leeway, wandering
only a degree or two off course, then doubled her error
in the other direction, gettin' back on track."

The crowd was cheering Cards second baseman
Hughie Cruz; the Mississippi boy approached the plate
with a mouthful of pebbles plucked from the infield, a
trademark, and he was rolling them around in his mouth
now, looking for a fastball. King Carl Hubbell threw him
a screwball instead.

". . . and she did do her homework," Mantz was saying. "But that wasn't flying. Like going over info on
airport facilities, weather conditions, custom problems.
And poring over detailed charts that Clarence Williams
prepared . . ."

Like the ones Amy ignored on her Mexico flight.

"Surely she did *some* flying," I said.

"Not near enough—she was hardly around. That goddamn Gippy had her tied up with advertising commit-

ments, radio shows, public appearances. . . . You know what she spent most of her time doin'? Writing the first four or five chapters of the goddamn book her husband's going to publish, when she gets home! *If* she gets home. . . ."

"It's that serious?"

Cruz popped out, and the crowd howled in disappointment.

Mantz touched my arm and drew my eyes from the field to his. "You want to know how serious it is? I don't think that bastard *wants* her to make it back."

I frowned in disbelief. "What? Aw, Mantz, that's just loony . . ."

He blinked and looked away. "Or at least, I don't think he cares."

"Mantz, find a mechanic—you got a screw loose. Amelia's his meal ticket, for Christ's sake."

I bought a beer off a vendor; Mantz declined.

"Heller, everybody on the inside knows this is Amelia's last flight—and that she plans to divorce the son of a bitch. I've heard them argue! It's an open secret she's been having an affair with somebody for the last year or two. . . ."

Now I blinked and looked away, feeling like Hubbell had hurled one of his screwballs at me.

Mantz was saying, "I think it's probably Gene Vidal, the Bureau of Air Commerce guy? But *whoever* it is, Putnam knows she's got somebody else, and he's pissed."

I shook my head. "G. P. doesn't want her dead. She's worth too much alive."

He got his face right in mine, eyes dark and burning; he smelled like Old Spice. "Maybe he figures, if she pulls it off, fine—I mean, he's got the five-hundred-dollar-a-crack lecture tours lined up, right?"

So her fee was going to double, out on the circuit, after the round-the-world trip. Not bad.

"But if she dies trying," Mantz continued, "then he's got a *martyr* to market . . . imagine what autographed first-day covers'd be worth if the *late* Amelia Earhart had signed 'em. What kind of sales he could rack up with the posthumous book? Movie rights? Hell, man, it's endless—plus, he doesn't have to suffer the embarrassment of being dumped by the celebrity wife he invented."

Dean, back on the mound, had just struck out Joe Moore on a high fastball. No beanballs all afternoon, so far anyway, not counting the close call of the first pitch of the day; Dean was slipping.

"Even if that's true," I said quietly, trying for a reasonable tone, "what the hell can we do about it? This flight's more important to Amelia than her husband—she knows what's riding on it."

Mantz's sneer spelled out his contempt. "Let me tell you about Gippy Putnam—I say to him, we got to paint the Electra's rudder, stabilizer and wing borders a nice bright red or orange, to make it easier to locate the bird if it goes down. He refuses. He says it's gotta be Purdue's colors—old gold and black!"

I shrugged, sipped the beer. "He's always cut corners for the sake of promotion."

Mantz's brow furrowed. "She almost died on the Atlantic crossing, did you know that, Heller? It's not just an exciting goddamn story for her to tell at those lectures—it happened, and it almost killed her. Storms, and mechanical malfunctions, engine on fire, wings icing up, plane damn near spinning into the ocean."

"I know," I sighed, hating the truth of what he was saying, "I know."

"If *your* wife narrowly escaped with her life like that, how anxious would you be to send her back up in the sky, on a flight ten times more dangerous? And yet Gippy's pushed her into this suicide run . . ."

Lefty O'Doul swung at another Dean high fastball and struck out.

"You were part of it, Paul," I said softly, no accusation in my voice.

But his face clenched in pain, anyway. "You think I don't know that? Listen, I love that girl . . ."

"I thought you had a new fiancée."

Myrtle Mantz had won her divorce decree last July, after plenty of embarrassment for Paul and Amy in the papers. Paul Mantz had steadfastly maintained, however, that theirs was strictly an employer/employee relationship.

"I love her like a sister," he said irritably. "Why do you think this is eatin' me up like a goddamn ulcer? I'm tellin' ya, Gippy sold her out."

I frowned at him. "How? Who to?"

"I don't know exactly. That's what I want to hire you to find out."

"I don't follow this. At all."

The Giants were at bat. Burgess Whitehead had singled, Hubbell had sacrificed him to second, with Dick Bartell up. Dean half-turned to second, then with no stop in his fluid motion, pitched one at the plate, which Bartell reflexively swung at, popping out to left field. But the umpire called it a balk, and Dizzy Dean threw his cap in the air and charged toward the umpire to talk it over. The crowd went crazy with rage and glee.

"Look," Mantz said, having to work his voice up a little, "let's just start with Howland Island."

"What is Howland Island, anyway?" I asked. "I never heard of the damn place before this flight."

"Nobody had, except some military types."

"Military?"

From the field, Dizzy Dean could be heard yelling, "I quit!" to the umpire, and he trundled toward the dugout. An uproar from the stands soon built into a thunderous chant: *"We want Dean . . . We want Dean . . . We want Dean . . ."*

Mantz really had to work to be heard over that. "That's the part of this thing that's putting that nosedive feeling in the pit of my stomach. See, the original plan was to use Midway Island for refueling—that's a Pan Am overnight stopover for Clipper passengers. They got a hotel there and even a golf course . . ."

"We want Dean . . ."

"Sounds ideal."

"We want Dean . . ."

"Yeah, only there's nowhere to land, no runway. Midway's strictly a seaplane port, by way of a sheltered lagoon."

"We want Dean . . ."

"So why didn't Amelia pick a seaplane for her flying laboratory, instead of the Electra?"

"*We want Dean* . . ."

"Actually, the Electra could've been fitted with pontoons . . . but those are expensive, many thousands of dollars."

"*We want Dean* . . ."

Mantz continued with a nasty smile: "Now you know, Eleanor Roosevelt damn near has a crush on Amelia; and FDR feels about the same way. So Gippy had Amelia write the president for help and permission to refuel the Electra in-flight over Midway . . . which by the way I considered inadvisable unless it was completely unavoidable."

Dizzy Dean, giving in to the crowd's urging, strode from the dugout back onto the mound.

I had to wait for the applause to die down before I could say, "That sounds expensive, too."

"Not if you can stick the government for it."

"And FDR okayed that?"

"Yes, sir."

"What does the government get out of it?"

Bartell singled to right; Whitehead scored, tying the game. The crowd roared in dismay.

"That's where Howland Island comes in," Mantz said. "And to answer your question, Howland Island is a desolate dab of nothing in the middle of nowhere, half a mile wide and one mile and a half long, covered with seagull shit."

"Just what is Franklin Roosevelt's interest in a bird-shit repository?"

He threw a hand in the air, rolled his eyes. "Hell, I don't know the politics, or the military ramifications, not really. But Howland and a couple other little islands are just about the only land between Hawaii and the Marshall Islands."

"So what?"

"The Marshall Islands belong to the Japanese. There's talk of the Japs and military expansion in the Pacific. This is all over my head, Heller, but even for somebody who doesn't read anything but the funny pages, it's not hard to figure: Uncle Sam musta needed an excuse to build a runway on Howland."

"And Amelia was it."

Down on the field was a flurry of play, and the crowd groaned in agony. Runs on hits by Lou Chiozza and Joe Moore had the score Giants 3, Cards 1.

Mantz said, "I heard G. P. say the government shelled out over three hundred grand, sending the Coast Guard dragging five-ton tractors over reefs and shoals . . . just as a courtesy to this famous civilian aviatrix, to aid her on her world flight."

I had to smile at what seemed like outrageous string-pulling and manipulation of the government on G. P.'s part. "That doesn't sound like a sellout to me, Paul. Sounds like you scratch my back, I scratch your back."

"It didn't bother me, either, at the time. G. P. wasn't even that secretive about it. Oh, he'd say, 'Now this is confidential,' but he got a kick out of telling how he'd conned the taxpayers into paying for Amelia's landing strip."

Hubbell was down there striking Cards out so quickly, it was hard to keep track.

"So," I asked, "why does it bother you now?"

Mantz's eyes narrowed. "This change of direction in flight plan—the first try was east to west; but now, all of a sudden, it's west to east."

"Yeah—Amelia told me it had to do with 'changing weather conditions.' "

He smirked and shook his head. "That's the story G. P.'s handing the press—'a seasonal change in wind patterns.' It's baloney—hardly any 'seasonal change' happens in weather along the Equator, and zero change in wind direction. Prevailing wind's always east to west, the opposite of wind in the northern and southern hemispheres. . . . Hell, that's why she chose flying east to west, in the first place!"

I was barely following him. "I don't know beans about flying, but it seems to me, bucking the prevailing wind is stupid."

"That's as good a word for it as any. And switching the flight plans to west to east meant everything from the previous attempt had to be scrapped—creating all kinds of problems, adding huge expense in a situation where scrimping would seem mandatory."

"What kind of added expense and extra problems?"

"Fuel, oil, spare parts, and personnel, in place for the east-west flight, had to be moved—for example, a mechanic dispatched from London to Karachi had to be assigned to somewhere else, Rangoon maybe, or Singapore. Credentials had to be reacquired, charts replotted, creating hours of work for engineers and mechanics at Lockheed."

"Well, what do you make of that?"

Dizzy Dean was back on the mound.

"I'm not sure. I never got a straight answer from either Gippy or Amelia on the reason for reversing the direction of the flight. The only way I can figure it is, it's got to be a directive from the same government quarters that funded the second try."

"Is that where the money came from? Uncle Sam?"

Dean hurled a fastball (what the papers called his fireball) at Lou Chiozza, or to be more exact, at Chiozza's head. Narrowly missing a beanball was a disconcerting experience, and Chiozza picked himself up from the dust, chastened.

"Well," Mantz said, "Gippy and Amelia sure as hell didn't come up with the dough, at least not all of it, not nearly. And listen, from the start, the military's been on this like ants at a picnic. You don't fly across the Pacific—particularly not when part of the plan is to land on a flyspeck like Howland Island—without the cooperation of Navy tenders, seaplanes and personnel."

"You said it yourself—Amelia has the President and First Lady in her pocket. She could pull that off."

Chiozza struck out.

"Heller, U.S. naval policy is that no nonmilitary flights get any assistance, whatsoever, with the exception of emergency aid. Every pilot in America knows that. Listen, Manning was a Navy captain, and Noonan is a lieutenant commander in the naval reserve, for Pete's sake."

"That's not surprising, is it? The military is where pilots get trained, for the most part."

Dean hurled his fireball at Jimmy Ripple's head. The

crowd roared in delighted approval; another Dizzy Dean beanball show was under way!

"Sure most pilots get their training in the military," Mantz said, "but does that explain why Amelia was driven around in a naval staff car? Or why we were given carte blanche at Luke Field in Honolulu, an Army-Navy airfield? Heller, Army Air Corps personnel dismantled the Electra in Honolulu and crated it for shipping back to Lockheed in Burbank, and we used a Navy hangar at Oakland Airport."

"What do you want me to do about it?"

His face was clenched with urgency. "Come back to California with me. I'll point you in the direction of some other people who, like me, were part of the inner circle and then got closed out, suddenly. You need to do some snooping around both Burbank and Oakland—"

"Whoa. I don't want this job, Paul."

Jimmy Ripple struck out.

"Why not?"

"If the government's in on this, if this is a military matter, if Amy's agreed to . . . to, what? Participate in some espionage mission of some kind? Then that's their business, and hers."

Mel Ott stepped up to bat, waiting for his fireball.

"But I don't think she even knows it's a government effort," Mantz said. "Or at least she doesn't realize to what extent."

Dean hurled the ball at Ott's head, Ott jumped out of the way, cursing. The umpire said nothing, did nothing.

"I think this is all Gippy's doing," Mantz went on bitterly. "I mean, Christ, Heller, you know Amelia! You've heard her speak, you were her bodyguard on that lecture series!"

"What's your point?"

"She's a goddamn pacifist, for cryin' out loud! She's not gonna willingly cooperate with the military."

Ott struck out.

"People make all kinds of deals with the devil," I said, "if they want something bad enough. And I know how bad she wanted this flight."

"I tell ya, if you can come up with proof that Gippy sold her out, I can get word to her, early in the flight."

Hubbell was back on the mound. No beanballs for him. He just played his game.

"And what," I said, with a single dry laugh, "she'll turn around and come home? Do you always fly without a parachute, Mantz? Do you always land on your head?"

His mouth twitched a grimace. "She needs to know she's being used."

"Let's suppose she is. Being used. Do I want to take on the military or the feds or whoever? No. Let Dizzy Dean argue with the umpire. I don't need that kind of grief."

"He's put her in harm's way, Heller. If she doesn't make it home, Gippy murdered her. Or the same as."

"I don't think much more of that bastard than you do, Paul. I'm sure he's made all kinds of, yes, deals with the devil . . . but I still don't see him working against Amelia, hoping she'll crash in the ocean. Not with those stamps on board, anyway."

". . . Somebody's been following me, Heller."

"What?"

"You heard me. I had a shadow ever since I got to St. Louis."

"Who?"

"How should I know?"

"You see the guy?"

"No. I can just feel it."

Dizzy hurled his fireball at Johnny McCarthy, knocking him down, into the dust. The umpire said and did nothing.

"I'm not doubting you," I said.

"Why do you think I wanted to meet you in some out-of-the-way place?"

"You mean with thirty thousand people around us?"

"It's one way to hide."

He was right. And down on the field, the Giants were charging out of their dugout (except Hubbell, ever a gentleman) and a full-scale brawl between the two teams was under way. Fists and spikes flying. The fans loved it.

"If you're being followed," I said, "then maybe the government, the military, *is* in on this."

"Yes!"

"In which case, I don't want to be."

When the brawl on the field was finally quelled, Dean was allowed to stay in the game (with a fine of fifty dollars) and he promptly, brazenly hurled another bean-ball at Johnny McCarthy. But the brawl did not resume, and McCarthy soon scored a double to left center and the game wound up Giants 4, Cards 1.

I thanked Mantz for inviting me to the game—it was worth the trip to St. Louis—and told him to forget about the fifty bucks for two days' work. All he owed me was for my train ticket and meals and a few other minor expenses.

And as the days passed, I read about Amelia's progress on her flight and all seemed to be going well. I was writing Mantz's suspicions off to his dislike of Putnam, which was something I could easily understand, and his frustration at being shut out of the inner circle.

On June 4, Mantz—back in Burbank—called me, at my office, and asked, "Weren't you around the hangar, last year, when Amelia and me had that tiff about her radio antenna?"

"Yeah. Yeah, I was—she didn't want to be bothered with unreeling it by hand or something."

"It's two hundred and fifty feet of trailing wire antenna, and yes, it is a pain in the ass to use. That's partly why I installed a Bendix loop antenna for her. But those Coast Guard boys aren't up on these latest gadgets, so it was vital she had that antenna along, as a backup, so the Coast Guard cutter near Howland Island can be sure to locate her."

"From your tone, I take it she left the trailing wire behind."

"I sent Putnam a telegram, expressing these concerns, before I left St. Louis . . . His letter of reply arrived in Burbank days after I got home."

"And?"

"She didn't leave the wire behind."

"Good."

"Right before she left Miami, she had the technicians shorten it and run it along the wings."

"And that won't do the trick?"

"Oh, it'll work out swell—for stringing Christmas tree lights."

"I'm not coming out there, Mantz."

"Don't bother. It's probably too late, anyway."

And he hung up.

I thought about what he had said, weeks later, when I heard the news that Amy's plane was missing, some-where between Lae and Howland Island, somewhere in the Pacific where a very expensive government rescue mission was in progress.

And that, finally, was the beanball that hit me in the head and prompted me to go back out to Burbank.

Ten

The bar was a South Seas refuge, the patter and spatter of a tropical storm on its tin roof, water streaking and streaming in lazy patterns behind opaque window glass that glowed with a yellow-orange sunset as foliage outside cast curious silhouettes; no music played, no native drums pounded, but there was the not-so-distant caw of strange birds, and earthen bowls in netting hung from the bamboo-beamed ceiling where churned lazily the blades of fans fluffing the blades of palms hovering over tiny teakwood tables with wicker furniture and coconut shell candles, each table situated within this bamboo-and-thatched-hut world so as to provide an island for two.

I had almost missed the place, and not just because I was a stranger in these exotic parts. The pair of interlocking, wooden-shuttered stucco boxes on North McCadden Place in Hollywood might have been a nondescript apartment complex but for the knee-high bamboo fence and the tropical thicket through which the bamboo-pole entrance peeked.

No sign announced this as one of the most popular joints in town; and it was too early—three-thirty-something in the afternoon—to put out the restraining velvet ropes. Of course, there would be no waiting for such regular customers as Rudy Vallee, Marlene Dietrich and Joan Crawford (whose framed pictures, among many others, peered from a wall through hanging fronds).

Right now, however, the bar was unpopulated, except for a few stuffed parrots, fake monkeys and a real bartender at his bamboo station. The "rain" on the false roof sprayed down the ceiling from garden hoses, and ran down the glass partitions of the "windows" to feed planters. The offstage bird calls came from a few real live caged parrots and macaws out in the open courtyard, where the palms weren't phony like the ones whose shadows fell on me; bunches of bananas, here and there among the fake vegetation, were real and could be plucked by a bold customer and eaten, free of charge.

Don the Beachcomber's was quite a joint, with a Chinese grocery just inside the door, a shop devoted entirely to different types and brands of rum (an idea whose time, I sincerely believed, had come), and a gift shop where fresh flower leis were available. Various meandering rooms presented themselves, with names like Paradise Cove, Cannibal Lounge and Black Hole of Calcutta, which was where I was waiting for my companion. This was the kind of joint where the lighting was so dim, just about any woman would look good, or at least mysterious.

Unfortunately, I was waiting for a man—and an airplane mechanic, at that.

Taking a cab from the train station, I had arrived at the United Airport at Burbank around two-thirty, and wandered into Mantz's United Air Services hangar only to find no sign of him. It was Tuesday, July 6, a mild breeze doing its best to downplay a blistering heat that defeated my lightweight maize polo shirt and tan slacks, turning them into sticky swaddling cloth. I hadn't warned Mantz I was coming; the day before, I'd gone back and forth about whether to stick my nose in this, then impulsively threw some things in a suitcase and caught a Sante Fe sleeper at Dearborn Station.

The vast hangar, nicely cool compared to the outside, was littered with small aircraft, among them several biplanes and Amy's little red Vega, though Mantz's *Honeymoon Express* wasn't among them. A trio of jumpsuited mechanics was at work; one of them was washing down a sleek little racing plane, a Travel Air Mystery S, which I recalled Mantz saying belonged to Pancho Barnes, an aviatrix pal of Amy's. Mantz allowed a number of fliers to store their planes in his hangar to make his "fleet" look bigger. The other two mechanics were working on the engine of another little red and white Travel Air, a stunt plane of Mantz's.

I recognized two of the three mechanics—the guy washing the racing plane was Tod Something, and one of the pair working on the Travel Air was Ernie Tisor, Mantz's chief mechanic. Pushing fifty, wide-shouldered, thick around the middle, hair a salt-and-pepper mop, the good-natured mechanic frowned over at me, at first, then grinned in recognition, then frowned again—it's a reaction I'd had before.

Rubbing the grease off his hands with a rag, he ambled over to me; his tanned, creased, hound dog's face was blessed with eyes as blue as the California sky under cliffs of shaggy salt-and-pepper eyebrows.

"Nate Heller," he said. He gave me half a smile; something odd lingered in his expression. "If you're looking for the boss, he's on a charter, sort of."

"What do you mean, 'sort of'?"

The half-smile continued and seemed strained. "Well, him and Terry and Clark and Carole went off to La Gulla."

Gable and Lombard. I was not impressed. I had met actors before. And Terry was Mantz's new wife, or soon to be, anyway.

I asked, "What's La Gulla?"

"A dirt strip down the Baja California peninsula."

"What attraction does that hold?"

Now he gave me a complete smile, not at all strained. "No telephones, no pressure. Rolling hills and mountain quail."

"Ah."

"They'll probably be back tomorrow morning, sometime." He seemed to be studying me.

"Something on your mind, Ernie?"

". . . You come out here 'cause of Miss Earhart?"

I shrugged. "Few weeks ago Paul asked me to get involved and, frankly, I passed."

"Asked you before she got lost, you mean."

"Yeah."

"Asked you, 'cause he thought something wasn't . . . kosher about this setup."

"Yeah."

His eyes narrowed in an otherwise expressionless mask. "And you turned him down, and now she's lost . . . and you don't feel so good about it."

"I feel lousy about it."

His mouth flinched, and at last I understood what the look in his eyes meant: they were haunted, those sky-color eyes. "Me too," he said. He glanced over his shoulder. Then he whispered: "Look, I wanna fill you in on some things . . . some things I saw."

"Okay."

"But not here."

"Some bar around here we could find a corner in?"

He shook his head, no. "Not *around* here, either. . . . I give you the address of a place, think you can find it?"

"I'm a detective, aren't I? That's what cab drivers are for."

"You don't have wheels? Wait a second. . . ."

He went inside Mantz's glassed-in office and soon he was handing me some car keys, and a slip of paper with Don the Beachcomber's address.

Still almost whispering, he asked, "Remember that convertible of Miss Earhart's?"

"The Terraplane?"

"Right. She keeps it here, leaves it with the boss; it's kind of a spare car. . . . I'm sure she wouldn't mind if you use it."

"Thanks."

"Of course, if the boss thinks I overstepped, he'll ask for the keys back and that's that."

"Sure."

"You go on and find that address. . . . See you there around four."

It was ten after four, and I had polished off a plate of chop suey; for California, it was early to eat, but I was still on Chicago time and my last meal on the train had been breakfast. The waitress, a sweet brunette in a lei and sarong, asked if I cared for an after-dinner drink. My choices included a Shark's Tooth, a Vicious Virgin and a Cobra's Fang. I opted for the house specialty, originated here: the Zombie. One ounce each of six kinds of rum blended with "secret ingredients. . . ."

I had braved two sips of the Zombie when Tisor wandered in, glancing around the otherwise still-empty Black Hole of Calcutta.

Forehead tight with worry and flecked with sweat, he wore a white shirt with the sleeves rolled up and chinos; in this context, he looked like a jungle trader who left his pith helmet and hunter's jacket at the door. He pulled out the wicker chair across from me and sat.

"Riskin' a Zombie, huh?" he asked, apparently recognizing the tall slender glass.

"You'll notice I'm not chugging it down."

"There's a house limit on two of those babies."

"This seems like kind of an unlikely hangout for mechanics, Ernie. If you don't mind my saying so."

"It's not a hangout, but sometimes for special events, goin'-away parties, celebrations. Best Chink food around."

I was sorry to hear that; the ersatz Cantonese chow here had nothing on the Won Kow in Chinatown back home, but maybe Ernie and his airfield pals hadn't made it to the local Chinatown. The waitress wandered over and Ernie ordered a beer and a plate of egg rolls to nibble on.

"That's what Jimmy ordered," he said, "a Zombie. The night of his goin'-away party, night he spilled the beans."

"Jimmy who? What beans?"

He sighed, shook his head. "Maybe I better get a beer or two down me, first."

I reached out and clutched his forearm. "Let's get a head start, Ernie. Who's Jimmy?"

"Jimmy. Jim Manhof." He didn't look at me as he spoke. "Skinny kid, mechanic, he was around when you was out here, last year. I don't know whether you met him, exactly."

I let go of his arm, leaned back. "I remember. You got a new man in his slot, I notice."

"Yeah. Pete. Good boy, Pete. Jimmy, uh . . . his work started slippin', and Mantz got on his ass and Jimmy finally quit. Last I heard, he had a job in Fresno, at Chandler Municipal."

"Good for Jimmy. What about the beans Jimmy spilled?"

He swallowed. Shook his head. "I never told Paul about this. I don't know why I'm tellin' you. . . ."

"I won't tell Paul. Think of me as your priest."

"I ain't Catholic."

"Neither am I, Ernie. Spill."

The beer arrived. The waitress smiled at me; she was very pretty but her crooked teeth would keep her out of the movies. To let you know the state of my mood, I didn't even ask for her phone number.

He gulped down half the beer, wiped the foam off his lip with a sleeve and said, "It was Jimmy put the acid on those rudder cables."

"No kidding?"

"He told me about halfway through the second Zombie."

"Nobody else heard him own up to that?"

"No. Tod was asleep, head on his arms like a kid snoozin' at his school desk; he'd already finished his second Zombie."

"Did Jimmy say *why* he put acid on Amelia's rudder cables?"

"Somebody hired him to . . . but it wasn't supposed to be sabotage, exactly. . . ."

"What the hell was it, then?"

"It was meant to be found, and repaired, before the plane took off. The guy that hired Jimmy said it was just a sort of . . . prank."

"A real knee-slapper."

"And of course, we did find it . . . Jimmy himself pointed it out to me. So, in a way . . . no harm was done. In a way."

"Yeah. What's the harm in sending a pilot off on a dangerous transcontinental flight, knowing her plane's been sabotaged? Hoping all the damage got noticed by her trusty mechanics?"

He was shaking his head. "I know. It's real, real shitty. But that's not even the shittiest part. The shittiest part is who hired Jimmy."

"Her husband, you mean. G. P."

His eyes popped. "How the hell did you—"

"I told you—I'm a detective."

I filled Ernie in on G. P.'s motive, the phony threatening notes that the rudder cable sabotage was meant to validate.

"He's such a raging asshole," Tisor said, shaking his head some more. "Lord knows what he's got her into now." And he ran a hand over his face and up into his salt-and-pepper hair. "Aw . . . Christ. Such a sweet kid. What's that bastard done to her . . ."

A parrot squawked in the courtyard.

"What do you mean, Ernie? What is it you've seen?"

He was holding his face in his hand and peering through the web of his fingers. "This is so goddamn dangerous. . . . We could both get our asses in one hell of a sling. What are you trying to prove, Heller?"

"You tell me," I said. It was an honest answer.

He stared at the flame in the coconut, as if its flickering held meaning. "This has to be some kind of . . . military business. The government's been on this thing like a heat rash since the first day. I mean, why else would everybody on Uncle Sam's payroll be so eager to please?"

"For example."

He was looking at me now, not the flame. "Before the first attempt, we did a lot of our prep over at March Army Air Base—near Riverside?"

"Military installations aren't usually available for the activities of private citizens, are they?"

"Hell no! That's strictly off limits! Yet, here we got the run of the place, with their mechanics pitchin' in with us, and, get this: armed military police outside the building."

"That's one way to keep the press out."

"But when we were at Oakland, we used the Naval Reserve Hangar, and got the same kind of help, and security. Don't you find that, I don't know . . . unusual? Kinda out of the ordinary, the Army and Navy throwin' in together like that?"

It was very odd. The Army and the Navy were separate entities, divided by rivalry, each with their own turf, their own hierarchies, their own agendas. What would it take to bring them together on one project?

The answer came to me at once, and made the skin

on the back of my neck crawl—or was that merely a reaction to my latest sip of Zombie?

"Their Commander-in-Chief could elicit their support and cooperation," I said.

He swallowed thickly. "You mean, the President."

"I mean, the husband of Amelia Earhart's pal Eleanor."

"We shouldn't even be talking about this."

The waitress brought Tisor his egg rolls and a second beer.

"Ernie," I said, "G. P. Putnam put his wife's fame—and her life—on the bargaining table. If the President of the United States was on the other side of that table, does that make it any more acceptable?"

"I didn't even vote for the son of a bitch," he said, biting the end off an egg roll.

I had. Twice. Thank God for the two-term limit, so I wouldn't have to do it again.

"You know, this kind of thing ain't that unusual," Tisor said. "It's an open secret in our business, Pan Am's in bed with Uncle Sam. Pan Am gets the contracts for overseas mail service, and the government gets . . . favors now and then."

"This is something Amelia would be aware of."

"Sure. Everybody knew what the government was gettin' out of the flight."

"An airstrip at Howland Island."

"Right. And Miss Earhart was okay with that, I'm sure. I know she appreciated gettin' this help from 'Franklin'—that's how she referred to him, y'know."

"I know."

"But when I heard about the change in flight plan, switchin' from east to west to west to east? I *knew* somethin' was up. Despite all the bull they handed the press about 'seasonal change in wind patterns,' any experienced pilot—any Pan Am pilot, for sure, which includes Fred Noonan—knew that switch made no sense."

Out in the courtyard, a parrot asked, *"Who's a fool?"*

"Ernie, can you make any sense of it? Why *did* they change directions?"

Having polished off the first egg roll, he picked up the second and gestured with it. "Well, first of all, think about the Lockheed Electra herself. She's the ideal plane for a military mission . . . particularly with those powerful military-issue engines."

"There are special engines on that plane?"

". . . Not the first plane."

"What do you mean, the 'first plane'?"

His eyes were hooded and his voice was very soft as he said, "Heller, you may not want to know this. I know I don't."

"You know where that woman is, Ernie? She's either floating on the ocean, or she's under it." I glanced around, gestured to the "atmosphere." "Or maybe she's on an island somewhere in the South Pacific, only she's not sitting under a fake palm tree at a varnished teakwood table eating a damn egg roll."

A macaw cawed.

"Between the crackup at Oahu and the takeoff in May," Tisor said, "the Electra was over at Lockheed's overhaul hangar."

"Which is also in Burbank."

"Yeah. Next-door neighbors of ours, but we weren't privy to the repair job. It was kept under wraps."

"Military guard?"

"Army. But I saw the plane when it was delivered over to our hangar, in fact I was there when Amelia saw it for the first time, and was she teed off! She said, 'Why did they have to do this? I loved my old plane. Who's paying for this?' Hell, all she wanted was some adjustment in front to make it easier to operate the rudder pedals."

"What did she get, Ernie?"

Now his eyes were wide. "A different fuckin' plane. Bright and shiny and new, from the nuts and bolts to the tires. You gotta understand about Electras, there's two basic types, the Model 10 Electra and the Model 12 Electra Junior. The Model 12's a little smaller, but faster, lighter. . . . This was a Model 12."

I frowned, leaned forward. "Didn't anybody notice? Didn't any reporters comment?"

He grinned and shook his head, no. "The similarities between the two models outnumber the differences, and besides, these're hand-built planes, no two alike. Lockheed tailors these birds to the specific needs of the customer; every ship's a hybrid. For example, this Electra had the advanced, constant-speed props of the Model 12, but overall it had the size and outward appearance of the Model 10—and the bigger engines I started to tell ya about, they probably made the gross weight similar . . . these were larger engines designed for military use, Pratt and Whitney Wasp Seniors, five-hundred-and-fifty-horse-power jobs. That baby had a greater effective payload than the original bird."

"You're saying Lockheed didn't repair her plane—they gave her a new one."

"Right." He chomped on the egg roll, chewed as he talked. "And a new one designed with a different purpose than the first one."

"A military purpose, you mean."

He nodded. "That change of flight plan doesn't make any sense from an aviator's slant—but it makes all the sense in the world if she was on a military mission."

"What sort of mission?"

A parrot in the courtyard asked the question again: *"Who's a fool?"*

He drew a breath, a deep one, then he leaned into the flickery light of the half-coconut; it turned his face shades of orange and yellow. "I wasn't over at Lockheed, when this ship was bein' put together—understand? What I'm gonna tell you now is secondhand, and don't ask me for the guy's name. I need your word on that, or I'm through talkin'."

"You got my word."

He settled way back in his chair, folded his arms; now his face was in the shadow of a palm blade. "I was askin' my friend, who's an airframe technician at Lockheed, about how things was goin', while the 'repairs' were under way? I was wonderin' what was takin' so long. Anyway, we were out drinkin', and he was in his cups . . ."

"You feed *him* Zombies, too, Ernie?"

His smile flashed in the darkness. "No. This was boilermakers. And maybe what I'm about to tell you was the boilermakers talkin', maybe it's pure bullshit. But I don't want to get my friend in trouble."

"Understood."

"First off, there's the ping-pong balls."

"Ping-pong balls."

"That Electra had ping-pong balls stuffed in every nook and cranny—nowhere they'd get in the way, but where controls go out to wing flaps, in wing spars, and so on."

"The point being?"

"Added buoyancy, in case they were forced to ditch in the open sea. I heard of that practice before, it's a little unusual, Dick Merrill did it once, but I just mention that to show you the extremes they was going to."

"That just sounds like a precaution to me."

He moved forward a touch, into the light. "Here's somethin' my friend told me about that wasn't no precaution. He said he cut two holes, sixteen to eighteen inches in diameter, to be used for installin' cameras."

"Cameras? What kind of cameras?"

"A pair of Fairchild, electrically operated aerial survey cameras that got mounted in the lower aft fuselage bay. Some Navy guys, technicians or engineers or something, installed 'em, and photoflash bombs in the aft."

I blinked. "Bombs?"

A thick hand waved that off. "They're not destructive, they just provide light for nighttime aerial photography."

"More good reason to use a lighter plane."

"Hey, the Lockheed Electra, either model, can fly high and fast, even without special modifications, like bigger engines. The plane I saw was a long-range reconnaissance aircraft with all the latest gadgets and goodies. With that customized bird, Amelia could climb higher and faster than the first Electra, zip off her official course and return on route without anybody the wiser; she can cruise at speeds up to, hell, two hundred and twenty miles per hour."

"As compared to what?"

He shrugged, rocked in the wicker chair. "One hundred and forty."

Alarmed, I said, "Then this elaborate sea search that's under way, all the rescue projections are based on the wrong aircraft specifications!"

He shrugged again. "Maybe not. After all, the military

knows the real specs. But look, this finally makes the west-east flight plan change make sense."

"How so?"

A shaggy eyebrow rose. "By flying west to east, from Lae to Howland Island, where American military personnel are waiting, the film could be retrieved, the camera equipment removed, and she could head home, to American Hawaii, in a non-spy ship, for a grand welcome."

I could think of another reason for the west to east change: that Coast Guard cutter, the *Itasca,* so involved right now in searching for Amelia Earhart, would have been posted (and waiting) at Howland Island, tracking Amelia's progress. Had she taken off *from* Howland Island, flying east-west, she would have been moving away from the ship, instead of toward it, as she undertook her mission.

Then she would have landed at Lae, a foreign territory, with her plane's belly filled with film from a spy mission; should something have gone wrong, and the local government confiscated that film, the international repercussions would have been devastating.

"The change of direction does make perfect sense," I said, "for a clandestine military operation."

"Polly's not a fool!" the parrot in the courtyard said.

"I've told you everything I know," he said. "And what the hell you think you can do with it . . ." He threw his hands up. ". . . is beyond me."

"Who else can I talk to?"

His eyes and nostrils flared. "Not my friend at Lockheed!"

I patted the air reassuringly. "I know, I know . . . I gave you my word. Who else was close to Amelia, and knows something . . . *and* thinks what Putnam did to his wife stinks?"

"Maybe you ought to talk to the secretary."

"What secretary?"

"Margot DeCarrie." He smiled, as if the mental image of her were a pleasant one. "Nice young kid, idolizes Miss Earhart, and Miss Earhart thought the world of her."

He was getting his present and past tense mixed up, where Amy was concerned; I knew the feeling.

"How come I never met the girl?"

"She only started with the Putnams when they got the new house, in Toluca Lake, just this year. She's live-in help. I'm friendly with her. You want me to pave the way?"

"You think she'd cooperate?"

"Living in that house, she coulda seen a lot. I know she's broke up about Miss Earhart's disappearance. She's a wreck. Take it easy on her . . . don't scare her . . . and I think she'll open up like a flower."

"I appreciate the help."

"I'll make a call . . . but I should warn ya—that guy Miller may still be there."

"Who?"

He gestured with an open hand. "I don't know his first name. It was always just 'Mr. Miller' . . . he's some kind of consultant. My guess is he's some sort of government intelligence guy. He's one cold fish. Him and Putnam was thick as thieves."

"What's he look like?"

"Tall, six foot one, maybe. Probably forty. Pale, like all the blood got drained out of him. Slim but not skinny—what they call it, lanky, like the actor, Jimmy Stewart?"

"Ever have a run-in with him?"

He shifted in the chair; these wicker things weren't all that comfortable. "He shooed me out of the hangar, once in a while, if him and Putnam and some of these others, military people, more guys in dark suits, was havin' a conference or somethin'. He smiles but he never shows his teeth, and his tone is always, 'fuck you,' no matter how polite the words. . . . I got a feeling he's a serious bad apple."

"I'll take that under advisement."

"Okay. I'll call Miss DeCarrie. They got a public phone out front." He pushed the wicker chair back, stood. "Should I set something up for tonight?"

"My dance card is free."

He ambled off, almost bumping into the waitress, who then hip-swayed over in true Polynesian style, though my guess was she was Jewish. She collected my long tall empty glass and, her voice high-pitched, melodic, asked me, "Another Zombie, sir?"

"You're a fool!" the parrot said.

Eleven

On Valley Spring Lane in Toluca Lake, a few blocks down from where Paul and Myrtle Mantz used to live, stood a similar Spanish-style bungalow, this one with a red tile roof rather than green, and stucco that was off-white rather than yellow, though at dusk the difference was negligible. A wing had been added to this cozy bungalow, however, giving it a one-story sprawl that overflowed onto the adjacent lot, making for a spacious lawn as immaculate as the greens of the golf course nearby. Palm trees provided shade and an oasis atmosphere, enhanced by the occasional cactus and even a century plant. Well-tended but thorny shrubs hugged the house and made me glad that this time I wasn't heading for the bushes with my Speed Graphic.

It was a little after eight when I rang the bell; a wooden slab of a door opened about a third of the way, enough to give me a good look at an Oriental houseman in Charlie Chan's white suit and black tie. He might have been thirty, he might have been fifty; whatever his age, he wasn't terribly impressed by my presence.

"I'm here to see Miss DeCarrie," I said, then told him my name. "I believe she's expecting me."

He nodded, closed the door, and when it opened again, just seconds later, it was like a magic trick: the deadpan Oriental replaced by a beaming young woman.

She was in her early twenties, as tall as Amy only more shapely, in the same sort of casual cowboyish clothes: a plaid shirt, tan cotton slacks and boots. She had a similar short hairdo, though unlike Amy's, hers was marcelled and dark brunette; she had a clear-complected, lightly made-up, heart-shaped face and wasn't as cute as Betty Boop, but damn near.

"Oh, Mr. Heller!" she burbled, as if we were old friends finally reunited, her eyes bright and brown and wide, "how wonderful it is to see you!"

She flung the door open and allowed me to move through the shallow, terra cotta–tiled entryway into a living room, casually tasteful in its modern furnishings, dominated by a fireplace of massive gray stone over which a mirror created an illusion of spaciousness, next to which French doors looked out onto a patio where the shapes of more palm trees and a garden were ghostly through sheer curtains. The stucco walls were fairly bare, though one side wall was taken up by a lovely oil portrait of Amy, in flying jacket, hand on hip, a breeze catching her scarf.

"I guess you've guessed I'm Margot," she said, her voice chirpy, her bee-stung lips forming a big smile; her eyes, however, were laced with red. "I feel like I already know you. . . . A. E. has told me so much about you. . . ."

"Thank you for seeing me," I said. "Are you sure there's no problem with your employer?"

"My employer is A. E.," she said, sticking her chin out proudly. "As for Mr. Putnam, he's at the San Francisco Coast Guard Station, with Mr. Miller, and isn't expected till tomorrow afternoon at the earliest."

She hooked her arm through mine and led me across the living room's Oriental carpet through an archway into the dining room, off of which a hallway led into the addition to the house. She had a clean fresh smell about her, soap not perfume, I'd bet.

"Ernie said you're looking into this," she said, walking me along. "I know it's what A. E. will want."

"Excuse me," I said, "but you act like she spoke of me often."

"Not often. But when she did, it was with great affection." She paused at a closed door. "Let's go in here—it's A. E.'s study. I think she'd like us to do our talking in her presence, so to speak."

I followed her in and she ushered me to a worn,

comfy-looking sofa in a corner of a rather spartan study, under a wall of photos that wasn't as excessive as Paul Mantz's office display, but close to it: aviation memories and signed movie star mugs. Double windows looked out onto the patio and a well-tended garden; they were open to let in the dry cool evening breeze that had replaced the sweltering day. A centrally placed card table with a typewriter was a typically informal Amelia Earhart "office," littered with books and typing paper and yellow pads. A more formal desk, a rolltop, took up one wall, and much of another was swallowed up by a trophy cabinet. Standing bookcases, a pair of file cabinets, and an easy chair made up the rest of the room.

"This looks like it might be Mr. Putnam's study, as well," I said, sitting down.

"It is—they shared it, but he hasn't been using it since . . . well, since." Margot closed the door. She wrinkled her nose, chipmunk cute, and said, "We'll opt for privacy. Joe's nice, but he's loyal to Mr. Putnam."

"Joe's the houseman?"

"Yes. A wonderful gardener, too. He also does the heavy chores; my mother does the rest."

"Your mother?"

She settled in next to me—not right next to me, but it was a good thing for her I wasn't Jack the Ripper, because she was assuming the best about me, not always the safest course for a cute kid like this.

"When my mother got the housekeeper position here—I'm a local girl, well, Glendale local—I just went crazy. I've been a fan of A. E.'s since I was twelve! I just adore her—you should see my scrapbooks. Did you know she had scrapbooks, too, when she was a girl? Full of stories about women doing work that was supposed to be a man's domain? And I'd been writing her fan letters since forever, and do you know, she answered every one?"

"Really?"

"So when Mother got this job, I just had to come around and meet A. E., and she was so wonderful, you just wouldn't believe, well I guess you would knowing her like you do, but I started coming around and, well, maybe I made a pest of myself, telling her how I was a graduate from the business college over in Van Nuys, dropping all kinds of hints, telling her how terrible it must be to be swamped like she was with so much fan mail and all, and anyway, finally she said, A. E. said, I guess I really could use a Girl Friday at that, and ever since then I've been in charge of fan letters, filing, and even the household accounts . . . I studied more than secretarial skills at business college, I have accountancy capability too you know . . . and I help out in a lot of other ways, meeting airplanes, showing guests around, and entertaining A. E.'s mother, who just went to stay with her other daughter, A. E.'s sister, Muriel, in West Medford, for a while."

"Is that right?"

"And you know it's funny, I don't really think A. E. feels all that close to her real sister, I mean I think she may kind of resent sending her checks all the time, actually I'm the one sending them lately, ever since A. E. disappeared, though I think Mr. Putnam may put a stop to it, but the thing is, we really did get close, we were more like sisters, I think, sometimes, than she was with her real sister, which is why I know what I know about you."

"What do you know about me?"

"That you love her, too. That's why you're here, isn't it?"

And then she turned away from me in sudden embarrassment and began bawling like a baby. I gathered her up like she was a hurting child, which maybe she was, and held her to me, let her hug me and bury her face in my chest and cry there. I had to wonder when Margot said she loved Amy, if it was the Toni Lake variety; but my hunch was not. This was about hero worship, not hormones.

As she began to settle down, I fished a clean handkerchief out of my pocket and gave it to her; she thanked me, dried her eyes and moved away a little, sitting with her hands in her lap, clenching the hanky. She looked very small, her face devoid of makeup now, a pale cameo.

"But you don't love *G. P.*, Margot, do you?"

A little humorless smirk dimpled her cheek. "No. Not

hardly. At first I accepted him . . . I mean, after all, A. E. married him, and she doesn't make many mistakes."

"That one was a whopper, though."

"He's a terrible man. Egotistical. Selfish. He's nothing more than a publicity-seeker, with no regard for anyone but himself."

"You're right."

She pressed her hands to her bosom and looked across at the trophy case. "A. E. made me feel so good about myself. . . . She made me feel I could conquer the world."

Margot had lapsed into the past tense about Amy, too. It was tough not to.

She turned her gaze upon me, and it was so earnest, I wanted to laugh—or cry. She asked, "What can you do about this, Mr. Heller?"

"I figure once I've had my arm around a girl, she's earned the right to use my first name."

She liked that. "Thanks, Nathan. You're everything A. E. said you were. . . ."

"Let's not jump the gun. As for what I can do—I'm not even sure why I came out to California, Margot. It was an impulse."

I told her about Paul Mantz trying to hire me—weeks ago, while Amy was still on American soil—to look into the funny business surrounding the world flight, and how I turned him down. How I may have missed the chance to head this disaster off before it started.

"Oh dear," she said, looking at me with tenderness and pity, "you must feel terribly guilty!"

"You really know how to lift a fella's spirits, Margot. . . . If the Coast Guard and Navy can't find her in the ocean, I'm not sure what good I can do in Burbank. But I do know I don't want G. P. getting away with this."

Her eyes got teary again and her lower lip quivered. "I don't think he cares if she comes back. . . . I don't think he wants her to come back. . . ."

"I suspect you're right. But first things first—I'm still trying to piece together what's really going on here."

Her expression turned firm; dabbing the new tears away with my hanky, she asked, "How can I help?"

"Tell me what you've seen." I gestured around us. "What unusual has happened here at the house?"

She drew air in and then blew it out through a Clara Bow pucker. "Ooooh, so many things. . . . One of the things that struck me was all the military people parading through."

"What kind of military people?" I sat sideways on the couch, to look right at her. "You mean, like the Navy chauffeur who drove her around in a staff car, sometimes?"

"Well that, but these were very high-ranking officers, Army and Navy both. They'd come over and meet with G. P. and A. E., or sometimes with just G. P."

"You remember any names, Margot?"

She nodded. "There was a General Arnold, and a General Westover. . . ."

Generals were dropping by?

"This was after Mr. Miller moved in," she elaborated. Then she shuddered. "Such a cold man."

"In what way? Who the hell is he?"

"He's with the government, too—the Bureau of Air Commerce. I think A. E. put up with him only because she's so friendly with his superior, Mr. Vidal. Mr. Miller is the 'coordinator' of the flight."

"What does that mean?"

"Who knows? His first name is William, and I've never heard him called Bill; G. P. just calls him Miller. Most everybody seems to, although I wasn't raised that way. I call him Mr. Miller. And other things, to myself."

"When did he move in here?"

"In April, after the last of the meetings with Mr. Baruch. But he's not here all the time, he has an office in Oakland—"

"Wait, wait, what meetings with who?"

"There were three meetings between G. P. and A. E. and Mr. Baruch starting in, uh, late March I believe, with the last one in early April."

"This is Bernard Baruch we're talking about."

"Yes. He's a gentleman in his sixties, early sixties, I would say; somewhat heavy-set but not fat. Beautiful white hair, glasses that sit on his nose. A nice man. Soft spoken, well spoken. Do you know him?"

"Not personally."

Maybe they didn't get around to current events at that business college in Van Nuys, but I knew who Bernard Baruch was, even if my newspaper of choice was *The Racing News.* Self-made Wall Street millionaire, philanthropist, so-called "park bench sage" . . . and advisor to FDR.

That was Bernard Baruch.

"Margot, did you take notes at these meetings?"

"No, but I was around . . . I overheard some things, things I probably shouldn't have. I know A. E. was upset after the meetings, though it was all very . . . civilized. I don't think she ever agreed to do what he wanted . . . or maybe I should say, what the President wanted."

"What was that?"

She frowned; worry, not anger. "I think he asked her to volunteer to help the government. . . . What would an 'intelligence operation' be exactly?"

"That would be spying, Margot. He must have asked her to use her plane to spy."

Her eyes widened, in a blend of disbelief and fear. "I can't believe she'd do that!"

Apparently I had put into words something that she had barely dared think.

Then she released her grip, her eyes hooded now, and the fingers of one hand rose to touch her lips, lightly, and when she spoke, her usual rush of verbiage slowed, as if each word had to work its way around the fingers poised protectively there.

"And, yet," she said, "it does make sense, with those generals coming around, later. You see, I heard Mr. Baruch say that the military would . . . what was his language exactly? 'Assist' is only part of it, I believe the words were . . . 'underwrite her enterprise.' Does that mean . . . ?"

"It means Baruch offered government financial backing to remount the world flight."

Her eyes narrowed. "I can tell you this, I was the one who handled the accounting on the first try, so I know what kind of money was spent, and on what. This time, the second time around, it was very different—no bills came in at all. Not for aircraft expenses or repairs or hangar storage or even fuel. Nothing."

I frowned. "Was Amelia aware of this?"

"Yes. . . . She was really very blue, which was a big contrast from before, when she was flying to Honolulu. She was so enthusiastic, and lighthearted and laughing."

Amy had always said she flew for the "fun of it."

I asked, "Did you ever ask her why the military was getting so heavily involved?"

"Yes. Sort of. . . . I didn't put it that way exactly, though. I think I was more concerned about the people who'd been close to her who were being driven away, and shut out, her friends, people she trusted."

"What did she say?"

"She said to me, 'We can't always do what we wish.' "

A hell of a statement from a woman who had made a lifelong habit of doing exactly what she wanted.

"Who was getting 'shut out,' Margot? Obviously, you kept your job."

"Oh, there's a lot of examples. There's that boy up in Oakland who she took under her wing—Bobby Myers? I know she felt bad about that, but I heard Mr. Putnam tell her he was a 'snot-nose snoop,' and to stay away from him."

"Who is this kid? How old is he?"

"Thirteen, fourteen, maybe? He's one of the amateur radio buffs that were going to monitor the flight. A man named McMenamy set up a whole network of radio operators, partly to help Mr. Putnam with material for progress-report press releases. He got shut out, too."

"Who, did? The kid, you mean?"

"Both of them."

I reached behind me in my hip pocket and pulled out the little notebook I kept tucked next to my wallet; I removed the nubby pencil stuck in the spiral. "What was this guy's name again?"

"Walter McMenamy. He lives in L.A., some kind of radio expert, works for Mr. Mantz, sometimes."

I wrote that down. "And the kid's name?"

"Bobby Myers. I heard Mr. Miller tell Mr. Putnam that he had to 'pull the plug on those ham radio morons.' I've never heard such cruel things as that man says."

For hanging out in a house where presidential envoys and generals came constantly calling, this kid led a sheltered life.

She continued: "The list is really long, Nathan, of aides and advisors and volunteers, tossed out with the trash." A thought flashed through her eyes. "Like Albert Bresniak, the photographer."

"Spell that name."

She did, and I wrote it down, and she explained, "Mr. Putnam picked him, personally, to be A. E.'s 'official photographer.' Very young, maybe twenty-two, very talented boy. He was supposed to go with her on at least some of the flight."

That made sense. Putnam had a deal with the Hearst papers—they had been publishing excerpts from Amy's flight journal that had been cabled and phoned home— and a photographer along on several legs of the flight would mean some nice exclusive photos.

"Was this photographer, Bresniak, scheduled to go on the first attempt?"

"No. Mr. Putnam approached him in April or May, I think. Albert was ready to go along clear up till a few days before A. E. took off. Mr. Miller was furious when he found out about Albert being invited. I heard him really bawling out Mr. Putnam."

"And then Albert was suddenly part of the legion of the unwanted."

"Yes. . . . Nate. There's something else I need to tell you. It's quite personal, but I think it's something you should know."

"Shoot."

A knock came at the door, but before either of us could respond to it, Joe—the houseman—leaned in and said, "Miss DeCarrie—Mr. Putnam and Mr. Miller pull in drive."

"But they're not due yet!"

"Mr. Putnam pull in drive. Mr. Miller with him."

And then Joe shut the door and was gone.

"Criminey," she said. "He wasn't supposed to come back till tomorrow . . ."

"We got nothing to hide," I said. "I'm not going out a window or anything."

I walked her into the living room, where Putnam—impeccable as always in a double-breasted gray worsted and black and white tie—was just coming in, saying, "What do you expect me to do, Miller? Indulge in public sobbing?"

And the man coming in behind him said, "All I'm saying is, you came off cold-blooded to that reporter. 'I have confidence in my wife's ability to handle any situation . . .'"

Putnam stopped his companion's conversation with the raised hand of a traffic cop, nodding toward Margot and me.

"We have company," Putnam said. Behind the rimless glasses, his cold dark eyes were fixed on me in that unblinking gaze of his.

William Miller—looking like an undertaker in a black worsted suit and a black silk tie whose small red polka dots were like drops of blood—formed an immediate smile, a small noncommittal smile developed no doubt as a reflex. He was fairly tall, medium build, his hair prematurely gray and receding on an egg-shaped skull, complexion ashen, eyes dark and intense under dark ridges of eyebrow, his mouth rather full, even sensual, the only hint of emotional content in an otherwise cold countenance.

"Who have we here?" he asked, in a pleasant, even soothing baritone.

"Heller?" Putnam said, answering Miller as if he weren't sure he was really recognizing me.

"G. P.," I said. "You weren't expected."

"Neither were you," he said. "What the hell's this about?"

We were standing near the entryway, facing each other awkwardly like gunfighters who forgot their six-shooters.

"I'm concerned about your wife," I said. "I came out here to offer my sympathy and help."

"Mr. Heller called," Margot said, with a smile as tellingly strained as Miller's was ominously casual, "and I

invited him over. I hope I wasn't out of line, Mr. Putnam, but I knew he was a friend of A. E.'s . . ."

"Why don't you leave us alone, Margot," Putnam said.
"Go to your quarters."

She nodded and said, "Yes sir," flashed me a pained
smile, and was gone.

"You want something to drink?" Putnam asked me.
He was slipping out of his suitcoat.

"Why not?" The Zombie had pretty well worn off.

"Joe!" he called, and the houseman appeared and
took Putnam's jacket. Miller made no move to remove
his, nor did he move to take a seat; just stood there with
that small meaningless smile, his arms folded, his weight
evenly distributed on both Florsheimed feet.

"Bring Mr. Heller a rum and Coke," Putnam told Joe.
"Manhattans for Mr. Miller and myself."

Miller gestured, no. "I'll pass, tonight, thank you,
Joe."

Joe nodded, disappeared, while Putnam loosened his
tie, unbuttoned his cuffs, rolled up his sleeves, saying,
"Nate Heller, this is William T. Miller. He's with,
uh . . ."

He left it for Miller to fill in, which he did: "Bureau
of Air Commerce."

We shook hands; his grip was cool, also firm but he
didn't show off.

"Mr. Heller runs the A-1 Detective Agency in Chicago," Putnam told Miller. "He did some work for me,
a year or two ago. Accompanied A. E. on one of her
lecture swings."

The tiny smile settled in one cheek; like Putnam,
Miller rarely blinked. With these two standing staring at
me, it was like having a conversation with a wax museum
exhibit. "You're a little off your beat, aren't you, Mr.
Heller?"

"Every time I leave Chicago," I said pleasantly,
"somebody says that. Do you think I should be staying
in my own back yard?"

Miller's shrug was barely perceptible. "There's something to be said for home team advantage."

A phone rang in the nearby hallway, and Putnam

called, "I'll get that, Joe! Just concentrate on those drinks!"

Miller and I stood facing each other, and I worked at giving him just as unconvincing a smile as he was giving me, while Putnam dealt with the phone call. We didn't speak; we eavesdropped—not that we had any choice. Putnam was on a long-distance call and was working his voice up to an even more obnoxious level than usual.

"Well, Beatrice," he was saying, "I know what you're going through. Who could know better than I? . . . Yes. . . . Yes, I know, dear. . . ."

I asked Miller, "Do you know who he's talking to?"

"Yes."

"Who?"

He thought about whether or not to answer, then did: "Fred Noonan's wife."

"Beatrice," Putnam was saying, "I have a hunch they're sitting somewhere on a coral island, just waiting for a ride home—Fred's probably out sitting on a rock right now, catching their dinner with those fishing lines they had aboard. There'll be driftwood to make a fire, and . . . Bea, please . . . Bea. . . . For Christ's sake, Bea! Look, one of two things has happened. Either they were killed outright—and that comes to all of us sooner or later—or they're alive and'll be picked up. . . . Keep your chin up, Bea. . . . Bea?"

Miller's smile was gone; faint disgust had replaced it.

Putnam came strutting back, shrugging, saying, "She hung up on me! What the hell's wrong with that woman? What does she want from me?"

"This is what I was talking about," Miller snapped.

"What is?"

But Miller said nothing, and Joe came in carrying a little tray on his palm with my rum and Coke and Putnam's Manhattan on it.

"Let's sit out on the patio, shall we, gentlemen?" Putnam asked, plucking his drink off the tray.

I took mine also, sipped it.

"Actually, G. P.," Miller said, glancing at his watch, "it's been a long day . . . so if you'll excuse me."

"Nice meeting you," I said.

Miller said, "Pleasure, Mr. Heller," shooting me the

meaningless smile one last time, and slipped past us into the dining room, turning toward the hallway to the new wing.

Soon Putnam and I were seated on the patio in white basket-weave metal lawn chairs, a round, white-metal, glass-topped table between us. Stretched out before us was a beautifully landscaped back yard washed ivory by moonlight, with stone paths, a trellis with climbing flowers, a fountain, potted agaves, and a flourishing vegetable garden.

But Putnam, leaned back in his chair, was glancing skyward. "It's comforting to know she's under this same sky," he said, and sipped his Manhattan.

I gave the star-scattered sky a look, thinking, *What a crock,* and said, "I'm sure it is."

"Who are you working for, Nate?" he asked, still looking at the sky. The moon was reflected in the lenses of his rimless glasses like Daddy Warbuck's eyeballs.

"Nobody."

" 'Fess up. Who hired you? Mantz?"

Maybe Mantz had been right: maybe G. P. did have him followed in St. Louis.

I said, "I came out here because of Amelia."

Now he looked at me, and half a smile formed; he raised his Manhattan glass and sipped. "Nate Heller? Working gratis? Has hell frozen over?"

"Does everybody have to have an angle?"

His expression turned astounded and amused. He gestured with the Manhattan glass almost as if he were toasting me. "You didn't come here thinking *I'd* hire you? What could you do for A. E. that the Army and Navy can't?"

Well within earshot were the open double windows of the study where Margot and I had spoken; I wondered if Miller was sitting in that darkened room right now, listening in, like a good little spy.

"Yeah, the Army and Navy," I said, and took a swig of rum and Coke. "I notice you got them doing your dirty work . . . or is it the other way around?"

"What's that supposed to mean?"

"Interesting houseguest you got there. He looks like John Wilkes Booth on the way to the theater."

He leaned forward. "Why were you bothering my secretary?"

"I thought she was your wife's secretary."

"What has that stupid girl told you?"

I sipped my drink, shook my head, grinned. "How did you manage it, G. P.? How did you get Amelia to go along with you on this one? Or did you keep her in the dark about a lot of it? Of course, you had Noonan aboard, and he was Naval Reserve, and ex–Pan Am, the spy airline; was *Noonan* the real pilot of this mission?"

He smirked dismissively and sat back, sipped the Manhattan again. "What kind of gibberish are you talking?"

"I mean, Amelia's a pacifist. You'd think the last thing she'd do is the military's bidding. On the other hand, if her wonderful friends in the White House leaned on her, maybe . . ."

He was staring into his back yard. "I don't know what you're talking about."

"I'm talking about you funding this flight by selling your wife out to the government. I've barely waded into this thing and already I'm drowning in the government's involvement, from airstrips on Howland Island to cameras in the belly of that second Electra Uncle Sam bought her."

That last one startled him. He gestured with the hand that held the Manhattan glass. "If what you're saying is true . . . and I'm not saying it is, I'm not saying it isn't . . . that would only make my wife a patriot."

"Extra, extra, read all about it: we're not at war right now. I seem to recall, in the campaign, FDR getting lambasted with a 'warmonger' label, for wanting to beef up the Army and Navy."

"I seem to recall him winning the election, anyway." G. P.'s face was expressionless now; his voice empty. "Please leave."

"Maybe I do have an angle, at that. Like you said, G. P. Maybe there is a way for me to make a buck out of this." I leaned across the table. "Can you imagine the kind of dough the *Tribune* would pay for a scoop like this? Colonel McCormick would dearly love to drag FDR's aristocratic ass through the mud. I think they'll like exposing you, too—we can start with you hiring that guy to put the acid on those rudder cables."

His face remained impassive, but the hand holding the Manhattan glass trembled.

I snorted a laugh. "You know, it must have killed you, when you had to put a lid on so much of your publicity effort, once the military lowered its veil of secrecy. Here you trade your wife's good name and maybe her life away, to fund the biggest flight of both your careers— and you can't even properly exploit it! It's a pisser."

The glass snapped in his hand. He dropped the shards to the tabletop; his palm was cut, bloody. But he ignored it and said, "I would never risk my wife's life. I love her. How can you accuse me of these atrocities? Do you actually imagine I don't love her?"

Those unblinking eyes had filled with tears; maybe it was his cut hand.

"That's the oldest murder motive in the book," I said. "A woman you love that doesn't love you, anymore. . . . Better bandage that up."

"You go to hell."

"Probably. But I got a hunch I'll be running into some familiar faces."

I rose, and didn't go back in the house, just walked around it, skirting a fancy Cord roadster in the driveway, and walked half a block down to where I had parked the Terraplane. For all my indignation, I was driving an automobile that belonged to Putnam, and even though I'd been told he wouldn't be around, I had rightly figured it might make sense to leave it out of sight.

As I was starting up the car, the rider's side door opened and Margot slipped in beside me, wearing a red silk kimono, belted tight around her. She was out of breath.

"Oh, thank God, I wanted to catch you before you left," she panted. "What did you and Mr. Putnam talk about?"

"Not the weather. Margot, you better get back in there before he notices you're gone. You may get fired for talking to me, anyway, and letting me in the house and all."

Her heart-shaped face was lovely in the moonlight. "I

don't care. At this point, I don't care. . . . Nathan, we hadn't finished talking."

"I thought we had."

She touched my arm with cool fingers. "No. There's something . . . important . . . and personal. You have to know it."

"What is it?"

"Can we go somewhere? Where are you staying?"

"Lowman's Motor Court."

Her anxious expression melted into a nostalgic smile. "That's where you spent time with A. E., isn't it?"

"Christ, how much did she tell you about us?" That wasn't like Amy; she was usually so private.

"She told me a lot. . . . We could talk in your room."

I wasn't sure what she had on her mind, but looking at her was enough to put something on mine.

"First tell me," I said, and touched her face. "What's this personal something you need to share?"

"Well . . . we were in the kitchen, having coffee, A. E. and me . . . it was just two days before she left . . . and I can't remember her exact words, but she said when she came back she was going to give up flying, give up celebrity, and 'just be a woman.' "

"What does that mean?"

"I think it's because she thought she might be pregnant. . . . Nathan? Nathan, are you all right?"

". . . You go back in now, Margot."

She leaned toward me. "She didn't mention your name or anything, but I knew she'd just seen you in Chicago and—"

"Good night, Margot."

And she stepped out of the Terraplane, and padded down the sidewalk in her kimono like a geisha. I drove back to the motor court, where a bed waited but not sleep.

Twelve

Nine o'clock the next morning found the sun slanting through high windows like swords in a magician's box, seeking out Ernie Tisor and the other two mechanics who were busy at work on an older plane, mending a fabric wing with "dope," the liquid tightening agent that filled the hangar with a pungent bouquet.

Shielded from sun and smell within his glassed-in office, Mantz—typically dapper in a navy shirt, white tie, and tan sport jacket—sat at his desk, flipping through some paperwork; famous framed faces on the wall behind him seemed to be looking over his shoulder, while others noticed me coming in. Though airfield and hangar noise had entered with me, he didn't look up.

"What is it, Ernie?" he asked.

"It's not Ernie," I said, shutting the door behind me. I was wearing the same yellow polo shirt and tan slacks as yesterday and they probably looked like I'd slept in them, which I had.

His brow furrowed, his eyes widened. "What the hell are you doing here?"

I pulled up a chair and sat opposite him. "I've had warmer welcomes. I thought you wanted to hire me."

He threw the papers on his desk and smirked in disgust. "It's a little late for that, isn't it? You look like you fell off a moving train."

"I didn't get much sleep last night."

His smile was as straight as his pencil-line mustache. "Don't tell me Nate Heller's developing a conscience. Little late for that, isn't it, boy?"

"Just *how* late, do you figure?"

The smile disappeared; he leaned back in his swivel chair, and began to rock. "I talked Amelia through ditching the Vega, before the Pacific flight, and I did the same thing where the Electra's concerned, before this one. But it's not the kind of thing you can really prepare for—and you don't exactly wanna go out over the water and practice."

"Assume the best."

He tented his fingertips, stopped rocking. "Okay, let's say she wasn't over choppy waters, first of all. Then let's say she lowered her flaps at the right moment, glided on in perfectly, stalling out at just the right height above the water, and let's also say the plane stayed in one piece after impact—and, classically, the tail section'll break off in a ditch like that—you still have the plane in a nose-down floating posture, due to the empty fuel tanks and the heavy engines. Assuming she and Noonan overcame all that, based on the Electra's specs, I give her nine hours at best before that ship sank."

"Even with the ping-pong balls?"

He frowned. "What ping-pong balls?"

"I understand they stuffed every spare space on that plane with ping-pong balls for better flotation."

A harsh laugh rose from his chest. "That's a new one on me. Maybe it *would* buy 'em more time; if they could drop the engines in the sea, they might make a boat out of that plane and float for a good long while."

"Could they do that?"

"I sure as hell don't know how. They did have a life raft and other emergency equipment on board, but in those waters, they'd be better off staying in the plane, if it's floating."

"Why? They could paddle the raft."

There were no teeth in his smile, and no humor, either. "Those are shark-infested waters, Nate. What the hell *are* you doin' here?"

I rubbed my burning eyes with the heels of my hands. "I'm not trying to find Amelia and Fred. I'm pretty goddamn sure they're not in Southern California."

Another harsh laugh. "You are a hell of a detective, aren't you?"

"You were right, Paul . . . dead right: G. P. did get Amelia tangled up in some kind of espionage mission."

He began rocking again; his eyes were half-closed, but he was looking at me with a quiet intensity. "What can we do about it, now?"

"There's a lot of rich Republicans who don't like FDR."

"What's that supposed to mean?"

I laughed. "I can hardly believe I said that; if my old man knew what I was thinking . . . he was an old union guy from way back. Socialist to the bone. I've been a Democrat myself, as long as I can remember."

"I still don't follow you."

I leaned an arm on his desk. "I made a wisecrack to G. P. last night—"

Alarm widened his eyes. "You saw G. P.?"

"Yeah. In that bungalow with gland trouble, down the street from your old digs. I had a little chat with him, and before that, I talked to that cute secretary that works over there."

Now the eyes narrowed. "You see that guy Miller?"

"Sure did. Kind of like an All-American version of Bela Lugosi, isn't he?"

He was sitting way forward, shaking his head. "What in God's name are you getting yourself into? Don't think you're getting *me* in—"

"You called me, remember?"

"Over a goddamn *month* ago!"

"Like I was saying, I made a wisecrack to G. P. about going to the *Tribune* with this lovely story, and on reflection, I don't think it's such a bad idea. This is the kind of bullshit presidents get impeached for, if somebody doesn't shoot 'em first."

He held both palms up, as if he were balancing something invisible. "What good does that do Amelia?"

"Probably nothing. But it puts G. P.'s nuts in a wringer, and everybody from the White House down who thought it was a good idea to con Lady Lindy into playin' Mata Hari'll find themselves all over the front page and out of work and maybe in jail."

"You really didn't get any sleep last night, did you?"

"I caught about two hours, after the sun came up. Don't you like my idea?"

"Wouldn't it just be easier to kill G. P.?"

"I don't rule that out. I'd rather have him publicly humiliated first."

Mantz was gazing at me as if I were insane; imagine that. "You're not joking, are you?"

"Not in the least. You take that cocksucker up for a ride, I'll toss him out of the plane. Deal?"

"You need some rest. . . ."

"I'm not looking for you to subsidize my investigation, Mantz. I'm off the clock; call it a busman's holiday. All I ask is for a little information, a little help; I need you to approach some people and set up some meetings."

He was shaking a hand in the air, as if waving goodbye. "Look—I was all for this . . ."

"*You* pulled *me* in."

". . . but that was when Amelia hadn't left the country, yet. We coulda done some good. We coulda saved her. But right now, her best chance is the government, the Coast Guard, the Navy, that they find her. And if she's workin' for them, it benefits them to find her—they gotta be spendin' millions on this search—"

"Further proof you were right. Since when does the government, who can barely get Congress to give 'em two nickels for defense, go spendin' that kind of dough looking for a downed stunt pilot?"

His expression was grave. "I'm sorry, Heller. I'm out."

"You got a charter today?"

". . . No."

"You do now." I reached in my hip pocket for my notebook. "I want to talk to these radio nuts. . . . McMenamy, who I understand has done work for you, and this Myers kid, in Oakland."

"Well . . ."

"You want dough? Here." And I dug in my front pocket for my money clip, and tossed two double saw-bucks on his desk. "That cover the charter?"

"You want me to fly you to Oakland to talk to a fourteen-year-old kid with a ham radio."

"That's right. And I want you to set up a meeting for me here, with the other guy, McMenamy."

"Heller . . . stop. . . ."

"Earlier, you assumed the best. Now let's assume the worst: she crashed in the ocean and if she was unlucky and didn't die on impact, the sharks made screaming meals out of her and Noonan. That's a menu courtesy of G. P. Putnam and Uncle Sam."

"I'll make the calls," he said. "And take your goddamn money. Get it off my desk."

"Okay," I said, and put the twenties back in my money clip, not giving a damn whether he took them or not.

That's how far gone I was.

Within the hour, Walter McMenamy was seated before me at a table at the back of the Burbank terminal's Sky Room restaurant. He'd been doing some work at Patterson Radio Company for his friend Karl Pierson, chief engineer for the firm and a fellow amateur radio enthusiast.

"We're designing an entirely new type of short-wave receiver," McMenamy said, his voice soft yet alive with enthusiasm. Probably in his mid-thirties, and despite his businesslike dark suit and navy and red tie, McMenamy came across as a husky kid, his oblong head home to a high forehead with dark widow's-peaked hair, and boyish features: bright eyes, snub nose, full, almost feminine lips.

"Thanks for dropping everything," I said, "to come talk to me."

It was midmorning, and we were drinking Coca-Cola on ice.

"It's my pleasure, Mr. Heller," McMenamy said. "I've been busting to tell somebody, and when Paul said you're looking into this mess, you couldn't keep me away."

"What have you been busting to tell somebody?"

He leaned forward. "Well, did Paul fill you in on what my role was to be, on the first attempt at the world flight?"

"Yes he did."

McMenamy had been retained by the Putnams, at Mantz's advice, as a technical advisor, selecting and in-

stalling the latest radio equipment in the Electra. He'd
also been enlisted to assemble volunteers among fellow
members of the Radio Relay League, a worldwide short-
wave radio club, to follow the Electra, particularly over
the more isolated regions on its flight path. A base station on Beacon Hill, near Los Angeles, was selected for
optimal reception.

"We had a big responsibility," McMenamy said, obviously relishing the thought, "providing en route communications that'd help ensure Amelia's safety, and Mr.
Noonan's—particularly weather reports and forecasts."

"And you could relay information to G. P. Putnam,"
I said, "to feed the press."

He nodded. "Day-by-day progress reports. It would
have really built public interest."

"What happened, Mr. McMenamy?"

"Call me Walt."

"Call me Nate."

He shrugged. "I don't know what the heck happened,
Nate. I used to see Amelia a couple of times a week,
but after the Luke Field crackup, I never spoke with her
again. She came back from Honolulu on the *Malolo* . . .
why are you smiling?"

"Sorry. I took a trip on the *Malolo* once. Just thinking
about what a small world it is."

"Not so small when you're going around it in an airplane. Anyway, we went down to meet the ship, Karl
and I, wanting to be waiting there to let Amelia know
that her bad luck, cracking up the Electra and all, hadn't
dimmed our faith in her. That we were game for a second try, if she was. . . . Boy, were we in for a surprise."

He seemed to want me to ask: "How so?"

He leaned forward again and spoke in a near whisper:
"She came down the gangplank surrounded by Navy
personnel—officers and, what, Shore Patrol or MP's?
Anyway, it was a combination of brass and armed
guards, and they whisked her right past us and into a
Navy staff car."

"Did she see you?"

He sat back, smirking disgustedly. "Oh, yes. She acknowledged me with this . . . pitiful smile . . . but didn't
say a darn word! And that was the start of it."

"Of what?"

He was shaking his head, his expression gloomy. "Of the government completely taking over. Some Naval Intelligence officers, plainclothes guys, met with Karl and me at a restaurant. They said any messages from Amelia, that came in from the Beacon Hill station, would go through them, and then to the press. We weren't to initiate contact with Amelia, either—just monitor her messages as they came in, which hardly any did. Some of what they released was false. They also swore us to secrecy."

"Why are you telling me, then?"

A faint smile formed on the babyish lips. "Two reasons. First, Mantz says you're okay. Second, Amelia's missing. If we'd been allowed to maintain contact with her, if we hadn't been shut out—who knows?"

"They didn't shut you out entirely . . ."

"The only reason for that is they needed our technical expertise and equipment. We had better gear than the government. And they knew we'd be able to monitor Amelia's signals anyway."

"I'm sure they didn't like that."

"No. But we were doing it under their watchful eye."

I glanced around the restaurant, which had only a scattering of patrons. "You think you're under their watchful eye right now?"

"I don't think so. I don't think I was followed here. We shut the Beacon Hill operation down a couple days ago . . . but I still listen at home."

"You say that like you heard something."

His face might have been young, but his eyes suddenly seemed old. "I still am . . . at night. The daytime frequency, 3105 kilocycles, I don't pick anything up; too weak. But at night, on 6210 kilocycles, I'm still hearing her . . . she's still out there."

I leaned forward. "What are you hearing?"

"The prearranged signal—two long dashes, if they were on water, three if they were on land. She's been sending the two long dashes. Ask Paul—he's heard them."

"Christ. And the Navy, the Coast Guard, they know?"

"Of course they do. I've heard a voice, too, weakly,

through the static . . . SOS, SOS, KHAQQ, KHAQQ . . ."

"I know what SOS is . . ."

"KHAQQ—her call sign."

"And she's still there—on the water?"

He swallowed, and nodded.

Mantz popped in the restaurant, spotted us and strode over. "You boys getting along all right?"

"Fine," I said. "You didn't tell me you heard her signal."

McMenamy, sipping his glass of Coke, watched Mantz reply.

"Hell, Nate, it could have been anybody. There's a lot of sick hoaxing going on right now. . . . Look, this Myers kid, in Oakland, there's no phone in his house, but I got the airport manager to send somebody over . . . and you'll be glad to know I've got this high-level conference between you and Jackie Cooper all arranged, for three this afternoon."

"I appreciate this, Paul," I said, and I meant it.

"I'll fly you over in the *Honeymoon Express.* . . . Been a while since you flew in a Vega, I bet."

"A while," I said.

The Duck Air Service Cafe at Oakland's Bay Farm Airport, its walls decorated with framed flying photographs and pennants commemorating air shows and competitions, had wooden booths along windows that looked out on the airfield and its hangars. The interior of the glorified shack was a dark-stained oak, except for a small gleaming counter with wrought-iron stools and leather seats. Pies and cakes and ice cream were served up from behind the counter by Mom, while Pop made the sandwiches in a small kitchen in back.

The afternoon was warm but not sweltering, ceiling fans churning the air like big propellers; those flies that flypaper strips hadn't shot down were dive-bombing the handful of customers in the place, which included me and Mantz, on one side of a booth, and young Robert Myers on the other.

I had bought the Myers kid a "snail," which was his word for a cinnamon roll, and a glass of milk; he was wolfing them down, whether out of hunger or in competition with the flies, I couldn't tell you.

He was a tall, bony kid with dark alert eyes, a strong nose and chin, and a shock of unruly blond hair in need of a barber; like a lot of kids in their early teens, his body approached manhood while his features still had a softness to them, as if not yet fully formed. He wore a crew-neck T-shirt with dark blue neck and sleeve trim, and his denim trousers were sailor-style denims—judging by how high they rode over his black speedsters, this was at least his second summer in them.

"Amelia never heard a snail called a snail before, either," he said, chomping on the roll; his voice hadn't changed yet. "I call her Amelia 'cause she said to. She always called me Robert, 'cause she knew I didn't like Bobby, since it's what my sister calls me when she gets mad."

Mantz and I traded grins.

"Well, then, I'll call you Robert, too," I said, "if that's okay. And you call me Nate."

"All right, Nate. I can't tell you how glad I am that somebody's come to talk to me about all this. I about been bouncing off the walls, worryin'."

"Why?"

He gulped some milk. "Jeez, I don't even know where to start."

"In the detective business," I said, knowing he would be impressed by that, "we like to keep it tidy, orderly."

He dabbed off his milk mustache with a paper napkin. "Start at the beginning, you mean."

"Yeah. How did you happen to meet Amelia?"

He shrugged, nodded out toward the airfield, where a two-engine job was taxiing. "I been hangin' around the airport since I was a kid."

"That long?"

"Oh yeah, I can spend hours just watching the airplanes and ground crews, and there's all sort of famous fliers around. I talked to Jimmy Doolittle and Howard Hughes and Bobbi Trout. Something interesting's always goin' on out here, parachute jumps, air races, powder puff derbies . . . that's when I first met Amelia. But I didn't really get to know her till fairly recent—when she was gettin' ready for the world flight. The first time she tried it, I mean, early this year. It was almost like she went out of her way to pay attention to me and be friendly and all—since she's a big-time celebrity, you might think I'm spreadin' it on thick, but I'm not: she treated me like a little brother."

Mantz chimed in, "Robert's not exaggerating. Amelia took a liking to the lad."

"Like, when she'd buy me a snail, she'd have it heated up for me. . . . Said it was better warm, and was she right! I just wasn't used to the finer things of life."

Mantz and I traded smiles again.

"She had such pretty hands," the boy said, looking through me. "Dainty and delicate, though her fingers were awful long. . . . She'd sit and drink her cocoa. . . ." He swallowed. I think he was holding back tears; I knew the feeling.

Then he went on: "You know, it's four miles from my house, to here, and when she'd come along in that fancy Cord car of hers, she'd pick me up. . . . Sometimes her mother was with her, and she was a nice lady, too."

"You want another glass of milk, Robert?" I asked.

"Sure!"

I called over to Mom behind the counter for one, and got fresh Cokes for Mantz and me, too.

"Mr. Mantz may not realize it," Robert said, "but this airport was real different, once prep for the flight got started. No more races, no more air shows, everything kind of shut down except for preppin' the world flight. And lots of strange people around."

"Strange, how?"

He nibbled at his snail. "Men in suits. They looked like businessmen. And sometimes military people. . . . A General Westover came around, everybody seemed real impressed."

They should. Westover was the head of the U.S. Army Air Forces.

The kid was saying, "Mr. Putnam would go in the office hangar and talk to them . . . usually without Amelia. It was almost like the hangar office was off limits to her, and I heard her complain about it, too—'What is

he doing? Who are these people? What are they talkin' about?' "

I turned to Mantz. "You saw this kind of thing, too?"

Mantz nodded. "But I wasn't involved on the Oakland
end, much. Noonan and the new mechanic, Bo
McKneely, were handling things."

"The security guard at night," Robert said, waving a
fly off his snail, "he was a Navy reservist."

"How do you know that?" I asked. "Were you out
here at night, much?"

"No, but my sister had a crush on that Navy guard
and was always bothering me about talkin' to him for
her. He'd show up kind of late in the afternoon. . . ."

"If security was tight, Robert, what were they doing
letting you hang around?"

"On the first try, before she crashed her plane in
Hawaii, things weren't so tight. Reporters were takin'
pictures and doing stories about Amelia. . . . As for me,
I'm kind of a mascot around here, I guess . . . as long
as I don't get in the way, mess with tools or bother the
mechanics or anything. Sometimes I run errands and
help out a little. Like that time I helped you, Mr. Mantz,
with that battery."

"That's right," Mantz said, with a little smile. "You
did help me haul that into the plane, didn't you?"

"Big green heavy-duty Exide battery," the kid said,
nodding, " 'bout three times the size of a car battery.
That's how she's sendin' her messages, I bet."

Mantz said, "Out of fuel, she couldn't be using the
radio, otherwise; she'd need the right engine running to
keep the plane's batteries charged."

"I got to watch the first takeoff from the hotel bal-
cony," Robert said, basking in the memory. "Amelia
invited me—can you picture that? Me with her Hollywood friends with their fancy clothes and flashy jewelry!
But you shoulda seen the dirty looks Mr. Putnam gave
me. He woulda never put up with me bein' around if
Amelia hadn't told him to. . . . Wasn't any fanfare on
the second takeoff."

I sipped my Coke. "You and Mr. Putnam didn't hit
it off?"

Robert frowned, shook his head. "He's a nasty person.

Sometimes he had his son with him, called him 'Junior'? He's a nice kid, I don't know, a year or two older than me. Not wild or anything . . . quiet."

"Well behaved," Mantz agreed.

"Well, I saw Mr. Putnam slap him, yell at him, really dress him down, for *nothin'*. . . . Once in the washroom over in the terminal building, Mr. Putnam hit him for 'not washing up' good enough."

"You ever have a run-in with him?" I asked.

"Run-in! Run *down* is more like it!"

I waved a fly away from me. "What do you mean?"

"Well, this one day a man in an Army uniform . . . I don't know what rank, but he sure wasn't a private . . . came in the cafe here, while I was sitting at the counter with Amelia and Mr. Noonan. Havin' snails and milk, like always. This Army man had a bunch of papers for them to sign, 'releases,' he called them, or 'clearances' or something, I don't know. . . . Anyway, Mr. Noonan said maybe I better leave, and so I did, and when I came out, Mr. Putnam spotted me. He came over, shouting at me, 'What did you see in there?' I said, 'Nothing.' And I started walking away, and he blocked me and started yelling! About how I'd seen and heard a lot of things I wasn't supposed to, calling me a 'punk,' saying things like 'Don't you have a home?' He told me to stay away and stop snooping around."

I glanced at Mantz, who was frowning, then asked, "Did you say anything, Robert? Or just walk away?"

"Heck, no, I didn't walk away! I yelled right back at him—said I had as much right as he did to come around the airport. He looked like was gonna grab me . . . only I'm not small, like his son, and he musta thought better of it. But he started yelling again: 'If I catch you around here again, you'll disappear and no one will know where to find you!' Then he kinda stormed off."

Mantz was shaking his head in disgust.

I asked, "What did you do, Robert?"

"Started to walk home. I just thought he was a real nut, I was ticked off, and you know how it is when you're mad, and the thoughts are sorta racing . . . I wasn't gonna let him scare me away, there was no way I wasn't comin' around the airport anymore, it's my

home away from home. And while I was walkin', it's
kind of a lonely stretch of road, and it was kinda late,
hopin' to hitch but figurin' I was probably out of luck,
I heard a car comin' and thought, great! Finally a ride!
Only it was this big black Hudson and Mr. Putnam was
driving. He was looking at me all pop-eyed and crazy
and you don't have to believe me, but I swear he aimed
that big car right at me and *gunned* it. I jumped out of
the way, into the ditch—he was going so fast, driving so
crazy, he sort of lost control and almost went in the
ditch himself; he slammed on his brakes and started
backing up, and turning around! If this other car hadn't
come along just then, and picked me up, I don't know
what woulda happened."

"Maybe," Mantz said softly, "it was an accident and
he was backing up to come see if you were all right."

"I don't believe in Santa Claus," Robert said. "I
haven't for a long time."

"That's a good policy," I told the boy. "Did you tell
the police? Or your parents, or anyone?"

He shook his head and his blond mop bobbed. "No.
Mr. Putnam's rich and famous. I'm just a poor kid.
Who're they gonna believe? But at least he left me alone
after that. Of course, it was just a few days before the
flight, the second flight. Did you know she took film
along, a lot of film?"

"Really?" I asked, giving Mantz a sideways glance.

"Did you help with that, Mr. Mantz?" the boy asked.
"I mean, everybody knows you're famous for aerial
photography."

"No."

Robert gestured out the window. "Well, I saw some
Navy people deliver some big boxes to the hangar. A
big white seal was on all the boxes—it said 'Naval Air
Photography, USN,' or something close to that. Mr. Putnam had those Navy guys load 'em on the plane. I think
they put 'em way in the back. . . . That's what they made
her do, isn't it? Take pictures of islands she flew over.
Islands that belong to the Japanese, right?"

Mantz and I exchanged startled looks. *How could this
kid know that?*

He was still talking, lost in memory: "She made me

promise, you know. Before she left. She told me she was going on a very secret and dangerous mission and that if I heard anything had happened to her or Mr. Noonan, I was supposed to tell somebody . . . my mother . . . the police . . . or somebody . . ." He sighed. "Well I finally have."

"It must feel good, Robert," I said quietly, "to get this off your chest."

He grinned, but it was a halfway, qualified grin. "It does, 'cause when I called the police, the man just laughed at me."

"You called the police about what Amelia told you?"

His forehead tightened. "No . . . not exactly . . . it was about what I heard on the radio."

"What do you mean, radio?"

"We have a Philco, it's a super-heterodyne that gets short-wave transmissions. It's a family hobby—my dad and brother and me. We put up a sixty-foot copper mesh antenna."

I took a last swig of Coke and said, "You don't have a phone in the house, and you have a short-wave radio with a sixty-foot antenna?"

"Oh, it gets more than short wave. We listen to Jack Armstrong, Tom Mix and the Shadow, too!" He shrugged. "I've heard dozens of transmissions from Amelia, since she took off from Lae . . ."

I blinked, then looked over at Mantz who rolled his eyes, when Robert wasn't looking.

The boy was saying, "I listen every night. . . . It's summer, and my dad works nights, and Mom doesn't care if I stay up; I mean, she knows how much trouble I have sleeping with my brother in the same bed, snoring. So, I'm just fooling around, twisting the dial, and I come onto this woman's voice saying, 'That was close! We just cleared the tail fifty feet!' I couldn't believe my ears! It was *Amelia's* voice! On *my* radio! It didn't take me long to figure out what I was hearing—I mean, reading about the flight in the paper every day, for a month! What I heard was Amelia on takeoff, when she was just leaving the airstrip."

"Robert," Mantz said, gently, "you know there have been some radio recreations, some dramatic—"

"Not happening at the exact same time as when she took off! I'm sorry, Mr. Mantz—I didn't mean to be rude. It's just—I know what I heard." His speech picked up speed, as if his conversation were lifting off a runway after a long taxi. "And then she was talking to a radioman back on Lae, named Balfour, saying Mr. Noonan had passed her a sealed envelope with a note about a change of flight plans. She seemed really peeved. . . . The radioman said he didn't know about the change, that his orders were to give her weather reports. She said something about flying north to Truk Island."

It was like listening to an idiot savant rattle off trigonometry equations. "You remember all this?"

He nodded, blond shock bouncing. "I wrote it down. I got my school notebook and I've been writing everything down."

"There's more?"

"Dozens of transmissions over the last few days!"

I sat forward, not really buying any of this, but impressed with his imagination. Mantz looked amused.

"She came on later, more relaxed, not so mad, even giggling a little, as she called out the names of islands she was flying over, trying to pronounce them—I heard her mention the tip of Rabaul, for instance. She lost contact with Lae about three hundred miles out, but I heard her say Noonan was getting good pictures of the Caroline Islands."

"And you're hearing all this over your Philco?" I asked.

"Sure! I heard her talkin' to that ship, the *Itasca*, too! I heard her make her first contact with 'em, when they asked her to identify herself and she said, 'The name is Putnam, but I don't use that.' "

I had to chuckle; that did sound like her. Even Mantz was smiling a little, though I could tell he figured this kid was spinning a yarn.

"I listened all night," Robert said. "She came on naming islands as she passed over them, sayin' they were off her left or right wing . . . Bikar, Majuro, Jaluit, I'm leavin' a few out but I got 'em written down. . . . She said there was plenty of good light and they could see the islands fine. Then she had trouble getting the *Itasca* to hear her—here I am, in my living room in California, and I can hear her fine! I mean, there's static and everything, and she kinda comes in and out, but I heard her asking *Itasca* to turn on their lights, sayin' she must be circling the ship, but she couldn't come down because it was too dark, she got there too early. Then it just got worse and worse. . . . They weren't answering her. . . . She kept saying her fuel was low. She told the *Itasca* she was gonna try for Hull Island, but they didn't hear her, and that's when she spotted the Japanese fighter planes."

"Fighter planes."

He nodded, wild-eyed. "One was above her, the other two were near her wingtips; they fired on her! Machine-gun bursts!"

"Look, kid—" Mantz began.

The boy just kept going, gesturing with both hands. "They were trying to force her to land at Hull, but when she looked down, she saw these ships offshore—a fishing boat, and two battleships—but they were able to outrun the Japs in the Electra, it was much faster. Mr. Noonan had her fly toward an island called Sydney, just a hundred miles away, and all the time she was still callin' the *Itasca,* no response. And then one engine sputtered out—they could see the island! But then the other one went out, too, and I heard her say, 'Oh, my goodness! We're out of fuel!' "

As silly as this story was, hearing Amy's familiar "Oh, my goodness!" from this kid's mouth sent a chill up me.

"I heard the plane make this awful loud thud—you'd think it would have sounded more like a splash, but it didn't—and I waited for seconds that seemed like hours before she came back on, saying, 'We missed the trees and the coral reef. . . . We're on the water.' She said Mr. Noonan injured his head, shoulder and arm and she stopped transmitting to go check on him. . . . Then it was morning, and I lost them. . . . I'd been listening twelve hours or more."

"Is this the story you told the police?" I asked.

Mantz was leaned back with a hand over his eyes.

"Oh, you listened to a lot more of it than the desk sergeant on the phone did. . . . They're still out there,

Nate . . . Mr. Mantz . . . Amelia and Mr. Noonan. I've
been listening to them every night. She comes on every
hour and doesn't stay on long—conserving the battery.
They're floating on the water. . . . They're hot and
they're hungry and Amelia's really mad, she keeps saying, 'Why are you doing this to us? Why don't you come
get us? You know where we are.' Things like that. It's
real sad. But they are still alive. . . . Isn't that a relief?"

I nodded.

He leaned forward, puppy-dog eager, looking from me
to Mantz and back again. "Would you like to come to
my house and listen, tonight? I'm sure my mom and dad
wouldn't mind."

"Thanks, kid," Mantz said, with a sick smile. "I think
I'll take a rain check."

I put a hand on Mantz's shoulder. "Paul, can I have
a word with you, for a minute? Outside?"

His eyes narrowed. "Sure."

"Robert, you think you can handle another snail?"

The boy beamed. "Boy, could I! Warmed up and
everything?"

"Live a little," I said, and nodded over to Mom behind the counter, who smiled and took care of the order,
as Mantz and I headed outside.

He dug a pack of Camels out of his sports coat and
lighted one up, saying, "You can't believe any of that
baloney. Tell me you don't."

There was runway noise and I had to work my voice
up. "How do you explain some of what he knows? The
names of those islands, for example?"

Mantz smirked, shrugged, blew smoke out his nose
like a dragon. "I never heard of those islands. Maybe
he made 'em up."

"Maybe he didn't."

"Maybe he's got a Rand McNally atlas in his house.
Look, he and Amelia were friends, all of that stuff he
told you was legit. . . . But now he's stayin' up at night,
with his head filled with what he's readin' in the papers
about his famous friend, and he's listening to staticky
garbage and his imagination is running wild."

"Is it possible for that Philco to be picking her up?"

"Sure." The cigarette bobbled in his mouth as he

spoke. "McMenamy thinks he's heard her, too—of course, he hasn't heard twenty or thirty exciting episodes like Robert has!"

Through the window we could see the kid chowing down on another snail.

I said, "I don't understand how either of them could be hearing what the *Itasca* and the rest of the Navy and Coast Guard can't."

Mantz raised an eyebrow. "Well, the Electra's radios sure can't transmit over any considerable distance, but there's always 'skip.' "

"What's skip?"

"A freak but common phenomenon. Sometimes radio reception turns up hundreds, even thousands of miles away."

"And that's what Robert could be hearing?"

"I think Robert's hearing pixies."

"I'm going to take him up on his invitation."

"You gotta be pullin' my leg! You can't—"

"Go home. I'll catch the train back to L.A. to-morrow."

"Heller—"

"I'm going over to Robert's to listen to the radio. Who knows? Maybe Jack Armstrong, All-American Boy, will win the big game."

"I'm an *Amos 'n' Andy* man myself," Mantz said, pitching his cigarette, sending it sparking to the ground. "And I'm takin' my plane back to Burbank, before I miss tonight's installment."

The Myers house, though in a heavily residential section on the north edge of Oakland, sat alone on a small hill, a shingled bungalow absurdly dominated by that sixty-foot copper antenna Robert had told us about. That, at least, had been no exaggeration.

The boy had hitchhiked home, on the understanding that I would drop by after supper, his parents suitably warned. Robert knew I planned to check in at the Bay Farm Airport Hotel, which I did, and it was there that he tracked me down.

"I thought you didn't have a phone," I said into the

receiver, as I sat on the edge of my bed in the hotel room.

"We don't," the kid's voice said, "but our neighbor does. My folks want you to come over for supper. My mom's a really good cook."

I accepted, and drove over there in a buggy that Mantz's friend, airport manager Guy Turner, loaned me, a '32 Ford station wagon with BAY FARM AIRPORT stenciled on either side. When I parked out front, the hangars of the airport four miles away were visible from the hill the house perched upon.

Dinner was pleasant enough, in the small dining room of the cramped, modestly furnished home—meat loaf and mashed potatoes and creamed corn, served up by Robert's mother Anna, an attractive woman in her thirties. His father Bob, Sr., a solid-looking quiet man, a little older than his wife, worked night shift in a canning factory. Robert's sister, a cute blonde, probably seventeen, and a younger brother, maybe twelve, were fairly talkative, not at all put off by the presence of a stranger.

I had been introduced as a friend of both Paul Mantz and Amelia Earhart, and as a detective who was interested in checking out the short-wave transmissions Robert had reported. They understood I was not from the police, and I implied I was working for Mantz, whom both parents had met at the airport on an occasion or two.

Questions about what Chicago was like predominated, and the father—who had said little throughout the meal—finally said, over apple pie, "You think there's somethin' to this? What Robert's been hearing on the radio?"

"That's what I'd like to find out."

"Paper says there's lots of hoaxers."

"I know."

"Any fool with a short wave can get on and pretend to be the King of England."

"Sure."

"Lot of sick-in-the-head people in this world, you ask me."

"No argument," I said.

"Robert's always been creative," his mother said. She

had lovely eyes and a nice smile, and Robert and his sister had gotten their blond hair from her, though Anna's was now a dishwater variety. She had the haggard look of an overworked, underappreciated working-class mother.

"You mean Bobby's always been a nut," his sister said.

The younger brother laughed, too loud.

"Shut it," the father said, and they did.

The mother smiled and laughed, nervously. "Brothers and sisters," she said. "You know how it is."

After supper, the father took off for work with his lunch pail in hand, and Mrs. Myers did the dishes, declining my offer of help. Her daughter pitched in, while the younger brother hung around the living room with us, as Robert sat me down on the couch across from the fireplace and the square-shouldered Philco console, which was not yet turned on.

For several mind-numbing hours, Robert showed me the charts and notes and maps he'd created, the supposed physical evidence of the transmissions he'd been hearing. He spread these out on the coffee table before me, and walked me through them, explaining his methods, reading aloud, and I could follow very little of it.

I had begun to suspect that Robert was, indeed, a "creative" young man, and possibly a seriously disturbed one.

Around nine o'clock, Mrs. Myers excused herself, having shooed the younger brother off to bed already (after the boy showed me the flying wings badge he'd sent for from a radio show called *The Air Adventures of Jimmy Allen*). The daughter had gone over to a girlfriend's house to spend the night, or anyway that's what she told her mother. Soon the house was dark, and I was on the couch and Robert—ring notebook and pencil at the ready—was kneeling in front of the Philco, as if it were an altar, bathed in its green glow, twisting the knobs, the dials, searching for Amelia.

And finding static.

"You'll see," he said. "You'll see."

This went on for some time. I sat with a hand covering my face, feeling like a moron, pitying this kid, exhausted,

having slept very little over the past thirty-six hours,
wondering why the hell I didn't go back to Chicago
where I had paying clients.

"*Oh my goodness, did you hear that?*"

The voice came from the Philco.

"*Fred just said he saw something!*"

"I told you!" Robert said, gleeful. He began writing,
recording what he heard.

I sat forward.

"*Did you hear that, Itasca? Please hurry, please,
please hurry!*"

Amy's voice. It sure as hell sounded like Amy's voice.

Another voice, fainter, male, but picked up over her
microphone: "*It's them! The Japanese!*"

"They're going to be saved!" Robert said, turning to
me, eyes glittering in the near darkness. He kept writing.
My heart was racing.

The male voice again, faint but shouting: "*So big! The
guns are so big!*"

I stumbled off the couch, and found myself crouching
next to Robert, a hand on the boy's shoulder.

The voice that seemed to be Amy's said: "*They're
lowering small boats . . .*"

"Thank you, God," Robert was saying, as he scribbled
cursive notes. "Thank you, God, for letting someone
find them."

Amy said, rapid-fire words: "*I'll keep talking, Itasca,
as long as I can. . . .*"

But static flared up.

They were gone.

"Is there anything you can do?" I asked the kid.

His terrified expression belied his calming words:
"They'll be back . . . they'll be back. . . ."

Finally, I heard the man's voice again: "*They're here!
They're opening the door!*"

And Amy said, "*Did you hear that, Itasca? They're
coming in!*"

Robert covered his mouth with a hand. He had
dropped his notebook.

Sounds of grunting, metallic banging around in the
plane, accompanied Amy's near screams: "*Oh my good-*

ness, he's resisting them! No, Fred—no! Oh, they're beat-ing him terribly. . . . Stop! Stop!"

And that was followed by a sound that could only have been a slap.

Then dead silence.

We listened for a long time, but all we heard was that awful deathly stillness, and static. He picked the note-book up and recorded those last terrible sentences. Fi-nally I helped the boy to his feet and we stumbled together over to the couch, flopping there, exhausted.

What had we heard? Cruel hoax? Or cruel reality?

"They're saved, though, right?" he asked. "It's better than nothing, the Japs saving them. Isn't it? Isn't it?"

Sitting there in the near dark, I nodded and smiled and put my arm around the boy, and pretended not to notice he was weeping.

He did me the same favor.

Thirteen

The sky was a glowing pastel blue with bright stars that created shimmering crosses if you looked right at them; the stars were electric, arranged in caricatures of constellations, and the sky merely the sculpted ceiling that rose in a gentle slope from behind the stage to shelter the posh crowd out on the mirror-varnished dance floor. They were gliding around to "A Foggy Day in London Town" as performed by Harl Smith and His Continental Orchestra, at the Club Continental, a shout away from Burbank's United Airport, formal in its linen-covered tablecloths, fine china and sterling silverware, intimate in its cozy booths, tables for two and pastel-tinted wooden paneling.

In my herringbone blue garbardine, the nicest suit I owned, I was underdressed. A good-looking brunette in furs and gown who might have been Paulette Goddard was dancing with a guy I didn't recognize but who, like most of the men on the dance floor, wore a tuxedo.

I found Mantz at one of those cozy booths, seated across from a cute blonde; he was in a white dinner jacket with a black bow tie, and she wore a yellow chiffon evening dress with an admirable décolletage.

"Sorry to track you down like this," I said. "But I'm leaving tomorrow morning, on the train."

"Glad you did," he said, and nodded toward his companion. "My fiancée, Terry Minor. . . . This is the guy I was tellin' you about, Terry—Nate Heller from Chicago."

"A real pleasure, Nate," she said, and beamed, offering her hand for me to shake; she had a firm, friendly grip.

"Pleasure's all mine, Terry," I said.

She was in her early thirties, not movie star pretty, but it was easy to see what Mantz saw in her, and I'm not just referring to her neckline. Her hair in hundreds of tiny blonde curls, eyes bright and blue, she radiated the same tomboyish appeal as Amy.

"Sit down," Mantz said, sliding over in the booth.

"I hate to think what he's told you about me," I said to Terry with a grin.

"I told her how you saved my behind," Mantz said, frosted martini in hand, "when Myrtle came gunnin' for me. . . . Considering why you were hired that night, that was pretty white of ya."

He was fairly well oiled, good-naturedly so.

Softly, I asked him, "Have you, uh, informed Terry about why I'm in town?"

"I've filled her in," he said. "We don't have any secrets."

"Speak for yourself," she said with a little smile, sipping her own frosted drink.

That made him smile; in addition to being well lubricated, he was lovesick over this cutie.

"So . . . you've come to your senses, then," he said. "You're finally givin' up on this foolheaded fishing expedition."

I gave him half a smile. "Are you forgetting what fool headed me there, in the first place?"

That made Terry giggle, but her steady gaze let me know she didn't take this subject lightly.

I waved a waiter over and ordered a rum and Coke. "Hell no I'm not giving up. I'm heading home and sell my story to the *Trib.*"

"Figures," Mantz snorted. "Leave it to you to find a way to make a buck out of this."

"I'm not in it for the money," I said testily. "But what's the harm of having your cake and eating it, too?"

Now the orchestra was playing "I've Got You Under My Skin."

"There are some damn dangerous people involved in

this affair, Nate," Mantz said. "That bird Miller, for one."

"Frank Nitti's a friend of mine," I said.

"What's that supposed to mean?"

"It means I've run into tougher birds than William Miller."

Last night, I'd told young Robert not to mention to anyone, even his parents, what we'd heard on the family Philco; but assured the boy he'd be hearing from me. I'd gone from the Myers house to the Bay Farm Airport Hotel, where after my day and a half of no sleep, I collapsed on the bed in a comalike pile. I didn't wake up till noon, and took the train back to Los Angeles, catching a cab to the Burbank airport. There, late afternoon, I spoke with Ernie Tisor, to see if he'd be willing to come forward with what he knew, explaining that it would be to the press, not the authorities. He was willing. Mantz had left for the day, but Tisor mentioned his boss's plans to take Terry out for dinner and dancing at the Club Continental. Then I'd driven the Terraplane to Lowman's Motor Court, where I still had a room, from which I called both Margot DeCarrie and Walter McMenamy, to see if they were willing to come forward, too. Both said yes.

And, after a shower and a shave, I'd finally gotten out of that yellow polo and tan slacks and into my garbardine.

At the moment, Mantz was looking at me with his eyes round under a furrowed brow. "You don't really believe you heard Amelia and Fred getting nabbed by the Japs?"

I'd just shared with Mantz and his fiancée the results of my slumber party at the Myers kid's house.

"If it was a hoax," I said, sipping my rum and Coke, "it was a hell of a job."

Mantz smirked, shaking his head. "You do know, don't you, that the *March of Time* did a reenactment of the flight, the day after Amelia disappeared? And so many calls came in, at Pearl Harbor, they flashed the *Itasca* that Amelia was transmitting!"

"I think I know the difference between Amelia's voice

and Westbrook Van Voorhis," I said, referring to the radio show's announcer.

He put a hand on my shoulder; his speech was slightly thick. "Nate, every paper in the country's givin' banner headlines to any scrap of information on our missing girl, and that includes every rumor, false hope and practical joke. . . . These publicity-seeking radio hams are jammin' the airwaves with their phony broadcasts!"

"I'm enlisting McMenamy to check with his radio-ham pals," I said. "We'll sort out the pranksters and publicity hounds, and see if anybody else heard what that kid and I did, last night. Anyway, even without that, I got juicy stuff for FDR's enemies in the Fourth Estate."

Harl Smith and his boys were having a go at "Let's Face the Music and Dance."

"Excuse me," Terry said, gently, "but I don't see how this helps Amelia."

Mantz had said almost the same thing, yesterday.

"It doesn't," I admitted. "But it helps me."

"Make a buck?" Mantz asked.

"Sleep at night."

"You really wanna see G. P. get his tit in a wringer," Mantz said with a chuckle.

Terry didn't blink at his crudity.

I took a last gulp of rum and Coke. "Him and the other sons of bitches who put her at risk. . . . Pardon my French."

"I think you're very sweet," Terry said, stirring her drink with a swizzle stick.

"I don't get accused of that, often."

"Amelia's lucky to have a friend like you," she said.

With his fiancée's seal of approval, I figured this was the perfect time to spring it on Mantz.

I slipped an arm around his shoulder. "So, Paul, how about it? Will you come forward, when I'm lining up sources for the *Chicago Tribune*?"

He sighed; his mouth twitched. He glanced across at Terry who was looking at him, carefully.

"Sure," he said. "It might be fun to watch Gippy Putnam twist in the wind."

They invited me to have dinner with them, and I accepted, with no further talk of the Amelia matter. The happy couple shared Chateaubriand, and I tried the Lobster Newburg. Later, as the orchestra played "Where or When," I danced with Terry, who pointed out Mr. and Mrs. Joe E. Brown, Mr. and Mrs. George Murphy, and Marion Marsh with lanky, craggily handsome Howard Hughes, who you may recall was an acquaintance of Robert Myers. Hughes wasn't wearing a tux, either; we had that much in common.

As I was taking my leave of them at their booth, Mantz said to me, "If you haven't picked up your train tickets, Nate, keep in mind I can get you a discount on fares, if you fly United or TWA. You got to come by and drop off the Terraplane at my hangar, anyway."

"No thanks," I said. "I kinda had my fill of airplanes."

Traffic was light as I made my way back toward Lowman's Motor Court, and I wasn't speeding, in fact I was probably poking. My stomach warm and full, I felt a certain satisfaction knowing what I was going to do about Putnam and company. I did believe what Robert and I had heard last night, and had a small sense of relief knowing Amy was alive, though a nagging sense of dread about what she might be going through, a spy in the hands of the Japanese.

So I was surprised, as I loped along North San Fernando Road, when I heard the siren coming up behind me, and my first notion was they were on their way to some emergency. I pulled over to let them pass, but they rolled in behind me, a black patrol car, its side-mounted white spotlight hitting the Terraplane with its blinding beam.

Terraplane idling, I got out, shielding my eyes from the glare but still able to see a cop getting out on either side of the black Ford, the blouses of their dark uniforms bisected by the black leather straps of their holsters, badges gleaming on blouses and flat-crowned caps.

This was a somewhat undeveloped stretch, North San Fernando Road also being Highway 6, scrubby landscape on either side of us. A breeze was whispering through the underbrush; suddenly the night seemed chillier.

"What's the problem, officers?" I asked, meeting them halfway.

Their faces were pale blots; with that light in my eyes,

I could make out no features, but the first voice was older: "Okay, boyo—lean your hands against the side of the car."

I gladly turned my back on the blinding light, heading back to the Terraplane, where I leaned against the sleek curve of a fender, waiting for the frisk. It came. My gun was back in the motel room, which was a good thing, I guessed. I felt my wallet leave my back pocket; my little notebook was in the motel room, also.

"Does this car belong to you?" the second one asked; he was young, or anyway younger.

"No it doesn't."

"You're damn right it doesn't," the older cop said. "This car was reported stolen."

Christ! Putnam. Somehow he got wind I was using Amy's car, and he set me up, the prick.

"This is a misunderstanding," I said, and risked looking back with a small smile. "I was loaned this car."

"That may come as news to the guy you pinched it from," the older one said. "You're going to have to come with us, boyo."

A night in jail loomed ahead. No reason to fight it. Mantz could straighten it out tomorrow morning; this was just Putnam's way of getting back at me.

The older officer took me by the arm and hauled me around; a little rough, nothing special, par for the copper course. I knew enough not to cross him.

"Hey, Calvin," the younger one said, gazing into my open wallet as if it were a crystal ball. "I think this guy's a cop. . . ."

Calvin, still holding onto my arm, snatched the wallet from his young partner's grasp and held it close to his face. "What's this. . . . Chicago Police Benevolent Association? . . . You on the job?"

"I work private now," I said. "I was on the Chicago department for ten years." That was a five-year lie.

I could now make out their faces. The older one had sharp features and dull eyes. The younger one had a bulldog mug that would make a great cop face, in a few years, but right now it looked a little silly.

"Ten years, you say," the older one said. "Why'd you step down?"

"Disability," I lied. With my free hand, I gestured to the arm he had hold of me by. "Took one in the shoulder."

He blinked and let go of my arm as if it were hot. "How'd it happen, son?"

I'd gone from "boyo" to "son"—an encouraging raise in rank.

"Stickup guy," I said, as if that explained it.

They nodded, as if I'd explained it.

The older cop's sharp features softened. "You didn't really steal this car, did you, son?"

"No. It was loaned to me. Like I said."

The two cops looked at each other, then the younger one's bulldog mug wrinkled into a plea of mercy, and the older one nodded.

"Look, friend," the older one said, promoting me again, "this was a roust. We were supposed to haul you in. Keep you busy."

"Why?"

"We don't know." The younger one shrugged. "A guy tipped us you'd be driving down this road sometime this evening, and we been keepin' an eye out."

I jerked a thumb toward the Terraplane. "*Was* this car reported stolen?"

"No," Calvin said, shaking his head, a thumb in his gunbelt. "But the guy said you'd buy the story."

I nodded. "And you'd just put me in a holding cell for a few hours."

"Yeah," the young one said. "And call a number and let this guy know we had ya . . . then again when we let ya out."

Didn't these clowns know they might have been setting me up for a rubout? No self-respecting Chicago cop would do that—for less than a C-note.

"What did this guy look like?"

"Gray hair, dark eyebrows, dark suit," the younger one said. "Medium build, maybe six feet. Respectable-looking."

Miller.

"What did he pay you?"

"Sawbuck each," Calvin said.

Life was cheap in California. I dug in my pocket, but the younger one said, "No! Your money's no good."

I don't think his partner appreciated this magnanimous gesture, but he let it go.

In fact, he said, "We ain't gonna be party to rousting a brother officer."

"Thank you, fellas," I said.

And they tipped their hats to me, walked back to their black Ford, cut the spotlight, and headed back toward Burbank.

A few minutes later, I pulled into Lowman's Motor Court, wondering just what the hell I'd gotten myself into. If Miller was military intelligence, willing to buy off local cops to set me up in some fashion, I needed to head home in a hurry, back to my contacts at the *Trib.* The sooner this was in print, the better.

I didn't remember leaving the lights on in my cabin, and in retrospect you'd figure a guy in my business would be smarter; but the truth is, if I was smart I wouldn't be in my business, and nobody had been parked in my stall, or the two stalls next to mine, which was the last in the row of cabins, so when I stepped inside and found the two guys tossing my room, I was genuinely surprised.

And they were surprised to see me, as after all I was supposed to be in a holding cell in Burbank or Glendale or somewhere. So I froze and they froze. . . .

They were the best-dressed shakedown artists I ever saw, clean-shaven men in their late twenties in dark well-pressed suits with tasteful striped ties and clean collars and flourishes of hanky in their damn breast pockets and lighter-color fedoras with snappy snugged-down brims. The one nearest me was larger, with the blank expression of a college boy on an athletic scholarship; the other one was smaller but sturdy-looking with a blandly handsome face out of a shirt ad. Neither had taken off his coat to search the place, which was turned well and truly upside-down, bed stripped, mattress on the floor, drawers out of the dresser, the couple chairs upended, nightstand lamp sitting on the carpet, my suitcase on the floor, my clothing scattered. They were insurance investigators poking around the aftermath of a tornado.

The dresser, though its drawers were stacked atop each other on the floor, remained upright, and on it were a few key effects of mine, specifically my little notebook and my nine-millimeter Browning.

It took perhaps a second and a half for all of that to register, and another half-second for one of the clean-cut customers—the one nearest me, who'd been thumbing through a Bible withdrawn from the nightstand drawer, perhaps seeking guidance—to lunge at me, straight-arm slamming the door behind me, sealing me within the cabin, and with his left hand, in a blow as casual as it was powerful, slapping me with the Bible.

The Good Book taught me a lesson, sending me to my knees; but I'd learned other lessons long ago, and swung an elbow up into his groin, not once, but three times, eliciting a howl and sending him tumbling back, cushioned by the mattress on the floor, though I don't think it did him much good.

The smaller intruder, his face white and wide-eyed with alarm, was reaching inside his suitcoat and I doubted it was for his card. I was still on my knees—the bigger guy was busy rolling around, clutching his balls and yowling in pain—and my fingers found that Bible and I flung it at the smaller bastard, and its pages fluttered like wings as it flew past him, crashing into the far wall, but startling him enough to send his fedora flying and gain me time to get to my feet, grab the nightstand lamp from the floor, and hurl it at him like a bomb.

This missed him also, smashing into, and just plain smashing, the dresser mirror, but at least it kept the bastard on his toes. The bigger one seemed to be emerging from that fetal ball he'd been rolling around in, and I stomped him in the stomach before charging toward the smaller guy, who was clawing under his suitcoat. If he wanted a gun, mine was right next to him, on the dresser, and when I reached him, I snatched the nine-millimeter in my grasp, shaking off shards of mirror making brittle rain, and whapped the barrel across his face, breaking his nose in a shower of of blood, twin streams of scarlet shooting from his nostrils, and when his hand emerged from inside his suitcoat, he indeed did hold a gun, a short-barreled .38, but it didn't last long, fumbling from his unconscious fingers as he tumbled backward, in a crumpled pile that would do his nicely pressed suit absolutely no good at all.

I turned back to the bigger intruder, who was pushing up off the mattress, a very tough man in a nice suit; his hat had flown off too, his face a mask of the rage that had overridden the pain from my elbows in the nuts and stomp to the stomach. He was digging under his suitcoat and probably wasn't looking for his comb; I pointed the nine-millimeter at his face and said, "Let's play Wild West and see who wins."

Something registered in his eyes, and his hand froze within the coat, and I leaned forward and slapped him with the nine-millimeter, like he'd slapped me with the Bible, and his eyes did a slot-machine roll before he fell backward onto that mattress again.

Something was grasping at my pants leg, and I glanced over my shoulder and down where the smaller guy had crawled over—tears streaming down his face with its shattered nose and blood trailing into his mouth like a dripping scarlet Groucho mustache—and I shook him off, as if he were a dog trying to hump my leg. I pointed the gun down at him and said, "This is my best suit. Get blood on it at your own risk."

He was breathing hard and then he started to choke on the blood in his mouth from his nose. I said, "Shit," and stuck my gun in my belt, reached down and picked him up by the lapels and sat him on the bed's box spring, to help him not strangle on his own blood. I'm just that kind of guy.

The bigger one, asprawl on the mattress, was still unconscious. I removed his gun from its shoulder holster, turning myself into a two-gun kid by stuffing it in my waistband next to my nine-millimeter; then I looked in his inside suitcoat pocket for his billfold. The name on his driver's license was John Smith and he resided in Encino, California; no pictures of a wife and kids, no business cards, no nothing. The other guy, who was sitting there whimpering and snorting blood, didn't protest when I checked out his billfold.

His name was Robert Jones, and he lived in Encino,

too. He also had no wife and kids, nor any sign of being in any sort of business.

A knock came at the door. Had somebody finally noticed the slight commotion? The mild hubbub?

"Yeah?" I called.

The voice was timid, male. "Mr. Heller, are you all right? It's the manager. Should I call the police?"

"No! No, I'm fine."

The timid voice tried for strength. "Mr. Heller, please open the door. I'm afraid I have to *insist*. . . ."

I dug in my pocket for my money clip, figuring a sawbuck ought to pave the way to a little silence. With some luck I could catch a night train to somewhere; a sleeper sounded mighty good right now. Maybe a double sawbuck . . .

I opened the door and William Miller's hand holding a damp white cloth reached out and the overwhelming odor of chloroform accompanied my final thought, which was to wonder if I'd ever wake up again.

Groggy, my mouth filmed with a medicinal aftertaste and the thickness of sleep, with perhaps just a hint of Lobster Newburg, I blinked under the glare of a high overhead light, a conical shaft of brightness that singled me out in a darkened room. For the second time tonight, I was in the spotlight. If this *was* still tonight. . . .

I sat slumped in a chair, a simple metal folding chair, and my hands were free; I ran one of them up over my face and felt the stubble of beard and ran my fingers into my scalp and massaged. My Florsheimed feet were roped to the legs of the chair; another rope looped my midsection, tying me to the chair. I was in the pants of my garbardine suit and in my white shirt, my suitcoat gone, my tie gone. And needless to say, the nine-millimeter and .38 I'd stuffed in my waistband were long gone.

The glare of the overhead lamp made it hard to focus, but gradually I achieved a sense of where I was. Beyond the cone of light I sat within was a vast, cool darkness, but a certain amount of light—moonlight and perhaps electrical light—came from high distant windows. The smell of gasoline and oil and wing dope wafted through the drafty structure. Gradually, dark bulky shapes within the darkness made themselves known, like beasts crouching in jungle night shadows.

A melodramatic response, perhaps, to being held captive in an airplane hangar, but justifiable. I had knocked the shit out of a couple of Miller's cronies and now Miller had me—or someone Miller had turned me over to had me—and the only reason I had any hope of getting out of this alive was that I wasn't dead yet.

Footsteps echoed in the cavernous room, footsteps in the darkness, hollow clops punctuated by gun-cock clicks.

Then I could make out the outline of him, moving out from between the large shapes that were parked aircraft, and finally he stepped just inside my circle of harsh light.

"Forgive the precautions," William Miller said in that mellow balm of baritone.

Again his lanky frame was draped in a dark undertaker's suit, navy with a red-and-white-striped tie. It was hard to see where his gray hair began and the grayish flesh left off. He stood with folded arms, his full lips pursed in an amused smile, but his eyes dark and cold under the black ridges of eyebrow.

"Stand a little closer," I said. "I can't hear you."

He waved a scolding finger my way. "Don't make me sorry I didn't bind your hands, as well. You did quite a thorough job on Smith and Jones."

"Are they military intelligence? Or am I contradicting myself?" My tongue felt thick and my head throbbed with a headache almost as blinding as the glare of the overhead lamp. But I was damned if I'd let him sense that.

Now his hands had moved to his hips. "Are you aware that the FBI has a file on you?"

"I'd be flattered if I gave a damn," I said. "Is that who they were?"

He chuckled. "I understand you once spoke to Director Hoover 'disrespectfully.' "

"I told him to go fuck himself."

The dark unblinking eyes had fastened on me, appraisingly. "You also prevented him from being kidnapped by the Karpis and Barker gang. And I understand, from

Elmer Irey, that you were helpful last year, in the ongoing IRS investigation of the late unlamented Huey
Long's confederates in Louisiana."

"If this is a testimonial dinner," I said, "go ahead and
roll out the cake with the stripper in it."

He began to pace, slowly, measured steps, not ner-
vous, in an arc that traced the edge of my circle of light.
"I also gather that you're a friend of Eliot Ness, that
you aided him on various matters when he was with the
Justice Department and, later, the Alcohol and Tax
Unit."

"Yeah, I'm a regular Junior G-man. You can untie
me now."

"I wouldn't go that far," he said ambiguously. "You're
also a known confidant of the criminal element in Chicago. You left the police department under a cloud, and
you've had frequent dealings with members of the Ca-
pone mob."

"So which is it? Am I a public-minded citizen, or a
lowlife crook?"

His mouth smiled faintly but there was no smile in his
eyes, at all. "That's up to you. . . . You mind if I make
myself comfortable?"

"Please. Come sit on my lap if you want."

Miller chuckled again. "I like your sense of humor.
Very droll."

That was a new word for it.

He stepped outside the circle into the darkness, but
my eyes were accustomed enough to that darkness that I
could make out his movement. He took something from
somewhere and came walking back. Another metal folding chair. He placed it at the edge of the pool of light
and sat. Crossed his legs. Folded his arms. Smiled
meaninglessly.

"You see, we're aware that you're considering going
to the press with what you've learned," he said. "I mention these various aspects of your life and career to show
why we feel you might be willing to cooperate with your
government . . ."

It was out in the open now.

". . . and, if you decline to help, to remind you how

easily we might discredit you and anything you came up with."

I laughed once but it was loud enough to echo. "So all you wanted was to talk this over with me? Is that what your friends 'Smith and Jones' were doing in my cabin? Looking for me? Under my bed? In my suitcase and dresser drawers?"

"Actually, we were looking for this. . . ." And he withdrew from his side suitcoat pocket my little notebook; he held it up as if it were an item on auction. ". . . and anything else pertinent, any other notes or documents you might have assembled."

Then he tossed it to me.

I caught it, and thumbed through. All the pages relating to Amy were missing.

"Everyone you've spoken to, we'll be speaking to," Miller said.

"Tied to chairs?"

His smile broadened. "No. . . . You're really the only one who requires . . . special treatment."

"You forgot the kid gloves."

Now the smile disappeared. "We intend to appeal to the patriotism of these individuals, Mr. Heller. . . . We don't anticipate any problems with any of them. Mr. McMenamy would surely not like to have his ham radio operating license pulled, nor would any of the other buffs who've reported hearing similar transmissions. The Myers youth is . . . a youth. He's unlikely to make a fuss and, even so, who would pay attention? Miss De-Carrie will understand that it was Miss Earhart's wish to cooperate with her government, and will respect the wishes of her employer and friend. Mr. Mantz and Mr. Tisor occasionally work on government contracts and I'm sure will do the right, public-spirited thing."

"Or you'll yank whatever licenses they need to do business. You bastards'll turn me into a Republican yet."

"Mr. Heller, stumbling around in the dark . . ." And he gestured to the blackness of the hangar surrounding us. ". . . flying blind as you have, you've imperiled a top-secret government operation. We are trying as best we can to . . . stage-manage what could become an international incident of such proportions that the next world war could be precipitated."

The volume of his voice had gradually risen; it was now reverberating in the vast chamber.

"And, Mr. Heller, speaking with a certain insider's knowledge of both military and naval intelligence, I can tell you with all honesty and no small regret that your country is at this time in no shape to enter such a conflict."

This was a new one on me: I'd never been accused of almost precipitating a world war, before.

I said, "I'm just supposed to take your word for all this."

Both feet on the floor now, he folded his hands in his lap and tilted forward. "Mr. Heller, the disappearance of Amelia Earhart is big news. But how long do you think the disappearance of a corrupt private detective would sustain the interest of the American people?"

Were there others in the darkness around us? I sensed as much, but couldn't be sure.

I said cheerfully, "Too bad your boys Smith and Jones didn't stop by my motel a little earlier. . . . They might have intercepted that detailed letter I sent my attorney."

He sat back and folded his arms again and the soft mouth formed a sort of kiss. Then he said, "All right. . . . Now we've exchanged threats. Mine is not empty, whereas yours is a fairly pathetic improvisation, but let's treat each other with a little mutual respect, nonetheless. I'll pretend I believe there's a real chance that such a letter exists. And I won't remind you that a blowtorch to the soles of your feet might elicit the truth in this matter and/or the name of your attorney. I won't insult your intelligence in that manner."

"You're a swell guy, Miller. I feel so good with the security of my nation in your principled hands."

"You're a funny one to talk about principles. . . . You forget I've read your FBI file. You have a reputation for looking the other way, when money's involved."

"Then let's see the color of yours."

"An interesting notion, and I don't rule it out . . . but I think in this instance we've gone past your innate avarice and passed into an . . . emotional realm. You see

I'm aware—unlike Mr. Putnam, who is cooperating with us, but knows less than he thinks he does—of your . . . this is delicate . . . *friendship* with Mr. Putnam's wife."

Funny how a guy threatening to torture me with a blowtorch a few seconds ago now felt the need to indulge in arch euphemism.

"I'll tell you this," I said. "I know Mr. Putnam's wife well enough to know that she wouldn't get in bed with the military. She hates war."

"Yes, and she cooperated with us for that very reason . . . and because she and her husband could not get sufficient backing for the world flight, otherwise."

I leaned forward as far as the rope around me would allow. "Why Amelia? Why drag a public figure, a *beloved* public figure, into your dirty business?"

He sighed. "This was a service only she could provide, Mr. Heller. As the most famous civilian aviatrix in the world, she enjoyed an unparalleled advantage: the freedom to fly anywhere in that world, including places where her own country was banned."

I sneered at the son of a bitch. "She was a civilian, and a heroine to America, and you cheapen that into making her a spy? Not to mention putting her life at risk!"

He waved that off. "That Lockheed of hers can outrun any unfriendly plane—and Mr. Noonan is *not* a civilian; he's the anchor of this mission. We did not consider Miss Earhart to be in any danger. Even the Japs would think twice before shooting down Amelia Earhart because she was off course!"

"Off course in a plane whose belly's packed with aerial survey cameras."

That rated a shrug from Miller. "The world would write that off as the Japanese trying to cover up for their ill-advised actions. Which is something the Japs, who are hardly stupid, would figure out for themselves."

"Then what the hell happened? It looks like they *did* fire on her. . . ."

Another shrug. "Just trying to force her down. . . . She did stray off course, after her mission was accomplished. It's unfortunate. . . ."

"You screwed up."

Something like regret touched the impassive features. "Actually, Amelia did. She's not really much of a flier."

"You *knew* where she was, when she was radioing for help. You knew she was down in Jap waters."

He said nothing.

"But you didn't go in after her, did you?"

Now he put his hands on his knees and leaned forward just a bit, as if lecturing a precocious but difficult child. "Mr. Heller, we believe Japan is building military bases throughout the tiny islands of the Pacific. They are forbidden by treaty to do this, but their islands in the Marshalls, Carolines and Mariana groups are closed to 'foreigners' like us. We believe they're fortifying for war, Mr. Heller, violating their covenant with the League of Nations."

"And you want to prove that."

The tiniest shrug. "We at least want to know it. The President has to know, if he's to carry out his responsibility to provide our country with an adequate defense, should the Philippines or Hawaii be attacked."

"Sounds pretty far-fetched to me."

He stood. His voice was firm; though he wasn't speaking terribly loud, echo touched his words: "Amelia agreed to cooperate. She did this in part as a favor to her friend, President Roosevelt. If you make this public, you will not only go against her wishes, but tarnish her image not just here, but abroad."

I raised a forefinger. "Plus start the next war. Don't forget that."

"Your actions may endanger her—might cause her captors to . . . destroy the evidence."

"Execute her, you mean."

"We believe she's alive. We prefer to keep her that way."

"I doubt that. The best thing for you people is for her never to be seen again."

"We're not monsters, Mr. Heller. We're soldiers. But so is Miss Earhart."

I had to laugh. "She'd slap you for that. . . . Did your people hear what Robert Myers and I heard last night?"

An eyebrow arched. "Frankly, no. . . . But various of our ships in the Far East fleet have intercepted coded messages sent by Japanese vessels and shore installations in their Mandated Islands back home to Japan . . . messages that indicate Miss Earhart and Mr. Noonan are indeed in Japanese hands."

"Jesus! Why don't you negotiate their release, then?"

"We can't admit we sent Earhart and Noonan," he said, "and the other side can't admit they have Earhart and Noonan. That is the reality of world politics on this very shaky stage."

I looked at him for a long time, his oval face with its lifeless features, the dead eyes, the soft mouth. Then I asked casually, or as casually as a man tied in a chair could ask, "You just shared top-secret information with me, didn't you, Miller?"

"Classified material, yes."

"That means if I don't cooperate, you're going to kill me."

The mildest amusement puckered the soft lips. "Oh, Mr. Heller . . . I would never do that. You're a citizen of the United States of America, the country I love, the country I serve."

"You'd have somebody else do it."

"Precisely."

I held out my hands, palms up. "These are free because you want me to sign something."

"Perceptive. . . . Yes. It's a contract, actually."

"A contract?"

He withdrew the document, folded lengthwise in thirds, from an inside suitcoat pocket. "A backdated contract. You've been working for the government, in the capacity of investigator. As such, you're subject to a policy of strict confidentiality."

"Really," I said, taking the contract, reading it over quickly, finding it surprisingly simple and in keeping with what he'd outlined. One portion remained to be filled in. "What are you paying me?"

"You've suffered a lot of inconvenience, Mr. Heller, and had considerable travel expense. What would you say to two thousand dollars?"

"I should throw this in your face."

"Have I insulted you, suggesting you take payment to walk away from a matter so personal to you?"

"Make it five."

I agreed to take their money, for two reasons. First, money doesn't know where it comes from, and this foul sum would spend just like money that smelled better. Second, this would convince Miller and those he represented that I would forget what I'd seen and heard.

"You *are* going to try to get her back," I said, as I signed the contract, using my leg as a desk.

"Of course . . . but it will be delicate. It's difficult for a country that denies responsibility to arrange the release of prisoners whose captors deny their presence."

He took the contract from me, then looked sharply into the darkness just over my shoulder and nodded and footsteps came up quickly behind me and a hand reached around in front of me and again a chloroform-soaked cloth masked my face.

I awoke in a private compartment of a train eastbound for Chicago. I found my nine-millimeter in my packed suitcase. Neatly folded in my billfold was a five-thousand-dollar check from the Office of Naval Intelligence. In the inside suitcoat pocket of my blue garbardine, which I wore, was my copy of the contract, with Miller's signature.

Legal and aboveboard.

On July 19, the Navy abandoned its efforts and declared the search for the Electra over. Though intercepted radio messages (never made public) indicated Amelia Earhart and Fred Noonan had been picked up by the Japanese almost two weeks earlier, the Navy used the continuing search as an excuse for continued, expanded reconnaissance of this strategic area of the Pacific. They were not allowed into Japanese-controlled waters, however, though the Japanese professed to be helping in the search.

Ten ships, sixty-five airplanes and four thousand men had scoured two hundred and fifty thousand square miles of Pacific Ocean in a four-million-dollar effort. Not a trace of the Electra or its crew or even a life raft turned up. No oil slick, no scrap of floating debris. Nothing.

One month to the day after the search for Amy ended,

Paul Mantz married Terry Minor in Hollywood's fabled wedding chapel, the Wee Kirk o' the Heather. When the papers covered it, they described Mantz as "technical advisor for Amelia Earhart," and quoted him as saying, "It's time to get on with our lives."

Miller apparently got to everyone I'd talked to, because no one came forward, and I certainly didn't go to the papers.

I was a good American, after all; and anyway, I had no desire to be the government's next disappearing act. But as the days and months passed, I would open the paper each morning, looking for the headline announcing her return. Amy's good pal President Roosevelt wouldn't let her rot in some Japanese jail, would he? An arrangement would be made; some exchange; something that would allow both countries to achieve their goals and the honorable Japanese tradition of saving face.

But the headline never came. Amelia Earhart had vanished from the pages of the papers as completely as she had somewhere over the Pacific. She had flown out of the news and into the pages of history, where she lay prematurely buried.

Dead-Stick Landing

May 6–June 4, 1940

Fourteen

The mural behind the Cine-Gril bar depicted early Hollywood days, Charlie Chaplin, Mary Pickford, Douglas Fairbanks, way back when movies couldn't talk, a dozen years ago. The soothingly air-conditioned lounge was cozy but large enough for a bandstand and postage-stamp dance floor (Russ Columbo's radio show was broadcast out of here) and the lighting was subdued, but not so much so that you couldn't be seen if you wanted to. That ultramodern material, Formica, covered the front of the bar in deep red, with horizontal stripes of chrome and indirect lighting from under the lip of the mahogany countertop. The blue leather and chrome stools were shaped like champagne glasses and I was perched on one of them, sipping a rum and Coke.

I was a little early—the meeting was set for four-thirty, and I'd arrived here at the Roosevelt Hotel, by cab, having arrived by train at the impressive new Union Station on North Alameda around three. Checking in, washing up and slipping into my Miami white suit, black-and-white-checkered tie and black-banded straw fedora, I'd ambled through the pale chamber of the impressively decorative, Spanish Colonial-style lobby trying to inconspicuously spot movie stars among the potted palms, plush armchairs and overstuffed couches. I'd made several trips to Hollywood—including one late last year—and my pals at the Barney Ross Cocktail Lounge and the Dill Pickle deli always looked forward to my blasé rundown on any Tinseltown somebodies I'd set eyes on. The joke was the few starlets, would-be matinee idols

and low-rent agents clustered here and there, chatting—
not a seat taken, no one wanting to be seen "waiting"—
were sneaking peeks at me, not realizing I was nobody.

The first person in Hollywood I recognized was in the
movies all right, but most tourists wouldn't have known
his name any more than his Gable-mustached, nearly
handsome face: Paul Mantz—in a single-breasted hunter
green sport jacket with gathered waist and double-patch
pockets, a yellow open-neck shirt, and light green
slacks—sauntered into the Cine-Gril, put his hand on
my shoulder, ordered a martini in a frosted glass from
the black-jacketed bartender and then said hello.

Other than a touch of gray at the temples and perhaps
a slight further receding of his hairline, Mantz looked
the same: dark alert eyes, familiar cocky set to his thin
mouth and jutting jaw.

"How's married life?" I asked him, as he stood next
to me, not taking a stool.

"Much better the second time around," he said. "I'm
a dad now, you know."

"No, I didn't," I said. I'd had my own ruminations
over fatherhood since I'd seen him last. "Congratulations."

"Well, two kids were part of the package," he said,
accepting the frosted martini from the bartender, finally
sliding up onto a stool. "Terry was Roy Minor's widow,
y'know, the racing pilot? His kids, good kids, Tenita and
Roy Jr., are mine, now . . . but Terry and me have our
own boy—Paul Jr. He'll be two in August."

"Hope business is good, with all those mouths to
feed."

Half a smile dimpled one cheek. "Real boom in war
pictures. The country may not wanna get into this scrap,
but they sure like to see it at the movies. Also, test
flights and aerial camera jobs for Lockheed. Charter service is doin' great, including a branch in San Francisco—
set up two amphibians at the Golden Gate Expo and
flew thousands of gawking Midwest bumpkins like you
over the fair. Oh, and the Vega crashed—ground accident, I was fully covered."

"No more *Honeymoon Express*?"

"Oh, sure, but it's a Lockheed Orion, now. You keepin' busy?"

I shrugged. "Retail credit, divorce work, a little industrial espionage now and then."

"Industrial spying? You doin' it, or stoppin' it?"

I let him have half a smile. "I'm a priest to my clients, Paul. Don't expect me to violate a sacred trust."

"Unless there's a buck in it. . . . Don't look so hurt."

"That was acting," I said. "When in Hollywood. . . . What can you tell me about this little business conference?"

He swirled his martini in its glass. "What have they told you?"

"Not a damn thing. Margot DeCarrie called, asked if I'd come out here and listen to a business proposition; she offered train fare, two nights' lodging and meals, plus a C-note and a half for my trouble and other expenses."

"And that's all she told you?"

"She said she represented the Amelia Earhart Foundation. Does that mean she's working for Purdue University?"

"Naw. Purdue set up the Amelia Earhart *Research* Foundation, but that was active only when Amelia was alive."

"You think she's dead, Paul?"

He didn't quite look at me. "Probably. I think she probably crashed into the sea. She bit off more than she could chew, Noonan missed the island, she was tired, and tried to land too high over clear water, or misjudged the distance and flew into a heavy roller. Either one would've killed them instantly."

I didn't tell him what I knew; the confidentiality clause in the agreement I'd signed with Uncle Sam precluded that. In fact, according to the terms of my contract, I hadn't even been in California in 1937.

"But 'probably' isn't 'absolutely,' is it, Paul?"

He nodded, gazed into his martini, as if an answer might be floating there. "She was a great lady," he said. "It's hard to let go."

"Is that what this is about?"

"I should leave the particulars to the others," he said. "Margot and the rest'll be here soon enough."

"This, uh, Amelia Earhart Foundation. . . . Does G. P. have anything to do with it?"

"Hell no!" Mantz's chuckle was edged with bitterness. "Not with me involved."

"You two were never exactly bosom buddies. Do I detect a further deterioration in the relationship?"

He sipped the martini. "Amelia and I were involved in several businesses, including my charter service. But we both signed a contract that gave the surviving partner the entire business. Gippy, as executor of the Amelia Earhart Estate, is suing for half, just the same."

I frowned. "How the hell can there be an estate? Doesn't it take seven years to be declared legally dead, anymore?"

Mantz raised an eyebrow. "Not if you're married to Gippy Putnam. I don't know what kind of strings he and his lawyers pulled, but Amelia's been legally dead since late '38, I think, or early '39. Gippy's been screwing over Amelia's mother and sister, too, makin' sure they don't get a share."

"He always was a classy guy."

"Well, he's scramblin' for dough. The estate was smaller than you'd think, at least that's what I hear. They had a lot of their own money tied up in the world flight. I heard he had to sell the house in Rye; the book 'by' Amelia, about the last flight, got rushed out but didn't do so hot. You do know he remarried, don't ya?"

"No!"

My response seemed to surprise Mantz, who shrugged and said, "Got a good amount of play in the papers out here."

"Not in Chicago. Remarried . . ."

Mantz was nodding. "Last year about this time, to a good-looking brunette who got a divorce from a successful lawyer in town—one of these Beverly Hills housewives who hit the garden club circuit. I hear Gippy picked her up at one of his 'Amelia' lectures . . . that's how he's makin' most of his money these days."

"Didn't take him long to get back in circulation."

"Hey, just a few months after Amelia disappeared, he

went off on one of his 'expeditions' and took this *other* good-lookin' gal along for company. . . . They say he was shacked up with her for months, after they got back from the Galapagos or wherever the hell. Till she got sick of his browbeating and foul temper."

"Jeez, Paul—you turned into a regular Hedda Hopper."

That made him smile. "Hey, I figure you might enjoy the dirt on Gippy, since you love him about as much as I do."

"Maybe more," I said.

"Ah," Mantz said, swiveling on his stool, "here's our little party now. . . ."

In a white frock with a cardigan collar and white buttons down to the navy and white polka-dot sash that served as her belt, pretty Margot DeCarrie had just entered the Cine-Gril, and behind and on either side of her were two well-dressed gents who each carried the unmistakable air of the business executive.

Margot—brunette hair longer now, a sea of curls nestled under a white beret—beamed upon seeing me; her cutie-pie heart-shaped face, its babyish mouth turned cherry red by lipstick, not to mention her Betty Grable frame, would have been the envy of many a starlet, white high-heel pumps doing nice things to her bare, untanned legs. She was hugging a patent leather bag under one arm, a small briefcase in her other hand.

"Nathan, it's so wonderful to see you," she said as she approached; some of the chirpiness had matured out of her voice. "Paul, I'm glad you could make it. . . . Nathan, this is Elmer Dimity, the manufacturer and inventor."

This was said as if I was supposed to recognize the name, so I said, "Oh, yes."

Dimity was solidly built and rather tall, in a dark suit whose lapels were trimmed with scarlet suede, and his scarlet tie bore a diamond stickpin, an ensemble that sent a mixed message of austerity and flash, solemnity and goofiness. His dark hair was combed back, his face a long oval, his nose a beak dropping over a small, indecisive mouth, his chin rather weak as well; but the eyes behind the wire-frame glasses were strong and alert, and his expression was open, friendly.

"Heard a lot about you, sir," he said, in a somewhat high-pitched, clear voice.

We shook hands and there was power in it, but no showing off.

Dimity picked up the introductions from Margot, gesturing to the other man, saying, "And this is James Forrestal, late of Wall Street."

"Make it Jim," Forrestal said, stepping forward to present a small hand for me to shake. His grip tried a little too hard to impress.

He was much smaller than Dimity, and in fact was shorter than Margot, yet his frame was slimly athletic within a pinstriped vested gray serge suit with four-in-hand black-and-gray-striped tie, apparel that made no allowance for the Southern California weather.

"And I'm Nate," I said.

Forrestal's spade-shaped face had a combative Irish look, dominated by the flattened nose of a pug; but his features otherwise reflected business-executive restraint: intense blue-gray eyes, thin lips compressed into an uncompromising line, and a ball-like cleft chin. His iron-gray hair was cut short and swept neatly back.

His small hard eyes appraising me, Forrestal asked, "Are you a Jewish fella, Nate? You don't mind my saying so, you have an Irish cast."

"So do you, Jim," I said. "My looks are my mother's fault. The name's my father's, but he wasn't raised Jewish and neither was I."

"Were you raised in your mother's faith?" Forrestal asked. "Are you a Catholic, then?"

Margot and Dimity were clearly embarrassed by this line of questioning.

"No, Jim," I said. "I'm afraid I'm not much of anything. The only time I pray is when I'm in a jam, and then it's pretty nondenominational."

"Like most people," Mantz said with a nervous chuckle.

"I'm not a religious man myself," Forrestal said, rendering our conversation even more oblique.

Mantz gestured toward the grill, which was sparsely populated this time of day. "Shall we find a table?"

Soon, our drink orders placed, we were gathered at a

red Formica-topped table, settled on chrome-tubing chairs along a beige-drapery-flanked wall of mirrored Venetian blinds that allowed us to watch the world pass by along Hollywood Boulevard; Grauman's Chinese was just across the way, that grandiose pagoda with movie star foot- and handprints at its gates, the mysteries of the East Americanized into a tourist mecca. I sat near the window with Mantz beside me; Forrestal was directly across from me, his gaze unnervingly steady, Dimity next to him. Margot sat at the head of the table, facing the mirrored blinds.

She tented her fingers—the nails of which, I noticed, were the same cherry red as her lipstick—and began: "As I'm sure you know, Nathan, Mr. Dimity . . ."

"Elmer," he interrupted cheerfully. "I can't be the only 'mister' at the table."

"Well," Margot said, touching his hand, "I'm going to call you Mr. Dimity because you're my boss. . . . And Mr. Dimity *is* my boss, Nate, and a wonderful one—I'm working full-time for the Amelia Earhart Foundation, as executive secretary."

"This little whirlwind is our *only* full-time employee," Dimity added. "And the only person on the payroll. I'm the chairman of the board, and strictly a volunteer. Jim here is a board member, though he's asked not to have his name on the letterhead, so that there's, uh . . . no misunderstanding."

That was provocative; but I let it go for the moment.

"Mr. Dimity is also *founder* of the Foundation," Margot said proudly.

"Swell," I said, getting a little weary of this mutual admiration society. "What is it?"

"The Foundation?" Dimity asked. "Well, our mandate is to 'inspire the study of aeronautical navigation and the sciences akin thereto.' "

"Ah," I said, as if that had answered it.

A white-jacketed waiter brought us our drinks. Actually, I'd held onto my rum and Coke, but Mantz was onto a second martini. Dimity had ordered a Gilbert, Forrestal a whiskey sour and Margot a stinger.

Then Dimity jumped back in: "But our primary objective is to conduct an expedition to clear up Amelia's disappearance."

"An expedition?"

"Yes. We hope to send a search and rescue team to the Pacific to discover whether our friend is still alive, and if not, find an explanation to the mystery of her disappearance."

I couldn't tell them what I knew, which was that to find Amy, going into Japanese-held taboo territory would be a necessity.

Instead I merely said, "That would be extremely expensive."

"Yes, we know," Dimity said, and sipped his Gilbert. "Tens of thousands of dollars, which we intend to raise. I'm not the only friend Amelia had in business and industry, and in the higher echelons of society and finance. We already have the blessing of Amelia's mother, and of course Mr. Mantz here, and the President and Mrs. Roosevelt."

The latter surprised me. Why would the government sanction an excursion into its most embarrassing, top-secret impropriety?

I played a hunch. "Uh, Mr. Forrestal . . . Jim. What does that mean, exactly—'late of Wall Street'?"

He lowered his whiskey sour and his mouth tightened into a slash of a non-smile. "I recently resigned as president of an investment banking firm, Dillon, Read and Company."

"And what are you doing now?"

Forrestal's smile froze and he waited several long seconds before replying, "I'm with the administration."

Knowing, I asked, "What administration would that be?"

"The Roosevelt administration." He took another sip of the whiskey sour, perhaps to provide time to see if his answer would be enough to satisfy me; my gaze was still on him, so he finally added, "I'm, uh . . . an administrative assistant to the President."

"Sort of a troubleshooter."

"You might say."

"And you flew here, from Washington, D.C., to take this meeting with me?"

"I had several other meetings here, but yes, primarily. The President, and particularly Eleanor, were close friends of Amelia's, and they are wholly supportive of the Foundation's efforts."

Even if they didn't want their man's name on the Foundation letterhead.

"I take it, then, Jim, that you were also a personal friend of Amelia's . . ."

"I knew G. P. and his wife, yes. We traveled in something of the same social circles, in New York."

Smiling innocently at Dimity, I asked, "And you, Elmer? You have a great passion for this cause, obviously. What was your connection to Amelia?"

But it was Margot who answered, leaning forward, reaching past Mantz, to touch my hand. "That's what I started to say, before I got off the track. . . . I thought you knew, Nathan, that Mr. Dimity was one of Amelia's closest friends and business associates."

"No I didn't," I admitted.

Margot continued: "Mr. Dimity developed a training unit for parachute jumpers. . . ."

"It's a two-hundred-foot tower," Dimity interjected, "with a safety line attached to a standard parachute harness. Designed primarily for military use. Amelia helped me out by taking the first public jump from one of my towers."

This was ringing a bell. Amy had told me that after G. P. had left Paramount, and needed some cash flow, he'd involved her with several publicity campaigns for a parachute company; she had also fondly mentioned the well-intentioned owner of the firm, who had become a supporter and something of a hanger-on.

"Amelia helped me gain public attention for several other of my aeronautics inventions," Dimity said, then had another taste of his Gilbert. Behind the wire frames, his eyes were distant with memory, his voice soft as he said: "I owe much of the success of my company to that kind and generous lady."

"Well, I know you didn't pay my way out here to ask me for a contribution," I said, which got a chortle out of Dimity and a smile from Margot. Forrestal's reaction was only a little less expressive than a cigar store Indian's. "And adding my name to your membership board sure won't gain you any prestige."

"We have a job for you," Dimity said. "We are probably at least a year away from mounting our expedition, hiring a ship and crew. . . . This is no idle effort, Nate, it's my intention to go along, and Miss DeCarrie feels the same way. Having Amelia's personal secretary aboard will lend our expedition credibility."

This was starting to sound about as credible to me as launching an expedition to the Island of Lost Boys to look for Peter Pan.

"Of course," Dimity was saying, "this assumes that all goes well with fundraising."

"An opportunity has arisen," Forrestal said, joining in belatedly, his whiskey sour glass empty, "that may help the fundraising effort."

"Have you heard of Captain Irving Johnson?" Dimity asked me.

"No."

"Or perhaps, Captain Irving and Electa Johnson?"

"Them either."

Margot said, "Captain Johnson and his lovely wife, when they're not sailing around the world, are active on the same lecture circuit as Mr. Putnam . . . the sort of places Amelia used to speak."

"And they talk about sailing around the world, I gather."

"Yes," Margot said. "They have a schooner."

"Isn't that what you serve German beer in?"

"No, Nathan, it's a big sailing vessel . . ."

"That was a joke, Margot. The, uh, Johnsons is it? Sail around the world, and then they go on a lecture tour; then they sail some more, and repeat the process?"

"Yes," she said, a little embarrassed.

"They write books together," Dimity said, "and perhaps you've seen their articles in the *Geographic*."

"My subscription just lapsed," I said.

Captain and Mrs. Irving Johnson were part of the adventuring and voyaging fad that had turned Amelia Earhart into a star, the same public fascination for exploring that had made G. P. Putnam and his instant books successful, and public figures out of Lindy, Admiral Byrd, Frank Buck and the rest of that hardy bunch.

Forrestal said, "Captain Johnson and his wife are out on a world voyage right now."

"But they are willing to divert from their cruise," Dimity said, "to accept a two-thousand-dollar commission from the Foundation. For four weeks, Captain Johnson will sail the Gilbert and Ellice islands. It is our hope that he will discover enough new information about the Earhart disappearance to fuel our fundraising efforts for a full expedition."

"That might be helpful," I admitted. "Do you want me to run a full background check on the captain, and make sure he's not just some con man?"

"Captain Johnson is quite reputable," Forrestal said.

Mantz said, "I've heard of this guy, Nate. Johnson's on the up and up."

"What we want," Dimity said to me, "is for you to go along."

"Me? Do I look like a sailor?"

Forrestal said, "Yes. But that's not the point."

"Nate," Dimity said, "I need a representative on that ship. Someone who can make sure the captain does his job, thoroughly earns his two thousand dollars. . . ."

I said to Mantz, "I thought you said he was on the up and up."

Dimity pressed on: "I can't, in good conscience, spend the Foundation's meager funds on a preliminary expedition without sending along a representative of our group."

Shaking my head, I gulped down some rum and Coke and said, "You know, I don't speak a whole lot of South Sea Island languages."

"You've survived in the Chicago jungle," Forrestal said.

"Nate," Dimity said, "I need a man who's physically and mentally tough. You *knew* Amelia . . ."

There was that past tense again.

". . . and you know the right questions to ask. If by chance, some delicate or dangerous situation arose, you could handle yourself . . . or so I've been told by those I've spoken to."

"Why don't *you* go?" I asked Dimity.

His expression mingled chagrin and regret. "I can't leave my business for a month. . . . We'll pay you twenty-five dollars a day and all expenses."

"That would wind up costing you close to a thousand bucks," I said. "The Foundation got that in its coffers?"

"No," Dimity admitted. "I'm paying for this myself. I can afford it."

"I don't think so."

"I certainly can!"

"I don't mean I don't think you can afford it, Elmer. I mean, I don't think this is a job for me."

He frowned and said, "I will guarantee you one thousand dollars."

"It isn't the money," I said, and for a change it wasn't. I didn't think the government would want me taking part in this, not after they bought me off and had me sign that agreement. But on the other hand, fucking Forrestal was sitting across from me. . . .

"Why don't you sleep on it?" Forrestal suggested.

"Yes, Nathan," Margot said, "you have two nights paid for here at the hotel, and your train tickets don't take you back till Wednesday. We can meet for lunch tomorrow."

I considered that.

Then I said, "All right. I'll sleep on it. But I'm warning you, Elmer, Jim . . . Margot. I don't think I'm your man."

"Fair enough," Dimity said, smiling as though I'd already accepted the job.

"I need to be going," Forrestal said, and he rose.

Everyone else at the table got to their feet too, and I shook Forrestal's hand—oddly, his grip was damn near limp, this second time—and he flinched me his tight non-smile and left.

Dimity said, "I need to get going, as well. Margot will contact you about time and place for luncheon tomorrow."

"Fine," I said, shook his hand, and he strutted out.

Mantz, Margot and I sat back down.

"That guy thinks 'no' is a three-letter word," I said.

"He's devoted to Amelia's memory," Margot said ad-

miringly, apparently not recognizing the death sentence
of her words.

Mantz put a hand on my shoulder and said, "Hey, I'd
invite you to the house tonight, but I'm afraid Terry and
I have plans. You think you can find supper in this town,
by yourself?"

"He doesn't have to be by himself," Margot said. "I
don't have plans."

I looked at the cute kid with her cherry-red lips and
bright blue eyes. "That's pretty brazen. You gonna twist
my arm if I spend the evening with you?"

She laughed, and it was nicely musical; brunette curls
bounced under the white beret. "We'll swear off any
discussion of the subject. No Amelia Earhart Foundation. Not even any Amelia Earhart."

"Okay," I said. "It's a date."

Fifteen

Margot, it seemed, lived in a Roosevelt Hotel apartment, which also served as the Foundation's Hollywood base; the official office was in Oakland, home of Dimity's company.

So around seven I met her in the lobby. I was still in my white linen suit but Margot had slipped into an elegant little black bengaline dress with puffy three-quarter sleeves and no cleavage but nicely form-fitting, and brother was it a nice form. Her turban and gloves were that cherry red of her lipstick, and so were the toenails peeking from the open-toed black patent leather pumps.

"Ever been to Earl Carroll's?" she asked, looping her arm in mine.

"No. Can we get in without reservations?"

"Mr. Dimity has a membership; we're guaranteed seats. I just hope you won't forget about me, with all those pretty girls around."

"I don't think there's much chance of that," I said, drinking in the smell of her. Since we first met, she'd switched from soap to Chanel Number Five.

Hollywood Boulevard was bathed in dusk, that time of day movie people call "magic hour," giving neons a special glow, muting colors, coolly air-brushing the handiwork of God and man much as gauze over a camera lens plays Fountain of Youth for an aging actress. We joined the parade sauntering along the celebrated Boulevard, a good-looking couple getting admiring looks from tourists and locals alike, Grauman's Chinese across the street, then Grauman's Egyptian on our side of the

street, high-tone department stores and lowly five-and-
dimes, exclusive shops and postcard parlors, and when
we turned down Vine, we soon saw the Brown Derby,
not the one shaped like a hat, but the rambling Spanish-
style affair with a neon derby riding stilts on the red clay
tile rooftop while below a gaggle of fans with autograph
books in hand waited to waylay celebs at the canopied
entrance.

Earl Carroll's topped them all, starkly modern in its
geometric grace, no pillars for this pastel green palace,
rather vertical shafts of white neon. Like Grauman's
Chinese, movie star autographs in cement were on display, not at your feet, but right in front of you, on the
outer wall, CARY GRANT, GINGER ROGERS, BOB HOPE,
JIMMY STEWART, ROSALIND RUSSELL, dozens more,
stretching to the sky, where to their right a haunting
electric visage loomed, the face of a beautiful woman, a
graceful Art Moderne rendition, ivory neon brushstrokes
against the building's jade, her head tilted enigmatically
above the impresario's neon name, the arc of her cha-
peau outlined with the blue-electric words THROUGH
THESE PORTALS PASS THE MOST BEAUTIFUL WOMEN IN THE
WORLD. I ushered my beautiful woman under the blush
of pink and blue and yellow lighting and through the
chrome entryway, into a foyer that wasn't much—just a
black patent-leather ceiling, columns of pastel light, a
gilded streamlined statue of a nude goddess, and a stair-
case so wide and grand it might have risen to heaven,
not the men's and ladies' rooms.

The rose plush-carpeted dining room/auditorium, its
walls green satin-draped, wasn't any larger than a couple
airplane hangars, seating for a thousand on half a dozen
terraced areas with pink table settings and matching
chairs under a ceiling that appeared at first to undulate
with gracefully curving fringed curtains but on closer
look consisted of thin tubular stripes of blue and gold
neon fluorescence, which seemed to lead into a similar
curving curtain of fringed light above the stage, feeding
into thirty-foot light columns on either side.

Margot and I sat alone at a table for four, with only
a row of banquet-size tables between us and the foot-
lights. The apparel for men ranged from my own fairly

casual white linens to tuxedos, though most of the women wore fancy evening wear, wanting to compete as best they could in a theater whose stage show, "Broadway to Hollywood," starred nary a Cantor nor a Jolson, but "60 of the Most Beautiful Women in The World." The joint was packed, though our terrace nearest the stage was perhaps only two-thirds full.

"Members of the Lifetime Cover Charge Club are always guaranteed a seat in the inner circle," Margot explained, sipping another stinger.

We'd finished dinner, which—despite a menu courtesy of Chef Felix Ganio "of the Waldorf-Astoria"—was just adequate. But how could a mere filet mignon measure up to thousands of feet of neon and the promise of sixty showgirls?

"What do they pay for that privilege?" I asked.

"A thousand dollars. . . . Mr. Dimity's status here has been very handy, wining and dining potential Foundation members."

We had both already broken our promise, several times, not to discuss the Amelia Earhart Foundation. We had also established that Margot was between boyfriends and that she was having the time of her life, hobnobbing with famous people and helping Amelia's "cause."

Actually, quite a few famous people were seated around us: Mantz's charter customers Gable and Lombard, Tyrone Power and Sonja Henie, Jack Benny and his wife Mary Livingston, Edgar Bergen without Charlie McCarthy (but with a lovely blonde), all seated at various tables of larger parties otherwise consisting of people I didn't recognize.

Okay, I was a little impressed. But famous folk occasionally wandered through the cowtown I called home, and I'd done a job for Robert Montgomery out here last year, an impressive, classy guy; but most movie actors were, like George Raft, smaller than you'd think, with off-screen dialogue that didn't exactly sparkle.

What even a thick-headed former cop like yours truly was starting to figure out was that I, too, was being wined and dined for the Foundation's cause; and I was starting to wonder if cute, curvy Margot was part of the package. And if you think any of that would stir indignation in my breast, you haven't been paying attention.

A nattily attired, almost skeletally thin, delicately handsome gent who might have been Fred Astaire but wasn't was winding through the inner-circle crowd, smiling, joking, shaking hands with the celebrities who seemed delighted, even honored, by his attention.

"Who is that?" I asked Margot.

"That's Earl Carroll himself," she said.

Carroll and his *Vanities*, of course, had been the chief rival to Florenz Ziegfeld's *Follies* in its Broadway heyday. The *Vanities* had gone nuder than the *Follies*, and showman Carroll was frequently in trouble with the law; he was notorious and flamboyant in a fashion that explained the admiration flowing from the Hollywood royalty at his tables.

"He's coming this way," Margot whispered.

"You're Nate Heller!" he said, as if I were a celebrity too, his smile as dazzling as it was insincere.

"Mr. Carroll," I said, and we shook hands, "nice little hole in the wall you got here."

His strong-jawed face had a surprising sensitivity, his cheekbones high, gray-blue eyes piercing, his dark, slightly graying hair combed way back; he smelled of lilac water, smelled better than a lot of showgirls I'd dated.

He sat next to me, leaned in chummily. "We make Broadway look provincial, don't you think? Got anything in Chicago that compares?"

"Not sober. How long you been open?"

He looked up at his glittering neon ceiling. "Year and a half. You know, I was on the verge of bankruptcy when I called every last one of my markers in, to make this place a reality. Now I'm back on top."

"Well, congratulations. How is it you happen to know who the hell I am?"

A tiny smile drifted across his lips. "You're sitting in my inner circle, aren't you? Listen, I just wanted to make sure you and your lady friend have a good time this evening. I wanted you to know you're welcome . . ."

And he slipped his arm around me.

". . . and if this little morsel you're with doesn't work

out," he whispered into my dainty ear, "just let me know if you see something in the show that appeals to you . . . and it's always good to have a second choice if an item is sold out."

He rose with a sly wink, handing me his card; I slipped it in my pocket, as he continued along his glad-handing way. What was this son of a bitch, my guardian angel?

Margot, smiling like a pixie, leaned across the table and touched my hand with a gloved one. "What did that devil whisper to you?"

"He was hoping I could talk you into trying out for the chorus," I said.

She blushed; it was legendary that Carroll's showgirls had to audition in the nude. "No, really. . . ."

I ducked the question with my own: "Carroll wouldn't happen to be a member of the Foundation, would he?"

Her eyelashes fluttered. "What makes you think that?"

"Well, he's a flier, isn't he? A pilot."

"How do you know that?"

"Remember when he landed a plane in the middle of New York? It was in all the papers."

"Oh, yes," she said, as if having to recall, "he landed in Central Park, in the middle of winter."

"That publicity hound makes G. P. look subtle."

"Mr. Carroll *is* a great admirer of Amelia's," she admitted, somewhat embarrassed.

"Hey, it's okay," I said, and patted her hand. "I used to be a Chicago cop. I thrive on bribes."

The show was an eye-popper. The sixty showgirls, who sang well and handled patter nicely, flitted about floating platforms and revolving stages, near nudists in feathers and sequins, sometimes to classy numbers like "The Blue Danube," courtesy of Ray Noble's Orchestra, and other times in more traditional burlesque fashion.

One running gag had shapely brunette headliner Beryl Wallace (Carroll's girlfriend, Margot told me; no doubt one of the "sold out" items) fleeing from a comic, first in a negligee with the funnyman flashing scissors, later in a hula skirt with him pushing a lawnmower, finally in tin pants with her pursuer wielding a blowtorch.

But spectacle and yards of near nudity were the hallmark, as when the sixty babes displayed themselves on one hundred feet of stairs. I was terribly distracted, watching this buffet of blondes and redheads and brunettes, knowing I could call their boss and select one or two or three; it ruined the damn show for me. I like to think if I pick up a showgirl for a cheap one-night fling that my boyish charm had something to do with it. Call me old-fashioned.

Maybe that was why I turned a little morose on the walk back. Margot looped her arm in mine as we strolled through the Boulevard's valley of bright lights, a streetcar clanging its unsophisticated way down the center, occasionally.

"What's wrong, Nathan?"

"Aw, nothin'."

"I think I know."

"Yeah?"

"You think I'm trying to use you."

That made me smile. I came to a stop and she took my cue and I faced her. The night was alive with headlights of passing cars, brand names outlined in neon, searchlights announcing the premiere of a major motion picture, or maybe the opening of a drive-in barbecue stand. I gathered the small, shapely creature in my arms, the slick material of her dress slippery under my touch, and I kissed her.

It was sweet and it was real.

"I've been wanting to do that for a long time," I said.

"I've been wanting you to," she admitted, her eyes dancing with reflected light.

"I just had to make sure."

"About what?"

"That you were as sweet a kid as you seem to be."

"Am I?"

"I'm not sure I care now," I said. "Let's go back to our hotel."

She snuggled against me as we walked, and I was deciding whether to take her to my room or try for hers, when she said, "Do you ever wonder?"

"Wonder what?"

"If . . . if she had it."

"Had what?"

"The baby. Your baby."

I stopped again. We were in front of the Egyptian Theater with its white columns and looming color caricatures of Egyptian deities. "You sure know how to kill a mood, kid."

"I'm sorry." Her lower lip was quivering.

I put an arm around her shoulder and walked her along. "No, I don't wonder about that at all," I lied, and led her to the hotel and inside, and soon we were stepping into an elevator, which we had to ourselves. It was one of those automatic jobs, no operator. I pushed my floor button, 7, and she pushed hers, 11. Lucky numbers.

"You want to come up?" she asked, perkily hopeful. "We can order coffee, maybe some cake or something, from room service. . . ."

"I don't think so."

"Are you mad at me?"

"No. And I'm gonna hate myself in the morning. But I'm tired. And you're just too sweet a kid."

She slipped her arms around me and kissed me softly, tenderly. "You're so romantic. . . . You still love her, don't you?"

"The problem is," I said, "you still do."

A little bell announced my floor. I touched her face and said, "See you tomorrow, kid."

"Maybe breakfast?"

"Sure," I said, stepping into the hallway. "Breakfast."

And the doors began to close over that cute mug, the cherry-red lipstick a little mussed, and before she was gone, she waved like a child. I sighed and dug my handkerchief out and rubbed the gunk off my mouth. Just me in the hallway. No Margot. No Earl Carroll girl. Of course, I did still have that card. . . .

I worked the key in the door and had it open only halfway when I saw him, sitting in a wooden armchair next to an open window in the small, modernly appointed hotel room, a book in his lap. Thoughtful of him, letting in that gentle breeze whispering the sheer curtains, because otherwise my room would have reeked of the smoke from the pipe clenched in his teeth.

"Took the liberty of making myself at home," Forrestal said, mouth flinching that non-smile around the stem of the pipe. He hefted the book; the jacket said: *To Have and Have Not.* "Took the opportunity to catch up on my reading—it's this fellow Hemingway's latest. Little raw for my tastes."

"I'm afraid I'm a *Police Gazette* sort of guy myself," I said, closing the door behind me.

"I have to ask you to forgive my rudeness," he said, taking the pipe out of his mouth, rising, tossing the book on my nearby dresser with a clunk. He still wore the same suit and tie as this afternoon, but it looked as crisp as if he'd just put it on. "There are matters we need to discuss . . . privately."

Suddenly I was glad I hadn't brought Margot back to my room. This little man with the broken nose and stiffly dignified air represented President Roosevelt, or least that was what I'd been told. But there was something ominous about all this.

"Oh-kay," I said, and sat on the edge of my bed near the foot, where on the luggage stand my suitcase rested. "Why don't you sit back down, Jim, and we'll talk."

He waved a hand dismissively. "Not here. . . . Mind if I use your phone?"

"My room is your room."

He flinched another non-smile and went to the nightstand and used the phone, speaking to the desk, asking for an outside line. His back was to me, perhaps so I couldn't catch the number he dialed; I took the opportunity to slip my nine-millimeter out of the suitcase, and into my waistband, buttoning my suitcoat over it.

"Yes," Forrestal said to somebody. "He's here. . . . He'll speak with us, yes."

He hung up and turned to me and said, "We need to take a little ride."

I gave him a smile that didn't have much to do with smiling. "Those aren't friendly words in Chicago. Not in my social circles, anyway."

He chuckled, as he relighted his pipe with a kitchen match that he flicked to flame with a thumbnail. "I assure you this is a friendly ride . . . and, uh, you won't be needing that weapon."

"Nothing much gets past you, does it, Jim?"

"Nothing much."

"Me, either. You *aren't* armed." I stood and patted my coat over where the gun was tucked. "I'll just keep this with me. It's not polite to go to a party without bringing a little something."

He shrugged, as if it mattered not a whit to him, and brushed by me, on his way out. I'll be damned if I didn't follow him, into the hallway, onto the elevator.

And we rode down, his eyes on the floor indicator, he asked, "Pleasant evening with Miss DeCarrie?"

"Swell. Plus, Earl Carroll gave me the pick of the litter."

"Really." That seemed to almost amuse him. "You pick a pup?"

"Night is young."

Soon we were standing at the rear of the hotel, the loading area adjacent to the parking lot, which was fairly full. It was approaching midnight, and the brittle mildly drunken laughter of a pair of well-dressed couples accompanied them from a cab that deposited them, and they stumbled past us in furs and jewelry and black tie to the stairs up into the hotel, perhaps calling it a night or heading to the Cine-Gril.

A minute or so passed and a black Lincoln limousine with a leather-covered roof and white sidewalls rolled in, pulling in front of us, like something out of a Rockefeller's funeral. The rear windows were curtained. From where I stood, I couldn't see the driver.

A Roosevelt Hotel doorman stepped forward and opened the rear door for us; Forrestal gestured for me to step in first, and I stepped over the running board and inside. Seats faced each other in the rear of the limo, with a gray-curtained division window providing privacy from the driver; the interior was spacious and dark leather and seated way over to the left, by a gray-curtained window, was William Miller.

"Sorry for the hugger-muggery," Miller said in his radio announcer's baritone, bestowing me a bland smile. As always, he wore a dark suit; his tie was so dark a red it was nearly black, too. But then, what would a hearse be without an undertaker?

I sat across from Miller while Forrestal slid in beside him.

"You never quite sound like you mean it," I said to Miller, "when you're apologizing to me."

Miller's feminine lips kissed me a little smile. "That must be why I'm not attached to the diplomatic corps."

The limo began to move. We were taking a tour of Hollywood with our curtains closed.

I sat with my hands on my knees. "Let me start off by saying what a swell job you government boys have done negotiating Amelia's return."

Forrestal was still smoking his pipe; its pleasantly pungent aroma was creating a minor fog. He and the lanky Miller made a Mutt and Jeff pairing, albeit a somber one. These guys were a lot of laughs. Like a barrel of monks.

Eyes hard and cold under the ridge of black eyebrow, Miller said, "The Japanese steadfastly deny any knowledge of the whereabouts of Miss Earhart or her plane."

"You left out Fred Noonan."

A tiny shrug. "So I did. How tactless. Or Noonan, either."

I shook my head, grinned. "Somehow I can't buy Uncle Sam backing Elmer Dimity's sailboat safari. What's really going on here?"

"We would like you to accept the Foundation's commission," Miller said.

"What, to keep an eye on them?"

"Not precisely. The Navy has long since conducted a thorough search of the Gilbert and Ellice Islands; Captain Johnson's efforts there are almost certainly destined to be redundant."

I gestured over at Forrestal. "Hey, you can ask your pal Jim, here—I didn't tip Dimity and Margot that their skipper'd have to get into Japanese waters, to make their time and money worth spending."

Outside, the occasional sound of a band playing in a nightspot provided sporadic background music for our conversation. With the frequent honk of a horn and general traffic sounds, my guess was we were gliding down the Sunset Strip.

"I appreciate your discretion," Miller said. "You've

honored your contract with us. . . . In fact, I'm here to bring you back into the service of your government."

I shook my head, no. "They haven't passed the draft *yet,* bud. . . ."

Miller leaned forward ever so slightly. "Nate, the information we have is limited . . . our intelligence in the Japanese-held sectors of the Pacific is sketchy and secondhand, to say the least. But we have reason to believe Earhart and Noonan were picked up either by a fishing boat or a launch from a battleship." A slight bump in the road sent him leaning back into his cushioned seat. "There's been speculation that they have been transferred to Tokyo, but our best educated guess . . . aided by some very indirect intelligence . . . convinces us she's being held on an island called Saipan."

"Never heard of it," I said.

The black ridge of eyebrow lifted in a facial shrug. "Few in America have. It's a jungle island in the Western Pacific, in the Marianas chain, fifteen miles long, five miles across at its widest point. The Japs have a 'development corporation' there, Nan'yo Kohatsu Kaisha. They specialize in sugar production, operating three plantations growing sugar cane, and two mills producing crude sugar."

"Isn't that sweet."

We seemed to be at a stoplight.

"Not really. We believe Nan'yo Kohatsu Kaisha is largely a front for military construction. We know they have a small seaplane base at Tanapag Harbor, and believe they're building airstrips all around the island. Saipan is only 1,250 nautical miles from Tokyo, potentially the most important supply base and communications center for the Central Pacific."

"And this is where you think Amelia and Noonan are being held?"

Forrestal got into the act. "There's a military prison on the island. We believe that when war comes, and it will, Saipan will likely become headquarters for Jap military operations in that part of the Pacific."

I blew out some air. "For having sketchy intelligence, you fellas know a lot."

Things had quieted down outside the limo; perhaps we were rolling through a residential area now.

"Not really," Miller admitted. "Except for a few details that we will in time share with you, you already know damn near as much as we do."

"Then why are you so convinced Amelia is still alive?"

Forrestal responded to that one, the small dark eyes fixed on me like gunsights. "She would be a valuable propaganda pawn to the enemy, in the early days of the inevitable war . . . as evidence that we committed acts of espionage, of war, against Japan during peacetime."

"Also," Miller said, "she'd make a valuable prisoner for them to swap, should we have any Japanese envoy or ambassador or prominent citizens in our hands, after open hostilities begin."

Forrestal was nodding. "And these are among the reasons that we would like to extract Miss Earhart from Japanese hands, before the war begins."

"Why the hell didn't the Japs tell the world they had her in the first place?" I asked. "And embarrass us *then*?"

Somewhere a dog was barking.

"Amelia Earhart is a beloved figure around the world," Miller said. "That admiration, particularly among young women, crosses all borders. That means the Japs would have to release her, at some point."

I frowned at this logic. "Even if they painted her as a spy?"

Miller gazed at the gray curtained window, as if he were taking in the scenery. "I believe so. And therein lies one of the reasons they've held her, and it's a time-honored one: she knows too much. She knows the nature and the extent of the military build-up by the Japs in the Pacific, particularly on Saipan, if indeed she's being held there. Acts of war that she could and no doubt would report."

A nasty thought formed and I reluctantly expressed it: "Then why haven't they quietly killed her and buried her on that hellhole?"

"Because of the factors we mentioned before," Miller said with a small, inappropriate smile. "Her propaganda value, her worth in a prisoner exchange . . . but also there's the wealth of aviation knowledge in her mind. What she and Noonan know about the Electra."

Forrestal frowned at Miller. "I don't believe it's necessary to get into that."

"Into what?" I asked. "If you want my cooperation, gentlemen, you'll need to be as forthcoming as possible. I have one motivation here: getting Amelia back from the Pacific where you lost her."

Forrestal shook his head, no, but Miller sighed and said, "One of the reasons we know she's alive . . . or at least why we know that she was kept alive, for a time . . ."

Forrestal gripped Miller's arm. "Bill, no."

Miller lifted Forrestal's hand off, as if it were something distasteful that had landed there, and gave him a smile that was really a frown; then his face turned sober as he looked at me and said, "The Japanese fighter plane is known as a 'Claude' . . . also as a 'Zero.' A well-designed, successful plane, particularly up against the Chinese, who were notoriously lousy pilots, by the way. But the Claude, the Zero, has had, chronically, a drawback . . . it's inclined to crash."

"Yeah," I said, "I'd call that a drawback in an airplane."

"This is due to its underpowered engine. That's one of the things, I believe, that's prevented Japan from moving against us, up till now."

I was in over my head, but I asked, "What is?"

"Our aircraft far surpass theirs . . . to go up against us, they needed to improve the handling and the rate of climb, in their fighter planes. A company called Mitsubishi has been developing the new Zero. . . ."

"I'd prefer you didn't continue," Forrestal said to Miller, petulantly.

"Christ . . . I think I'm ahead of you." I sat forward. "By sending Amelia and her 'Flying Laboratory' into enemy territory, we handed those bastards a schematic for a better plane!"

Miller nodded once, almost a bow. "You are a perceptive individual, Mr. Heller. A true detective. Our intelligence reports indicate that the new Zero incorporates many of the Electra's best features . . . retractable landing gear, double radial engine, automatic carburetor, and the embarrassing list goes on."

My brain reeled. "You're telling me we handed the Japs the specs for a plane they can use to *invade* us?"

Outside, silence, the limo moving through sleeping streets.

Miller shifted uncomfortably in his comfortable seat. "Worse than that—we managed to do that by way of *Amelia Earhart's* plane. And, to add to the potential embarrassment and crushing indignity that implies, very possibly they've induced her to share her knowledge of that aircraft with them."

"What, she's working *with* the Japs?"

Miller blinked several times, a fairly rare occurrence. "She may have felt somewhat . . . misused by her government."

"Oh, really? Whyever would she think that?"

He ignored the sarcasm and gave me a straight answer: "Because she wasn't made aware of the flight over Japanese waters until the very last minute."

That fit the Myers kid's story of what he'd heard on his Philco, Noonan handing Amy an envelope with a change of "flight plan."

"What did she think the cameras in the fuselage bay were for?" I asked Miller. "Home movies?"

He held up two hands, as if in surrender. "We told Miss Earhart—and it was absolutely true—that her mission was to take reconnaissance photos over Italian-held Eritrea's military and commercial airfields . . . at Massawa, Assam and Asmara."

"Where the fuck is that?"

Forrestal reared back slightly, as if offended by my harsh language. Fuck him.

"Africa," Miller said. "I met her personally at Darwin, Australia, and took home the film she'd shot up to that point."

"Yeah, and handed Noonan his new secret orders behind Amelia's back. Hell, if I was her, I'd be drawing blueprints of the White House for those Japs."

And I let the gray curtain up next to us, to show them what I thought of their secrecy. The palm trees of Beverly Hills were gliding by, a tropical dream in the moonlight.

Miller only smiled the meaningless smile. "No you wouldn't. . . . Are you going to help us?"

I snorted a laugh. "If Amelia's stuck in some military prison on . . . where?"

"Saipan."

"Saipan . . . then what the hell good does it do me to go along with Captain Johnson on his wild-goose chase through the What's It Islands?"

"That's only your cover, or at least part of it. You need to understand the high opinion we have developed of you, where your special . . . qualities are concerned."

"Gee, thanks."

"You're good with your fists, you're good with a handgun, you're smart, resourceful, and you know the ins and outs of this delicate situation as no other civilian does."

"If you're looking to head up my fan club, Miller, there's an opening."

"In addition, you have a personal stake here, by way of your . . . relationship with Miss Earhart. You need also to understand that, while a private citizen, Captain Johnson is also a Naval reserve officer."

"So you've recruited him, too."

"In a word—yes. He'll help you prepare your reports for Dimity's Foundation, as if you'd been with the Johnson cruise all the while."

That got my attention. "What do you mean, as if?"

Miller's baritone was calm, soothing; he'd missed his calling—he should have been a hypnotist. "You'll only go partway with Johnson, Nate," he was saying. "You'll really be working for us, for the Office of Naval Intelligence, not 'Dilly-Dally' Dimity, as we call him . . . though you can keep the money he pays you, which we intend to match with our funds. This adventure should prove as lucrative as it is interesting."

"Why do I think I'm going to be signing another contract?"

"Because you are," Miller said, leaning forward to pat me on the knee. "You see, we've arranged a separate expedition for you . . . to Saipan."

Sixteen

I sat on a netting-shaded cement verandah, sipping a rum and Coke, outside a Quonset-hut "hotel" rented by the Navy to Pan American Airlines. The naval base on this scruffy, hot, humid island—Guam, the sole U.S. territory in the midst of the Japanese-controlled Marianas islands—was on Commar Hill, where the evening had turned out surprisingly cool. The floor show consisted of small, cat-eyed, long-tailed lizards chasing flies in the pools of light that spilled here and there from our corrugated-tin Hilton.

"Geckos," William Miller said.

"Excuse me?"

"That's what those little lizards are called." Miller, in a white short-sleeved shirt and dark trousers, was stretched out on the deck-style chair next to mine. He was smoking a cigarette and the cool salty breeze was turning the blue smoke into a native girl's hula.

"I've seen bigger lizards," I said. I was dressed almost identically, except my trousers were a light khaki.

He allowed me a faint smile. "The rest of the *Clipper* passengers will be taking off at four A.M. You get to sleep in till five."

"Are you going on with them to Manila?"

He shook his head, no. "I'll stay here at the base and wait for your return."

"I like your optimism."

"You'll make it."

"And if I don't, the government saves a grand or so."

He dropped his cigarette to the cement floor, reached

out his foot and ground it out. "Is there someone you'd like to see get that money?"

I had given him sarcasm; he'd given me a straight, if sobering, answer.

"No," I said. And wasn't that a sad goddamn thing? Didn't that say something about the state of my affairs? The only person I could think of to bequeath my riches to was somebody who might or might not exist, a child that Amy may or may not have had on an island where she possibly was, or possibly wasn't.

He glanced at his watch. "Johnson should be here for our little chat, shortly. He and his crew are eating over at the Navy mess."

We had eaten, and well, on the *Clipper*. The famed flying boat had lived up to its storied reputation. We were served our steam-cooked meals by the steward on tables with white linen cloths, china, silver and water goblets (no liquor was served) in a lavish, spacious lounge where the ten passengers sat in roomy, well-padded seats facing each other, five abreast. A second passenger compartment, aft, served as a sort of game room, with wicker chairs at tables for cards or checkers. Another cabin, further aft, converted to sleeping berths, but we only used them on the first leg of the flight, from San Francisco to Honolulu.

That first leg had seemed endless. The *China Clipper* had lifted off from the Alameda seaplane base on San Francisco Bay on a beautiful afternoon, accompanied by only the gentlest breeze. Sunshine had glistened off the hull and wings and prop blades of a white, red-trimmed four-engine ship that seemed at once sleek and ungainly, its wing riding atop the fuselage like a perfectly balanced teeter-totter. Once the lines had been cast off, we'd made several circles on the bay, warming the engine up, before surging forward, only barely flying at first, under the heavy burden of fuel, finally gaining altitude, cruising into an afternoon that stubbornly refused to let go of the day.

Many hours later, when darkness finally sheathed the ship, the *Clipper* settled in between layers of cloud and cruised along. My traveling companion, William Miller, wearing a dark suit and dark blue tie, to add a festive touch to our flight to the tropics, pointed out to me that we were flying a route charted by Fred Noonan.

"Isn't that reassuring," I said.

Dawn took its time arriving, too, and out a window, at breakfast, I spotted the familiar shape of Diamond Head; the last time had been from the deck of the ocean liner *Malolo*. And after only twenty and a half hours, we were landing at Pearl Harbor to a typically flower-strewn welcome. Meanwhile, the *Clipper* was loaded up with staples of the island Naval bases—crates of fresh fruit and vegetables, mostly—while limos with Pan Am drivers escorted the passengers to the Royal Hawaiian Hotel for a leisurely evening of dining and dancing and the sight of Oahu's starry purple sky, golden moon, ebony ocean and white breakers. Then dawn slapped us back to reality and we were soon aboard the *Clipper* for the easiest leg of the trip, the mere 1,380 miles to Midway.

The entire briefing for my mission took place in hotel rooms, along the way, and of course the passenger cabin of the *China Clipper*, over the four days of flying. Only ten passengers were aboard—me, Miller, and four wealthy couples, two from New York, one from Los Angeles, one from Dallas—the little California to Hong Kong six-day jaunt, after all, cost $950, one way, one tickee. The cabin soundproofing was remarkable, allowing conversation in a normal, even hushed, voice.

So Miller and I sat apart from the paying customers and played endless games of checkers—which ended invariably in deadlock—while the government agent filled me in on my distressingly detailed cover story, suggested plans of action and various routes of escape. At no time was anything hand- or typewritten given to me; everything, like a pill, was administered orally.

"That saves us the annoying necessity of having to eat the papers," Miller said, and I was never sure whether he was kidding. Probably not. A sense of humor didn't seem to have been among his government-issue materials.

Out the window occasionally I'd spot one of the many little islands that we seemed to be following like bread crumbs to the atolls of Midway, where a beautiful lagoon waited for us to touch down. Waiting too were attentive white-uniformed Pan Am staff at the landing float with its long, pergola-style deplaning dock. A brick walkway led to a sprawling white-pillared hotel, its two wings spread like open arms, gathering us up into a sanctuary of Simmons beds, bathrooms with hot showers, classy lounges with wicker furniture and tasty exotic meals served by white-uniformed native stewards.

On the spacious verandah that evening my bosom pal Miller sat with me as we watched an unruly surf crash upon the encircling reef, and observed bald-headed, turkey-looking birds that would run crazily along the beach, flapping their wings in takeoff, invariably nosing over in a feathery flurry of a crash landing in the sand. Most of my fellow passengers found this endlessly amusing. Takeoffs that wound up in crash landings were never my idea of a good laugh.

"Gooney birds," Miller told me. "In fact, some people call Midway itself 'Gooneyville.' . . . They're really Laysan albatrosses."

"Is that something I have to remember? If so, I'm really glad that one wasn't written down; I'd hate to have to swallow the definition of a gooney bird."

"No," Miller said humorlessly. "You needn't remember that."

So of course I did.

The next day's hotel, at Wake, was almost identical to the one at Midway, but the island itself was a barren, cruelly tropical atoll that had been home to hermit crabs and nasty rats and not humans, until flying boats like the *Clipper* had come along. It was a world with no fresh water, shade or harbor, a wind-blown bevy of scrubby sand dunes. For recreation we were offered air rifles and the chance to go rat hunting. I passed.

The cliff-bordered harbor at Guam had been arrayed with Navy warships and a few freighters. A small yellow bus with a small yellow driver had taken us along a scenic coastal road, dotted with big beautiful poinciana trees bursting with red blossoms. It was almost enough to make me forget about Wake; but my stomach was unsettled, and scenery, barren or bountiful, had nothing to do with it.

My *Clipper* cruise among millionaire tourists was coming to an end; I wouldn't even have my warm and won-

derful friend William Miller at my side, before long. I
would be embarking on what might charitably be called
an adventure, what more realistically might be termed a
fool's errand, and what most likely was a suicide mission.
Two thousand dollars, give or take a buck, half from the
Foundation, half from Uncle Sam, was all I would haul
to shore; good money, in these Depression days, but
only if I lived to spend it.

Why the hell was I doing this?

It was a question I had asked myself over and over
again, on the various legs of this journey; and the answer
was Amy. Amy and what she had told her flighty secretary, in confidence, about a possible child on the way.
Whenever I had looked out a *Clipper* window at shimmering Pacific waters, I knew why I'd come. It was waters like these she'd disappeared over.

Now, on a verandah in Guam, outside a Navy Quonset
hut, I took a last swig of my drink and looked out
toward the ocean. By *Clipper*, Saipan was only an hour
or so away. But I wasn't going by seaplane.

Miller was on his feet and so was I. We had been
joined by a singular physical specimen in a light-blue
denim shirt with rolled-up sleeves, darker denim trousers
and white rubber-soled shoes. Leathery tan, his sun-
lightened brown hair cropped short, he regarded us
through the narrow slits his eyes hid behind, the strength
of a slenderly hawkish nose offset by a shyly boyish
smile. His bull neck led naturally into a massive upper
torso, then tapered to a wasp waist; his wrists were small
but his hands were big, blunt and powerful—he extended
one to Miller and they shook.

"Skipper," Miller said, "good to see you again. This
is your passenger."

"We don't normally take on passengers, Mr. Heller,"
he said, without having to be told my name; his voice
was a New England drawl. The boyish smile was still
alive as he held his hand out.

"This is Captain Irving Johnson," Miller said, as Johnson and I shook. His grip was firm but not obnoxious.
"Pull up a chair, Skipper. Can I get you something to
drink?"

Easing into a wicker settee, he said, "Maybe a lemonade." I must have reacted to that, because Johnson said, "I run a dry ship, Mr. Heller. No drinking, no smoking, either . . . hope that won't be a problem."

"Not at all, Captain. I understand your crew pays *you.* That's a neat trick."

Miller had stepped away to summon a steward to get Johnson his lemonade.

Johnson's shy smile settled on the left side of his face, as he said, "My bride and I've come up with an interesting way of living. . . . We go out for a year and a half, sail around the world having the time of our life, with a crew of young people who pay us for the privilege."

"If I'm not out of line asking, what do you charge these amateur adventurers to play Barnacle Bill?"

"Three thousand dollars per."

I let out a slow whistle. "You turn rich boys into slightly less rich men."

He shrugged. "We make sailors out of them. Standing watch day and night, steering, handling sail, rigging, even sailmaking. Everybody works, which is why you'll be an exception."

"Hey, I'm just thumbin' a ride—and I appreciate the favor, though it seems like an awful risk for you."

Miller was back, joining Johnson on the settee. "The skipper here is generally regarded as the best all-around schooner master on the seas."

"I don't doubt that," I said. "But sailing into Japanese waters . . ."

Johnson leaned back, a knee locked in his palms. "We'll drop anchor outside Saipan, beyond the three-mile territorial zone."

"Who's going to take me in?"

"I will. And Hayden, my first mate . . . he's no rich kid, he's a real sailor."

I glanced at Miller. "Who am I on this ship?"

"You're Nate Heller," Miller said. "The skipper has told his boys that, should anyone ask, you were along for the full four-week cruise of the Gilbert and Ellice Islands."

"Captain," I asked, "is your crew aware this is a government mission?"

"They are," Johnson said, nodding. "They know none

of the particulars, just that we're doing the red-white-and-blue a favor. They're good kids, obviously from good backgrounds, and can be trusted."

I looked at Miller again. "This sounds a little free-wheeling to me."

Miller's shrug was barely perceptible. "We'll have a talk with the boys at the first available moment."

A native steward brought Johnson his lemonade. The skipper nodded his thanks to the man, and sipped at the tall cool glass. "You can have them briefed at Nauru," Johnson said to Miller.

"Frankly, Captain," I said, "I'm surprised you're out in these waters with your boatload of silver spoons, considering what's going on in this world."

Geckos were chasing flies; catching and eating them, too, in those spilled circles of light.

"I was worried the war might dog our tracks out on the high seas," he admitted. "And I have my wife and two young sons with me, after all. . . . Maybe the time has passed for carefree sailing into the world's faraway places."

Or maybe, like Amy, he was a well-known civilian with a handy, credible cover for reconnaissance.

I tossed a nod back toward the tin-hut hotel behind us. "It certainly hasn't stopped millionaires from taking pleasure cruises."

"My schooner is not the *China Clipper*, Mr. Heller," Johnson said, the smile turning wry. "You're stepping into the past when you set foot on my deck. The *Yankee* was sailing the North Sea before any of us were born."

And in the Guam harbor the next morning, anchored among the warships and freighters, the *Yankee* indeed looked as if she had sailed out of the past into a harsher, less pleasing present, this majestic white-hulled schooner, nearly a hundred feet long, like a pirate ship of good guys, as the American flag painted on her bow attested.

My travel bag in one hand, with the other I shook hands with Miller, dockside, and he asked, "Any final questions?"

"Yeah. What do you mean, 'final'?"

And he actually laughed. "Good luck, Nate."

"Thank you, Bill," I said, and meant it. He had

worked hard, preparing me for this mission. He was one cold son of a bitch, but then I was a smartass bastard, so who was I to talk?

Captain Johnson, at the wheel, invited me to stand beside him as we cast off and glided out. Brown-as-a-berry rich kids scurried around his deck in shorts and no shirts and no shoes, as he called out to them, "Foresail! . . . Mainsail! . . . Forestaysail! . . . Jib! . . . Maintopsail! . . . Fisherman staysail!" One by one they were set, then finally a massive square sail dropped from the yardarm, and a triangular one rose above it, thousands of square feet of sail, a skyscraper of canvas.

"Spend much time at sea?" the Skipper asked.

"Does Lake Michigan count?"

He laughed. "On Lake Michigan, do you run into swells two hundred yards from crest to crest?"

"Well, Chicago *is* the Windy City. . . . I've had some ocean voyages, Skipper. I think I can survive one day of this."

And one day was all my tour of sea duty with the *Yankee* would amount to: a long day, ten hours, and after sundown, we would drop anchor and spend the night, so that come morning Johnson and his first mate could row me to the next stop on my itinerary: Tanapag Harbor. Saipan. The town of Garapan.

In the meantime that long day did prove a restful journey into a simpler time. It was a sunny day with a warm breeze, the ship sailing steadily along, the ocean shimmering with sunlight. The boys—and two pretty girls in their twenties were along, too, which considering the dozen young men aboard made for interesting arithmetic—began the day ambitiously, scraping and varnishing the teak trim, splicing ropes and lines; the two girls, a blonde (Betsy from Rochester, New York) and a brunette (Dorothy from Toronto), were sewing canvas covers and mending sail. By afternoon, the barechested sailor boys and the two girls in shorts and boy's shirts were sprawled here and there on the deck, bathed in sun, or reading in the shade of dinghies.

Belowdeck had a warmth due to more than the sun streaming through the skylights; painted ivory with varnished teak trim, the big main cabin had built-in upper and lower bunks on either side. Down the middle was an endless teakwood table where, between meals, cards were played, books were read, letters written. In the forward galley, Fritz the cook (one of the few crew members getting paid) made the most of powdered milk, canned butter and wax-coated eggs. Lunch was particularly memorable—turtle stew with curry, baked beans, fried onions and johnnycakes.

Watching these young people work and play was a reminder of life's little pleasures. Johnson's wife Electa, Exy to one and all, was a compact curvy blue-eyed blonde in a blue-and-white-striped top and blue shorts, and who could blame Johnson for running off to sea in her company? She spent much of her time with her two young sons, a two-year-old and a four-year-old, who nimbly navigated the deck, balancing on forebooms, bouncing on sails.

"They're fearless," I said to her.

Exy's smile was a dazzler. "The *Yankee*'s their home. They never lived anywhere else. . . . You're in their back yard."

The two kids had their own cabin below, down the hall from the Captain and Mrs. Johnson's cabin, the engine room and bathroom. There was also a double stateroom for Betsy and Dorothy, who may just have been two more of the "boys" on this trip but nonetheless did not make use of the main cabin's dormlike bunks.

I had been assigned my own bunk, for my one night aboard the *Yankee,* six and a half feet long by three feet wide, thirty inches between my thin mattress and the slats of the bunk overhead. The wall next to me was bookshelves, as was the case with every bunk, and the main cabin had an entire wall devoted to books. This was a well-read, and often-reading, crew, reflecting the hours they had to kill, and their good breeding.

The ship's first mate, Hayden, a tow-headed, long-legged, sinewy middle-class kid from New Jersey, twenty or so, passed along the skipper's orders with an offhanded ease. Sometimes, seasoned sailor that he was, he seemed to be acting as an interpreter between Johnson and the rich kids playing sailor. Of course, some of these "kids" were in their late twenties and early thirties. The wealthy crew included a doctor, a photographer, a radio expert and a guy who knew his way around the ship's diesel engine. Even so, Hayden had the respect and obedience of them all.

The young man had a serious mien but an explosive smile, and was devoted to Johnson. Thinking about what was coming tomorrow morning, I decided to look for a chance to talk straight with Hayden about what he was getting into.

After a turtle-steak supper, the crew gathered on deck to see what kind of sunset God had in mind for them. The sea turned a glaring red, and the water danced with phosphorescence, as if an underwater fireworks show was, going on. The childlike joy on the faces of these pampered, hardened mariners as they leaned at the rail was both touching and a little sickening. Life wasn't this simple, anymore. These were Depression times; war times. They were hiding, out here in the open. But who the hell could blame them?

Betsy, the blonde from Rochester, kind of sidled up next to me as we studied the sunset; she had a freshly scrubbed soapy smell that reminded me of Margot, B.C. (before Chanel), and her hair was a mop of curls almost as cute as her blue-eyed, apple-cheeked, lightly lip-sticked mug.

"Everyone says you're a mysterious government agent," she said.

"Everyone's right," I said. "Particularly the mysterious part."

"It's too bad. . . ."

"That I'm mysterious?"

"That you're not going to be on the *Yankee* except just tonight. That isn't very long."

"No it isn't. Isn't that a shame?"

She licked her lips and they glistened. "Terrible. . . . Want to sit with me downstairs?"

Her hand locked in mine, and she led me through the deckhouse down the companionway to the main cabin, where I sat with her at the table, getting dirty looks from at least six of the rich sailor boys. We talked a little about my being from Chicago and how she hated Rochester; she also hated the all-girls schools she'd attended. Under the table, she rubbed her leg against mine.

After some guitar playing and folk-song singing, the crew headed for their bunks at eight o'clock. Betsy waved and smiled and went off to her cabin with Dorothy, giggling.

I lay in my bunk for about an hour, sorting through the memorized information Miller had fed me, an actor going over his lines, feeling the same sort of butterflies in my stomach, and it wasn't seasickness. A little after nine, I swung out of the bunk and padded up to the deck, where the breeze had turned cool with a kiss of ocean mist in it. I knew that kid Hayden was standing watch and this would be my chance for a word alone with him.

The young man was stretched out on his back in a dinghy, ropes for his bed. His hands were locked behind his head, elbows winged out; bare-chested, in shorts, legs long and gangly, he was studying the starry sky with wide-eyed expectation.

"You always stand watch on your back?" I asked him.

"Mr. Heller," he said, sitting up, his voice a breathy second second tenor. "Is there a problem, sir?"

"Naw. Just thought I'd see if you wanted some company. Eight o'clock's a little early to hit the rack for this Chicago boy."

He swung out of the dinghy, bare feet landing lightly on the deck; he was aware that every movement up here was conveyed below, where the others slept.

"Would you like some coffee? I have a pot in the skipper's deckhouse."

Soon we were sitting on a bench on deck, sipping coffee from tin mugs, contemplating the stars scattered on a cloudless, richly pastel blue sky shared with a sickle-like slice of yellow moon. It was unreal, like an imitation sky in a Hollywood nightclub.

"The skipper says you're a real sailor," I said to the lad, "which I take to mean you're not paying three grand for the fun of sailing around the world."

"I wouldn't mind having three grand," he reflected. "I'd buy my own ship. No, I'm getting paid, one hundred a month. Johnson didn't want to pay me anything, you know, said the experience of a voyage around the world would be pay enough. But I drove a harder bargain."

Words tumbled out of this kid's mouth without modulation, dropping off at the end of the sentence as his breath gave out. It was as if he were issuing the words to float before him for review.

"Yeah, you really held his head under the water on that deal," I said.

He regarded me with steady eyes, his smile turned a sardonic shade rare in one his age. "The lure of this life isn't money, Mr. Heller. It's the utter simplicity."

"Your skipper's taking in a pretty penny for sharing this simple life with these spoiled brats."

"Well-heeled vagabonds, I call them. You see, that's why I'm probably destined to be a mate, not a master. Johnson doesn't have to deal with just the ship, but with the land—finance, lectures, photographs for the *Geographic*. He's practical. I'm romantic. He's tolerant. Half the time I want to toss these rich babies overboard."

"They love you, you know."

A grin blossomed. "Well, I pride myself on treating them harshly, and they thrive on the punishment. Maybe it'll make men of them . . . if the war doesn't do it first."

The world, by way of the ocean, stretched endlessly before us, seeming empty, nicely empty. No people.

"It is coming," I said, "isn't it?"

"Oh, it's here. It's everywhere . . . back home they just won't admit it."

The gentle rolling of the ocean beneath the boat was lulling. The lapping of water splashing against the hull made a sweetly percussive music.

I asked him, "Do you know what you're getting yourself into tomorrow?"

A smile twitched; he was gazing out at the waters. "I know where we're taking you."

"It's a risk that isn't worth a hundred a month."

"The skipper asked me to go along, and I'm going."

"For what it's worth, I'm tellin' ya, take a pass. There's a motor on that dinghy; Johnson can take me by himself."

"No, I think I'll go along."

"I thought you liked the lure of the simple life."

"I do. But I like things lively, too." He laughed, but it came out more like another word: Ha. "You know, the skipper seems immune to the finer things . . . tobacco and booze and these island girls."

"He has a pretty wife."

"Exy's a princess, but me, I'd leave her home." He sipped his coffee, stared out at the moon's yellow reflection on the ocean. "This one time . . . we'd been sailing west and north of Tahiti . . . we lay to at a quay in a lagoon near Raiatea. This broad-beamed copra schooner draws up alongside—with a cargo of beautiful girls. Twenty of them or more, lining the rail nearest our ship, clinging to the rigging. Ravishing creatures."

"You run across boatloads of babes out here frequently, do you?"

He shook his head. "Regretfully, no. This was a charter out of Papeete, a planter named Pedro Miller, friend of Nordhoff and Hall's."

They were the authors of the bestsellers about the mutiny on the *Bounty* and its aftermath.

"They invited us aboard . . . wine, music, laughter, dancing. I met this black-haired girl who did this grass-skirt dance. . . . I was walking with her into the village when I glanced back and noticed the skipper standing on the *Yankee* deck, near the wheel, arms crossed, Exy sitting on a skylight. Wonder what he was thinking?"

"Probably that he was going to get laid, too, but not have to worry about South Sea Island crotch rot."

He bellowed a laugh, then suppressed it, not wanting to wake anyone below. "You're a cynical one, aren't you?"

I put a hand on his shoulder. "Hayden, you may think *you're* a romantic . . . but right now you're looking at the biggest romantic sap in the South Pacific."

He put a hand on my shoulder. "Well, I'll be with you tomorrow . . . and my pistol will be under a tarp at my feet."

"Let's hope you can keep it there."

His eyebrows lifted as he cocked his head and grinned at me, and nodded in agreement. Then his eyes narrowed in good humor. "Say, uh . . . I see Betsy took a shine to you."

"Yeah. Cute kid."

"You always been this irresistible to women?"

"Just lately." I stood; stretched. "Think I'll go below. Wake me if a schooner of native girls stops by."

"Okay . . . but I don't think you have to worry about catching the creepin' crud from Betsy."

"Oh?"

"She's a nice girl, but a tease. She's got half the crew crazy over her and is the cause of more cases of blue balls than you can shake a stick at."

"That's an image I'd rather not linger over, kid. G'night."

"G'night."

As I was coming down the companionway, there she was, cute Betsy, waiting on the steps; she wasn't in her nightclothes—still the shorts and a loose-fitting boy's shirt that she bobbled under.

"Sit with me," she whispered. "And talk."

I was tired, but I sat, on the stairs; she snuggled next to me, wanting to be kissed. So I kissed her, all right. I put my tongue in her mouth and one hand on her soft full left breast and another on her rounded rump and she pulled away, wide-eyed, and said, "Well! I never . . ."

"That was my impression," I said.

And she jumped to her feet and bolted down the stairs and disappeared into her cabin.

The next morning, after breakfast in the main cabin, I emerged from the bathroom in my dark suit with clerical collar and received bemused looks all around, particularly from Betsy. She sat before her plate of powdered eggs and fried potatoes with her eyes as wide as a pinup girl's, and I leaned in and kissed her cheek, and whispered, "Bless you, my child."

There was laughter 'round the table, but good-natured, though Betsy flushed and hunkered over her eggs. I thanked the crew for their hospitality and friendship, and kissed Exy on the cheek, too, and ruffled the hair on the two tykes' heads.

From the deck of the *Yankee,* the island that was Saipan was a vague shape in the distance, but rising at its center, like a green peaked hat floating on the sea. Another island could be seen as well, off to the right, smaller, flatter.

"That's Tinian," Johnson said. He wore a navy blue, anchored skipper's cap, white shirt with rolled-up sleeves, loose brown trousers and white deck shoes. He pointed toward Saipan. "That anthill in the center of things is Mount Tapotchau, fifteen hundred feet of her." Then he traced the horizon with his hand. "The coastline here on the western side is almost completely fringed by reefs, except for the mouth of the bay. Few years ago the Japs dredged a deep-water channel to the shore, to improve the anchorage. You'll see some good-size ships in that harbor."

Hayden was on the other side of me, but his eyes searched not the horizon but the sky, which was as gray as cement. "I've seen prettier days," he commented.

Tiny brown shapes were moving away from the island. Boats?

"Sampans," Johnson said. "Okinawan fishermen. They'll travel for days, looking for flocks of terns, meaning schools of sardine and herring are nearby. And that means bonito and tuna."

"That's a relief. I thought it was the Jap armada."

"Not yet," Johnson said with the faintest smile. "Not yet."

Soon we had set off in the dinghy, Captain Johnson minding the motor, with Hayden on the middle seat and me up at the bow. My nine-millimeter Browning was in the travel bag, under several more changes of clerical wear; other than underwear and socks, my real clothing had been left behind. In my right hand were clutched two envelopes, and in my left a passport.

From where I sat as we putt-putted across choppy water, warm wind whipping our hair, I was watching the *Yankee* recede, and I felt a pang of regret out of proportion to my brief stay on Captain and Mrs. Johnson's ship. It seemed to me I was leaving America, perhaps Western civilization itself, behind; and the faintly decadent sweetness of rich boys paying big bucks to play Popeye, and a rich girl who wanted a shipboard romance with a mysterious government agent (strictly above the waist, you understand), lent a bittersweet flavor to this

lonely ride under a broodingly gray sky on rough gun-
metal waters. Then the *Yankee* disappeared and I looked
over my shoulder.

The shape of the island was no longer vague. A long
undulating beast, with the central hump of Mount Tapotchau, crouched on the ocean's surface, a study in brilliant greens and dull browns, myriad jungle shades. But
we were not approaching a primitive world: the tiny
boxes of buildings indicated a city, and toy boats that
were massive freighters hugged a concrete pier. We were
skirting a coral reef now, heading toward a much smaller
island, just a glorified sandbar.

"Maniagawa Island," Johnson said, with a nod. "That
marks the entry to the harbor."

As we drew closer, Saipan was dashing my expecta-
tions: the island seemed larger than I'd imagined, as did
the surprisingly thriving town of Garapan that spread
out upon the flatland beneath the hills. The little city
had banished the tropics from its confines; but on either
side, coconut palms swayed as per South Sea Island routine, and flame trees, with their dazzling scarlet flowers,
dotted the coastline, exotic flourishes of flora.

Garapan, however, might have been a port city in the
northeastern U.S.A., with its rectangular concrete wharf
embracing freighters and fishing boats alike, the factory
sprawl and towering black chimney of a sugar refinery,
and row upon row of boxy houses in grid formation. As
we neared the formidable jetty, other details filled in: a
train pulling in along the pier, warehouses, telephone
poles, streetlights. So much for leaving Western civilization behind.

The dinghy chugged into the harbor unnoticed; we
pulled alongside the concrete pier, cut the motor, but
did not tie up. Over at left, near a smaller, separate jetty,
two flying boats floated near the refueling tanks and repair shed and ramps of a modest seaplane base. Down
from us, at right, native workers in loose scruffy pants
and usually no shirt and no shoes (like the rich boys on
the *Yankee*) were unloading heavy sacks—sugar, Johnson said—from a freight car of the quaint-looking little
steam-engine choo-choo that rested on narrow-gauge
tracks; other workers were hauling sacks up a gangplank

into a freighter. Supervising were pith-helmeted Japanese in white linen jackets over buttoned-to-the-neck, high-collar shirts with white trousers and white shoes; it was not quite a uniform. . . .

Someone in a real uniform had noticed us, however.

Muscular, spade-bearded, perhaps twenty-five, he wore a light-green denim shirt, open at the neck, with matching shorts and cap, and this uniform would not have been impressive at all, might even have seemed silly or childish, had that revolver in a black holster not been on his hip.

"Naval officer," Johnson whispered.

Our one-man welcoming committee pointed a finger at us: Uncle Samurai Wants You. Well, at least it wasn't his gun. He seemed unhappy. He told us so, in a spew of Japanese.

Johnson responded in Japanese; it sounded clumsy and halting, but our host considered the skipper's words carefully, then called out and another denim-dressed officer trotted over, a chubby individual who received some instructions, and trotted off again.

Then our spade-bearded welcoming committee unsnapped his holster, and withdrew and pointed his long-barreled .38 revolver at us. The tarp between Hayden and me covered a similar gun. But there was no need to go for it; our host was just keeping us covered.

Behind him and his gun, beyond the warehouses and the train tracks, sat a typical jumbled waterfront—bars, cheap restaurants, small stores, wooden-frame buildings mostly, a few brick. Very few automobiles were in sight; people walked, or rode bicycles.

"How much of their lingo do you know?" I asked Johnson in a near whisper, as we bobbed in our boat.

"That one sentence," he said. "It was a request that he bring an English-speaking official to meet an important visitor."

Our host barked at us in Japanese; my psychic translation was: "Shut up!" I heeded my instinct.

We weren't kept waiting long. When the chubby officer returned, I thought at first he'd summoned one of the men supervising the unloading of the train. Positioning himself before us, feet planted, hands clasped behind him, was a small, somber, rather skeletal-looking gray-mustached fellow in that white pith helmet, linen jacket and trousers getup.

But on closer look, there were differences: the linen jacket had epaulettes, the pith helmet bore a gold badge, and a revolver in a cavalry-style holster rode his belt—arranged for a fancy right to left cross-draw.

"Mikio Suzuki," he said in a calm, medium-pitched voice. "Chief of Saipan Police. This is closed port."

"Captain Irving Johnson of the civilian ship, *Yankee*," the skipper said. "I apologize for this unscheduled stop. We are anchored beyond your three-mile zone. I do not ask to come ashore. I'm here to drop off a passenger."

He appraised me and my black apparel and white collar with placid skepticism. "Chamorro missions need no new missionaries. Two priests already."

Johnson said, "Please do us the courtesy of looking at Father O'Leary's papers."

I blessed him with a smile as I handed my passport and the two envelopes up. He examined the passport, then withdrew and unfolded each letter; he read them with no visible reaction.

Johnson and I traded tiny shrugs; Hayden had his eyes locked onto these men with guns looming on the pier, his hand draped casually between his legs, hovering over the tarp.

Then Chief Suzuki spoke to the spade-bearded officer, a guttural command that might have been my death sentence.

But within seconds, I'd been hoisted up and out of the dinghy, Hayden handing me my travel bag and a tight smile, while the Chief of Saipan Police carefully refolded my letters, inserted them in their envelopes and returned them to me, with a bow.

"Welcome to Garapan, Father O'Leary," Chief Suzuki said.

I half-bowed to the chief, then nodded to the skipper and his first mate, who were already putt-putting away from the pier.

Father O'Leary was on his own in Saipan.

Seventeen

The main street of Garapan bisected the waterfront, whose typical seediness was quickly replaced by a wholesomely bustling downtown thoroughfare that, with minor changes, might have been small-town America. One- and two-story structures, sometimes wood-frame, sometimes brick, occasionally concrete, were shoulder to shoulder along the telephone-pole-flung asphalt street—office buildings, restaurants, a bakery, hairdressing salon, hardware store, fish market, the larger storefronts with awnings, smaller shops with modest wooden overhangs, even a picture show (although a samurai movie was playing). The apparel, too, seemed oddly Western—white shirts, white shorts, black shorts—though there was the occasional parasol-bearing housewife in a white cotton kimono, out grocery shopping.

A major difference—besides signs and hanging flags that bore the graceful hen scratchings of Japanese script—was how bicycles outnumbered automobiles. Another was a pervading, unpleasantly pungent odor of copra and dried fish, a near stench at odds with the neatness and cleanliness of Main Street Garapan, as were the occasional Chamorro men, dusky natives of the island, loitering at alleyways and along the wooden sidewalks, dirty and disheveled in their tattered clothes and unshod feet. It was as if the Japanese were a hurricane or tidal wave that had displaced them, and they hadn't gotten around to tidying up yet.

The sky remained gray but little breeze accompanied this persistent threat of rain. The temperature was mild—probably seventy-five degrees—but mugginess undermined it: I was sticky in my black jacket and clerical garb, lightweight though it was.

As I walked along, travel bag in hand, at the side of the white-uniformed chief of police—who was about as talkative as the stone dogs outside the Oriental Gardens restaurant on West Randolph Street—I was getting discreet but amazed glances from almost everybody.

"They don't see many foreigners around here," I said.

"No." He kept his eyes straight ahead as we marched along, didn't even look at me when we spoke.

"But you said you have priests."

"Two. For Chamorro, the missions. Spanish priests. Darker skin than you."

The morning was still young, and clusters of giggling children, knapsacks on their backs, were heading for school, and an occasional straggling fisherman trudged toward the pier. Handcart peddlers wound their way among the bicycles and pedestrians, hawking in their language, making it sound as if torture were being performed on them, while postmen and policemen on their rounds pinged the bells on their bicycles to clear a path.

Of course, nobody dinged a bell at the chief of police, who was diminutive of stature but towering in bearing; in fact, everybody was clearing a path for us, as we left a trail of intimidation and astonishment in our wake, the chief and the foreigner.

"You have a nice town here," I said.

"We have factory, hospital, post office, newspaper, radio station, electric light."

"It's a modern place, all right."

On the other hand, they didn't seem to have indoor plumbing. The side streets were unpaved and dusty, and lined with an assembly of bedraggled stores and ramshackle private homes with tin roofs; outhouses were easily glimpsed, even if they did lack our traditional half-moon.

We were four blocks from the waterfront when the street opened onto the town square, built around a rather grand, official-looking white wooden two-story building, colonial-style with pillars and double doors. The place was like an ice cream salesmen convention:

everybody going in and out wore white suits or white shorts and white shoes with white Panama hats or white pith helmets or white military caps.

"Court of Justice," Chief Suzuki said, quietly proud. "My office here."

But we didn't go in; the chief had paused at a black sedan parked out front. He barked at a cop in white shorts, caught on his way into the courthouse; the cop bowed, on the run, went inside and shortly thereafter another servile young copper in white shorts, white cap and black gunbelt came trotting out and saluted the chief. The chief gave him some instructions, the young copper said, "*Hai,*" and opened the rear sedan door for me.

I took my cue, and the chief got in after me, with the young copper going around the front to play chauffeur.

"Would it be impolite of me to ask where we're going?" I inquired, as we pulled out between bicycles. The backseat was roomy; it wasn't a limo, but this Jap buggy with its cushiony black interior was comfortable, even though it rode like a lumber wagon—they'd have to go some to catch up with American automaking.

"Forgive my rudeness," Chief Suzuki said. "I escort you to meet *shichokan.*"

"Oh. Local official of some kind?"

"Yes. What you call 'governor.' " He pondered that for a moment. "Not governor of *Nan'yo chokan*; he is not *chokunin.* He is governor of *shicho.*"

"You mean, he's the governor of Saipan?"

"Not Saipan only. Governor of all Mariana Islands."

"Oh . . . but not of Micronesia."

"Yes." He seemed pleased that his intelligence and communications skills were overcoming the limitations of the slow-witted child in his care. "I instructed Lieutenant Tomura to call ahead. The *shichokan* . . ." He chose his words carefully. ". . . anticipation our arrival."

Then he leaned back, happy with himself over that memorable sentence.

"Does the, uh . . . *shichokan* speak English?"

"Yes. Not as well as mine. But he does speak."

We passed a pleasant park with a bandshell, yet another confounding familiarity in this foreign place; somehow it was oddly reassuring when we glided by a pagodalike shrine on a tastefully landscaped plot.

"Buddhist?" I asked.

The faintest frown passed over the chief's stone visage. "Shinto."

"I see. You mind if I roll the window down?"

"Please," he said.

It was warm in the car, and the only breeze available was the one stirred up by our movement. The chief rolled his window down, just a little, a nice politeness on his part.

"Do you mind my asking what the population of Garapan is?"

The chief said, "Fifteen thousand people. Few thousand islanders."

Glad he broke it down for me.

I had expected a native village with a small garrison of Japanese troops treating the place like a prison camp; instead, I was in a boom town, attested to by the contemporary residential neighborhood we were rolling through, bungalow after bungalow rising three or four feet off the ground on stone or concrete pillars with neat little yards and gardens of papaya, guavas, mangoes; despite modern construction and style, the little houses wore tin roofs whose grooves sluiced rain to gutters down to cisterns. Occasionally a stone building dating to the period of Saipan's German domination would rear its head, or a hacienda-style abode going back to the Spanish days. Primarily, however, I was witnessing the boxlike houses—some wood-frame, mostly of newer, cement construction—in the classic gridlike layout of the modern factory town.

But what were they making in this factory town? Were these thousands of people (and natives) all employed by the sugar refinery, and the service industries of the downtown?

On the fringes of the city, finally, were clusters of the poor indigenous housing I'd expected, the thatched wooden shacks before which sat heavy-set middle-aged native women in faded sarongs fanning themselves with palm leaves. I felt strangely reassured.

"Where are the native children?" I asked. I'd seen very few, except a handful of filthy bare-assed toddlers.

"In school. We bring these simple people *kansei.*" The chief winced in thought, briefly, realizing I wouldn't understand the meaning of that final word. "Rules," he explained. "Law from society."

"Civilization?"

He nodded, as if to say, *Not quite, but close enough.*

As we left the city, moving along the wide, well-paved road that seemed to be leading us into the green hills, bright red hibiscus grew along roadside hedges beyond which stood guardlike rows of palms, their broad leaves whispering with a hint of wind. Then our sedan turned down, and up, a gently sloping gravel road boarded by blooming flame trees, a riot of red and orange under the dull gray sky.

We ended up in a crushed-stone cul-de-sac, where a number of other black sedans were parked, their radio antennas bearing tiny white flags with red suns. We came to a stop, and the young copper came around and opened the door for his chief. I was reaching for the travel bag at my feet when Chief Suzuki said, "You will not be needing."

So I left the bag behind—and the nine-millimeter tucked away inside, rolled up in my spare priest attire. The young cop chauffeur stayed behind, too, as I followed Chief Suzuki up a wide crushed-stone path through an immaculately landscaped Oriental garden, with perfectly squared-off hedges and flawlessly rounded bushes, to stone pillars bordering stone steps that rose in landings up a terrace at whose crest sprawled a lattice-work-decorated white wooden structure, red-roofed, cupola-surmounted, swimming in a sea of red, yellow, white and purple chrysanthemums, emerald explosions of palm trees standing watch.

This would seem to be the governor's mansion.

At a slant-roofed portico awaited a Naval officer in a green denim uniform—long pants, jodhpurs, a black-holstered revolver, and something else: a samurai sword. I decided I liked the more casual uniform better.

We were immediately ushered inside, into a world of sliding wooden-frame rice paper walls, hardwood floors

and Buddha-belly vases of dried flowers. We removed
our shoes, trading them for slippers, and were escorted
into a large sunken octagonal chamber that might have
been the living room, but was more a receiving-area-
cum-office. The furnishings were sparse but of an impressive dark-lacquered teakwood: three chairs arranged
before a massive desk, behind which a higher-backed
chair awaited an important posterior.

The possessor of that posterior was a short, heavy-set
individual of perhaps fifty, wearing the same white uniform as the chief of police, but with a black string tie,
and without a gunbelt, or samurai sword either. His face
was pleasant and round, fat enough that his features
were getting lost in it, distinguished by a mustache and
goatee, his thinning black hair combed forward and plas-
tered to his forehead like a spreading spider.

Chief Suzuki, with a half-bow, said, "*Shichokan,* this
Father Brian O'Leary from Milwaukee, United States
of America."

"Father O'Leary," the *shichokan* said, in a surprisingly bassy, rumbly voice, bowing. "You honor my
house."

I returned his bow. "You do me honor, sir. May I
present my letters of introduction?"

The *shichokan* nodded.

I withdrew from my inside jacket the two envelopes
and handed them to him.

"Please sit," he said to me, and with a nod extended
the invitation to Chief Suzuki.

We took chairs opposite the desk as he got back behind it, settling into his teakwood throne, where he put
on round-lensed wire-frame glasses and read the letters.
One, on embassy stationery, was from the German Ambassador to the U.S.A.; the other was from Sean Russell,
Chief of Staff of the Irish Republican Army, currently
in the States on a fundraising tour, and laying low after
several major London and Liverpool bombings.

They were not forgeries. Wall Street boy Forrestal's
connections with wealthy supporters of the I.R.A. had
made both letters possible; and the real Father Brian
O'Leary of Milwaukee, a former I.R.A. advocate ap-

palled by the recent spate of bombings, had lent his cooperation. It was a solid cover story.

Seeming mildly confused, the *shichokan* removed his
glasses and rested them on the table, by the two letters,
which he had not returned to their envelopes. "You are
Irish? Or American?"

"I'm an American citizen," I explained. "My parents
were from Dublin. There are many of us in the United
States who aid and support the I.R.A. in their righteous
war on England. The reason I have come is to seek
your—"

The *shichokan* raised a pudgy hand in a "stop" gesture, smiling; his head looked like a cookie jar with a
face on it. A face with Fu Manchu whiskers, that is.

"Before we go on," he said, in that bass that rumbled
up out of his squat body like an echo up a canyon, "I
will need to show your letters to *kaigun bukan*. I hope
you will forgive this formality."

I loved the way he made it sound like I had some
kind of choice in all of this. And, of course, I had no
idea what the hell a *kaigun bukan* was.

"Not at all," I said.

He folded the pudgy hands as if in Christian prayer.
"I have taken liberty of calling him. He should be arriving soon. . . . Tea?"

A lovely young woman in a flower-print kimono
served us, and we sipped from delicate hand-painted
porcelain cups as the *shichokan* asked me how I liked
his island and I told him how swell I thought it was.
Chief Suzuki said nothing, barely sipping his tea. Then
the *shichokan* inquired if I would like to visit the Spanish
mission while I was on Saipan, to meet with my fellow
priests, and I declined.

"I came to your island on matters of state," I said,
"not of church."

"In Shinto religion," the *shichokan* said good-naturedly, "there is no division. . . . Ah! Captain Tatehiko."

The governor rose and so did we, turning to see a
slim, surprisingly tall naval officer, in the more formal
jodhpurs and sword uniform, embellished with campaign
ribbons, striding across the hardwood floor; that he, too,
wore slippers made him seem somewhat absurd though

no less formidable. I placed him in his mid-forties, a
warrior with Apache cheekbones and cuts in his face
where his eyes should have been. He half-bowed to us.
We all returned the compliment.

"Captain Tatehiko no speaks English," the *shichokan*
informed me. "Please to sit. I will speak to him of what
we have said."

Chief Suzuki and I returned to our teakwood chairs
while Captain Tatehiko—who was apparently the liaison
officer between the Navy and the colonial government—
stood with crossed arms, like a sentry, listening to the
shichokan, who had remained standing. Then the *shichokan* handed the letters to Captain Tatehiko and stood
beside him, pointing at words as he read/translated.

Tatehiko listened to all this expressionlessly, then nodded curtly and took the third chair, beside Suzuki, as the
relieved *shichokan* took his seat behind the desk, again.

"Father O'Leary," the *shichokan* said, leaning forward, hands flat on his desk. "Why do you honor us
with visit?"

I stood, to lend some weight to my words. "The I.R.A.
has since January of last year been waging a bombing
campaign against Britain. Unfortunately our resources
are limited. The quality of our explosives, homemade or
stolen, has not always been the best."

"Forgive please," the *shichokan* said, holding up his
palm again. "I must translate as we go."

And he translated for Tatehiko. Then he nodded to
me to continue.

I did: "We have been discussing an alliance with Germany for many months. Arrangements are being made
for Sean Russell to go to Berlin. He seeks aid to fight
the common British enemy."

I paused, to allow the *shichokan* to translate for Captain Tatehiko, which he did.

Then I went on: "I am acting as a courier in hopes
that Mr. Russell, or some other I.R.A. envoy, can go
to Tokyo to build a similar alliance with your imperial
government. Britain bedevils you by aiding China; they
hold island territories in these waters that are rightfully
yours. With funding and supplies, the I.R.A. can mount

a sabotage campaign aimed at key British war industries."

Again I paused, and again the *shichokan* translated.

"The I.R.A. can damage the British transportation structure," I said, ticking off a list on my fingers. "It can demoralize the British public. And it can cripple the British aircraft industry. But we need funds, arms and supplies. That is the substance of the message I have been asked to convey."

And the *shichokan* translated.

And I sat.

Captain Tatehiko mulled all of this over, briefly, then spoke in Japanese, at some length, while the *shichokan* listened intently.

Then the governor said to me, "Captain Tatehiko thanks you for your message, and your friendship. Your message will be conveyed."

"That's all I ask," I said. I looked at the Captain, said, "*Arigato,*" and nodded.

He nodded back.

The *shichokan* said, "Some time may pass before we have a reply to your message. Captain Tatehiko will speak to Rear Admiral who will speak to Naval Ministry. I will do same with *chokunin* of *Nan'yo chokan.*"

"I understand," I said. "However, I have arranged passage on a German trading ship due to dock at Tanapag Harbor two days from now. Back to the American territory, Guam."

Captain Tatehiko spoke to the *shichokan,* apparently asking for a translation, which the *shichokan* seemed to provide. Tatehiko spoke again, and now it was the governor's turn to translate for me.

"Captain Tatehiko say that if you stay longer, we will arrange safe passage to Guam at a later date." The *shichokan* held his open palms out in a gesture of welcome. "Will you be our guest until that time?"

"I would be honored."

The *shichokan* beamed. "You honor us, Father."

Both Chief Suzuki and Captain Tatehiko excused themselves to pursue their official duties, but I remained behind, at the *shichokan*'s insistence, for luncheon, with the promise of an island tour thereafter.

My pudgy host and I sat in another room, on woven straw mats in the usual cross-legged Nipponese style, with a sliding door drawn back on a view of green hills rising into the mist. Two lovely young women in colorful kimonos attended our every whim, keeping first our tea-cups filled, then later serving tiny warm cups of sake, which I sipped guardedly. Lacquered trays with small dishes of food—seaweed, rice, pickles, miso paste—were set before us. The stuff was lousy.

It wasn't like I didn't know or appreciate Japanese cuisine. There was a place back home, on Lake Park Avenue, called Mrs. Shintani's where they cooked suki-yaki on a little gas stove right at your table, thin slices of beef, crisp fresh vegetables, the warm aromas rising to your nostrils like undulating dancing girls. Take a young lady to Mrs. Shintani's for an intimate evening of heavenly dining, and I dare you not to get lucky.

This tasteless goo wouldn't get you to first base.

"I hope you enjoy meal," the *shichokan* said. "We eat only finest imported food. Sent from home in can, jar, sack."

"Aren't there farms here?" I asked, my chopsticks finding a pinch of flavorless seaweed. "I know there's fishing."

The *shichokan* made a sour face. "Island food. We do not eat the harvest of primitive people."

On a tropical paradise, surrounded by waters teeming with fish, where coconuts and bananas and pineapples flourished, where native farmers raised chickens, cattle and hogs, these proud people ate canned seafood and seaweed out of jars. This was my first real indication that they were nuts.

The roly-poly *shichokan*'s tour of the island was fairly brief—an hour and a half or so—but illuminating. Riding in back of another black sedan, with a white-uniformed driver, our route was at first scenic, following hard dirt roads south through lush foliage, stopping to take in a small bay, a tidal pool, a blowhole and several craters. Then, apparently to demonstrate to his new I.R.A. friend the capabilities of the Japanese, the *shichokan* paused to allow me to take in the panorama that was Aslito Heneda airfield.

Two vast crushed-coral runways, two service sheds
with spacious crushed-coral aprons, five dark-green
wood-frame hangars and a similarly constructed terminal, Aslito Heneda was a modern airfield in the shadow
of an ancient mountain. The facility had an unmistakable
military look, but as we coasted by, I caught sight of no
fighter planes, no bombers—the only planes on the
apron were a pair of airliners—and a few parked automobiles, with some civilian activity around the terminal
building, a small ground crew on the field.

"Great Japan Airways," the *shichokan* explained.
"People come to work Saipan. Some come for vacation
from Tokyo."

Later, the *shichokan* pointed out a flat stretch of land,
which looked to have been recently cleared, and said,
"Marpi Point. We begin clear second airfield soon."

Saipan didn't seem to be in dire need of another commercial airport; in fact, Aslito Heneda was barely used
for that purpose. In his sly way, the *shichokan* was letting his I.R.A. ally know that, though military aircraft
and combat units were not yet in place, the island was
undergoing heavy-duty fortification.

He was less coy back in Garapan, when we rolled past
the chainlink-fenced-off Chico Naval Base with its
sprawl of barracks skirting the seaplane base with its
ramps and repair shed, and modest population of two
flying boats. Within that fenced-off area, there was no
sign of any military personnel.

"Those buildings full by next year," the governor
bragged. "With *konkyochitai* . . ." Noticing my confu-
sion, he thought about that and came up with a translation: "Battalion. Also, a *bobitai,* defense force. Five
hundred men. And *keibitai* . . . guard force. Eight hundred navy troop."

Our sedan headed back up the main street, and turned
over onto a side street parallel to the waterfront, my
spider-haired chubby tour guide proudly pointing out an
imposing low-slung complex of concrete buildings on
golf-green grounds—a modern hospital specializing in
tropical diseases ("Dengue fever, big problem Saipan").
Across the street was a small park, where a few palm
trees and stone benches attended a towering pedestal on

which stood a larger-than-life-size bronze statue of an older Japanese gentleman in a business suit, a hand in his pocket, an oddly casual pose for such a formal monument.

"Baron Matsue Haruji," the *shichokan* said, answering my unasked question. "Sugar King, bring prosperity to Saipan."

On a side street nearby, however, the tour turned less cheerful, as the sedan pulled over by an undeveloped overgrown plot of land, a reminder of the jungle this town had been carved out of. Across from us were two one-and-a-half-story concrete buildings with high barred windows. The building at right was long and narrow, stretching out like an endless concrete boxcar; across a crushed-stone area, where several black sedans were parked, a similar but much smaller building squatted, a concrete bungalow with four barred windows. Probably the maximum-security section.

"Father," the *shichokan* said quietly, "we give you trust. We show you . . ." He searched for the words and found perfect ones. ". . . good faith."

"That is true, *Shichokan*."

He nodded slowly. His bassy voice was somber as he said, "We ask a favor."

I nodded in return. "You honor me, *Shichokan*."

"We would like you to speak to two American prisoners. . . . Pilots."

My heart raced but I kept my voice calm. "Pilots?"

"Spies."

I gestured toward the concrete buildings. "Are they held in that prison, *Shichokan*?"

"One is. Man."

"There is a woman, too?"

"Yes. She is famous woman in your country. . . . She is call 'Amira.' "

I was trembling; I hoped he didn't see it. "Amelia," I said.

"Yes. Amira." He grunted a few words in Japanese and his driver pulled out into the street, turned at the next corner.

I said nothing; my heart was a fucking sledgehammer,

but I said nothing. He had brought up the subject. It was his to pursue.

We hadn't gone far—maybe six hundred feet—when the sedan came to a stop again, opposite another concrete building, a two-story one; it loomed over its neighbors (a low-slung general merchandise store at left, a single-story frame house at right) looking at once modern and gothic, a church designed by Frank Lloyd Wright. Its four upper-floor windows, divided by decorative pillars, were tall and narrow, and the lower floor—which had a shallow, one-story extension to the street—had arched windows that cried out for stained glass.

But it wasn't a church.

"Hotel," the *shichokan* said. "This hotel—Kobayashi Ryokan—run by military. Keep honored guests, like honored friend, here. . . . Also political prisoners."

An interesting mix.

"The woman is here?" I asked, with a casual gesture to the building.

"*Hai*," the *shichokan* said. "Second floor. . . . Please go to hotel. You expected. Your questions answered."

He gave me half a bow, and my door was opened by his driver; I damn near fell out of the sedan, or into the driver's arms. But within moments I was crossing the dusty, unpaved street, watching the sedan roll away, with—framed in its rear window—the *shichokan*'s inanely smiling face. I approached the boxy gothic structure, and went in.

The one-story extension served as the hotel's minuscule lobby: at right, nobody was behind the check-in counter; at left, under a churning ceiling fan, straining their rattan chairs, sat two massive Chamorro men, playing cards on a rattan table with a deck turned splotchy from sweaty, dirty fingers. Also on the table were the kitchen matchsticks they were betting, a pack of Japanese cigarettes, two long black billy clubs and a sheathed machete.

They were the first native males I'd seen wearing shirts; in fact, they wore suits, only soiled-looking, threadbare, as if these were hand-me-downs from the Japs.

But that seemed unlikely, because these were two very

big boys. One of them was hatless, with a thatch of black hair atop a cantaloupe head with watermelon-seed eyes in walnut-shell pouches of skin in a litchi-nut-toned face so unwrinkled, it was as if neither thought nor emotion had ever traveled across that arid plain. Twenty years of age or maybe fifty, he was just plain fat, bursting his seams.

Such flab made him less dangerous than the other one, a bull-necked mass of muscle and fat in a straw fedora, with a face so ugly, features so flat and blunt, so wrinkled, so pockmarked, the white knife scar down his right cheek seemed gratuitous.

The worst part was the eyes: they were not stupid; they were hard and dark and glittering and smart. He looked at me above a hand of cards clutched in knife-handle fingers and said, "Six."

At first I thought he was making a bet, but when a frown tightened around the hard dark eyes, I asked, "Pardon me?"

He was missing a front tooth; the others were the shade of stained oak, approximately the tone of his skin. "Six."

"That's, what? My room number? Room six?"

He played a card. "Six."

"Do I need a key?"

"Six!"

That seemed about as close to getting directions as I was going to get, so I entered the main building through a doorless archway, making my way down a central corridor, my shoes echoing off the hardwood floor. Doors to rooms were on either side of me; the walls were plaster, not rice paper. Stairs to the second floor were at the rear, but there seemed to be no exit down there. Fire inspectors apparently played it fast and loose in Saipan.

Okay, Room 6. I stopped at number 6, tried the knob, found the door unlocked. Slippers awaited me just inside the door, and I traded my shoes for them. The pale yellow plaster walls were bare; a tall sheer-curtained window looked out on the side of the wood-frame residence next door. Though this was a Western-style structure, the room was in the style of a Japanese inn: a "carpet" of fine woven reed, padded quilts on the floor for a bed, two floor cushions to sit at a scuffed, low-riding teakwood table. No closet, but a rack with a pole was provided. The only concession to any non-Japanese visitors was a dresser with mirror.

My travel bag was on the dresser.

I checked inside, found my nine-millimeter; both the clip I'd loaded into the weapon, and my two spare clips, seemed untampered with. Weapon cradled in my hands, I looked up and saw my face in the mirror, or anyway the face of some confused fucking priest holding a gun.

Then I looked at the ceiling, not for guidance from the Lord, but thinking about what the *shichokan* had said: the woman, "Amira," was on the second floor. . . .

So what should I do? Go upstairs and start knocking on doors? And take my nine-millimeter along, in case I needed to bestow some blessings?

A knock startled me, and I didn't know whether to tuck the gun away in the bag, or maybe in my waistband, with the black coat over it.

"Father O'Leary?"

Chief Suzuki's voice.

"Father O'Leary, can speak?"

I returned the nine-millimeter to my bag, and opened the door.

Chief Suzuki stood respectfully, his pith helmet with the gold badge held in his hands. "I hope you find comfort."

"Thank you. It's nice. Please come in."

Suzuki gave me a nod that was almost a bow, stepped inside and out of his shoes, and I closed the door.

"Those two in the lobby," I said, "do they work for you?"

He frowned. "Jesus and Ramon? Did they give you trouble?"

"No. I just saw their clothing, and the billy clubs, and wondered."

"Billy . . . ?"

"Billy clubs. Nightsticks, batons?" I pantomimed holding a billy and slapping it in my open palm.

That he understood. "They are . . . native police. Ten Chamorro work with us—internal security. We have Jesus . . ." He traced a finger down his right cheek, in imitation of the bullnecked pockmarked Chamorro's scar.

I nodded that I understood who he meant.

He continued: "We have Jesus on guard here many time. Jesus is my top *jungkicho* . . . detective. Jesus takes care of his people."

All of a sudden Suzuki was sounding like the priest. But what I figured he meant was, Jesus took care of investigations into crimes among the Chamorro.

"Well," I said, "he didn't give me any trouble. . . . The *shichokan* said you wanted a favor, involving a woman in this hotel."

"Yes," Captain Suzuki said. "May I sit?"

"Certainly. . . ."

Soon we were seated on floor mats facing each other.

His skeletal, gray-mustached countenance was grave, and regret clung to his words like a vine on a trellis. "Some people think the woman in this hotel . . . in the room above yours . . . should receive mercy. They say she is a fine person. A beautiful person."

Trying not to betray the chill his words had sent through me, I said easily, "If she is who the *shichokan* says she is, she is a famous person, too. Important."

"Yes. This is true. Nonetheless I disagree—she came here to carry out duties as a spy, and it cannot be helped. She should be executed."

And then Captain Suzuki asked his favor of Father O'Leary.

Eighteen

The room directly above mine was number 14. Chief Suzuki did not accompany me up the stairs, nor were there any signs of Jesus Sablan or Ramon Reyes, the chief's Chamorro watchdogs; Jesus and Ramon were apparently still down in the lobby, playing rummy with smeary cards. I was alone in the hallway; according to the chief, right now only a few guests were registered at this hotel, whose rooms were reserved by the Japanese for honored guests—and prisoners.

My two knocks made a lonely echo.

From behind the door came a soft, muffled, "Yes?"

Wrapped up in the sound of that one spoken word were so many hopes and dreams carried with me across the months, across the ocean, a single word spoken in that low, rich, matter-of-fact feminine voice I never thought I'd hear again.

"Amy?" I said to the door, my face almost rubbing against its harsh, paint-blistered surface.

But the door didn't reply. The voice on the other side of it had granted me only that one word. . . .

I looked both ways, a kid crossing the street for the first time—stairwell at one end, window at the other, no Chief Suzuki, no members of his Chamorro goon squad, either. I kept my voice at a whisper, in case someone was eavesdropping across the way.

"Amy—it's Nathan."

It seemed like forever, and was probably fifteen seconds, but finally the door creaked open to reveal a sliver of the pale, lightly powdered elongated oval of her face.

Under the familiar tousle of dark blonde hair, one blue-gray eye, sunken but alert, gaped at me, as half of the sensuous mouth (no lipstick) dropped open in astonishment.

"You know what I hate," I said, "about seeing a married woman?"

The door opened wider and displayed her full face with the astonished expression frozen there, though her lips quivered and seemed almost to form a smile. ". . . What?"

"Always meeting in hotel rooms."

And she backed away, shaking her head in disbelief, hand over her mouth, eyes filling with tears, as I stepped into the room, shutting the door behind me; she was thin but not emaciated, her face gaunt but not skeletal. She wore a short-sleeve mannish sportshirt and rust-color slacks and no shoes and looked neat and clean.

That's all I had time to take in before she flew into my arms, clutching me desperately, and I held her close, held her tight, as she wept into my clerical suitcoat, saying my name over and over, and I kissed the nape of her neck, and maybe I wept a little, too.

"You're here," she was saying, "how can you be here? Crazy . . . you're here . . . so crazy . . . here. . . ."

Our first kiss in a very long time was salty and tender and yearning and tried not to end, but when at last she drew away from me, just a little, still in my arms, and looked at me with bewilderment, she didn't seem able to form any more words, the surprise had knocked the wind from her.

And so she kissed me again, greedily; I savored it, then pulled gently away.

"Take it easy, baby," I said, running a finger around my clerical collar. "I got a vow of celibacy to maintain."

And she laughed—with only a little hysteria in it— and said, "Nathan Heller a priest? That's good. . . . That's rich."

"That's Father Brian O'Leary," I corrected, stepping away from her, taking a look around her room. "If anyone should ask. . . ."

Her living quarters were identical to mine, save for a few additional allowances for an American "guest": a well-worn faded green upholstered armchair and, near the window looking onto the neighboring house and the rooftops beyond, a small Japanese-magazine-arrayed table with a reading lamp and an ashtray bearing the residue of several incense sticks. Incense fragrance lingered, apparently Amy's antidote to the ever-present Garapan bouquet of dried fish and copra.

But she had the same woven-reed carpet, padded quilts for a bed, low-slung teakwood table with floor cushions. On the clothesrack, among a few simple dresses and the inevitable plaid shirts, hung the oil-stained, weathered leather flight jacket she'd worn when she flew me in her Vega from St. Louis to Burbank. I checked the walls—including behind her dresser mirror—for drilled holes, found nothing to indicate we were being monitored. I didn't figure we had much to worry about: the Japanese weren't exactly known for their technical wizardry.

Nonetheless, we both kept our voices hushed.

"What are you doing here?" she asked, studying me with wide eyes that didn't seem to know whether to be filled with joy, disbelief or fear. "How in God's name did you . . . ?"

"Does it matter?"

"No," she said, with a sigh of a laugh, "hell no," a rare swear word from this proper creature, and she flung herself into my arms again. I squeezed her tight, then held her face in my hands and studied it, memorized it, and kissed her as sweetly as I knew how.

"Why did do you this?" she asked, cheek pressed against my chest, arms clasped around me, grasped around me, as if she were afraid I might bolt. "Why did you . . . ?"

"You know me," I said. "I was hired. Works out to a grand a week."

And she was laughing quietly into my suitcoat.

"You just can't admit it, can you?" She looked up at me, grinning her wonderful gap-toothed grin. "You're a romantic fool. My mercenary detective . . . coming halfway around the world for a woman. . . ."

There was something I had to ask, had to know, though I knew she was brimming with so many questions she didn't know where or how to start. With us standing there, in each other's arms, I said, "I thought . . . maybe . . ."

She was studying me now, almost amused. "What?"

"That there might be . . . someone else here with you."

"Who?" She winced. "Fred? He's in that horrible jail . . . poor thing."

"No, I . . . Amy, was there a baby?" It came out in a rush of ridiculous words. "Did you have your baby and they took it away from you?"

She smiled half a smile, and it settled on one side of her face; she touched the tip of my nose with a finger lightly, then asked, "Who told you I was pregnant?"

"Your secretary."

"Margot?" The grin widened. "I bet you slept with her."

"Almost. How about you?"

She slapped my chest. "I shouldn't have confided in that foolish girl. I hope you're not too disappointed. . . . I hope you didn't make this trip just to be a father . . . but most men would be relieved to hear it was a false alarm."

I hugged her to me, whispered my response into her hair. "I am relieved . . . not that I wouldn't mind being a father to a child of yours . . . but to think our kid would be caught up in these circumstances."

She drew away, her eyes hooded in understanding, nodded, taking my hand, leading me to the quilted sleeping mats on the floor. We sat there, cross-legged, like kids playing Indian, holding hands.

Her smile was a half-circle of embarrassment. "Nathan, I'm afraid . . . it was something else . . ."

"What was?"

"What I thought was the baby. There never will be a baby . . . not in these circumstances, or any other."

"What do you mean?"

She squeezed my hand. "What I thought was pregnancy, Nathan . . . was early menopause . . ." Shaking her head, her expression grooved with wry regret, she added, "The, uh, symptoms *are* similar."

I slipped an arm around her, pulled her against me. "You picked a hell of a climate for hot flashes, lady."

She laughed softly. "I didn't feel a thing . . . I was so ill with dysentery when they brought me here . . . can you imagine? I arrive at the dysentery capital of the world *with* a case of the world-class trots. . . . They had me in the hospital here for many, many months . . . I almost died."

"Were you ever in that jail?"

She rolled her eyes, nodded vigorously. "Oh my goodness, yes . . . the 'calaboose,' they call it. Same cellblock as Fred—that dirty little building with the four nasty cells. But I only lasted three days. I passed out and woke up, I don't know . . . six months later."

I frowned. "Then you really did almost die. What, were you in a coma?"

She shrugged. "Or they kept me doped up. I don't really know. . . ." She studied me through narrowed eyes, as if only now she had convinced herself I wasn't an apparition. "What are you doing here, Nathan? Who sent you on this harebrained expedition? G. P.?"

My laugh was harsher than I intended. "Not hardly. He had you declared dead, I don't know, two years ago; he's already remarried."

The blood drained out of her face; so did the emotion.

"Hey," I said. "I'm sorry. . . . I don't mean to be so cold about it. . . ."

"It's all right. It's just . . . I knew he didn't love me, anymore. And I never loved him, not really. But we were . . . a kind of team, you know? A partnership. I think I . . . deserved a little better from him, is all."

"You're preaching to the choir on that one."

She flashed me the gap-toothed grin and slipped a finger in my collar and tugged. "Preaching to the preacher, you mean. What's this about? Who *did* send you, you wonderful lunatic?"

"The same star-spangled bunch who sold you out," I said. "Uncle Sam and assorted nephews."

And I filled her in, giving her a brief but fairly complete rundown, from my unofficial investigation in July of '37 (she was fascinated and astounded to learn that I'd heard her capture on the Myers family Philco) to my current mission, right up to my role as I.R.A. emissary

Father O'Leary—leaving out what Chief Suzuki had asked of me.

Then it was her turn, and she told how she and Noonan had been picked up by a launch from a battleship, and were held in a place called Jaluit where a doctor tended to injuries Noonan had received ditching in the water; they were bounced from one Japanese Naval station to another, islands with names like Kwajalein, Roi, Namor, and finally to Saipan, where they were interrogated by Suzuki and others—they denied being spies, having dropped their photographic equipment into the ocean—and were jailed.

"After my collapse in my cell, and that long stay in the hospital," she said, "I was brought here to the Kobayashi Ryokan. And I've been treated more or less decently, ever since. I'm really under a kind of house arrest."

"You mean, you can come and go as you please?"

She nodded, shrugged. "Within boundaries. There are always at least two of those native police lackeys watching me, here at the hotel—day and night; if I leave, they're my shadows . . . even when it's just a trip out to the privy."

"How short a leash are you on?"

"I can venture out into the Garapan business district. Like a child, I have an allowance. I can get my hair done. Go to the movies. Stop at a teahouse—they don't make cocoa here, unfortunately, so I've finally learned to drink tea and coffee, at this late date. But always my Chamorro chaperons are nearby."

"You mean, if we wanted to leave right now," I said, "we could go for a walk—we'd just have a couple of fat ugly tails on our behinds?"

"Yes." She gripped my hand, tight. "But Nathan . . . don't underestimate them—particularly the one named Jesus." Her eyes took on a momentary glaze. "Lord Jesus, the islanders call him. His own people are frightened to death of him, even the ones he works with. He's terribly cruel."

I looked at her carefully. "You sound like you speak from experience. . . ."

"I know he's tortured Fred, many times."

"It's more than that."

She nodded in admission, and shared the unpleasant memory: "Shortly after I got out of the hospital, Lord Jesus came to my room, this room, and tried to make me admit I was a spy. . . ." She tilted her head to one side and pointed to her neck, where there were several nasty burn scars.

"Cigarettes?" I asked. A cold rage was rising in me.

She nodded. "But Chief Suzuki came in and saw what Jesus was doing, and put a stop to it."

I didn't bother to tell her that she'd just described an interrogation technique that dated back to the time of the original Jesus. Except for the cigarettes.

"This room has become a kind of . . . sanctuary for me," she said. Then her tone turned bitter. "But I always remember that, whenever they want, any of them can come right through that door . . . torture me, rape me, whatever they please. . . . It's a pleasant enough prison, Nathan—but it's a prison."

"Let's go for that walk," I suggested. "A priest and his parishioner."

She nodded, springing to her feet with girlish enthusiasm. "Just let me grab my sandals. . . ."

We went out through the lobby—a Chamorro clerk in a high-collared white shirt and bemused expression was at the check-in desk, now—and Jesus and Ramon were indeed still playing cards at their matchstick-, billy club- and machete-littered table. Under his misshapen straw fedora, the blunt-featured, knife-scarred, pockmarked puss of Lord Jesus frowned up at us in a startling mixture of indignation and contempt. How dare we interrupt his life?

"Catching some air," I explained. "In Six—remember?"

He sneered at me, baring mahogany teeth and the space for one.

And then we stepped out onto the wooden sidewalk where a cool yet muggy afternoon awaited under a steel-wool sky. We strolled by the general merchandise store with its shelves open onto the street, dolls and cloisonné vases, cakes and confectioneries, condiments and bean curd, its salesgirls in colorful kimonos. But the passers-by were less formal, men in shorts, women in Western-style dresses, not a parasol in sight; a few young men on bicycles. A pair of green-denim-uniformed officers on a motorcycle and sidecar rolled by, in the direction of Chico Naval Base. This time, I couldn't catch anybody even stealing a glance—word about my presence, here, must have gotten around.

"For such a striking couple," I said, "we're not attracting much attention."

Not counting Jesus and Ramon, of course, who were behind us about a half a block; they were so fat, only one could walk on the boardwalk—the other had to trod along kicking up dust in the hard-dirt street, making an obstacle for bikes. The billy clubs were stuck in their belts like pirate swords; Jesus had the sheathed machete stuck there, too—all he lacked was the parrot and eyepatch.

"Oh, I'm old hat around here," she said with a little smile. "They call me 'Tokyo Rosa.' "

"Why?"

"Tokyo because I attract so much official attention. Rosa because it's a female name in English they know from somewhere."

I gestured toward the little park where the sugar baron's statue loomed and we headed over there.

"It's usually prettier here," she said, as we sauntered along. We were close enough to the waterfront that we could see gray patches of ocean between trees and buildings. "Saipan sunsets are amazing, and the waters are so many different, clear shades of blue."

"It almost sounds like you like it here," I said.

A tiny grimace tightened her face. "I guess I deserve that. But I'm always aware of what Fred's going through."

We could see the prison, on its little jungle side street, as we walked. The boardwalk had given over to a simple well-worn grassy path.

"According to Chief Suzuki," I said, "your navigator's been pretty uncooperative, even belligerent."

"Fred's never given them a shred of information, never admitted to anything . . . but he's been through a living hell for it."

That made sense. Leaning on Noonan and taking it

easy on Amy wasn't chivalry on the part of the Japanese, rather their chauvinist supposition that the male team member would be the leader, and would hold the military secrets. To some degree, they may have been right—after all, Noonan had been working for the Navy, all along.

I asked, "Do they let you see him?"

"Once a week or so we talk, when he's allowed out into the exercise yard." She looked in that direction and I could see the area she meant, a grassless parcel beside the larger, boxcar-like cell blocks. "He's very strong. Resolute. I admire him terribly. . . ."

She wiped tears from her eyes with her short sleeve and smiled bravely and I looped my arm through hers and walked her into the little park, where we settled onto a stone bench, alone in the shadow of the baron's statue and sheltering palm trees.

"I'm going to get you out of here tonight," I said.

Her eyes widened with hope and alarm. "You can do that?"

Jesus and Ramon were watching from across the street, sitting on the stone steps out in front of the hospital, like a couple of gargoyles who'd fallen off the roof.

"You need to understand something," I said. "My mission to Saipan was defined by such patriots as William Miller and James Forrestal as 'intelligence gathering.' They didn't send me in here to rescue you, just to find out whether you and Fred were here or not. Alive and well, or hung by your thumbs, it didn't matter—are our missing people in Saipan or aren't they? That was the extent of why I was sent."

She nodded. "I follow you."

"Trust me, you don't. I was told, if you were here, not to 'play hero,' but to leave you behind, with the assurance that your pal FDR and naval and military intelligence would decide what to do about it . . . whether to negotiate the release of the American prisoners, or mount a full-scale rescue operation."

Wincing in thought, she said, "I guess that makes sense. . . ."

"No it doesn't. I played along with them, so they'd send me in here, but baby, my sole point in taking this seagoing safari was to bring you home with me. You think I got a particle of confidence in the government's ability to negotiate your release? How have they done so far?"

She sighed a laugh. "Not wonderfully well . . . and I guess they did figure there was a pretty good chance I was on Saipan, in Japanese custody, or they wouldn't have sent you in here, looking."

"Now you're gettin' your head out of the clouds." I gently touched her arm. "Do you really think FDR would send some kind of full-scale military raiding team into Saipan, to save his wife's canasta partner in what would clearly be an act of war?"

Her eyes seemed suddenly empty. ". . . No."

"Yes—*no*. And I knew, coming into this masquerade party, that once Father Brian O'Leary had disappeared off their island, the Japs would figure out my real purpose. That I had come calling to ascertain the condition and whereabouts of Earhart and Noonan . . . in which case, what kind of future do you think would've been in store for you?"

"Continued detention? Imprisonment . . . ?"

I let out a heavy sigh. "I'm going to say this, and you're going to have to be strong. I don't want our audience to detect any undue reaction."

Jesus and Ramon had brought their shopworn deck of cards with them; Ramon was dealing, on the hospital steps.

"Say what you have to," she said.

"Faced with the knowledge that the United States military has confirmed your presence in their custody, your Japanese hosts would take steps to remove any and all signs that you'd ever been here."

She said nothing, her expression blank. I didn't have to spell it out. She knew. She and Noonan would be executed. Buried anonymously on this island, or dumped as chum into the ocean to attract bonito.

"You'd be part of an incident that never happened," I said. "Which, at the end of the day, would suit both governments just fine."

Her eyes and nostrils flared. "Nathan, I can't believe . . ."

"That FDR would rather have you dead, than a Japanese propaganda tool? That he'd rather have you in an unmarked grave, than living evidence that the United States committed an act of espionage and war? Didn't they tell you what you were getting into, baby? If you're captured, you're on your own. That's the cardinal rule, the unwritten law of espionage: your government never fucking heard of you."

She looked as though I'd struck her a hard blow in the stomach; and hadn't I?

"Maybe," I said, "if our ambassador told their ambassador that we knew for a *certainty* that Amelia and Fred were in Japanese hands, *maybe* the Japs would quietly return the two of you. Very damn doubtful, though. It makes more sense that you would simply disappear. That's the Japanese face-saving way, in which case America saves face, too—the U.S.A. wouldn't have to see Amelia Earhart's mug turning up on Jap recruiting posters."

"Then . . ." she began, in halting horror. "Then . . . why did you come? If you knew—"

"Amy, full-scale war is around the next corner. Your death sentence has been passed already; it just hasn't been carried out yet. No, I knew going in that I had to bring you back with me, or leave you to die. You said it yourself: that hotel room may be pretty damn nice for a prison cell, but a prison cell is exactly what it is."

"Yes," she admitted. "Yes it is."

"Now—are you ready for where this really turns nasty?"

She laughed hollowly. "You're kidding, right?"

I nodded up toward the mustached statue of the sugar baron. "Don't let 'em kid *you,* baby. Garapan isn't a boom town 'cause of sugar; Saipan isn't thriving 'cause of dried fish, or sheds full of copra. The chief product here is war . . . they haven't harvested it yet, but they're planting, and the yield is gonna be something fierce."

She thought that over, and swallowed, and said, "And how does that affect me?"

"Understand, they've kept you here because Saipan's been a suitably out-of-the-way pimple on Nowhere's ass; not a bad place at all to keep a famous person like you

under wraps. But with the fortification of this floating
fly speck, and its advantageous position in the Pacific—
perfectly located for either side, where long-range bombers are concerned—Saipan's going to be a major target
of the coming war. So, I gather from my new best friend
Chief Suzuki, a decision has to be made about you and
Fred Noonan."

"A decision."

"Yeah—about finding you a new home. One possibility is Tokyo. The imperial government, the chief tells
me, is impressed by your propaganda value. They feel
you might possibly be . . . turned. That you might come
over to their side, and became a major embarrassment
to your homeland."

"But I've only cooperated to keep Fred and me
alive," she said, half-enraged, half-defensive. "I mean,
of course I felt betrayed and abandoned, by G. P. and
Franklin . . . but that didn't turn me into some kind
of traitor!"

It had to be asked: "How exactly have you cooperated?"

She smiled nervously, shrugging. "Well, you know,
they fished the Electra out of the waters . . . they put
her in slings and hauled her up onto the deck of that
battleship that picked us up, Fred and me. I don't exactly
know how they got the plane to Saipan . . . Fred said
on a barge, though I heard later someone actually flew
it here, and badly, crash-landing through some trees onto
the beach near the harbor. . . . Anyway, Chief Suzuki,
who's been very nice to me, said that things would be
better for me, and for Fred too, if I would answer a few
simple questions about my ship."

"Did you?"

"Yes, out at Aslito field. Over a period of several
months, I spoke with pilots and engineers, about the
plane and its various capabilities. I mean, it wasn't a
fighter plane, what was the harm? These engineers were
from a Tokyo firm called, uh . . . Mits-something."

"Mitsubishi?"

"Maybe. . . . Anyway, they made all sorts of repairs,
and we took the ship up a few times . . . that was the
last time I was in a plane. Just a passenger, though. Far

as I know, the Electra's still sitting in a hangar out at Aslito airfield. It's certainly not going anywhere without its engines."

I blinked. "Without . . . its engines?"

"Yes, the last time I saw the ship, maybe six months ago, the engines'd been removed."

Shipped off to Tokyo for further study.

I didn't have the heart to tell her that her flying laboratory had become the blueprint for the revamped Japanese fighter plane, the new and improved Zero. Her own disdain for war, and her love for flying, had created in her a deadly naïvete. On the other hand, it had helped keep her alive.

"Is, uh, Fred aware of how you've cooperated?"

The idea of that seemed almost to frighten her. "No! Oh my goodness, no—I've never admitted any of this to him. I know he wouldn't approve, and it would just agitate him. He has it so terrible, as it is. . . ."

"I'm afraid, Amy, that Fred's problems are going to be over very soon. That 'nice' Chief Suzuki informs me that the imperial government has approved Fred Noonan's execution."

I'd hit her with so many blows, she was almost punchy; she could barely reply. "W-what?"

"There's no way to sugar-coat this. I heard it from Suzuki's own lips. Fred Noonan is considered a dangerous prisoner, uncooperative, belligerent, but most important, he's a spy, and as such will be executed . . . and Chief Suzuki feels that you, despite being a fine and beautiful human being, are also a spy, and should face the same fate."

"Why did he tell you this?"

"Because he asked me . . . or rather, he asked Father O'Leary of the I.R.A. . . . to ascertain your true feelings about the Japanese."

She was shaking her head, as if she were reeling. "True feelings . . . ?"

"Are you sympathetic enough toward the Japanese, and bitter enough toward FDR and the United States, to come over to their side, as a valuable propaganda voice? To help them demonstrate that, as early as 1937, the United States committed an act of war upon imperial Japan?"

She was holding her head in her hands as if trying to keep it from exploding. "How this nightmare could become a greater nightmare, I never imagined . . . but it has . . . it has. . . ."

"The chief also wanted me to ascertain whether or not your sympathies could be maintained even after the execution of your cohort. Of course, they may try telling you he died of dysentery or dengue fever—"

"Horrible . . . horrible."

I took hold of her by the upper arms and swung her so that she directly faced me; I locked her eyes with mine. "Look, Amy. Love of my life, I don't know if I can spring Fred Noonan out of that concrete pillbox. But you, you're out walking around. The security around you is laughable. You think I can't get around those fat fuckers across the street? I can get you out of here. Tonight."

She was moving her head, as if shooing away flies. "Not without Fred . . . we can't leave Fred. . . ."

"It's too risky. I'm one man with one gun. A pair of native goons with nightsticks I can take out. Spring your guy out of a maximum-security cellblock . . . probably not."

Her mouth tightened; her jaw was firm; her eyes stony. "Then I'll stay. I'll talk to them. I'll convince them I'll cooperate if they'll spare Fred."

"They won't. They've decided. Sentence has been passed, baby. . . ."

She shook her head, firmly; her mouth was a thin narrow line. "No. After all we've been through, I can't leave him behind. I couldn't live with myself, couldn't look at myself in the mirror, knowing I'd abandoned somebody who'd been through what I'd been through, *worse* than I'd been through, no, you have to find a way, Nathan. You have to take us both . . . or leave us both behind."

I let go of her, sighing, throwing my hands up. "Even if this were possible, Amy, think about what you're saying, think of who you are, what you represent to so many people back home. Think of the young girls, cutting out stories about you from papers and magazines and pasting them in scrapbooks, like you did every time you saw some woman succeeding at a man's task . . . are you going to take their symbol, the symbol of American womanhood, and turn it into a smiling face on a red sun on a Jap flag?"

"If I have to," she said.

The breeze was picking up; palm fronds rustling.

"Yeah," I sighed. "And I don't blame you, either."

"When you came here," she said, "you didn't know where you'd find me, *if* you'd find me. I could have been in a prison cell. What would you have done, then?"

"I'd find a way to blast you the hell out."

She gripped my arm. Tight. "Then find a way. We can't leave Fred behind."

There was no moving her on the subject.

So I told her Suzuki and the governor had asked me to talk to Noonan—perhaps Noonan would reveal his secrets to an American priest; it was certainly worth a try, the Japs thought, before they killed him. I would accept their invitation, I told her, and look the jail over firsthand, and see what I could come up with.

This put some spring in her step as we walked back, that gray sky darkening, whether into evening or worse weather, I wasn't quite sure; the temperature was dropping and that cool breeze, carrying the smell of ocean, was driving out the copra and dried fish odor, or at least diminishing it.

I left her in her room, after a long slow kiss that promised wonderful rewards to a hero who succeeded at his impossible task, and went down to the lobby, where Jesus and Ramon were back at their old stand, their greasy hands filled with greasy cards.

"Tell Chief Suzuki," I said to Jesus, "that I need to see him."

Lord Jesus turned his face toward me, a flower seeking sun, and showed me those brown teeth again; it wasn't a smile. "I look like your errand boy?"

"No," I said, "you look like the chief's errand boy."

He thought about that, rose, brushed by me, in a stunning wave of body odor, and—without asking the clerk's permission—reached across the counter and used the phone. He spoke in Japanese. His eyes had told me he wasn't stupid, Suzuki had called Jesus his "top" native detective, and Amy said not to underestimate him; I was starting to see why: this beast spoke at least three languages.

When he trundled back, I had pulled up a rattan chair myself and was shuffling the deck of cards; I'd wash my hands, later. Ramon, whose eyes weren't smart, looked at Jesus as if his friend might have an explanation for my aberrant behavior.

"Chief be here soon," Jesus muttered.

"Fine," I said, shuffling. "You boys know how to play Chicago? Seven-card stud, high spade in the hole splits the pot? What are these matchsticks worth, anyway?"

I'd won a few thousand yen when the chief showed up; that was only a couple dollars but Jesus seemed pretty resentful, just the same.

"You have talked to Amira?" Suzuki asked me. He was in the company of yet another member of the Chamorro police auxiliary, a shorter but no less burly boy with a billy club in the belt of his threadbare white suit.

I nodded. We were still in the cramped lobby. Leaning toward Suzuki confidentially, I said, "Why don't we walk over to the jail? I'd like to talk to the other pilot, now. I'll fill you in on the way."

"Fill in?"

"Tell you what Amira told me."

He left the short Chamorro in Jesus's stead, bidding his top *jungkicho* to tag along with us. Jesus kept a respectful distance, the billy and machete stuck in his belt, crossing in a menacing X.

On the way to the jail, I told the chief that Amelia had indicated she would be cooperative; that she was truly enamored of the Japanese and would willingly collaborate.

"She accept death of pilot?"

That was how they referred to Noonan: pilot.

"I didn't get that far," I pretended to admit. "She seems loyal to him. Must he die?"

"Animal man," Suzuki said, shivering in disgust. "Throws food. Strike at jailer." He shook his head, no. "No mercy for pilot. You talk to him now?"

"Yes," I said.

At the jail, in a small office that but for its desk and filing cabinets was itself a concrete-walled cell, Chief Suzuki introduced me to a compact, brawny police officer, in the usual white uniform but minus gunbelt and sword; this was Sergeant Kinashi, a smiling mustached man in his thirties, the warden of Garapan Prison who, in prison guard tradition, did not wear weapons around the cells and prisoners.

Sergeant Kinashi spoke no English, but he was very gracious, in fact sickeningly solicitous, to the visiting Irish-American priest, as he led us from the boxcar main cellblock to the nearby, smaller building, the four-cell maximum-security bungalow. Though we were within the town of Garapan, the prison was set off by itself, surrounded by jungle overgrowth, which provided shade as well as an ominous backdrop, palm trees hovering like guard towers. A little parade of us—Sergeant Kinashi, Chief Suzuki, Lord Jesus and me—went up the short flight of steps and inside.

The space between the prison wall and the four barred cells allowed guards and visitors a shallow walkway; the prison wall at our backs provided most of the light, with barred windows that let in air (and flies and mosquitoes) and cut down on, but did not nullify, the fusty fragrance of body odor, shit, piss and general stagnation. None of that prissy, irritating disinfectant odor you run into in American jails; just pure, natural stench.

Each cell had a single high window, narrow and barred; eight feet by eight feet, the cells would have made generous closets. They had thatched sleeping mats and, in one corner, a built-in open-top concrete box three feet square, a toilet for prisoners, an airfield for flies.

Of the four cells that made up this small solid building, the one at far left was empty, the center two were occupied (a pair of Chamorro cattle rustlers, the chief said), and at far right, regarding us through his cell bars with skeptical eyes, his arms folded, stood a tall skinny white man with a bushy curly beard, dark brown mixed in with gray. He wore a filthy, occasionally ripped, crumpled-looking khaki flight suit; his feet were sandaled.

Under a mop of widow's-peaked, dark brown graying hair, he had a long, hawkish, weathered, grooved, defiant mask of a face, eyes dark and wild in deep sockets. A nasty angular white scar streaked his forehead. His teeth were large and yellow and smiling within the thicket of beard.

Fred Noonan was home, when I came calling.

"We honor you with visit," Chief Suzuki said with low-key contempt. "American priest. Father Brian O'Leary."

"I'm a Protestant," Noonan said, his voice a gravelly baritone, "but what the hell."

"In our culture," I said to Suzuki, "it's traditional for holy men visiting prisoners to have privacy."

"Cannot open cell door," the chief said, shaking his head, no.

"That's fine," I said, gesturing to the closed door between Noonan and me. "Just leave us alone like this."

"I will have Jesus stay, protect you," he said, nodding to the massive Chamorro.

"No thank you," I said. And then I said, pointedly, "I need to be alone with the prisoner to do what I need to do."

"Ah," Suzuki said, remembering I was on a mission for him, and nodded. He bellowed a few Japanese phrases, and the warden, Lord Jesus and the Chief of Saipan Police left me alone with my one-man flock.

I checked out the window and could see Sergeant Kinashi heading back into the main building, while the chief and his *jungkicho* were huddling for a smoke, standing well away from our cellblock bungalow.

Noonan stood near the bars with his arms unfolded; they hung funny, sort of askew.

My eyes were drawn to these poor twisted limbs. "What did they do to you?" I asked.

"I got smart with the bastards, Father," he said, "and they broke my arms. It was that good-lookin' fellow named after our savior. They didn't set 'em or anything. No sissy casts. Just let 'em heal naturally. I coulda used a miracle, Father. But I didn't get one. . . . You wouldn't have a drink on you, by any chance?"

"No."

"Picked a hell of a way to dry out, didn't I?"

I glanced out the window one more time; the two men were smoking, talking.

"Do your neighbors speak English?" I asked, nodding toward the cells where the dark faces of the rustlers looked at me curiously.

"They can hardly speak their own native gibberish," he said, eyes narrowing in their deep sockets. "Why?"

"Listen," I said, moving close. The smell from the cell was as foul as a rotting corpse. "We're only gonna have a little bit of time."

"To do what? Who the hell are you?"

"It's not important. . . . Nate Heller."

His eyes narrowed even tighter, and glittered. "I know that name. . . ."

"Old friend of Amelia's."

He began to nod, smile. "More than a *friend*. . . ."

Apparently, on their long flight, he and Amy had shared a few secrets.

"Listen," I said, "the Yellow Peril out there thinks I'm an I.R.A. priest. . . ."

Noonan, an Irishman himself, chuckled. "Not a bad way to get onto this hellhole island. But why would you want to?"

"Our loving uncle sent me to see if you and Amelia were guests of Hirohito."

"The answer is yes. . . . I hope you didn't come alone."

"Afraid I did—I got a way out of here tonight, though." I glanced around the concrete bunker. "Is there any way I can bust you out of this hatbox?"

He laughed the most humorless of laughs from deep in his sunken chest. "A small army couldn't . . ." Then, with sudden urgency, he said, "But you can take Amelia! They her got in this hotel over—"

"I know. I spent the afternoon with her." I slipped a hand through the bars and onto his shoulder; and squeezed. "But she won't go without you."

He backed away from my touch, eyes so wide they filled the sockets. "That's crazy! She *has* to. . . ."

"When do they let you into the exercise yard?"

"Not more'n once a week, and I was just out there yesterday. No set schedule."

"Damn." I checked the window again; Mutt-san and Jeff-san were still smoking. "Fred. If you'll forgive the familiarity . . ."

"I'll let it slide this once."

My hands gripped the bars as if I were the prisoner. "Chief Suzuki sent me in here to see if you'd spill your guts to a priest . . . a last-ditch effort to get something out of a very stubborn prisoner."

He was studying me like he must have studied his charts. "You sayin' what I think you're sayin'?"

"You're under a sentence of death. Today, tomorrow, a week, maybe two. But probably no more. I'm sorry."

Another hollow laugh. "*You're* sorry . . ."

"Amelia's under the same death sentence. She thinks she can manipulate these clowns, but we know better, don't we? She's already spilled a lot, Fred, about the souped-up aspects of the Electra. . . ."

The yellow teeth clenched in the nest of beard, and he spat, "Damn it, anyway. That's a pacifist for you. Damn it. . . . Listen, Nate, you gotta get her offa this island. She doesn't deserve this fate." He shook his head. "Me, I knew what I was getting into. I'm military; she's civilian. It was wrong how they used her . . . hell. How *we* used her. She didn't even know we were flyin' over the Mandates, till—"

"I can get her out tonight, Fred."

"Then *do* it!"

"*You* have to do it. You have to help me convince Amelia to leave you behind. Can you think of some way to do that?"

He lowered his head; he laughed but no sound came out. Then he said, "Yeah."

"I mean, some message. . . ."

"I know what you mean."

". . . I'm sorry."

"*You're* sorry."

I was. It was a hell of a thing I was asking.

"I better go," I said.

I offered him my hand, and, twisted arm or not, he shook it, with a firm grip worthy of the adventurer who had helped chart the Pacific for Pan Am, not to mention his country.

I turned away.

"Heller! Nate. . . ."

"Yeah . . . ?"

"I got a wife." He swallowed and his eyes were brimming with tears. "Didn't have her very long, but she was a honey. Mary Beatrice. Some people call her Bea, but I like Mary. That's what I call Amelia, too. . . . Smartest thing I ever did, marrying that girl, followed by the dumbest. Would you tell her something for me?"

"Sure."

". . . Make it something nice."

"It'll be a fuckin' poem, pal."

He grinned through his beard and held a thumb's-up. "Do me another favor—call 'em in here. And hang around, a while, would you? Keep me company? Moral support?"

"Well, sure. . . ."

He snorted a laugh. "Tell ol' Chief Suki-yaki that I got something for him."

I nodded, went to the door and called out. "Chief, the prisoner would like to speak with you. He has something for you!"

The chief smiled, pleased that his strategy had worked, obviously thinking that my priestly counsel had loosened the prisoner's tongue. He sucked a last drag on his cigarette, sent it trailing sparks into the high grass, and marched toward me, with Lord Jesus completing the procession.

As they were entering, Noonan whispered, "You might want to stand to one side, Father . . . this could be messy."

I didn't know what the hell that meant, but I moved to one side as Chief Suzuki, Lord Jesus just behind and to the left of him, positioned himself before Fred Noonan's cell.

Chin high, regally proud, the chief asked, "You have something for me, pilot?"

"Oh yeah," Noonan said, his grin as wild as his eyes, and he reached back into the open concrete box of shit and piss and grabbed a big handful and hurled it; the stuff sluiced through the bars and spattered the clean white uniforms of both the chief and Lord Jesus, and clots of dung clung to both their faces like lumpy awful birthmarks.

Noonan stood right up against the bars of his cell and howled in laughter at them. He was still laughing when Lord Jesus stepped snarling forward and swung the machete back and down, between the bars, and through the top of Noonan's head, between his eyes, splitting his hawk nose, the machete handle extending like a new one.

When Lord Jesus yanked the machete loose, as if from a melon, Noonan—silent now—felt backward, blood geysering the cell wall, brightening his gloomy surroundings, depending on me to deliver his message to Amelia.

Nineteen

The Nangetsu was a shabby wood-frame pagoda-roofed two-story, just another crummy Garapan storefront, only the windows facing the street were not glass showcases, but tightly closed double-shuttered affairs, in a section of the waterfront Chief Suzuki referred to as the town's *hana machi*—"flower quarters." This was one of a cluster of similar buildings huddled like conspirators between warehouses and fishery sheds: *ryoriyas,* which Chief Suzuki translated as "restaurants," though that definition would soon prove to be loose. It had been an easy walk over here from the prison, for the chief, his favorite *jungkicho* and me.

After a fawning greeting inside the door from a short chubby fiftyish woman in a scarlet Dragon Lady slit dress, we moved through the front half of the restaurant, where steamy food smells erased the waterfront reek. The dimly lighted room was an odd combination of shabby and elegant, unpainted, unvarnished rough-wooden walls and ungainly tile floor laid right on the dirt, but the wall decorations were elaborate Japanese murals and splayed silk fans, as Japanese men (no young men, late twenties or older) in white bathrobes sat on cushions at low-slung red-trimmed black lacquered tables while attractive women in colorful kimonos served them. When the women had finished serving their cups and bowls of this and that, they were joining the men at the tables.

The Chief of Saipan Police had taken Father O'Leary to a whorehouse.

We were ushered by the chubby Dragon Lady down a short corridor, where a sliding rice paper door gave entry to a small room that was mostly a sunken tub of steaming water. We were here, after all, to bathe, my companions having been the recipients of flung dung, which was not an Oriental delicacy but a gutsy final statement by one hell of an American.

I remained somewhat shell-shocked; I'd seen my share of savagery in the wilds of Chicago, but I'd never witnessed a murder quite like the one I'd just seen at Garapan Prison. The immediate aftermath had been a chilling display of bizarre face-saving. Chief Suzuki—who one might expect to rebuke his Chamorro protégé for showing a certain lack of restraint, in his machete-wielding response to Fred Noonan's shit-hurling affront—had turned to Jesus and, feces still dripping from his face, bowed to his dusky associate in respect and thanks.

We were now in a sunken hot steaming tub of water, to get the shit washed off (none had gotten on me, thanks to the late Fred Noonan's warning). This was also Suzuki's way of rewarding Jesus Sablan for defending the chief's honor. Jesus was clearly the only Chamorro in this brothel, and I'd noticed the chief placing a fat handful of funny money in the madam's palm, doing some quick whispered explaining to her while nodding in Jesus's direction.

As we relaxed in the steaming water, sipping glasses of *awamori,* a potent mullet brandy, the chief—whose body was smoothly scrawny—said to his associate, "I send for new clothing. I ask *shakufu* burn dishonored clothes."

I gathered *shakufu* referred to that barmaid madam who'd walked us back here.

Lord Jesus said nothing—his eyes were wide and moving side to side as he luxuriated in the steaming, scented, oil-pooled water, in what was obviously a new experience for him; hell, maybe bathing itself was a new experience for him. He was a curious combination of brawn and fat, cords of sinew alternating with flaps of flab, his heavily muscled outspread arms surrounding half the tub.

Then the chief turned his gaze upon me. "With pilot dead, is Amira lost?"

"Only if you tell her the truth about his death," I said, matter-of-factly. "I believe you can still count on her cooperation."

Lord Jesus, leaning back limply with his glass of *awamori* in hand, had an expression of bliss, his eyes half-shut, his mouth open in moronic ecstasy. I wondered if he'd worn a similar expression when he pressed the glowing red tip of a cigarette to Amy's gentle throat.

"Pilot die dengue fever?" Suzuki suggested.

"*Hai,*" I said, smiling, nodding, as if this were a brilliant notion.

Water had gotten on his gray mustache and it was dripping down his smile. "You tell her for us? Make her believe?"

"You honor me with this mission," I said. "I am sorry I failed with the pilot. I will not fail again."

"No apology," Suzuki said. "Barbarian pilot is better dead. Deal with woman now."

"I can tell you, as an American, that the woman's value to your country, alive, would far outweigh the alternative."

Suzuki frowned, not understanding. "All-turn . . . ?"

"Kill her," Lord Jesus said.

I wasn't sure whether he was explaining the meaning of what I'd said, or making his own suggestion.

Soon three slender geishas had padded in, stepped from their cheap faded rayon kimonos and slippers, and slipped down into the tub, where they began washing us.

"If you have religion problem," the chief said, apparently noting that I was ill at ease, "please to say."

"Actually, yes," I said. Normally I wouldn't have minded a Madam Butterfly soaping my privates, even if I did seem to have drawn a somewhat withered flower. I had a feeling Saipan was where Tokyo shipped their aging talent.

"If you don't mind," I said, putting my barely touched glass of *awamori* down, "I'll walk back to the hotel. Any man's death is troubling to a man of the cloth."

The chief nodded solemnly; he had regained considerable dignity since the shit got cleaned off his face. Lord

Jesus was lost in the nirvana of a massage from a geisha whose ability to hide her distaste was miraculous.

I smiled at my geisha, trying to send her a message that my rejection of her charms wasn't personal, and she smiled back with a sadness in her eyes as old as her country. As I climbed out, she brought me towels and a robe.

Drying off, I said to the chief, "I'll talk to the woman tonight, and report to you tomorrow."

"Thank you," Chief Suzuki said with a respectful nod. *"Konichiwa."*

I exited the brothel into a late afternoon that had turned ugly and cold, under a rolling, growling charcoal sky. Gun-metal waves were splashing up over the concrete jetty; a trio of immense freighters anchored in the harbor took the rough waters stoically, but fishing sampans tied to a concrete finger of a pier seemed almost to jump out of the water. This was not good. But it would not stop me. Turning up the collars of my priestly black suitcoat, I walked against the wind, the hotel only a few blocks away.

This time when I knocked, the door opened right now and there she was, standing before me, blue-gray eyes at once shiny with hope and red with despair, mouth quivering as if not quite daring to smile, hoping I'd returned with the foolproof plan that would liberate Fred Noonan and send us all happily home.

But she knew me too well; she knew the little smile I gave her did not bode well.

"Oh my goodness . . ."

She took a step back as I moved into the room, which had turned dark and cool with the afternoon; she still wore the short-sleeve mannish white shirt and rust slacks, her feet bare. I shut the door, as she asked, "You can't help him?"

I took her arm, gently, and walked her to the chair by the window, which she had lowered, but not all the way, the cool wind sneaking in to riffle the covers, the pages, of the magazines on the table, colorful images of smiling Japanese.

Kneeling before her, like a suitor, I enfolded her hands in mine, gazed at her with all the tenderness I could summon and said, "No one can help him now. Amy, they executed Fred this afternoon."

She didn't say anything, but outside the wind howled in pain; her chin quivered, tears trickled. Slowly, she shook her head, her eyes hooded with grief.

"That's why they wanted me to talk to him," I said, patting her hand. "To give him Last Rites."

A spattering of rain had begun; filmy curtains reached out in ghostly gesture.

She swallowed. "How? Was it . . . quick?"

"It was quick," I said. "They shot him in his cell, right in front of me. Couldn't do a damn thing . . . I'm so sorry."

My lies softened the blow only slightly; but she mustn't know the sacrifice he made, and had to be spared the grotesque details of his death.

Still, she knew Noonan too well not to come close, within a consonant actually, saying, "I bet he spit in their eye."

"Oh yes."

"Nathan . . . it hurts."

Still kneeling, I held out my arms to her, like Jolson singing "Swanee," and she tumbled into my embrace and we kind of switched around so that I was sitting in the chair, she was in my lap like a big kid, grabbing tight, face buried in my neck, the tears turning from trickle to downpour, as outside the sky imitated her.

We were like that for several minutes, and then the rain was coming in, so I eased her to her feet, and walked her to the padded quilts, where she sat, slumping. I closed the window, leaving an inch for air, switched on the reading lamp, whose translucent tan shade created a golden glow. Sick of playing priest, I removed the suitcoat, and the clerical-collared shirt, and in my T-shirt went over and sat beside her. Our legs were stretched out laxly before us, our arms hung loose, puppets whose strings had been snipped.

She was staring into nothing at all. "He suffered so. They were so terribly cruel to him . . . it makes me . . ."

And she covered her face and began to weep, sobs racking her body. I put my arm around her, patting her back as if comforting a child, but I knew there was nothing I could say or do. Could I even understand what she was going through? Could anyone, except Fred Noonan?

Finally she looked at me with wide red-rimmed eyes, her lightly powdered face streaked with tears, and said, "I feel so guilty, Nathan. So guilty . . . I've had it so easy, compared to Fred."

"Nothing to feel guilty about," I assured her. "It was out of your control."

"I didn't fight them, like he did. He was brave. I was a coward."

"You were in prison, too."

She shook her head, no, violently, no. "Not like him. Not like him."

"Well, he's free now. Be happy for him."

She blinked some tears away. "You really look at it that way?"

"I saw how he was living. He was glad to go. Believe me. Wherever he is, it has to be a better place than that."

Thinking that over, she lay down, resting her head in my lap, pulling her knees up, like a fetus, and I stroked that curly head of hair while she quietly cried and snuffled and even slept for a few minutes.

Finally, with her head still in my lap, she looked up and asked, "Can we really get out of here?"

"Yes. The schooner that brought me here, the *Yankee*, is anchored out beyond the three-mile limit. They've spent the day waiting to see if I'll need a lift home tonight—the captain and his first mate'll come in, in their motor launch, and pull up on the other side of that little island just off the waterfront—Maniagawa—and watch for me."

"When?"

"When else? Midnight."

Two escape routes had been arranged for me: Captain Johnson and his dinghy, tonight; or if I needed more time, in two days (as I'd told the *shichokan*), passage was arranged with a German trader. If I missed both my rides, I'd be on my own, though with Guam so nearby, a hijacked motorboat remained a viable third option.

"Is this rain going to be a problem?" she wondered.

The storm was rattling the window.

"It could be a help," I said. "What fools but us will be out in it?"

She sat up. Hope was back in her eyes. "We'll just . . . walk out of here?"

I cupped her face in my hands. "Baby, we'll just slip out the window in my room. Don't those native watch-dogs usually camp out in the lobby?"

"Yes."

I slipped my arm around her shoulder and drew her to me. "Well, they won't even know we're gone, till to-morrow morning sometime. They don't watch the back door, 'cause there isn't one, right?"

She nodded. "Originally, there was a side exit, but it was blocked off . . . this hotel *is* a sort of jail."

"So they only watch the front door."

She nodded again. "Where will your schooner captain pick us up?"

"Right on the dock. Right where he dropped me off."

The sky cracked like a whip, then a low rumble followed.

I asked her, "Do they check on you? Bring you meals or anything?"

"They hardly bother me. I take my meals at that restaurant across the street."

"Then all we have to do is sit tight for a few hours."

"Well . . . after all, we do have some catching up to do."

"We really do."

"Nathan. . . . Turn off that light."

"All right. . . ."

I got up and switched off the reading lamp and when I turned she was standing beside the padded quilts, un-buttoning the white blouse; beneath it was a wispy peach bra with (she revealed as she unzipped the rust trousers) matching silky step-ins. Her flesh took on cool tones of blue, as the reflected rain streaking down the window projected itself onto the walls, shadow ribbons of darker blue making abstract flowing patterns along the lanky curves of her body. She undid the bra and let it fall, baring the small, girlishly pert breasts, then stepped from the step-ins, standing naked, shoulders back, unashamed, legs long and lean and even muscular, clothing pooled at her bare feet, her slender shapely body painted with the textures of the storm, arms held out to me beseechingly.

It was time for Father O'Leary to take his pants off.

We made love tenderly, we made love savagely, we made up for lost time and laughed and wept, and when she rode me, her preferred posture, strong-willed woman that she was, her ivory body washed in the blue shadows of the streaky rain, she made love with an abandon and joy that she otherwise must have found only in the sky. I will never forget her lovely face hovering above me, gazing down with heartbreaking fondness, her face bright with joy, then lost in passion, drunk with sensation, and finally aglow with the bittersweet sense of loss fulfillment exacts.

Later, since we were after all in an unlocked room in the political "hotel" of our hosts, Father O'Leary and a fully clothed Amira sat on the quilts in the cool blue reflection of the rain coming down. A pitcher of water poured into her basin had allowed us to wash up and she mentioned that this current rain was welcome.

"Rainwater's important here," she said. "The ground water on this island has an awful, brackish taste."

"I thought it rained every time you turn around, in the tropics."

"We don't get much in the summer, but winter monsoon season is pretty fierce. Lots of frequent, short showers."

I wondered if she realized she spoke of Saipan almost as her home? And hadn't it been, for almost three years?

"This is shaping up like a typhoon," she said, looking toward the window. The shadows on the walls were darker, moving more quickly, and the wind sounded angry. The direction of the rain seemed to have shifted, coming down straighter, hitting the tin roof of the one-story house next door in hard pellets, unrelenting liquid machine gun fire.

She asked me questions about home, pleased that Paul Mantz had remarried ("That Terry is a terrific gal"); I gave her more details on her husband's remarriage, which only seemed to wryly amuse her, now. She had no idea her disappearance had been the center of such worldwide attention and seemed rather flattered, even touched. Bitterly, though, she commented that the multi-million-dollar naval search must have largely been an excuse to pry in these waters.

She also spoke of her life in Saipan, which was very solitary. Other than Chief Suzuki, Jesus Sablan and a few officials, like the *shichokan,* she knew of no one in Garapan who spoke fluent English, and—despite her ability to traverse the downtown—she had made few friends.

"The Chamorro family next door," she said, pointing toward the window, and the rat-a-tat-tat tin-roof rainfall, "has been kind." She laughed softly. "I got to know them on my trips to the privy . . . it's in back of their house. They have a little girl, Matilda, maybe twelve, a sweet thing. She knows some English, and I tried to help her with her homework, now and then. I gave her a ring with a pearl as a keepsake. . . . Her parents are nice, too, they give me fresh fruit, pineapples, mangoes, which is something I can't find at the Japanese market. Food's awful—everything's out of a can or a jar."

"I noticed," I said with a smile.

The room turned white from lightning, and the thunderclap was like cannon fire.

"Are you sure this rain won't be a problem?" she asked. "For us leaving tonight?"

"No, it's helpful," I lied. "Listen . . . it's getting close to time. I'm going down and check on the chumps in the lobby. . . . You better look around this room and see if there's anything you want to take with you."

Her laugh sounded like a cough. "I don't think I'll be looking back on this room with much nostalgia."

"Well, look over your personal items, things you brought with you . . . wrap up a little bundle, if you have to, but travel light."

She smirked. "Don't worry."

"I'll go down and distract the fellas. . . . Wait maybe a minute after I leave, then go down to my room and slip inside."

She nodded.

I was almost out the door when she clutched my arm.

I leaned over and kissed her. "We're gonna be apart for two, maybe three minutes," I said. "Think you can bear up?"

She shook her head, no; she was smiling but her eyes were moist. "I'm afraid."

"Good. That's healthy. Only the dead are fearless."

"Like Fred."

"Like Fred," I said, and touched her face, and stepped into the hallway.

It was empty. My hunch was the entire floor was vacant, except for Amy. The only other person I'd seen who seemed to be staying here was the desk clerk or the manager or whoever he was, who had the first room off the little lobby. I moved down the stairs, and through another empty hallway.

In the lobby, the check-in desk was unoccupied, and the ceiling fan whirred sluggishly over two Chamorro assistant coppers in their threadbare white suits. I knew them both: fatso Ramon, of the cantaloupe head and blankly stupid countenance, was seated in the rattan chair where Jesus had been previously plopped; and across from him was the short, burly officer who Suzuki had brought in to sub for Jesus. They were playing cards, of course, with what seemed to be the same greasy deck. Billy clubs and matchsticks again littered the rattan coffee table.

"Where's Jesus?" I asked Ramon.

"Paint town red," Ramon grinned. It wasn't as nasty as Jesus's grin but it was nasty enough.

"Oh, he's still out with the chief?"

Ramon nodded, fat fingers holding the smeary cards close to his face, eyes almost crossing as he studied his hand.

Then I asked the burly character, who had a lumpy sweet-potato nose and pockmarks (though the latter weren't nearly in Jesus Sablan's league), if he knew how to play Chicago. His grasp of English was obviously less than that of Ramon, who having played a few hands with me this afternoon, frowned at my apparent interest in joining them.

"No!" Ramon said. "No play. Go hell."

This rebuff was fine with me. I didn't really want to

play cards with these wild boars; I was just keeping them busy long enough for Amy to slip down the stairs and into my room.

Which, a few seconds later, was exactly where I found her, wearing her weathered wrinkled flying jacket, pacing and holding her stomach; my room seemed darker than hers, perhaps because my window onto the house next door did not overlook its rooftop.

"I feel sick," she said. "Sick to my stomach, like before going onstage to give a stupid lecture. . . ."

I was digging the nine-millimeter out of my travel bag. "Do you get butterflies before you take off in a plane?"

"Never."

I checked the chamber; the bolt action made a nasty echoey click. "Well, this is more like takin' off on a flight than giving a lecture. So tell your stomach to take it easy."

She sucked in air, nodded.

Now, if only my belly would take that same good advice.

I slipped the extra clip into my suitcoat pocket. I wasn't taking anything with me but the clothes on my person, the gun in my hand and Amy. That leather flight jacket was apparently the only keepsake she was taking along. Thunder rumbled and cracked, sounding fake, like a radio sound effects guy shaking a thin sheet of steel.

She swept into my arms and I held her tight, and her eyes widened as she looked at my right hand with the automatic held nose upward. "Is there going to be violence?"

"Only if that's what it takes. Pacifists get off at this stop. . . . Okay?"

She swallowed. "Okay."

"If there is . . . violence . . . you have to stay calm. If you ran into trouble up in the air, you could stay calm, right?"

"Usually."

"Well, I need that world-famous nerves-of-steel pilot at my side, right now. Okay? Is she here?"

"She's here."

"Now." And I held her away from me and gave her

a goofy little smile. "Sooner or later in the life of a man having an affair with a married woman, the inevitable occurs."

She couldn't help it; she smiled back at me. "Which is?"

"Nate Heller goes out the window."

And I opened the window—no bars on this prison—and went out first, into the downpour, a splattering, insistent rain that was surprising in its power, my feet sinking into grassy, muddy ground several inches. The window was up off the ground a ways and I held my arms for her to slip down into, as if we were eloping, and then she was in my arms and she blinked and blinked as water drummed her face and she grinned reflexively, saying "Oh my goodness!"

And, as if she were my bride just ushered over the threshold, I eased her onto the sodden ground, where her slippered feet sank in almost to the ankle.

"This is going to be slow going!" I said, having to work to be heard over the driving rain and grumbling sky.

We were between the hotel and the house next door—there wasn't much space, not much more than a hallway's worth. So I got in front of her, leading her by the hand; my nine-millimeter was stuck in my waistband. We hadn't taken more than two soggy steps when the voice behind us cried out, "Hey!"

I looked back, past Amy, and saw him: Ramon, coming out of the outdoor toilet, buckling his pants with one hand and coming at us with the raised billy club in the other. His chubby body charged through the curtain of rain as if it were nothing more than moisture, his sandaled feet making rhino craters in the muddy earth, his eyes wide and dark and brightly animal, like a frightened raccoon's, only a raccoon would have had sense enough to flee and here Ramon was barreling right toward me, moving faster than a fat man had any right to move, and I pulled Amy back behind me, closer to the street, and thrust myself forward and just as Ramon entered the tunnel between hotel and house, my nine-millimeter slug entered the melon of his head, somewhere in his forehead, lifting the top of his skull in fragments, revealing in a spray of red that Ramon did indeed have a brain, before he tumbled backward, careening off the house next door, then splatting against the hotel, where he slid down its cement surface and sank into the mud like an animal carcass on its way to becoming a fossil.

Amy screamed and I rudely covered her mouth with my hand until her wide eyes and nodding told me she wouldn't scream anymore and she was trembling and crying as I stood there with a fucking monsoon dripping down my head, saying, "Nobody heard that gunshot, not in this shit . . . but I gotta go in and deal with the other one!"

"Why?!"

"Because Ramon here can't take a dump forever. The other one's gonna go checking on him, and I can't have that!"

"Are you going to kill him?"

"Not if he's smart."

And what were the odds of that?

So I left her there, in the passageway between hotel and house, rain pummeling her as she covered her mouth, her back turned to the horror of what had become of Ramon, and I moved out onto the street and inside the hotel where the burly Chamorro looked around at me, and I swung the nine-millimeter barrel across the side of his skull in a fashion that would not only knock out most any man, but probably fucking kill him.

Only this son of a bitch shook it off, and went for the billy club on the table.

I put a bullet in his ear that wound up going through his reaching hand, as well, though I doubt he felt it. He tumbled onto the rattan table, breaking it in a crunch of shattering straw.

Now he knew how to play Chicago.

Just down the hall, out of the first hotel room door, the Chamorro desk clerk stuck out his mustached face. His eyes were huge.

"He didn't understand that real cops have guns," I told him. I went over and reached across the check-in counter and yanked his phone out of the wall. "Do I have to kill you or tie you up or anything?"

He shook his head, no, crossed himself, and ducked back into his room.

Then I ran out into the rain, the nine-millimeter back in my waistband, and Amy came flying out from between the house and the hotel. I slipped my arm around her waist and we ran down the boardwalk. No one was around; the unpaved street next to us was a swamp no vehicle could have navigated. From across the way, in a seedy little bar, came the sound of a gramophone playing a Dorsey Brothers record, "Lost in a Fog," and Chamorro kids were dancing, boys and girls holding each other close, swaying to the record's rhythm, ignoring the staccato percussion of the downpour.

When we ran out of boardwalk, the grassy ground provided a terrible soggy glue, but we moved along, stumbling, never quite falling, slowed though not quite caught in this just-poured cement. Through the sheeting rain we glimpsed the concrete cellblocks of the prison, impervious to the pounding storm, then ducked out of the way as a tin roof, flung recklessly by the wind, went pitching across our path, carving a resting place in the face of a wood-frame warehouse. Exchanging startled looks, and grabbing gulps of air, we moved on, pushing past our old friend the sugar king in his park as palm trees bowed down to him.

Then, along the waterfront, we had boardwalk under our mud-coated feet again, and the two-story buildings around us lessened the squall's impact, though we were heading into the wind, and it took effort just to walk, our clothes so drenched they were heavy, our hair soaked flat to our scalps. A block away yawned the expanse of the Garapan harbor's concrete dock. We were early, maybe five, maybe ten minutes; would the storm have delayed Johnson? Would it have defeated him entirely, and had I blasted my way out of one dead end and into another?

And with these questions barely posed, bad luck rendered their answers moot.

Because just as we were passing through the *hana machi* section of the waterfront, where men who were men drank *awamori* and had their manly needs tended to by faded flowers, Chief Mikio Suzuki and Jesus

Sablan, drunk as skunks, came stumbling out of the Nangetsu, after an evening of revelry signifying the chief's gratitude for his top *jungkicho's* earlier display of loyalty.

Only drunks—particularly drunks who were outfitted in new, fresh clothes (even the Chamorro wore fresh white linens)—would have exited in the midst of this tempest, their finery immediately getting saturated.

But these were dangerous drunks, who looking across the liquefied goo of the unpaved waterfront street, recognized us, Amira and Father O'Leary.

And at first Chief Suzuki smiled.

So I smiled and waved and nodded.

But then Chief Suzuki frowned, even in his inebriated state smelling something fishy, not that difficult to do in this part of town, and he shrieked in Japanese at Lord Jesus, who also frowned, and they ran toward us.

We kept moving, too, toward the dock. We were on the boardwalk and the Chief and Jesus were trying to run across a sucking mucky morass. I drew my gun.

"Nathan!" she cried, and I just pulled her along.

"Amira!" the chief yelled. *"Leary!"*

I looked back at them and they were making progress but we were almost there, almost to where the cement apron of the waterfront led to the jetty itself.

Then a thundercrack that wasn't a thundercrack startled me and I looked back to see that Suzuki had pulled his gun, I'd forgotten he had one, his suitcoat had been buttoned over it, and I fired back at him. It caught him in the right shoulder but the drunken little bastard barely winced, just shifted his revolver to his other hand and fired again.

Amy screamed.

"Are you hit?" I yelled, putting myself between her and the chief.

"No! I'm scared!"

I fired again and this one caught him either in the chest or the shoulder, I wasn't sure which, but the gun fumbled from his fingers and was swallowed into the sludge. The chief just stood there, arms limp, weaving, whether from liquor or pain, who could say?

But what was worse, what was much worse, was Lord Jesus.

He was lumbering toward us, his right arm raised, hand filled with the machete, eyes showing the whites all 'round, teeth bared in a ghastly grimace of a smile. Lightning turned the street white and winked off that wide wicked blade.

I was still moving forward when I fired back at him, fired twice, hitting him once, somewhere in the midsection but it didn't even slow him down. Behind him I could see the wounded chief waddling like a penguin, heading back toward the Nangetsu, no doubt to call in the alarm signal, goddamnit! Still running, pushing Amy out in front of me, I fired back behind me again and this time caught Jesus in the left shoulder. He felt it, he yowled, but he was still coming.

We were on the cement now, and stretching before us, beyond the concrete jetty, were choppy but not impossible waters, rough wild waters but a sailor like Captain Irving Johnson could maneuver on them. . . .

Only there was no sight of him.

Maniagawa Island beckoned; you could almost reach out and touch it . . . but no motor launch in sight. Just rolling waves and angry sky.

And Jesus had made it to the cement, and his machete was poised to strike and my muddy feet slipped as I fired, the bullet taking a piece of his ear off but not important enough a piece of anything to stop him from lunging in and swinging that blade, and Amy screamed as I felt that blade carve through my clerical collar and the front of my suitcoat and cut the cloth and cut me, a gaping wide C from my right collarbone to my left hip bone and it was wet and stung but I could tell it wasn't deep, and I fired a round into the bastard's stomach and his yelp of agony was the sweetest fucking sound I ever heard. He tumbled face first to the cement, like a huge catch onto the deck of a fisherman's boat, and I turned with my upper lip peeled back over my teeth in what must have been one frightening demented smile, because Amy drew back from me in alarm.

Then she moved close to me, looking at the front of me. "He cut you! He hurt you!"

"I cut myself shaving worse than this." Gulping for air but getting mostly rain, unrelenting goddamn rain, I looked out into the restless waters and saw nothing but waves and dark sky; then lightning illuminated those waters, seemingly to the horizon, and showed me nothing new—no rescue craft. Had Johnson double-crossed me, at Miller's behest?

"Either we're early," I said, "or they're late."

"Or they're not coming!"

Out of breath, panting, I said, "That nice chiefy of yours is probably calling out the guard. We have to get out of here. Got any ideas?"

Breathing hard, too, she nodded. Thunder exploded as her arm thrust past me and I followed her pointing finger to the nearby, unguarded seaplane dock. The two flying boats floated there, tied at the ramp.

Right out in the open.

"Can you fly one of those things?" I asked.

She tossed her head; moisture beads flew. She was smiling, proud. "I'm Amelia Earhart," she reminded me.

"Oh yeah," I said.

And we ran, leaving the body of Lord Jesus behind, with no resurrection in the plans, ran across the cement, feet splashing, kids playing in the rain, and climbed a ridiculous little waist-high chain-link fence and scooted down the ramp. I untied the moorings, and she was already wading out into where the planes bobbed in the rough water. Then I was doing the same, climbing up onto the pontoon on my rider's side, as she climbed on her pontoon to get access to the cockpit.

That was when the shots started flying.

The police station was only a few short minutes' walk from the waterfront, even in the rain, and the chief's reinforcements were streaking toward us, getting their white uniforms wet, bullets zinging and careening off the flying boat's green fuselage.

The sound of a motor—and it wasn't the flying boat's, she wasn't in that cockpit yet—drew my attention back out to the water, despite the bullets I was ducking. A glowing light seemed to be coming around Maniagawa Island—a lantern! A kerosene lantern in Hayden's hand, the skipper riding the motor. . . .

"Forget the plane!" I yelled, looking across at her—her eyes were wild. "Swim for the boat!"

She hesitated, as if hating to miss the opportunity to fly once again, then a bullet whanged into the metal near her head and she swallowed and nodded, and dove in; so did I. I swam with my nine-millimeter clenched in my fist, but I swam.

We swam toward the launch as it moved over the bumpy waters toward us, and bullets made kisses around us in the waters. And then somebody, Hayden, was hauling me into the boat, and I gulped air, air with rain in it but air, and looked toward the water, looking to reach down for Amy, and she was swimming toward us when the bullets caught her, danced across the back of her leather jacket.

And then she seemed to slump forward into the water, and soon the jacket was all we could see of her, several boat lengths away, sort of puffing up, its weathered brown leather blossoming red, hanging there as if it were a floating flower; then it, too, disappeared, sucked down under.

Gone.

I was halfway out of the boat when the kid hauled me back in, yelling, "It's too late! Too late for her!" Bullets were flying all around us, and we were moving away from where Amy and her jacket had been, away from the little white figures on the jetty who were shooting at us, jabbering at us almost comically, tiny insignificant jumping-up-and-down figures that got lost first in the rain, then in the darkness, until they were gone, just a bizarre bad memory, a coda to an escape that almost happened.

Johnson's voice said, "How is he?"

Hayden's voice said, "Nasty cut."

That was the last voice I heard, except I thought I heard Amy's voice, one last time, saying the last thing I heard her say, so proudly, right before she ran toward that seaplane, a final plane she never flew.

"I'm Amelia Earhart," she said.

Rain on my face.

Darkness.

Epilogue

Return to Saipan—March 1970

Twenty

Late in June 1940, Captain Irving Johnson reported to Elmer Dimity of the Amelia Earhart Foundation as follows: "It is my opinion that the search be considered finished and that everything humanly possible has been done to find any trace of Miss Earhart."

Nevertheless, Elmer and Margot did not give up on their plans and a ship the Foundation had commissioned was waiting in the Honolulu harbor on December 7, 1941. The Foundation's Pacific expedition, interrupted by World War II, was never resumed, although successful businessman Dimity—and the Foundation—continued on for many years, extolling Amelia Earhart and researching her disappearance.

Captain Johnson was working at Pearl Harbor in the War Plans Office when the Japanese attacked; the *Yankee*'s last cruise ended in the spring of 1941, Johnson selling the ship and entering the Navy. He spent the war on the survey ship *Summer*, charting the islands and waters of the South Pacific for the United States government; perhaps this was merely a continuation of what he'd already been doing on the *Yankee*.

After the war, Johnson—looking for a new sailing ship—was alerted by his old first mate of a German brigantine seized by the British and held in England; called the *Duhnen*, the ship was purchased, renamed the new *Yankee*, and Johnson and his wife and family resumed their 'round-the-world cruises and continued to record their adventures (well, some of them) in bestselling travel books into the 1960s.

Their first mate did not join them, as he had another career to pursue. I would never have guessed that Hayden's chief interest, other than sailing, would be little theater; he did not seem the artsy type. But he had gone from the deck of the *Yankee* into a Hollywood career that was prematurely interrupted by the war; like me, Sterling Hayden served in the Marines, only Hayden got assigned to the OSS, through the auspices of Captain Johnson's good friend "Wild Bill" Donovan. Hayden's low-key macho and the weary poetry of the peculiar cadence of his speech lent themselves well to such films as *The Asphalt Jungle*, *The Killing* and *Dr. Strangelove*, wherein his General Jack D. Ripper saved the world from the loss of its "precious bodily fluids."

After Pearl Harbor, Howland Island was the next United States territory attacked by the Japanese; nonetheless, its perfect crushed-coral airstrips, long since overgrown, have never been used.

William Miller, Chief of the Air Carrier Division of the Civil Aeronautics Administration, died of a heart attack in Washington, D.C., in 1943. Doing a job in Hollywood, I received that news August of the same year in a booth at the Brown Derby on Wilshire, from Lt. Colonel Paul Mantz of the Army Air Forces First Motion Picture Unit.

"Well, that's a surprise," I said.

"That a guy as young as Miller would die of a heart attack?" Mantz asked over his frosted martini.

"That Miller had a heart."

Mantz's smile twitched under his mustache; he looked spiffy in his military threads. "You always were a sentimental soul. So, Nate—what's the story on you and Guadalcanal?"

"Got likkered up, lied about my age and found myself in boot camp with a bunch of kids. We saw rough action, but it was malaria that got me sent home early."

Mantz's expression told me he knew I was holding back, but respected a fellow soldier's right to privacy. Then, chewing a bite of Caesar salad, he grinned and said, "Hear the latest about Gippy?"

"Which story? Faking his own kidnapping to promote

that Hitler book? Or pretending to sue RKO for making that movie about Amelia?"

Shortly before the war, Putnam showed up at the Los Angeles DA's office with threatening notes to himself and a bullet-riddled copy of *The Man Who Killed Hitler*, which he'd just published. Later he reported firing shots at a man trying to break and enter the Putnam home. The fascist plot against him—widely covered in the papers—reached its pinnacle when G. P. was found— within hours of his staff reporting his "disappearance"— bound and gagged (but unharmed) in a house under construction in Bakersfield.

The 1943 film *Flight for Freedom* starred Rosalind Russell as an Amelia Earhart-like aviatrix and Fred MacMurray as her Fred Noonan-like navigator, who undertake an espionage mission for the government with heroically tragic results. Putnam loudly objected and rattled litigation sabers in the press. In fact, he had sold the rights to Amy's story to the studio and earned extra money by promoting the picture through his public protestations.

"Neither one," Mantz said. "Gippy's got himself commissioned as a major in Army Intelligence."

Putnam, who was also in the process of acquiring a new wife (his fourth—Margaret Haviland, an executive with the USO), served in China, reportedly briefing, and debriefing, squadrons flying bombing raids into Japan. He also visited American-held Saipan, supposedly to investigate the rampant rumors about two white pilots, a man and a woman, captured before the war by the Japanese, that were circulating among GIs who'd spoken to Chamorro refugees in Camp Susupe, a city of tents run by the Army for the former citizens of Garapan, which had been obliterated in June 1944.

Thirty thousand Japanese and thirty-five hundred Americans—Navy, Army, Marines—died in Operation Forager, the twenty-four-day battle for Saipan, the Pacific island hit worst by the war. I don't know that anyone ever bothered to total up casualties among the islanders, but many had to have died in the bombings; Garapan was reduced to rubble by June 24. Garapan Harbor thereafter was home to thousands of Allied

ships; while the seaplane base was destroyed, Aslito
Haneda was quickly rebuilt, expanded and renamed
Isley Field, handling hundreds of takeoffs and landings
each day, becoming an airbase for the B-29 Super For-
tress Bombers (the *Enola Gay* took off for Hiroshima
from neighboring Tinian). The Japanese never com-
pleted the airstrip at Marpi Point; nearby was Suicide
Cliff—there, and, near the north end of the island, at
similarly named Banzai Cliff, thousands of Japanese
men, women and children threw themselves to a rocky
death to avoid a worse fate at the hands of invading
barbarians.

One odd, persistent rumor that came out of the Pacific
theater was that Amelia Earhart was the voice of Tokyo
Rose, the infamous female disc jockey whose Japanese
propaganda broadcasts enticed American soldiers to listen to nostalgic songs from home interspersed with lies
about how Japan was kicking the Allies' ass. Major Putnam, while in the Far East, reportedly crossed enemy
lines to listen to broadcasts of an American woman per-
forming such propaganda, and rather defensively pro-
claimed the voice absolutely not to be Amelia's. He said
he would stake his life on it.

I have to admit, when the rumors that Amy might
have been Rose first found their way to me, I had to
wonder. Could she have survived that nightmarish rainy
night? Had those bullets not been fatal? Did the Japs
fish her out of the clear waters—we hadn't been that far
from shore—and revive her, and ship her off to Tokyo
as a propaganda tool, as always intended?

And hadn't she been known, in Saipan, as Tokyo
Rosa?

Sometimes, late at night, I could almost talk myself
into it. But too much was wrong. For one thing, there
was no "Tokyo Rose"; it was a nickname, possibly
picked up by GIs in Saipan who heard the "Tokyo
Rosa" moniker, attached by the Chamorros to Amelia,
and—in the way verbal storytelling evolves into legend—
got applied by GIs to any English-speaking female disc
jockey who turned up on Japan's regular propaganda
broadcasts.

Anyway, there was no single "Tokyo Rose," rather

dozens of female DJs who appeared on various Japanese radio shows, some with Japanese accents, others without, none of them using the Tokyo Rose appellation.

The myth grew so strong, however, that one of these women, who came forward and admitted having been coerced into doing some broadcasts—an American of Japanese descent who'd been visiting Tokyo when the war broke out—was railroaded into prison by such wonderful Americans as Walter Winchell and J. Edgar Hoover.

Amy's name came up in the coverage, however, because during the public witch hunt that put innocent Iva Togori away for the crime of her race, another Amy Earhart attended every day of the trial: Amelia's mother, though elderly and in poor health, traveling from Medford, Massachusetts, to San Francisco. Amy Otis Earhart told reporters her daughter had been secretive about the world flight, not sharing as much as she usually did with her mother.

"I'm convinced," Mrs. Earhart said, "she was on some sort of government mission, probably on verbal orders."

Also, I could see Army Intelligence, in 1944, with the end of the war looming, panicking that Amelia Earhart might turn up embarrassingly, and sending G. P. to check out those broadcasts. After all, in my debriefing—conducted by William Miller in June 1940—I had mentioned that Amelia was nicknamed "Tokyo Rosa" by the islanders. Maybe they put two and two together, and came up with egg on their face.

But the Japs wouldn't have used Amelia anonymously; they would have played up her celebrity, if they'd actually had her, and had actually turned her. No. Amy died that night, when we almost made it. If Chief Suzuki and Jesus Sablan hadn't come stumbling out of that brothel, we would have.

I didn't learn of Suzuki's death, incidentally, until many years later when J. T. "Buddy" Busch of Dallas, Texas, told me that a Mrs. Michiko Sugita—the daughter of Mikio Suzuki—had provided the first testimony by a Japanese national that placed Amelia Earhart on Saipan. Mrs. Sugita told Busch of hearing her father and other Garapan police officers discussing the female pilot, and whether or not she should be executed. Mrs. Sugita seemed embarrassed that her father's vote had been for execution.

The former chief of Saipan police had not been among those Japanese who flung themselves from the suicide cliffs. After hiding in the mountains for a while, Suzuki surrendered and cooperated with the occupying forces; due to fatigue he was transferred to a hospital tent, where a witness saw an islander and an unidentified American make him drink poison. The case was investigated by one Jesus Sablan, who had been appointed (by the Army) "sheriff" of Camp Susupe, due to his "police background"; the murder was never solved.

Aviatrix Jacqueline Cochran Odlum, Amelia's close friend, was the first American woman to set foot in postwar Japan; after her mission to investigate the "role of Japanese women" in the air war, Jackie reported seeing several files on Amy in Imperial Air Force headquarters. I did not meet Mrs. Odlum during those years of my relationship with Amelia, but sometime later, when she and her wealthy husband Floyd Odlum hired me on an industrial espionage case related to their cosmetics business.

"I didn't see anything that would lead me to think Amelia was captured and kept in Japan," Jackie told me, over dinner at the Odlum ranch in Indio, California. She was a bubbly blonde who might have been the missing Andrews Sister. "Certainly nothing to make you think she was 'Tokyo Rose.'"

She also showed me a precious memento Amy had given her before that last flight: a small silk American flag.

For whatever reason, G. P. Putnam returned from military service a different man, though staying involved with publishing and writing several more books. Plagued with illness, he lived in a Sierras mountain lodge, and later at a resort he ran in Death Valley, with his fourth wife, Peg, in what by all accounts was a happy if brief marriage. The postwar Putnam was apparently a much mellowed man, his outrageous promotional stunts behind him. He died of kidney failure in January 1950.

Paul Mantz's military service was stellar, and not just

because the movie actors serving under him included Clark Gable, Ronald Reagan and Alan Ladd. His unit shot over thirty thousand feet of aerial combat footage and hundreds of training films, and while most of his duty was stateside, as he operated out of so-called Fort Roach (at Hal Roach Studios), Lt. Colonel Mantz shot stunning combat footage over the North Atlantic and in Africa.

At war's end Paul was back at his old charter service stand, and enjoying his long and happy marriage to Terry. Radio commentator and Putnam-esque world traveler explorer Lowell Thomas hired Mantz to develop the multi-camera techniques for the famous Cinerama process; director of photography Mantz was perched in a chair in the nose of a converted B-25 bomber as he shot *This Is Cinerama.* Most of the famous aviation pictures of Hollywood's Golden Age included footage shot by Paul Mantz and his team of fliers; he died in 1965, in an airplane, when a stunt went wrong on the James Stewart picture *The Flight of the Phoenix.*

James Forrestal moved from his administrative assistant position at the White House to Under Secretary of the Navy, and in 1944, when Secretary of the Navy Knox died of a heart attack, Forrestal took over; in 1947 he became the country's first Secretary of Defense. He was credited with "building" the Navy, increasing the number of combat vessels from under four hundred to over fifteen hundred; he was considered "two-fisted" for taking frontline inspection tours, unusual for a ranking cabinet officer. He was also a virulent anticommunist and appeared to cheerfully despise Jews.

After President Truman forced his resignation, Forrestal—attacked in the press by Drew Pearson for war profiteering—apparently sank into a deep depression. Two months later, he fell—or perhaps was pushed—from the sixteenth floor of the Naval Hospital at Bethesda, Maryland, supposedly tying his bathrobe belt to a radiator and trying to hang himself, succeeding rather in falling to his death.

I didn't keep track of, or run into, any number of the other people from those days. Ernie Tisor was still working with Paul Mantz in the late fifties, but that's the last

I saw of him. Toni Lake, who walked away from five crash landings, was killed in a motorcycle accident in 1943. Earl Carroll and his showgirl girlfriend Beryl Wallace were killed in an airliner crash in June 1948. Dizzy Dean ruined his pitching arm and got traded to the Cubs; FDR ran for a third term. I never saw Myrtle Mantz again; Margot died a few years ago—she never married; perhaps she was pining for me—or Amy.

Fred Noonan's widow, Mary Bea, to whom I carried his message, married a widower, happily. For all her complaining about her family, Amy turned out to have a very loyal mother and sister, both of whom honored her at their every opportunity. Amy Otis Earhart, who never really gave up on the thought that her daughter might just show up one day, died at age ninety-five in October 1962.

From Boston to Honolulu, in dozens of towns across America, Amelia Earhart is honored with memorial plaques and markers, and streets and schools are named for her. Commemorative stamps have been issued; libraries and museums honor her with displays. Television movies and documentaries of her life frequently turn up on my Mitsubishi. And her luggage is still being manufactured and sold.

But also, the questions about her disappearance have developed into a cottage industry of research, expeditions and books of a sort that G. P. Putnam might well have published. Rarely did a researcher track me down, and even more rarely did I cooperate. With one or two exceptions, I didn't read their books, either. I didn't need anybody to tell me what happened to Amelia Earhart. Besides which, I was under contract to Uncle Sam to keep my mouth shut; it's like a deal with the devil— no escape clause.

And the government laughed off the Amelia-on-Saipan stories, though occasional documents surfaced due to the Freedom of Information Act that supported the "theory"; and scores of other letters and documents remain unclassified and or destroyed. But Admiral Chester W. Nimitz, wartime commander-in-chief of the Pacific Fleet, later Chief of Naval Operations, admitted that the truth about Amelia Earhart would "stagger the imagination."

In 1969, when I heard, after so many years, from Robert Myers—now a grown man, working in a sugar factory in Salinas, California—it sent me hurtling back to his parents' living room where we heard that exciting radio drama on the family Philco. Still peppy, he told me he was writing a book about his memories of Amelia and, on weekends and vacations, lecturing on the subject.

I was struck by odd resonances in what he'd said: the statue of sugar Baron Matsue Haruji somehow loomed over the career of Amelia Earhart's kid pal, now working in a sugar factory, supplementing his income out on the lecture circuit. I wondered if he'd ever spoken at the Coliseum in Des Moines; I wondered if it was even still there.

"She's alive," he told me excitedly, and over the phone, the voice, even with the deep, older timber of an adult, still sounded like a kid's. "She's a woman named Irene Bolam, and she lives in New Jersey. Fred Noonan's alive, too!"

"If he is, he's got a splitting headache," I said.

"What?"

"Nothing. Look, Robert, it's nice hearing from you—"

"Fred Noonan is this guy William Van Dusen. This former Air Force major and this author, they've researched both of 'em, and Van Dusen and Bolam, their backgrounds are phony. It looks like a witness protection plan kind of deal."

"I don't think they had a witness protection program in the forties."

"How do you know? If Amelia got turned into Tokyo Rose, maybe the government would want to . . . sort of, *bury* her."

"Robert, it's nice hearing from you again."

"You don't want to look into this for me?"

"Are you hiring me?"

"I can't afford that. I work in a factory."

"I work for a living, too, Robert. Thanks for the call. Good luck."

And that had been that. I didn't know whether to feel happy or sad for Robert Myers: his friendship with Amelia had given meaning to his life; yet it had obviously been painful for him, carrying around so many unanswered questions, going through his life a "kid" few took seriously.

I'd been there. I sat in the living room with him. I knew what he'd heard. He just didn't know where I'd been.

The book that claimed Irene Bolam was Amelia Earhart got its authors sued and itself pulled from the shelves. This made me suspicious, and one day in 1970, when I was visiting the Manhattan office of A-1, I took a side trip to Bedford Hills, New York. I found Irene Bolam in the bar with three other women in the clubhouse of Forsgate Country Club; these were ladies in their late sixties and they seemed to appreciate the attention of a good-looking kid like me, in his early to mid-sixties.

I knew at once which one was Irene. She bore a resemblance to Amy, though her nose was different, wider, larger; noses change, though, not always for the better. And the eyes were a hauntingly familiar blue-gray.

Standing next to the ladies, who looked pretty foxy in their golf sweaters and shorts, I said to Irene, "My name's Nate Heller. We had a mutual friend."

"Oh?" She beamed up at me. "And who would that be?"

"Amelia Earhart. I understand you were an aviatrix yourself, and flew with her?"

"That's right, I was in the Ninety Nines. . . . Oh, my goodness, I hope you don't believe that baloney in that horrible book."

The "oh my goodness" gave me a start: it was a favorite phrase of Amy's.

But this wasn't Amy. Amy couldn't look at me and not betray the feelings we'd had. If by some bizarre circumstance, this was an Amelia Earhart who had survived those bullets and been carted off to Tokyo, brainwashed by Tojo, returned home, and brainwashed again by Uncle Sam . . . if that ridiculous scenario were even possible, I didn't want to know.

Whether this was Irene Bolam, or Amelia Earhart, I

knew one thing for sure: my Amy wasn't in this old woman's eyes.

I sat with the girls and they had tropical drinks with umbrellas while I had a rum and Coke. One of the girls was a widow with a nice body and a decent face lift and I think I could have got lucky. But I was an old married man now, and had changed my ways.

Irene Bolam died in July 1982. She left her body to science and her family honored her wishes that her fingerprints not be shared with those who had been hounding her about her identity.

The Continental DC-10 circled lazily on its approach, as the island of Saipan made itself known through the clouds. We had left Guam forty-five minutes before—Buddy Busch, his two-man camera crew and me. At first glance the long narrow island appeared to be nothing more than a jungle with a mountain rising from its midst; but soon rolling hills, shell-pocked cliffs and white sand beaches disclosed their presence, as did roads, buildings and cultivated fields.

This was a slightly different view than I'd gotten from the *Yankee* or its dinghy, and I could finally understand what everyone had been raving about all these years: the ocean waters surrounding Saipan were dazzlingly blue and turquoise and green and yet transparent.

"Someday I'm gonna bring the wife along," Buddy said. "She dudn't believe me, 'bout how pretty them waters is. You been here before, Nate—ever see the like of it, anywheres else?"

"The folksier you get, Buddy," I said, "the less you're getting out of me."

Buddy was frustrated that I had yet to open up about my own Saipan experiences.

"And the stars at night . . ." he began.

"Are big and bright? Deep in the heart of Saipan?"

"Back in '45, every night, we'd be on our cots in our tents and Hoagy Carmichael's 'Stardust' would come driftin' across the camp, over the loudspeaker. . . . It was like he was singin' about Saipan."

"I doubt he was."

"Well," he said defensively, "*I* never seen the like of

it. Parade of damn stars traipsin' across the sky. . . . Or was I just young, and my memory's playin' tricks with me?"

"I ask myself that often," I said.

Even from the air, the scars left on this island by World War II were readily apparent, violent punctuation marks in a peaceful sentence: a tank's head poking out of the water a few hundred yards offshore; a barge marooned on the coral reef; a wrecked fuselage, half in the water, half on the beach—shimmering twisted metal in crystal-blue waters.

The DC-10 touched down at Kobler Field, near the former Aslito Haneda, aka Isley. We taxied over to a cement shed with a wooden roof emblazoned SAIPAN in white letters; this and two Quonset-hut hangars was the Saipan airport.

"This is my fourth time here," Buddy said coming down the deplaning steps, "and I never quite get used to how different it is from the war—no jeeps, or military trucks, no soldiers, sailors or Marines."

The tiny airport, run by Chamorros, was a surprisingly bustling place filled with the Babel-like chatter of many languages—tourists from all over the world coming to this vacation center, Europeans, Arabs, but mostly Japanese. Buddy had told me to expect that: Saipan was a combination war shrine and honeymoon resort for the Japanese.

"Yeah, and they're buyin' back this island they lost," he'd told me on the plane, "piece at a time."

A Ford van Buddy had arranged was waiting, and we loaded our suitcases and the camera and recording gear—which was ensconced in heavy-duty flight cases— into the back. The two-man camera crew was also from Dallas; Phil was clean-cut and owned the video production company that had gone in partners with Buddy on a documentary of our visit, and Steve was a skinny, bearded, longhaired good old boy who I took for a hippie until I realized he was a Vietnam veteran—both knew their stuff. I told them I didn't want to be on camera and they said fine, I could "grip."

"What is a grip?" I'd seen that in the end credits of movies and always wondered.

"It means you help haul shit," Steve said, ever-present cigarette bobbing.

Japanese machine-gun bunkers provided decorative cement touches on the road leading out of the airport. Beach Road itself, lined with flame trees, was a macadam fast track—back when the *shichokan* had driven me through this part of the island, the dirt road had been a glorified oxcart path. The cars outnumbered the bicycles now, but there were still plenty of the latter, often with Japanese tourists on them.

We passed through several native villages that had turned into modern little towns—Chalan Kanoa, which sported banks and a post office and a shopping district, as well as wood-frame houses and tin-roofed huts, vaguely similar to Garapan of old—and Susupe, which the army's tent city had evolved into, where we stayed at a motel called the Sun Inn, behind a ballpark by a high school.

"Now I know you think I'm probably just bein' a cheap bastard," Buddy said, as we unloaded our stuff into a motel that looked like it belonged next to a strip club outside the Little Rock, Arkansas, airport. "But if we stay in one of them new fancy tourist highrises, up in Garapan, we'll have trouble holdin' court with the locals we need to talk to."

The Sun Inn had a freestanding restaurant where we could sit and talk and sip coffee with our Chamorro subjects, in unintimidating surroundings.

"I'd like to bitch," I said, "but as a veteran of a hundred thousand interviews, I agree with you. Once we get checked in, you mind if we take a spin up to Garapan?"

"Not at all," Buddy grinned. "Kinda curious to see your old stompin' grounds?"

"I think that's 'stamping grounds.' "

"Not in Texas."

Garapan had not changed. It had gone away. This new city, called Garapan, wasn't even on quite the same patch of earth; it was further south, its resort hotels lining white Micro Beach. Buddy took me to Sugar King Park, where the statue of Baron Matsue Haruji lorded over what was now a small botanical garden; also on display amid the palm and flame trees—and popular

with Japanese children—was a little red and white locomotive, looking like the Little Engine That Could, resting on the last fragment of railroad track that once
circled Saipan. It was probably the locomotive I saw at
Tanapag Harbor, so very long ago.

"That statue is one of the handful of survivin' physical
remains of the original Garapan," Buddy told me. His
camera crew was catching some shots of the park, for
color.

"Looks like the Baron's got a bullet hole in his left
temple," I said, taking a closer gander.

"Yeah. Probably some jarhead, when we were occu-
pyin' the place, takin' target practice. . . . There's only
two buildings from old Garapan still standin'—if standin'
is the word." He nodded his head across the way, where
the walls of the old hospital poked above overgrown
grass. "That's the old imperial hospital . . . and, not
too far from here, the old Garapan Prison, which is all
overgrowed. We need to get shots of that."

"I'll pass," I said.

He frowned in surprise. "You don't want to go over
there to the prison with us?"

"If you don't mind, no."

"Well, we'll do it another day, then. We need to get
ahold of Sammy Munez, anyways."

Munez met with us in a booth at the back of the Sun
Inn coffee shop. Samuel Munez was a respected member
of the community, a member of the House of Represen-
tatives of Micronesia, and had avoided previous researchers into the Earhart mystery.

But Buddy Busch was an ingratiating guy, and after
three trips to Saipan, had made a lot of friends; the head
of a local car dealership—who had provided our van—
had arranged for us to meet with Munez, a compact, not
quite stocky Chamorro in his mid-thirties with pleasant
sad features on an egg-shaped head.

"You served in the Army here?" Munez asked Buddy.
Munez wore sunglasses, a yellow and green tropical-style
sportshirt and navy shorts. "Wartime?"

It was just Busch and me and Munez in the booth; no
camera crew yet. Buddy and Munez were drinking coffee
but the climate—eighty degrees that would have been

heaven if it hadn't been so damn muggy—had me drinking Coke.

"Yes I did," Buddy said, "only I was a Marine."

"You, too?" Munez asked me.

"I was a Marine," I said. "I was in the Pacific but not here. Guadalcanal."

"I have a souvenir a Marine gave me," Munez said, with a sly smile. His English was near perfect, though he had an accent, which had a jerky Hispanic lilt.

"Must be a lot of those on this island," Buddy said affably.

Munez patted his thigh. "Mine is from a hand grenade. Still in me. What is that called?"

"Shrapnel," I said.

Munez smiled, nodded. "The Marine who threw it was very upset. He apologize to us, bandage my leg himself. He thought we were Japanese. . . . You Americans were much kinder to us than the Japanese."

"Mr. Munez . . ." Buddy began.

"Sammy. All my friends call me Sammy."

"Well, Sammy, as I think you know, we're attempting to trace Amelia Earhart and her navigator Fred Noonan. Lots of people like me have come here, and lots of your people have told stories . . . but everything seems . . . secondhand. We need eyewitnesses."

Munez sighed and thought for a long while before he answered. "Mr. Busch . . ."

"Buddy."

"Buddy, I can find people to talk to you. But some will not. You stir up bad memories for Saipanese. Almost every family on the island lost family members during the Japanese occupation. We have survived centuries of occupation by doing nothing to invite punishment, nothing to invite reprisal. To come forward, even now, with public testimony, is to ask trouble."

"From the Japanese?"

He nodded. "They begin to rule our island again—in a different way. But those who speak against them might suffer. And during the war, there was a local police force of Chamorros who worked for the Japanese. These were bad men who tortured and punished their own people. Many of them are still here."

"Like Jesus Sablan?" I asked.

That I knew this name surprised Munez. He blinked and said, "Yes."

"I heard he was shot and killed, a long time ago," I said.

Buddy was gazing at me with golf-ball eyes.

"That is one reason why he is so feared," Munez said. "The story that bullets could not kill him. . . . Yes, he is alive and meaner than ten brown tree snakes."

"What's he doing these days?" I asked.

"He is in the junk business."

"He peddles dope?"

"No! Junk. He has a junkyard by where the seaplane base once was. He has Saipanese employees to haul scrap to the pier. War wreckage from the jungle. He sells it to the Japanese."

So the *jungkicho* was a junk king.

"He lives in a nice small house outside Chalan Kanoa," Munez was saying. "He is a man who likes his privacy."

"Does he like money?"

"That is his great love. What is your interest in this man, Mr. Heller?"

"It's Nate, Sammy. I just heard he knows a lot about Amelia Earhart and Fred Noonan."

Sammy nodded vigorously. "They say he knows more than anyone else on this island. He has offered to speak about this, before."

This was obviously news to Buddy. "I never talked to him."

"Others have. Fred Goerner. Major Gervais. But none would pay Jesus his price."

I sipped my Coke. "Can you arrange a meeting?"

"He won't meet with more than one man at a time. Some men attacked him once—one researcher who had Guam policemen with him who lived in Garapan during the war."

"Ah, and held a grudge."

"Yes."

"Well," I said cheerily, "Mr. Busch here would like to see the jail, and I have no interest. Perhaps you could arrange a meeting for me, with Mr. Sablan, while you and Buddy and his camera crew tour the old jail."

That seemed agreeable to everybody. We would need an extra set of wheels, but Buddy felt that would be no problem, he'd just call his car dealership pal.

Over the next three days, we interviewed Chamorros that Munez lined up for us; the idea was to talk to them informally at the Sun Inn coffee shop, and the best ones would be invited to speak on camera. We spent two days doing the pre-interviews, and another shooting footage with the better subjects, at the Sugar King Park, which provided a scenic backdrop.

Two farmers traveled together from the village of San Roque with similar stories of having seen the male and female fliers at Tanapag Harbor and later in Garapan. A retired dentist had not seen the two white people but, as his practice had been restricted to Japanese military officers and police officials, he'd heard much talk of the American fliers captured as spies; the officers had joked about the U.S.A. using women as spies.

Munez's sister, who was in her mid-sixties, had done laundry for the hotel, the Kobayashi Ryokan, and spoke of the American woman's kindness and gave a detailed description, even identifying Amy's photo.

A man who had been a salesclerk at the Ishi-Shoten, the general merchandise store next to Kobayashi Ryokan, spoke of often seeing Amelia in a second-floor window.

A pleasant middle-aged woman born of a Japanese father and Chamorro mother said her name was Matilda Fausto Arriola, and told of living in the house next door to the Kobayashi Ryokan. Her English limited, she chose to speak to us in the Chamorran language (which to me sounded like a combination of Spanish, French and bird calls) and Munez translated, but I knew she spoke the truth when she talked of Amy helping her with her homework, and giving her a gold ring with a pearl, which had been lost in the war. She told of the woman being followed everywhere by the Chamorran security police.

She also spoke of the burns she noticed on the white woman's neck—from cooking oil, she thought.

I didn't correct her.

Only one familiar face showed up: the desk clerk from the Kobayashi Ryokan, who turned out to have been the owner. He didn't seem to recognize me, which hurt my feelings—hadn't I spared his life? On the other hand, maybe he did recognize me, and that's why he didn't bring up the priest and the Chamorro who got shot in his lobby.

These and eight other witnesses told a story that provided the mosaic tiles for the following: American fliers, a man and a woman, had been brought ashore at Tanapag Harbor; the woman had short hair and dressed like a man, the man had a head injury. They were taken to the police station and then to the jail; the woman was only in the jail a few hours, and later turned up at a hotel used by the military to house political prisoners. No one seemed to know for sure what happened to these mysterious white people, but the consensus was that they'd been executed.

Buddy was generally pleased, and got some good interviews for his documentary—a few of the Chamorros spoke English, which was helpful. But he was frustrated not coming up with anything new. I suggested perhaps that the researchers had gone to the Saipan well once too often.

That made the Texan pout.

Munez said, "You might find it worthwhile to talk to Mrs. Blas—my sister says this farm woman knows something about Amelia—but she won't come into town. She doesn't come to town very often. You would have to go to her."

It wasn't much to go on, but on the fourth day, with no other interviews lined up, we followed a winding dirt back road into farm country, where the foliage was so thick, it was as though the van were moving down a green tunnel. Then suddenly the road was cutting through cultivated land, and Munez pointed out a modest tin-roofed woodframe farmhouse.

Mrs. Blas was a tiny, slight, dignified woman, probably around sixty but with a smooth lightly tanned complexion that would be the envy of many a younger woman. She wore a black and lime and white island print dress that was similarly youthful. Against a backdrop of swaying sugarcane, with Munez translating, she told a chilling tale.

First she recounted, as so many others had, having seen the two Americans, man and woman, at Tanapag Harbor; they were taken to the police building on the town square. But several years later she saw the woman again.

"She say she was working on the farm when a motorcycle driven by Japanese soldier go by with the white woman slump in the little seat on the side," Munez said. "The woman is blindfolded. Another motorcycle with two more Japanese follow. Mrs. Blas say she follow the Japanese soldiers without them seeing. They take the woman to this place where a hole already been dug. They make the woman kneel in front of that hole, tear the blindfold from her face and toss it in the grave. Then they shoot her in the chest. She fall backwards into the grave."

"Did this happen near this farm here?" a stunned Buddy asked.

Munez's translation of her answer was that it had been another farm, closer to Garapan. She had run from the place, afraid the Japanese soldiers would see her; but later she went back and saw that the grave had been filled in.

"Mrs. Blas," Buddy asked, his voice breaking, "is it possible you could find that place again?"

She said the grave was under the biggest breadfruit tree on the island, a tree she had been to many, many times. It seemed the Japanese took all the food the farmers grew, and her family depended on the fruit of this wild tree.

Soon we were back in the van with Mrs. Blas in the rider's seat of honor up front, Buddy Busch at the wheel, trembling with anticipation. I didn't know what to think. Old questions were stirring. Had the Japanese hauled Amelia out of the waters that night, only to execute her later? Or had they carted her corpse in a motorcycle sidecar, and what Mrs. Blas had seen been simply a further desecration of Amy's body before the unmarked grave took her?

But where Mrs. Blas directed Buddy was to an expansive parking lot covered with crushed coral on which bulldozers and tractors and other heavy equipment perched like stubborn dinosaurs that didn't know they were supposed to be extinct. All of this was behind a seven-foot chain-link security fence topped with barbed wire.

And there seemed to be no breadfruit tree within the fenced-off area.

Nonetheless, Mrs. Blas insisted, through Munez, that she could identify the exact spot.

"This looks like a road maintenance storage yard," I said. "That means government."

Buddy nodded. "We have some fancy talking and red-tape-cutting ahead of us."

That afternoon, in a jeep that Buddy's car dealer had loaned me, I headed toward Chalan Kanoa for a meeting with an old friend. Buddy and his camera crew were shooting Mrs. Blas at her farmhouse and then planned to get the Garapan Prison footage they needed. I made a stop at a hardware store, to pick up a machete, and was right on time, when I pulled up in front of the Saipan Style Center.

On the outskirts north of Chalan Kanoa, the Saipan Style Center was a tin-roofed, ramshackle saloon with a restaurant and trinket shop in front, the flyspecked show window with two beach-attire-clad mannequins apparently inspiring the joint's grandiloquent name. Moving through the small trinket shop, with its cheap made-in-Japan items—paper fans, windup toys, hula dolls—I pushed through the hanging bead curtain into the bar where a jarring cold front hit me, thanks to a chugging air conditioner.

The surprise of the chill was matched by the darkness of the bar. I took off my sunglasses and it didn't make much difference: the only illumination was courtesy of occasional Christmas tree lights haphazardly tacked on the walls, and a garish jukebox, out of which came Wilson Pickett singing "In the Midnight Hour," despite it being two o'clock in the afternoon. A half-dozen Chamorran males at the bar registered mild surprise at seeing a white man, then returned to their drinks. The waitresses—voluptuous Chamorran babes in unmatching bikini tops and hot pants—were much happier to see me, three of them swarming after me like sharks sniffing blood.

The first one that got to me claimed me, a heart-breakingly cute Chamorran dish with shocking absurd platinum-blonde hair.

"What's your pleasure, daddy?"

"Well, it's not my pleasure exactly," I said. "But I was wondering if Jesus Sablan was here."

Her lip curled into a sneer and she said, "You're not a friend of his, are you?"

"I'm his twin brother. We were separated at birth."

That made her laugh; she was no dope. "He's in the restaurant, havin' the special. And he's all yours."

Then it was through another beaded doorway and into the low-ceilinged, undecorated dining room and its dozen or so tables. It was early for supper, so nobody was back there but a bullnecked mountain of muscle and fat in an old Seabees cap and gigantic loose-fitting, well-worn army fatigues. He was hunkered over a plate of stringy, sticky seaweed, sucking it up like a kid sucks spaghetti.

I was wearing a black T-shirt with a khaki jacket over it, and khaki pants; the weather didn't demand the jacket but I had a .38 revolver in the righthand pocket. Just in case he recognized me.

I certainly gave him every opportunity. I stood right before the table, opposite him as he sucked seaweed, and the dark, pockmarked, knife-scarred, mustached face looked at me with cold contempt, but it was the cold contempt he reserved for everybody, not just priests who shot him in the stomach.

"You the American?" he asked, chewing.

He was probably sixty, but other than some white in his short-cropped hair (his right ear had a piece out of it), the thick Zapata mustache, and some added wrinkles that gave him a bulldog quality, he hadn't changed much.

"Yeah, I'm the American."

He poured himself a healthy glass of red wine from an unlabeled bottle. "Siddown. I don't look up at nobody."

I sat, with my hand on the revolver in the jacket pocket. "How much for your Amelia Earhart story?"

"It's a good story. What really happen."

"How much?"

He grinned; he had a gold tooth now, and the rest of the teeth were much closer to white than I remembered. The junk king could afford a dentist. "Two thousand," he said.

"I can get you ten."

The dark eyes flared. "Thousand?"

"No, ten dollars. What do you think? Come in with me, we can take these rich Texas assholes for twenty grand."

He frowned. "Fifty-fifty split?"

"Yeah, that's how you end up with ten." Time had made him stupid; or maybe too much of that cheap wine.

The eyes that had once scared me a little, because of the smartness in them, narrowed and perhaps something, in the back of his skull, was trying to click.

"Do I know you?" he asked.

"I never been in Saipan before in my life. You want in?"

"Let me hear it."

I leaned toward him. "They want to find Amelia Earhart's grave. Let's show it to them."

". . . I don't know where it is."

"That doesn't matter," I shrugged. "I got a bag of bones in my jeep—I brought 'em with me from the States."

"What kind of bones?"

"Female. Forty years of age. Dead thirty years."

"What'd you do, dig up some other grave?"

"That's right. Now if a Saipanese . . . somebody with a history that goes back to those days . . . could lead these Texans to a grave in the jungle. . . ."

He had started smiling halfway through that; he did still have some smarts. Not enough to save him, though.

"But first we got to bury those bones," I said. "Meet me tonight at the old Garapan Prison. We'll bury 'em near there somewhere. . . . Bring a shovel."

He was still grinning, nodding, liking it. "What time?"

"When else? Midnight."

We didn't shake hands. Just nodded at each other, and I left him to his plate of seaweed.

That evening, Buddy Busch, in the room we were sharing at the Sun Inn, was aglow.

"They're gonna let us dig," he said. "Problem is, they'll only give us tomorrow . . . Sunday . . . when the facility is closed, 'cause otherwise we'd get in their way."

So at nine the next morning, with the loan from the lot manager of a heavy front loader (and one of his men), the coral surface and an added two feet of topsoil were scraped away, and then the two Chamorran kids Munez had hired to dig got at it. Phil and Steve recorded the efforts, from various angles, and by three that afternoon, we were looking into a trench four feet by twelve, three feet deep. And very empty.

"How deep do you think those guards woulda buried her?" Buddy asked me.

"Well," I said, stroking my stiff left arm, "probably pretty deep."

"You know, if we're off a little, the real grave could be three feet away and we'd never fuckin' know it!"

But Steve called out, "Hey, what the hell's that?"

"That" proved to be the find of the expedition, and the centerpiece of Buddy Busch's documentary, *Grave Evidence: The Execution of Amelia Earhart.* The tattered piece of black cloth appeared to be a full-face blindfold, cut so that narrow strips on either side could be tied behind the wearer's head—attesting to this, the tie straps had a stitched hem.

Mrs. Blas herself identified the scrap of cloth as the blindfold Amelia wore to her execution by Japanese soldiers.

Because of the lime-based coral content of the soil, human remains would likely be swallowed up, over these years, ashes to ashes, dust to dust, and that blindfold might be all that was left of Amelia Earhart, if in fact she'd been buried beneath the missing breadfruit tree.

But even now, an aging Buddy Busch (a stroke and heart attack not enough to slow him down) is planning one last trip to Saipan (his sixth); meanwhile, a new generation of Earhart enthusiasts plans more expeditions to the Mariana Islands and other parts of the South Pacific.

Of course, if Amelia was buried in the brainwashed mind of Irene Bolam, the body they're looking for was donated to medical science and is a long-since discarded, cremated cadaver.

I have finally decided to tell my story because I figure nobody will believe me anyway, and if the government doesn't like it, they can sue me or go fuck themselves.

I believe Amy died in the waters of Tanapag Harbor that night, swimming with me, toward freedom; perhaps Chief Suzuki's boys did drag her body out, and the Japanese military did take her, blindfolded, to an unmarked grave near Garapan. Perhaps by the time you read this, Buddy or some other latter-day explorer will have discovered more evidence to pinpoint exactly where Amelia Earhart was buried.

Anyway, I'm confident of one thing.

They're more likely to find her body than that bastard Jesus Sablan's.

The press called her "Lady Lindy," but her family called her Mill. Schoolgirl pals preferred Meelie, certain friends Mary (Fred Noonan among them), she was Paul Mantz's "angel," and her husband used "A. E." To the world she was Amelia Earhart, but to me, and only me, she was Amy.

I Owe Them One

Despite its extensive basis in history, this is a work of fiction, and liberties have been taken with the facts, though as few as possible—and any blame for historical (and/or geographical) inaccuracies is my own, reflecting, I hope, the limitations of conflicting source material.

Most of the characters in this novel are real and appear with their true names. The characterizations of Margot DeCarrie and Myrtle Mantz are fictionalized, based upon limited reference material. Ernie Tisor, Jesus Sablan, Sammy Munez, Toni Lake and J. T. "Buddy" Busch are fictional characters with one or more real-life counterparts.

To my knowledge, the notion that Amelia Earhart may have been bisexual is new to this work. The possibility that she was a lesbian is a subject often broached but little explored, and the issue of her sexuality is clouded (as are her accomplishments and disappearance) by the tendency of those writing her biographies to view her through rose-colored glasses, sacrificing the person for a role model. She is depicted as a Victorian prude, and yet reports of her promiscuity persist; her mannish attire, and traveling with women companions, is offset by talk of youthful flings with older men and long affairs with Samuel Chapman and Eugene Vidal. Despite the claims of some biographers, her marriage to G. P. Putnam was obviously an arrangement, perhaps a sham. From these contradictions, my portrayal of her arose, organically, during the writing of this book.

The characterization of Robert Myers, although somewhat fictionalized, draws upon his book, *Stand By to Die* (1985), an earnest memoir distinguished by the author's personal relationship with Amelia Earhart. Some may view Myers's story with skepticism, but it is my privilege as a novelist to accept it at face value.

My long-time collaborator, research associate George Hagenauer, located books and articles, and in particular lent support in figuring out how to get Nate Heller to Saipan (and under what cover story). My other chief researcher, Lynn Myers, came up with rare Saipan material as well as the elusive G. P. Putnam autobiography, *Wide Margins* (1942).

June Rigler of Muscatine, Iowa, generously loaned me numerous books from her extensive Amelia Earhart collection; she also allowed me to sort through an extensive, decades-spanning clipping file on Amelia, entrusted to me in a piece of vintage Amelia Earhart luggage. June's clippings, from hundreds of newspapers and magazines, greatly helped broaden my picture of Amelia and her disappearance—in particular, a 1982 series of articles about the Irene Bolam controversy appearing in the Woodbridge, New Jersey, *News Tribune.*

Alice and Leonard Maltin graciously fielded several phone calls, providing instant in-depth research as the unpaid proprietors of the Toluca Lake Historical Society (phone number unlisted). Tom and Yuko Mihara Weisser also fielded impromptu phone inquiries; Yuko helped me figure out that the hotel referred to in *every* source as "Kobayashi Royokan" likely was the Kobayashi Ryokan, "*ryokan*" being Japanese for "inn."

In 1996, Jim Ayres of Muscatine moved his family to Saipan, where he and his wife took teaching jobs. In the midst of this traumatic relocation, he undertook on-site research for me, intersecting with the Department of Community and Cultural Affairs of the Commonwealth of Northern Mariana Islands. Jim and his family took photos and searched out books, magazine articles and visitor's bureau information, as well as photocopied the original testimony of Matilde Fausto Arriola, among others. He also located several video documentaries on the disappearance as well as a current travelogue on Saipan.

The key book Jim found is *Nan'yo—The Rise and Fall of the Japanese in Micronesia, 1885–1945* (1988), by Mark R. Peattie. In trying to imagine the Garapan of 1940—a city that had virtually ceased to exist by July 1944—I found in the Peattie book many major puzzle pieces (most discussions of Saipan focus on the invasion, and photos of the rubble of Garapan are as common as photos of pre-bombing Garapan are not). Other puzzle pieces were culled from various magazine and newspaper articles, notably a *Yank* article by Corporal Tom O'Brien on Camp Susupe. Others were gathered from *East Again* (1934), Walter B. Harris; *Lady with a Spear* (1953), Eugenie Clark; *Micronesia Handbook—Guide to the Caroline, Gilbert, Mariana, and Marshall Islands* (1992), David Stanley; *Saipan—Then and Now* (1990), Glenn E. McClure; and *Saipan: The Beginning of the End* (1950), Major Carl W. Hoffman, USMC.

Three biographies provided much information and many insights: *Letters from Amelia* (1982), Jean L. Backus, a warm life story illuminated by lengthy quotes from Amelia's letters to her mother; *The Sound of Wings* (1989), Mary S. Lovell, the most detailed biography, beautifully written and exhaustively researched, marred slightly by the author's inexplicable approval of G. P. Putnam (ironically, much of my negative view of Putnam is derived from material in Lovell's book); and *Amelia Earhart—A Biography* (1989), Doris L. Rich, an outstanding job with a slightly less rose-colored view of Amelia than Lovell's. These books tend to accept the notion that Amelia crashed into the sea; Lovell in particular spends time debunking disappearance theories.

Also consulted were the lavishly illustrated *Amelia, My Courageous Sister* (1987), Muriel Earhart Morrissey and Carol L. Osborne; *Amelia Earhart—Pioneer of Aviation* (1973), Julian May; *Still Missing* (1993), Susan Ware; and *Winged Legend* (1970), John Burke. A tribute with pictures, *Amelia—Pilot in Pearls* (1985), Shirley Dobson Gilroy, provided useful nuggets. Other biographical material was drawn from books bylined Amelia Earhart: *20 Hrs. 40 Min.* (1928), *The Fun of It* (1932) and *The Last Flight* (1937), as well as G. P. Putnam's puffy, unconvincing *Soaring Wings* (1939).

While I viewed several documentaries and one of the two television movies about Amelia, the work that really impacted this book was Nancy Porter's 1993 documentary, *Amelia Earhart—The Price of Courage,* which explores Amelia as a celebrity created and manipulated by the media.

The groundbreaking *Daughter of the Sky—The Story of Amelia Earhart* (1960), by Paul L. Briand Jr., endorses the notion of Earhart and Noonan winding up in Japanese captivity on Saipan. Still a good read despite all that has followed, *The Search for Amelia Earhart* (1966), by Fred Goerner, is the cornerstone of the Saipan scenario. The next major entry is the controversial (and withdrawn) *Amelia Earhart Lives* (1970), by Joe Klaas, covering the Joe Gervais investigation and presenting the Irene Bolam theory; entertaining but disorganized, this book is a peculiar mix of hard research and wild speculation. Also consulted was *Amelia Earhart: The Final Story* (1985), Vincent V. Loomis with Jeffrey Ethell. The "disappearance" book authors are often catty about each other's work—almost everybody bad-mouths Goerner, despite his pioneering contribution. A tour guide through the theories is presented in the excellent *Amelia Earhart: Lost Legend* (1994), Donald Moyer Wilson.

Two of the best inquiries into the Saipan theory are *Eyewitness: The Amelia Earhart Incident* (1987), Thomas E. Devine with Richard M. Daley; and *Witness to the Execution* (1988), T. C. "Buddy" Brennan (and his video documentary of the same name). My character Buddy Busch is a composite of Devine and Brennan, with some fiction tossed in; in particular, Brennan's research is the basis for Busch's, including the testimony of Mrs. Blas and the discovery of the blindfold. The story of the burning of the Electra, and Forrestal's presence on Saipan, derives from Devine.

Other books focus primarily on the flight itself: *Amelia Earhart—What Really Happened at Howland* (1993), G. Carrington, suspects an intelligence mission was undertaken, while *Amelia Earhart—Case Closed* (1996), Walter Rosessler and Leo Gomez, attempts to debunk that same thesis. The most convincing, coherent, credible inquiry into the government's role in the "last flight" is *Lost Star* (1993), Randall Brink.

Material unavailable elsewhere was found in the well-illustrated *The Earhart Disappearance—The British Connection* (1987), J. A. Donahue. Ann Holtgren Pellegreno's *World Flight—The Earhart Trail* (1971) charts her own recreation (sans disappearance, of course) of Earhart's "last flight" in an Electra in 1967; she includes her own insightful overview and summary of the disappearance theories. During the writing of *Flying Blind,* another woman "recreated" the Earhart flight, but Iowan Pellegreno did it first, and far more authentically.

A number of biographies provided the basis of characterizations in this book, in particular *Hollywood Pilot* (1967), by Don Dwiggins, an excellent biography of Paul Mantz. The autobiography *Age of Heroes* (1993) by aviator Henri Keyzer-Andre with Hy Steirman includes the fascinating possibility that the Japanese "Zero" fighter plane may have benefited from engineers having access to Amelia's "flying laboratory." The autobiographical travel books of Irving and Electa Johnson were essential in creating not only their characters but Heller's ocean voyage, specifically *Westward Bound in the Schooner Yankee* (1936) and *Yankee's Wander World* (1949). The only world cruise the Johnsons seem not to have written a book about is the one including the Amelia Earhart side trip; their article "Westward Bound in the *Yankee*" in *The National Geographic* (January 1942) purports to describe that trip, their third, but is in fact a condensation of their 1936 book on the first voyage.

Other biographies that proved helpful include: *Aviatrix* (1981), Elinor Smith; *The Body Merchant—The Story of Earl Carroll* (1976), Ken Murray; *Diz—Dizzy Dean and Baseball During the Great Depression* (1992), Robert Gregory; *The Forrestal Diaries* (1951), edited by Walter Millis with E. S. Duffield; *James Forrestal—A Study of Personality, Politics and Policy* (1963), Arnold A. Rogow; *The Hunt for "Tokyo Rose"* (1990), Russell Warren Howe; *Jackie Cochran—An Autobiography* (1987), Jacqueline Cochran and Maryann Bucknum Brinkley; *Wanderer* (1963), Sterling Hayden; and the biography of a business (Marshall Field's), *Give the Lady*

What She Wants (1952), Lloyd Wendt and Herman Kogan.

Material on the Irish Republican Army was drawn from *The I.R.A.* (1970), Tim Pat Coogan, and *The Secret Army—A History of the IRA* (1970), J. Bowyer Bell. Restaurant and nightclub color were derived from *Dining in Chicago* (1931), John Drury, and *Out with the Stars* (1985), Jim Heimann; baseball reference from *The Gashouse Gang* (1976), Robert E. Hood. The following WPA guides were consulted: California, Illinois, Iowa, Los Angeles, Ohio, Michigan and Missouri. Aviation references include *China Clipper—The Age of Great Flying Boats* (1991), Robert L. Gandt; *This Was Air Travel* (1962), Henry R. Palmer, Jr.; *United States Women in Aviation, 1930–1939* (1985), Claudia M. Oakes; and *Women Aloft* (1981), Valerie Moolman.

I would again like to thank editors Michaela Hamilton and Joseph Pittman for their support and belief in Nate Heller and me—Joe was extremely patient when I called into question my reputation for meeting deadlines by requesting extension after extension, as I attempted to meet the challenges of this material; and of course my agent, Dominick Abel, for his continued professional and personal support.

My talented wife, writer Barbara Collins, helped me through this difficult, rewarding project, providing frequent impromptu trips to the Muscatine Public Library, and constant insightful criticism, keeping me aloft as much as possible, and lovingly walking me away from crash landings.

One

The Chevy Chase Club was open for golf every day of the year, but the gun-metal sky threatened rain, a muted rumble of thunder promised the same, and only a madman would risk a round on a chill late March afternoon like this.

Make that a pair of madmen, and make me one of them.

I had an excuse, however; I was half of this ill-fated twosome because I was on the clock. No, not a caddy— a security consultant, as they said in the District of Columbia. Back home in Chicago, the term in use was still "private eye," even if these days I was an executive version of that ignoble profession.

After all, the A-1 Detective Agency was now ensconced in the Loop's venerable Monadnock Building on West Jackson in a corner suite brimming with offices, operatives and secretaries as well as a more or less respectable clientele. I could pick and choose which cases, which clients, were worthy of my personal attention, and those in that favored category had to be prepared to pay our top rate of a hundred dollars a day (and expenses) if they wanted the head man.

My golfing partner had wanted the head man, all right, but I was starting to think he needed a different sort of head man than the A-1's president. Specifically, the headshrinking variety.

Longtime client James V. Forrestal—immaculately if somberly attired in dark green sweater and light green shirt with black slacks and cleated black shoes—seemed the picture of stability. I was the one who looked unhinged, albeit spiffy, in my tan slacks, lighter tan polo shirt and brown-and-white loafers, having been encouraged to bring golf attire along, assured I was in for "perfect golfing weather." Then why were my teeth chattering?

Forrestal carried himself (and, today, his own golf clubs—the caddies weren't working today) with a characteristic aura of authority, as well as a certain quiet menace; he would have made a decent movie gangster with his broad, battered Cagney-like features, and wide-set, intense blue-gray eyes that could seize you in a grip tighter than the one his small hands held on that three-wood.

But on closer examination, the picture of stability started to blur. The athletically slim body had a new slump to the shoulders, his skin an ashen pallor, his short, swept-back hair had gone from a gray-at-the-temples brown to an all-over salt-and-pepper, and the eyes were sunken and shifting now, touched with a new timidity.

On the other hand, there was nothing timid about Jim Forrestal's golf game. After I'd hit my respectable two hundred yards, Forrestal strode to the tee and addressed the ball and gave it a resounding whack, then almost ran after it, all in about four seconds. Perhaps he was trying to beat the rain—God kept clearing His throat as we traversed the blue-green grass—but I suspected otherwise.

Forrestal played a peculiarly joyless form of golf, striking the ball in explosions of pent-up violence, expressing no displeasure at bad shots, no pleasure at good ones, as if the eighteen holes we were trying to get in were an obligation. He'd outdistanced my drive by fifty yards or so, and stood waiting with clenched-jawed impatience, foot tapping, as I used my two-iron to send my Titleist into a sand trap.

As for me, I hated golf—the game was something I put up with for the social side of business—and had no idea what the hell I was doing here, on the golf course or otherwise. I assumed, of course, this had something to do with Secretary Forrestal's rather unfortunate current situation. Politics never held much interest for me (the

Racing News didn't carry much coverage of the D.C. scene); but even an apolitical putz like yours truly knew what had been happening to Forrestal of late.

Much had happened in the nine years since I had done that "personal" job for Jim Forrestal. One of Washington's most powerful figures had, for the first time in a rather blessed life, suffered a humiliating fall from grace. This was the man who had built the vast fleets of the navy from a mere four hundred to over fourteen hundred combat vessels; who had—despite his extensive administration duties—made dangerous frontline inspection tours in the Pacific, landing under fire at Iwo Jima.

In 1944 he'd become secretary of the navy and, after Roosevelt's death, President Truman appointed the highly regarded Forrestal the first secretary of the defense, despite Forrestal having fought against the creation of such a position, believing the army, navy and air force should each be their own boss. After Truman's unexpected victory over Republican Tom Dewey last November, Forrestal alone among Roosevelt's holdover cabinet members seemed likely to stay on for the peacetime duration.

Or anyway, that's what most of the pundits had been saying, with a few key exceptions, specifically a guy who knew less about politics than I did—Walter Winchell—and, more significantly, Drew Pearson, the most powerful left-leaning muckraking columnist in the country.

In his various syndicated columns and on his national radio show, Pearson for over a year had been accusing Forrestal on a near-daily basis of everything from being a personal coward (by failing to stand up for his wife in a holdup, supposedly) and a Nazi sympathizer (because Dillon, Read & Company had done business with Germany in the twenties).

But from a political standpoint, the most damning was Pearson's claim that Forrestal had secretly made a pact with Tom Dewey to continue as secretary of defense under a new administration that, obviously, never came to be.

James Forrestal's resignation had been made public on March 3, and that this action was taken at the request of President Truman was no military secret. Louis Johnson, a key Truman fund-raiser, would take over Forrestal's position two days from now, in a patronage tradition that was easy for a Chicagoan like me to grasp.

All of which added up to, I was golfing with the most famous lame duck in the United States.

Soon to be a wet one: the sky exploded over us while we were approaching the tenth tee, and Forrestal—the golf bag slung over his shoulder damn near as big as he was—waved for me to follow him back to the white-stone porticoed clubhouse. He'd moved fast, and so had I, lugging my rented clubs, hugging a tree line, skirting the tennis courts; we got drenched just the same. A colored attendant provided us with towels, but we looked like wet dogs seated in the clubhouse bar.

Save for the bartender, we were alone, which was one small consolation, anyway. Forrestal ordered a whiskey sour and a glass of water but I needed coffee, to help me stop shivering.

We sat at a small corner table by windows that provided a front-row seat on the rolling black clouds and white lightning streaks and sheeting rain turning the gentle hills to the golf course into a hellish surreal landscape. Forrestal, hair flattened wetly, sat back in his chair as if he were behind his big executive desk at the Pentagon, calmly sipped his whiskey sour. He looked like the elder of an elf clan, and a wizened one at that. He probably only had ten or twelve years on my forty-three, but looked much older.

"Nate," he said quietly, "they're after me."

I tried to detect humor in his medium-pitched, husky voice, and could find none; no twinkle in the blue-gray eyes, either.

"Well, uh, Jim," I said, and smiled just a little, "it seems to me 'they' already got you. You *are* out of a job."

"You can lose a job and get another," he said, and the slash of a mouth twitched in a non-smile. "But a man only has one life."

Thunder rattled the earth, and the windows; cheap melodramatic underscoring, Mother Nature imitating a radio sound-effects artist.

"Have there been threats?"

He nodded, once. "Telephone calls to my unlisted number at home. Cut-and-paste letters."

I gestured with an open hand. "But someone in your position always hears from cranks."

Now he leaned forward conspiratorially, whispering, "Didn't you wonder why I wanted to meet you here?"

"Hell no." I waved to the rain-streaked window and the squall beyond. "Beautiful golfing weather like this?"

He dipped the fingertips of his right hand into his water glass, as if it were a fingerbowl, and then raised the fingers to his lips, moistening them gently.

Then he said, "My phones are tapped. Electronic bugs all through my house."

This wasn't making sense to me; I sat forward. "Why bring me in from Chicago? Why don't you call some of your friends in from the FBI or intelligence or something, and do a sweep?"

"That's who probably planted them."

I sat back. "Oh."

He began to shake his head, slowly, his eyes glazed. "We won the war, Nate, but we're going to lose the peace."

"What are you talking about, Jim?"

"I'm talking about Communists in government."

"Communists. In our government."

He nodded gravely.

"And that's who's 'after' you."

His eyes flared. "If I *knew* who wanted me dead, why would I hire you?"

"Who else could it be, Jim? Besides the Communists."

His whiskey sour glass was empty. He lighted up his trademark pipe, having to work a little to get it going. I was about to repeat the question when he said, "That prick Pearson, for one."

Lowering his pipe, which was in his left hand, he again dipped the fingertips of his right hand in his water glass and remoistened his lips.

"The S.O.B. made me out a coward, Nate." He was trembling; I'd never seen Forrestal tremble before, and I wasn't sure if it was anxiety or rage. "Told a pack of damn lies that made me out a yellow weakling who ran from danger when his wife was threatened! I wasn't even there, when that robbery occurred. . . ."

"Jim . . . Pearson's a newspaperman. All he's after are stories."

Forrestal's hand was clenching the bowl of the pipe as if it were a hand grenade he was preparing to lob. "Pearson is not a mere newspaperman. He's a crusader—a misguided one—and a pawn of the Communists. Hell, he may be a damn Russian agent; certainly it's no great stretch of the imagination to see him on Stalin's payroll."

"Maybe so. But you're still out of office."

His eyes narrowed and the thin line of his mouth almost curled into a faint smile. ". . . In four years I might assume another one."

"Under another president, you mean?"

An eyebrow arched. "I mean _as_ president."

It seemed to me, despite my political disinterest, that I had read something about the Republican party courting Forrestal; but looking at this gray-skinned, sunken-eyed shell of his former self, a man seeing Communists under his bed and the FBI in his pantry, I found it difficult to picture his face on a _Forrestal in '52_ campaign button. _In with Jim!_ I didn't think so.

The real irony, of course, the aspect of this that was truly odd and even creepy, was the extent to which this circumstance mirrored that "private" job I'd done for Forrestal in 1940. The parallel was so glaring, so disturbing, I couldn't seem to find a way to bring it up, to point it out to Forrestal. . . .

In the aftermath of that earlier investigation, Forrestal had told me he'd taken the troubled Jo to see a New York psychiatrist, that she'd been hospitalized with a diagnosis of clinical schizophrenia. Shock treatment had been part of the therapy, and I hated to hear that, because I didn't believe in that snake-pit shit. I even felt a little guilty about telling her I'd seen a shrink myself; the story about my father killing himself with my gun was true, of course, and I still carried guilt for it. But I'd never lost a night's sleep and wouldn't have seen a psychiatrist if voices were telling me to paint myself blue and dance naked in Marshall Field's window.

And now, almost nine years later, in the bar of the clubhouse of the Chevy Chase Club, with wind and rain rattling the windows nearby, I was seated with Jo Forrestal's husband—the secretary of defense of the United States of America (for two more days, anyway)—who was telling me a story that seemed chillingly familiar.

"You're a Jewish fella, right?" he asked, out of nowhere, pointing with the pipe stem.

"My father was a Jew," I said with a shrug. "My mother was Irish Catholic, like your stock."

He waved that off. "I don't practice the faith."

"I wasn't raised in any church. What's that got to do with people trying to kill you, Jim?"

His eyes narrowed to slits. "If I was a Jew hater, if I was anti-Semitic, would I hire a Jewish detective? Christ, my secretary is Jewish!"

"I'm still not with you, Jim."

He wet his fingertips again and patted his lips, saying, "I stood against Palestine, for the sake of my country, and that makes me a Jew hater? It's bullshit, utter bullshit."

"The Jews are trying to kill you, too?"

He nodded; beads of water clung to the upper lipless mouth like sweat. "They could be. It could be the Zionists. Why aren't you writing this down?"

"I can remember it. Anybody else want you dead, Jim?"

Now the pipe stem jabbed at the air. "Is that sarcasm? I won't tolerate sarcasm. This is very real."

"No it's not sarcasm," I said flatly. "Who else wants you dead?"

He pounded the table with a fist. "I don't know! I just know I'm being shadowed. I know they've got the house bugged, the phone tapped. You're the detective, Heller. Find out!"

"Okay." I sipped my rum and Coke, casually said, "Let's start with the other obvious question: *why* would somebody want you dead?"

"The obvious answer: I know too much." He dabbed more water on his lips. "Nate, I've done some bad things, trying to do good. Sometimes I'm afraid I've betrayed my country by trying to serve it. . . . Once I'm out of office, I'm a threat to all sorts of people."

I had a sick feeling in my stomach: fear. "If this is tied in with the intelligence community—what's this new branch called?"

Forrestal flinched a non-smile around the pipe stem. "The CIA."

"Yeah, a spook by any other name. Anyway, if that's what this is about, what do you expect a lowly private dick to do about it?"

He jabbed the air with the pipe stem again. "Don't do anything about it—just find out who the hell is after me! I can call in favors once I know who it is, whether it's the Zionists, the Russians, American Commies, or that bastard Pearson . . . and the list goes on!"

"The suspect list, you mean?"

"Call it that if you like." Forrestal reached behind him for his wallet and withdrew a check.

He held it out so I could see it: a three-thousand-dollar retainer for the A-1 Detective Agency.

"Nate, find out who wants me dead."

I took the check. "Jim . . . this is awkward, but there's something I have to raise. Doesn't all this seem a little—familiar, to you?"

He blinked. "What do you mean?"

"That job I did for you, back in 1940—for your wife? She thought 'they' were out to get her, too, from the Commies to the household help."

"That is an interesting coincidence," he said, nodding somberly. "Of course, there's a major difference."

I was putting the folded check into my wallet; mine was not to reason why, mine was but to keep my business afloat. "Which is?"

He shrugged. "My wife's a lunatic."

And he dipped his fingertips in the water glass and patted the moisture on the thin dry lips.

PENGUIN PUTNAM INC.
Online

Your Internet gateway to a virtual environment with
hundreds of entertaining and enlightening books from
Penguin Putnam Inc.

*While you're there, get the latest buzz on
the best authors and books around—*

Tom Clancy, Patricia Cornwell, W.E.B. Griffin,
Nora Roberts, William Gibson, Robin Cook,
Brian Jacques, Catherine Coulter, Stephen King,
Jacquelyn Mitchard, and many more!

Penguin Putnam Online is located at
http://www.penguinputnam.com

PENGUIN PUTNAM NEWS

Every month you'll get an inside look at our upcoming
books and new features on our site. This is an ongoing
effort to provide you with the most up-to-date
information about our books and authors.

Subscribe to Penguin Putnam News at
http://www.penguinputnam.com/ClubPPI